SECRET WARS:
AN ESPIONAGE STORY

Joe Goldberg

ISBN-13: 9781500345419
ISBN-10: 1500345415
Library of Congress Control Number: 2014911862
CreateSpace Independent Publishing Platform
North Charleston, South Carolina

This manuscript has been reviewed and approved by the Central Intelligence Agency Publications Review Board.

To Lynda,
Jessica, Sarah, and Benjamin.
Without you, there is nothing.

And to the patriots—you know who you are.

CONTENTS

AUTHOR'S NOTE

The journey that led to this being published, in any fashion, is almost a book in its own right. *Secret Wars: An Espionage Story* was first researched and written from 1999–2001, the nascent Internet days, when libraries, bookstores, and other "analog" resources were still the best means available to get information. On September 11, 2001, the working drafts were in proper format, the cover letter had been meticulously crafted, and all of it was bundled in nice packages ready to be taken to the post office. After the attack, I pulled out the cover letters and rewrote them with the theme, "If there isn't an interest in terrorism now, there never will be."

Agents and publishers disagreed, despite a few kind comments.

In 2001, publish on demand was basically a phantom concept, so *Secret Wars* languished for years in hard copy and on hard drives until January 2014. Then, what I took as several not-to-be-ignored coincidences, perhaps omens, motivated me. They lit a fire of remotivation in me.

A few more comments.

My mantra while writing this was to be as accurate as I could without going to prison. By signed secrecy agreement, which I wholeheartedly concur with, this manuscript was sent to the CIA's Publications Review Board for review and approval. I worried, back in 2001, that they would redact some of the details. I was happy when it was approved for publication, but surprised, perhaps a little disappointed, that not one word was changed.

With this said, I must state: This is a work of fiction. Any resemblances to anyone, living or dead, are purely coincidental.

There are real historical events inside—the bombings in Rome, Vienna, and Berlin; the bombing of Tripoli; and military actions in the Gulf of Sidra, among others. I did my best to be as historically accurate as possible in the context of my work of fiction, starting in 1999 and a decade and a half later, with digital access to newspapers, scholarly reports, news reports, and websites. Any actions or conversations of the few actual people are totally my creations, paraphrased themes from speeches, or direct quotes.

Real people suffered, fought, and died for freedom, and it would be irresponsible to devalue any of their actions or memories.

Real people have also been with me on this journey since the beginning or were born into it: Lynda, Jessica, Sarah, Ben. Thanks.

So here it is, finally. Not Hemingway, but what I hope you will enjoy as a good story. An espionage story.

Joe Goldberg
Summer 2014

PROLOGUE

FRIDAY, DECEMBER 27, 1985

All warfare is based on deception.
There is no place where espionage is not used.

—Sun Tzu

A few minutes after nine o'clock in the morning, four men dressed in light-colored jackets entered the main terminal of Rome's Leonardo da Vinci Airport. They maneuvered their way through the thousands of holiday travelers and mountains of baggage that filled the vast main passenger terminal. They approached a long queue of men, women, and children weaving back and forth in front of a ticket counter.

Each passenger shuffled slowly forward toward the El Al counter to check in luggage for the six-hour flight to Tel Aviv. Another line, composed of nearly identical-looking faces and just as long, waited at an adjacent counter to check in for the even longer flight on TWA 841 to New York. Hundreds more lounged in and around the nearby coffee shop, seeking a few moments of solitude from the stress of international holiday travel.

Security was tight within the terminal. Italian *carabineri* security forces, wearing bulletproof vests under their bright-blue uniforms, walked slowly in pairs, making certain their presence was known, their machine guns slung conspicuously under their shoulders.

The Italian government believed the increased security measures to be prudent, as worldwide tension had risen after a series of terrorist attacks against venues frequented by travelers. Within just the last few months, sixty people had been killed in the hijacking of an EgyptAir flight bound for Malta, and the Italian cruise ship *Achille Lauro* had been seized. Most dramatically, television images were still fresh in every traveler's mind of TWA 847's hijacking to Beirut, Lebanon, that summer.

Still, travelers never spoke on the subject, even the most seasoned ones. They collectively and silently knew Israel's El Al airline was a favorite terrorist target. Why tempt fate?

Conscious of the importance of its tourist trade, the Italian government planned to ensure that holiday travelers to Rome found themselves standing in the highest security area of the airport.

The four men moved to within fifty yards of the El Al passenger check-in counter. Without warning, one pulled two grenades from inside his jacket, released the pins, and rolled the explosives across the terminal floor into the crowded coffee shop. One grenade exploded, sending an ear-shattering echo across the terminal. Ripping open the front of their coats, all four men pulled out Soviet-made Kalashnikov rifles and began firing into the crowd.

Bullets sprayed wildly into the El Al and TWA counters as screams of panic mixed with the rapid gunfire, and the smell of gunpowder filled the air. Italian security forces returned fire from their mezzanine-level positions above the counter. Four plainclothes Israeli El Al Security Officers, who had been patrolling the concourse, charged the gunmen and opened fire.

Some of the panicked travelers fell to the floor, while others ran terrified from the gunmen, looking desperately for a place to hide. Crying and moaning now mingled with the sounds of the automatic gunfire. A father threw himself over his two children, but too late. His daughter was shot in the neck and chest and died instantly. His son was struck in the stomach.

The terrorists, yelling, "Kill them all," ran through the crowd, grabbing the heads of the people now lying flat on the terminal floor and shooting them at point-blank range. The advancing security guards shot and killed two terrorists as they ran. A third terrorist took refuge on the floor among the mass of wounded and dead passengers. Seriously wounded, the gunman reached for his rifle when he saw El Al security officers rapidly approaching. The guards shot him in the head, spattering blood across passengers and luggage.

Dozens of enraged travelers, seeing the bloodied fourth terrorist making his escape toward the terminal exit, grabbed, punched, and kicked him. They dragged him by his hair until stopped by police reinforcements, who captured him alive.

In a little over a minute, the terrorists and airport security had fired over three hundred rounds of ammunition. Bodies, luggage, and blood were strewn across the floor. Moans and wails of children rang through the hall. Glass from the airport windows, shot out by the gun battle, littered the sidewalks and street. Police-car and ambulance sirens wailed outside as helicopters circled above. Early body counts found fifteen dead and seventy-two wounded.

At almost the exact same moment, three gunmen entered Schwecht International Airport in Vienna, Austria.

Travelers and tourists stood on the black-and-white checkerboard floor in front of the El Al transit counter ninety minutes before their flight to Israel was scheduled to depart. One gunman rolled three smoke grenades into the departure hall. Austrian police and Israeli security guards fired back immediately, stopping the terrorists from reaching the El Al counter. Screaming, the gunmen fired wildly into the air and tossed four grenades into the crowd. Three exploded. Chased by security and police forces, they ran from the airport building and seized the car of an airport employee. As the gunmen pulled away, security forces shot at the car, killing one and wounding the other two.

Miraculously, only one airline passenger was killed. Forty-four were wounded, including the two El Al security guards.

In less than thirty minutes, in separate airports and countries across the European continent, bullets, glass, and shrapnel injured 116 people. Sixteen people lay dead. A few more would join them in the following days. Within an hour, camera crews and journalists would file their stories and send the images and words to a stunned world.

Mike Garnett believed that Christmastime provided the Soviets a perfect opportunity to launch an attack on the United States of America. The entire US government, from the president down, was on leave, recovering from overeating or yuletide and New Year's hangovers. He figured the Agency building was basically empty, except for the fifteen new loyal employees now scurrying through the building toward the exits. Perhaps a few other mopes were stationed in the Watch Office.

He had written a story about his theory for an eighth-grade writing assignment—a well-crafted series of Associated Press wire stories detailing, with chilling and precise accuracy, a Soviet victory in World War III. Missiles and aircraft launched while the American and NATO forces took weeks of leave, leaving behind understaffed installations and defense systems. It had taken him weeks to write it, with just the right amount of *Fail-Safe* meets *Dr. Strangelove*. Garnett thought it was a work of genius. His teacher, Mrs. Harris, fresh out of college, didn't get it at all. She wrote, with chilling precision, a big red question mark at the top of the page and handed it back. He had hated her ever since.

These thoughts rambled through his mind as he made his way past the empty desks that made up most of the Electronic Media Branch. It was a room in transition from battleship-gray Government Services Administration desks to the more modern modular cubicles. Stacks of colored folders, papers, and videotapes covered every surface. *One of the benefits of a vaulted room—you don't have to put shit away,* he thought. Bolted across the ceiling of the room were TV monitors permanently tuned to PBS, NBC, CBS, ABC, and CNN.

He maneuvered to his office, a small room with an exterior window on the third floor overlooking the front courtyard of the Central Intelligence Agency. A glass window had been installed on the office wall facing the branch so he could easily see the TV monitors, in case he was using the one in his office—an information junkie to the end.

He had granted leave to those on his staff who felt obligated to continue the government tradition, if not rite, of taking time off between Christmas and New Year. Being loyal government employees, all eight members of his staff took advantage of it, although he ordered the video technicians to rotate shifts to change tapes and check the equipment in the Tech Room.

That morning, C/DO/PO/EMB—Chief/Directorate of Operations/Propaganda Operations/Electronic Media Branch, or C/EMB for short—sat alone in the dead quiet epicenter of American intelligence. Scanning the *Washington Post* and *Washington Times,* he plugged his headphones into the large Zenith television on the credenza behind him.

His fingers started flipping channels, and, as was his habit, he started with NBC's *Today Show* to see what Bryant and Jane had on, then to ABC, and finally CBS. Within seven minutes, it was clear it was going to be an agonizing day of fluff stories covering the vital topics such as "How to Return Those Unwanted Christmas Gifts" or "What

One Should Do with Leftover Fruitcake." With the covert operations in Afghanistan, Nicaragua, Angola, and Cambodia pretty much shut down for the holidays, Garnett spent the rest of his time speeding through the recordings of the nightly and overnight news programs. There was little of intelligence interest.

Fortunately, Garnett knew he had CNN to save the day and left those tapes for last to keep him motivated. Barely five years old, the upstart cable station had quickly become a favorite news source for his group, if not the rest of the intelligence community. But even CNN was letting Garnett down, concerning itself instead with the beginnings of the year-end-review programming.

Just as he was about to give up, his eye caught a change on the CNN monitor. A "breaking news" graphic replaced the picture of the rambling anchorperson. Garnett hit the stop button on his VCR, flipped his Zenith's channel to CNN, and cranked up the volume to his headphones. A pretty anchor reappeared to give the details "as we have them." The image changed to blurry video with text superimposed along the bottom of the screen that told viewers they were inside Rome Airport.

From an angle above, bloody bodies and stacks of luggage lay covering the floor. Each body had a white card next to it with a large handwritten number. Security officials were zigzagging around the bodies, speaking into radios. The reporter relayed the details of a terrorist attack, including a few "sketchy" eyewitness accounts. Outside the terminal, the road was blocked with police cars and ambulances, their lights flashing against a field of broken glass. The text changed shifting the action to Vienna. According to the reporter, another terrorist attack had left more bodies sprawled across a black-and-white checkerboard floor.

Throwing off his headphones, he grabbed the receiver of his secure green line and quickly punched in the five-digit number of the Directorate of Operations Duty Office, or the DODO (pronounced by the staff like the extinct bird). The DODO was staffed twenty-four hours a day, seven days a week, with experts from all the intelligence organizations. Stocked with the latest communications equipment, the DODO was the around-the-clock eyes and ears of the CIA. But experience told Garnett that the DODO sometimes missed things.

EMB had taken the role of unofficial backup Watch Office many times. On the fifth ring, someone picked up the line.

"Five one four one five." Agency policy dictated that no one answer a phone with a name, just the line number.

"This is Mike Garnett, chief of the DO, TV Branch," he said quickly. "Have you heard anything on this Rome-and-Vienna airport thing?" Garnett waited.

"No. What have you got?"

"Listen to this." Garnett took the receiver and placed it by the TV monitor and cranked up the volume. The CNN reporter was retelling the same details over the same video Garnett had witnessed the minute before.

"Got that?"

"Yes," said the voice, and hung up immediately.

"You're welcome, bastard," Garnett said to the dead line.

He slipped a blank tape into his VCR and hit record. As a matter of normal operational procedure, the VCRs set by his techs were recording every important channel, but he wanted to make sure he had it, just in case.

When the video ran again, he punched the button on the black-and-white Mitsubishi printer hooked to his TV. Although the quality was marginal at best, he would have something to show anyone who needed a quick idea of the layout of the airport or a picture to attach to an intelligence report. He turned back to his phone directory and started calling all the other offices that needed to be alerted.

None of them answered.

By the last days of 1985, the chief investigating magistrates in Rome and Vienna were traveling back and forth between the capitals, piecing together the details of the attacks. They refused to release an official statement of their results, but privately, the investigators had collected enough evidence to formulate the likely scenarios surrounding the attacks. Members of the Italian and Austrian investigation teams lined up to supply the staff needed to follow hundreds of leads, talk to witnesses, and most important and satisfying, interrogate the surviving terrorists. All holiday leaves were canceled, which was not a problem, as most volunteered to skip their traditional family time. Law enforcement agencies across Europe and around the world worked around the clock.

In Austria, both of the surviving Schwecht Airport terrorists had already been charged with murder and attempted murder even as they were recovering from stomach and chest wounds at a Vienna hospital. Interrogators were happy to extract the information from the badly wounded terrorists but were disappointed to find the two captives were more than eager to tell their story. During their interrogations, the terrorists admitted their goal to seize as many passengers as possible, force them onto the El Al aircraft, and crash-land the plane into downtown Tel Aviv. The investigators determined that the terrorists had started in Beirut, Lebanon, around December 20. From there, they flew to Athens, Greece, where they split up, one traveling to Geneva, Switzerland, and then arriving in Vienna by train.

The other entered Germany, then moved to Budapest, Hungary, and finally went by train to Vienna. They entered Austria using fake Tunisian passports, conveniently the only Arab country whose citizens do not need visas. The investigators had already determined that the fake passports had been seized from two Tunisian guest workers in Libya expelled during a Libyan government crackdown on foreign workers the summer before.

Italian investigators were having even better luck uncovering details of the Rome airport attack. Under heavy security at Sant'Eugenio Hospital in a southern suburb of Rome, the surviving attacker claimed that eight additional guerrilla squads had been sent to Charles de Gaulle airport in Paris and Madrid airport. Other European airports were targeted, but security was too tight, and the attacks were aborted.

The terrorists, internally calling themselves Martyrs of Palestine, stopped in Geneva, where they received money and instructions from a terrorist support cell operating there. They left Geneva and traveled by train to Rome on December 2. Terrorist cell leaders in Rome provided false Saudi, Kuwaiti, and Moroccan passports the day before the attack.

Even before the Rome magistrate's preliminary interrogation report was sent to law enforcement, intelligence, and government officials, the world's media had already discovered the most important and chilling detail.

The terrorists had received financial support and shelter from the government of Libya, led by Colonel Muammar Qadhafi.

BOOK 1

JANUARY 1986

And ye shall know the truth, and the truth shall make you free.

—John 8:32

Engraved into the marble wall,
CIA Headquarters lobby, Langley, Virginia

CHAPTER ONE

"**W**e are in the deception business. And our mission statement is to cause...our...enemies...pain."

Mike Garnett always began his briefing with this standard line, pounding his fingertips firmly against the top of the lectern on each word for dramatic effect. In front of him sat the CIA's newest Career Trainee (CT) class—fifteen white males and two women, one of those Hispanic. *Another successful testament to the new equal employment opportunity program the Central Intelligence Agency is instituting.* The small movie theater was dimly lit, but Garnett could tell that his spectators were nearly comatose.

He welcomed the chance to express his views on the role of video in the overt and covert collection of intelligence, one of the reasons the CIA brought him and his TV degree in three years ago. Taking advantage of his zealousness, they had scheduled him to brief new CIA employee orientation classes.

Grabbing a book from under the podium, he started pacing in front of the movie screen, an act aimed at keeping his students awake. Garnett flipped open the book to a page marked with a card.

"According to the *American Heritage Dictionary*, propaganda is defined as a 'systematic propagation of a doctrine or cause or of information reflecting the views and interest of those advocating such a doctrine,' etc. I have no idea what the hell that means."

He let the book drop to the floor with a bang, startling their slumbering cerebral cortices.

"Sometimes we tell truths. Sometimes we tell less than the truth. We live in specters, illusions, ghosts, maybe sleight of hand. Is it trickery, like a magician? It's propaganda. It resides between the blacks and whites of politics, in the shaded unknown regions of gray. We piece our operations together across a complex network of unnamed case officers, spies, and technologies. Alone. Unknown. Underappreciated, given the danger. We put it all together to disseminate what we want, where we want, how we want."

Are they getting it?

"I can't tell you that much about our ongoing covert propaganda action operations, but I will tell you not to believe everything you read in the *Washington Post* or hear from the evening news." A few chuckles from some woke up the others. "All covert action operations revolve around 'findings,' an oversight system established by the 1974 Hughes-Ryan Amendment, for any historians in the audience. This law prohibits the funding of CIA covert actions unless and until the president 'finds' that the action is vital to national security. It also requires the president to submit the findings to the appropriate congressional oversight committees. Simply put, we are the most controlled area within the Agency."

Garnett took a sip of his morning Diet Coke, giving them a moment to let it sink in.

"However, my office, Propaganda Operations, Electronic Media Branch, has a second, more overt, no less difficult task. Most analysts, those in the Directorate of Intelligence, hardly ever visit the countries where they are considered the experts. We aid them by providing up-to-the-minute news and pictures on their relevant subject areas. Video is real time and personal. You would be surprised by the impact a few pictures can have on an analyst looking for new intelligence assessments, and even more surprised by the resistance to the use of video as an intelligence tool."

"Why?" *A question from the darkness!*

"Because video is television, and television is equated with *Charlie's Angels* and *Happy Days*. If a professor from an Ivy League school doesn't write it, then to the DI's intelligence experts, it's just Hollywood stuff. Listen, it isn't the library that revolutionaries storm to get their message out to the people when they are overthrowing a government; it's the television studio and radio station."

Murmurs from the crowd told Garnett his passion was finally getting their attention.

"Let me show you an example pulled from the world news reports as recently as today."

The red-and-blue NBC "block N" logo with the character-generated title *Today Show—Nicaragua* appeared underneath. The audience stirred to attention.

Off camera, a reporter narrated the segment. "Last night, Sandinista internal security forces raided the Managua headquarters of *La Prenza*, effectively shutting down the last remaining opposition newspaper."

The images caught a long shot of a narrow street in a business area. The camera quickly zoomed to the exterior of a small three-story building in the middle of the block. The windows on the first two floors were shattered—glass littered the sidewalk. People milled around outside, their faces saying they didn't have anything to do, so standing outside was the best alternative they could come up with.

The reporter continued as the video changed to dimly lit interior shots of an office in chaos. The lights of the camera caught broken ceiling tiles and light fixtures dangling by thin wires. Desks, paper, and machines, presumably printing presses, were tossed in all directions. The shot changed to a close-up of an older man speaking calmly in Spanish into a microphone. The graphic indicated he was the editor, and as he spoke, he became more agitated.

"We will not be stopped," a thickly accented voice-over translated as a fist pounded the air.

The video cut to stock footage of President Daniel Ortega, dressed in fatigues, seated at a U-shaped table surrounded by other men dressed in Nicaragua military uniforms. Another shot in the jungle, armed men sitting in camps—the Freedom Fighters, as the Reagan administration called them, Contras to the rest of the world. The CIA emblem appeared over the shot, then the video cut to C-130 planes dropping cargo. The story completed with a stand-up by the reporter in the street. Over his shoulder, the cameraman framed a medium exterior shot of the *Le Prenza* offices, the same people outside.

The segment ended after three minutes and forty seconds. The lights in the theater stayed down.

Garnett nodded toward the glass panel in the back of the theater. The technician immediately twisted the dimmer switch for the lights and pushed the play button on the top VCR in the rack. Behind Garnett, the theater screen blinked and lit up with the large CBS eye staring back at the audience with the title "January 1986, South Africa—Olson."

This segment opened with a long shot of the black township of Soweto. A few huts and stick fences broke up the barren brown landscape. The rest were on fire. Thousands of black residents ran in terror. Into the picture, heavily armed soldiers and armored vehicles entered, following the crowd. On top of the trucks, soldiers fired high-pressure water cannons at the fleeing people.

"These are the types of images award-winning BBC cameraman Rolf Olson used to capture—until recently, when the government of South Africa revoked his press credentials. He was expelled shortly afterward."

The images cut to a chaotic street battle between identical-looking government forces firing tear gas at rock-throwing young blacks…tear gas…tossing debris and retreating…tossing…retreating. The fighting intensified as the camera moved in close to the action. Another cut to a medium close-up of a thin, sandy-haired man with a beard, seated on a tree stump. Behind him were green rolling hills, a stark contrast to the scenes of South Africa.

"Olson, a native of Sweden and the winner of the Pulitzer Prize in photojournalism for his South Africa camera work, thinks he knows why he was finally expelled."

The camera pulled in to a close-up of his face as he spoke directly into the camera.

"I believe that they are afraid of the pictures. That is why. It is simple." The segment stopped after two minutes and fifty-three seconds.

The theater lights came up. Garnett watched the audience rub their eyes and blink.

"Afraid of the pictures, Rolf said. He's right. There is nothing more powerful and potentially dangerous than pictures.

"So what do you do with this?"

"We can manipulate images like these, create a reality around them, and disseminate them to whomever it is we want to influence—usually a wider audience, but there is no reason it couldn't be a single target." Garnett waited for any more questions. "I appreciate your attention. Good luck."

He was the last to leave, locking the theater door behind him.

CHAPTER TWO

The Intel Officer pretty much hated everything about his life.
Earlier in the year, he had hit middle age, which to him was forty
years old. He immediately started putting goop in his hair to keep it
black, crud on his teeth to bleach them white, and noticed his ass had
become so big it looked as if he were carrying France around in his
back pocket.

Twice divorced, with no children, he had been in Chicago longer
than any other Agency case officer. He wore the same stretched-out
gray slacks to work every day, alternating between the small-in-the-neck
white shirt and the tight-across-the-chest blue shirt. Still, as long as
there was a Republican in the White House, everything was right in
the world.

The Intel Officer knew he had one thing over all the new kids
coming into the Agency's station in Chicago: he could write. Not that
intelligence report writing was anything that his idol Hemingway
would recognize as writing, but when it came to the nuances of the
multisyllabic word and well-crafted sentence, he kicked the ass of every
other case officer in the station, if not the entire Domestic Collection
Division.

It was the only reason *they* let him stay in a job that was designated
as "mobile." Agency personnel in the field, if they wanted to get pro-
moted, were supposed to move every few years to avoid getting too
comfortable with their sources. To him, this was a bullshit regulation,
and after six years in Chicago, he wasn't going anywhere. He liked
the people, he liked the atmosphere, and he loved the fried ravioli at
Rosal's on Taylor Street.

They could force me to move, he thought as he climbed the wooden stairs of the University of Chicago's School of Economics, but *he* knew that *they* knew that no one had collected the quality of intelligence from the variety of sources that he had. And since *they* all knew it, why bring it up?

By the time he reached the top of the stairs, his heavy wool coat was soaked with sweat; he made a mental note to ignore that he was a few dozen pounds overweight. The Intel Officer entered the first dark-wood, glass-paneled door he reached, which had his appointment's named embossed in gold across it. Inside the narrow office, a pale-gray woman he had long ago nicknamed Bubbles sat behind an old desk too small for her frame.

She looked up at him with startled annoyance.

"Scott Cessna to see the professor." Intelligence officers got to pick their alias names. He liked planes.

She glanced at an appointment book on her desk, picked up a phone, and punched a button. A buzz came from behind the oak door opposite him. The Intel Officer had done this at least two dozen times over the past three years, and, although he was certain that she understood why he was there, she treated him as if she had never seen him before. But he had a rule for getting access to a source: never piss off the secretary.

"Mr. Cessna is here." He could hear the "Send him in" simultaneously through the door and from the receiver.

"The professor will see you now."

The Intel Officer smiled. "Thank you."

The room was no wider than the outside room but was twice as deep. Shelves overflowing with books lined the walls. One long table covered most of the floor space between the shelves, forcing anyone who wanted to get to the other side of the room to turn and shuffle sideways. A boy and girl, whom he assumed from their crew-neck sweaters and zombie smiles were grad students, stood rearranging books. At the far end of the table sat the professor of politics and international studies, University of Chicago, a long-time source of the CIA station in Chicago.

"That's all," he said, dismissing the students. The Intel Officer had to retreat back into the other office in order to make enough space for the students to leave, much to the annoyance of Bubbles.

When they had left, he reentered the office, where the professor motioned him to sit at the table. He had occasionally thought about retirement and that perhaps teaching was a viable next career, especially when he beheld the man in his Armani suit and fifty-dollar haircut. Always immaculate in appearance, the Intel Officer long ago gave him the nickname Professor Perfect.

"What's it like to have free servants?" the Intel Officer asked.

Professor Perfect smiled. "Wonderful."

Professor Perfect was augmenting his considerable college salary by charging big dollars consulting for corporations. Being one of the world's leading experts on the Middle East got him sojourns all over the world, bylines in the *Wall Street Journal*, and interviews on national news programs. The Professor's ego was never without an air hose to keep it inflated. But until he could afford it, the Intel Officer had a job to do, which at this moment consisted of sucking his source dry concerning his recent international trip.

"So how was your trip?" he asked as he pulled out his precious Waterman pen, his one luxury.

"Boring, mostly. Lots of meetings, nothing of note."

The Intel Officer started to scribble on his yellow legal pad, taking down any information he could glean. His source was playing his usual game of relaying drivel on which cities he had visited, dropping names of famous people, the menus of meals, making the Intel Officer wait for the nugget. And, as always, he played along. Showing attention to every detail. Asking follow-up questions or the spellings of names. Waiting. Patient.

Finally, after an hour, it arrived.

"However, there was an interesting conversation I had. In Libya."

"Oh? Can you tell me about it?"

He walked out of Professor Perfect's office an hour later. He didn't even notice that Bubbles had left for the day. His mind was already composing the intelligence report he would soon be sending to Headquarters.

CHAPTER THREE

The ultramodern General People's Congress Hall in downtown Tripoli, Libya, was packed with thousands of Libyan teenagers, mostly young boys and girls, none much older than seventeen, most closer to twelve. They had been bused in from schools and military training facilities in and around Tripoli. It was a good business, as some organizers received ten dinars from government officials for every one hundred voluntary "spontaneous demonstrators" they recruited.

The cool early January winter evening outside the building was replaced inside with the heat of three thousand chanting, giggling, and shouting bodies. The crowd stretched out the door of the hall and filled the streets surrounding the building. Draped in bright-green revolutionary scarves, they waited feverishly, getting shoved back into line by security guards. Ear-pounding chants of "Death to the US—Our Revolution is Forever—We will die for our Leader—Death to Reagan" continued hour after hour with a constant revolutionary zeal. Girls cried with hysteria, and several fainted from the heat and excitement.

In the back of the auditorium, Foreign Minister Abdallah Mukhtar felt the arthritis attacking his right knee, the result of a decades-old, career-ending soccer injury. He acknowledged that the pain in his knee was becoming worse as every year passed now that age fifty had arrived. The doctor-mandated stretches had to wait for the last three days with another crisis taking up his time. He had only a few aspirin, topical heat creams, and his ever-present cane to lean on.

His appearance was his one vanity. Diplomats and Libyan colleagues remarked that he looked more like a professor behind his wire-rimmed glasses than the man who had been at the forefront of Libyan diplomacy since coming to power almost twenty years ago.

Mukhtar was small compared to his peers. With an almost permanent smile accenting his round face, he kept his slightly graying hair short, wore no facial hair, and dressed impeccably in his trademark Italian tailored suits.

Mukhtar kept as far away from the crowd as possible to avoid being recognized. His reputation for honesty and diplomatic credentials had earned the respect of the international media, which placed him in the role of the country's official international spokesman and de facto lead for public relations. This time, he preferred to remain quiet. After he had been standing in the back of the hall for over an hour, waiting for the main speaker to arrive, his suit was soaked through with sweat. *It might be ruined.* He wished he had eaten more of the breakfast fruit his wife, Marwa, had sliced for him. To pass the time, Mukhtar read the reports from the Libyan press agency, *JANA*, which had caused so much trouble since their release. *What did they call the attacks? Heroic acts?*

"Idiots," Mukhtar whispered, so no one could hear. Even worse, they had attributed the comment to him.

The reaction to the article was swift.

Most Western governments, even the normally placid Italians and French, who relied on Libya for oil, condemned the comments. Some in those governments even suggested a break in diplomatic relations as a punishment. The American and British reactions were under-standable and predictable—the recall of citizens, a call for economic sanctions, and the movement of naval ships closer to the Gulf of Sidra. Some in the Foreign Ministry downplayed the events. He did not. He had read carefully the statement of US President Ronald Reagan:

> By providing material support to terrorist groups which attack U.S. citizens, Libya has engaged in armed aggression against the United States under established principles of international law, just as if he had used its own armed forces.

It was a vague, but not meaningless masterpiece of diplomacy. *They are giving us one last chance.* The Americans were doing all they could to

avoid using force but reserved the right of self-defense to stop terrorists. Whatever economic sanctions remained as a weapon would come
soon. His counterpart, Secretary George Schultz, was doing his job. *I
would like to do mine.*

Mukhtar had spent the better part of the last day crafting a response
to the *JANA* broadcast, trying to disassociate the Leader and affirm the
country's stance against terrorism to the world. Mukhtar knew it was as
good as he could do, true or not. *If they decide to release it.*

> We affirm the clear-cut, evident, and solid position of Libya to-
> ward international terrorism, which it neither supports nor spon-
> sors. On the contrary, it condemns it. We denounce every action
> that harms or threatens innocent lives. In the name of Allah, the
> Most Compassionate, the Most Merciful.

He watched fearsome-looking security forces escort foreign camera
crews and journalists to a special area in the front of the hall near
the podium. Members of the ruling Revolutionary Council, dressed in
their finest military uniforms, shouted slogans and chants into microphones. Mukhtar chuckled in amusement as the crowd chanted back,
reminding him of the cheering section at the soccer matches years
ago.

After two hours, the Leader finally stepped onto the stage.
Pandemonium broke out. Mukhtar witnessed the crowd surge forward,
almost overwhelming the tight security surrounding the stage. Camera
flashes lit up the hall like a lightning storm as journalists began scrib-
bling into their notepads. Camera crews fought for the best position.

Mukhtar had not seen him in a while, and he was surprised by
the fresh look on the face, magnified to gigantic proportions by the
huge screen at the side of the stage. Crowds always brought out the
best theatrics in the Leader, he remembered, and after ten minutes
of deafening cheering, they grew as silent as the desert as the Leader
began to speak.

For the next hour, without once looking at notes, the Leader smiled,
pounded his fist, brushed his hair, adjusted his clothes, threatened,

whispered, shouted, and lectured on the evils of the United States, the Sixth Fleet, and the Zionist State of Israel. Everyone had heard all the lines dozens of times before, and as the speech droned on, Mukhtar turned his attention to the once-hysterical crowd.

Silence replaced shouting. Much of the audience had fallen asleep in their chairs, occasionally being rudely awakened by security forces. Another thirty minutes passed, and the hall remained silent except for the same voice drowning out all other sounds.

Mukhtar had heard enough and waited for the right moment to exit out the back of the auditorium. His driver was asleep in the front seat of his car, and he jerked awake with the slam of Mukhtar's door. In a few seconds, he was heading home to Marwa through the empty, black streets of Tripoli. His driver would report his leaving early, but that was expected in a country where all citizens were members of the internal police force.

The sound of the Leader's voice was still pounding in his ears.

CHAPTER FOUR

The CIA's Domestic Collection Division is comprised of Agency stations based in key locations throughout the United States. Their purpose is to collect information from American citizens who interact in some way with foreign nationals. Domestic case officers, like their overseas counterparts, are charged with the collection of intelligence in support of presidential and congressional foreign policy needs. The division is the conduit to US citizens, with its jurisdiction and limitations for CIA activities expressly spelled out in Executive Order 12333.

Intelligence reports from the field are routed, by subject, to reports officers in the division office at CIA Headquarters in Langley, Virginia. Each report is treated as an irregularly shaped piece of an unknown puzzle. Reports officers carefully and critically review the information for accuracy and importance. Depending upon the sensitivity and content of the information, it is coded and sent electronically to the appropriate organizations within the vast intelligence community—the National Security Agency, the military intelligence arms, the Drug Enforcement Agency, the Federal Bureau of Investigation, and a half dozen or more acronyms and agencies. The dirty little secret of this process is that the amount of intel traffic coming in is overwhelming. Thousands of reports wait in a computer queue or sit in stacks on desks, and unless the staff is tripled, that is where many will stay. To offset this, CIA reports officers wield a grading system like a butcher's knife slicing any case officer who has sent too many irrelevant reports.

Most of her neighbors knew her as a mousy librarian for some obscure, tax-wasting government organization in DC. No one knew she was a twenty-year CIA veteran reports officer, and one of the best in the business. She was an expert in international finance, chemicals, telecommunications, insurance, nuclear physics, metallurgy, and dozens more esoteric topics collected from the stations across her region. Rarely did a case officer challenge her grades or comments. Experience kept the stack of backlog reports of her Midwest Branch to less than half of her regional rivals, a fact of which they were all aware.

When the Chicago cable marked Immediate Priority arrived at her desk, the Reports Officer was ready and waiting. The COS/Chicago had called her on the STU-III secure telephone asking for assistance in processing the report immediately. She whistled out loud at the intelligence, turning the heads of the three other people sharing the small office.

"Sorry," she said with a smile.

She had met the Intel Officer occasionally when he came in from the field, which was just shy of never she recalled. He was a nice enough guy, a little depressing, but few of his hundreds of reports needed any edits. *The sign of a professional taking pride in his work. I wish more were like him.* But on this one, she wanted to make sure. When she finished her review, it was still in its original form.

She added a series of designator codes, signifying which groups throughout the community would receive the details. The report was sent to a large spool printer entombed in an almost-soundproof cabinet just outside the door to her office. Carefully ripping along the perforated folds, she took a routing slip and wrote the office designations of only three Agency offices she felt had a need to know of the report's contents. A thin green Top Secret and red Priority flag where attached to the papers for good measure.

Until recently, she would have sent the report out through the Agency's antiquated but trustworthy pneumatic tube system. Tubes were one foot long with yellow-tinted glass on the sides and heavy felt-and-leather padding on each end. Every office in the building had a tube station designation—a combination of a letter and number. The sender would twist some colored rings on the end to tell the central tube room where it should be forwarded and stuff the tube into a pipe. Air pressure moved the tube to the tube room. But time had caught up with the system, which was being shut down in favor of new, less reliable, Wang computers. The decades-old system enjoyed a loyal following among the older employees who were clandestinely stealing a tube as a keepsake.

She picked up the intelligence and walked out of the office, knowing exactly what grade she would send back to Chicago.

CHAPTER FIVE

Garnett picked up the receiver and punched the buttons on the black-line, nonsecure desktop telephone. "John? You got those copies made yet?"

"Give me another ten minutes, and we're done," the voice replied from the Tech Room across the hall. "Unfortunately, you can't speed dub three-quarter-inch tape, and we're not going any lower than second-generation copies, so back off and quit wasting my time."

"At least you're not blaming the uncontrollable 'glitch' this time."

"Now that you mention it, I—"

Garnett hung up before his chief technician gave his usual techie excuse for why things always went wrong.

Garnett leaned back and looked out his window at the Agency auditorium, a silver dome called the Bubble. Fifty yards beyond the Bubble was a twelve-foot-high electronic fence, and beyond that were acres of trees surrounding the complex. He sometimes wondered which Civil War army might have been camped in these woods over a hundred years ago. They certainly had more important things to consider, such as disease, food, and not getting shot.

"No daydreaming allowed," came a voice from behind.

"Mind your own business. It's the only hobby I have time for."

Karen Olsen fell uninvited into his worn leather guest chair with a thud. A young, stocky, dark-haired girl with a thick New Jersey accent, she had one long eyebrow running across her forehead. A year before, Karen had transferred to Electronic Media Branch as his assistant after two years in a secretary's position in the Directorate of Administration. She was tough. A confirmed workaholic, she didn't like others who weren't. And she would tell you that or anything else on her mind.

"John was about to tell me a glitch story," he said.

"Techies. Without a glitch, or a bug, or a whatever, they would actually have to do some work without an excuse. As my father would say, 'a poor workman blames his tools.'"

"You're assuming they work. Who knows what they are doing in the dark over there."

"I don't even want to think about it," she answered, laughing too loudly for the small office.

"The truth hurts. Where do we stand?"

"Lots going on. John and his merry bunch of editing elves have worked pretty much through the night piecing together the Soviet update in Afghanistan. Wish someone could teach those mujahideen how to turn the camera on and off. We have thirty minutes of dirty feet in worn sandals scrambling over rocky mountain paths before we even see the sky and a Soviet helicopter. Nicaragua. Not much there. It's the same with Cambodia. Savimbi showed up on South African. Maybe enough for the VID."

The Video Intelligence Daily (VID) was Garnett's pet. It consisted of short videos of the previous days' overseas television coverage of relevant intelligence topics. His objective was to complement or make obsolete its old-school paper counterpart, the National Intelligence Daily (NID). The NID was a thin, top-secret report compiled by a small unit that collected and analyzed the top intel of the day. Each morning it was distributed to selected individuals in the CIA, Pentagon, State Department, Capitol Hill, and the White House. Garnett viewed the NID as an over-the-hill rival to his slicker, high-tech product. The proof of his vision was the specific request from the White House to receive the VID every morning for an executive who favored pictures over words.

Garnett and his young hand-picked team were the CIA zealots advocating electronic media as an intelligence source, which was heresy in an intelligence world mired in the tradition of PhD analysts writing scholarly reports. EMB took seriously their mission to spread the gospel for video. So far, in a few short years, Garnett had claimed success as three meritorious unit citations were awarded to EMB for covert operations—signifying the value of what they had accomplished—and now hung on his office wall. It also didn't hurt his ego that there were two individual performance awards with his name hanging there.

After he was hired, it had taken three years to persuade his peers to regard him as a professional covert action officer. Assuming command of a relatively new but high-profile propaganda position at age twenty-seven had left him vulnerable to attacks by the older, traditional members of the Agency establishment. It was only three years ago that he had been offered a position in the Directorate of Operations, virtually fresh out of the University of Iowa. Degrees in political science and broadcasting had made him a natural to take the position as chief of a new branch focused exclusively on media as intelligence tools.

After his training, Garnett found the Agency a strange world filled with a perspective not taught in any of his college courses. The naiveté of this safe life was quickly washed away on his first day when he reached his office and a woman walked up to him and asked, "Who the hell are you?" Garnett realized right away that he had entered a quagmire of chaos caused, he was told, by the dismantling of the covert action program during the Carter administration in the late 1970s.

Garnett was astonished to discover the CIA's electronic media propaganda program consisted mostly of a few friendly television assets in Latin America. For a small fee, each was willing to covertly accept and air short CIA-produced news segments. It didn't take long for him to realize that the real reason the assets were willing to take the materials, which were only marginally of propaganda value by any definition, was that videotape was scarce in most of the countries, and a free reusable tape was always welcome.

He launched QRSCAFFOLD, his code-named project designed to rapidly buildup and support CIA covert action propaganda initiatives around the world—and there were plenty. Soviet Union. Afghanistan. Poland. Nicaragua. Within a year, EMB was a new and improved asset in the Agency's global arsenal. And they were in demand. Even the entrenched "Old Boy Network" that ran the CIA gave Garnett and his team credit for a series of surprisingly successful propaganda operations. It was a crash course in the culture and intricacies of the espionage business.

The invisible truth Garnett had learned about a deception operation was that if they weren't looking for it, they never saw it coming.

"How about Libya?" he asked Karen.

Since the airport attacks, Garnett had ordered his team to collect and retain any video on Libya. A shelf in the editing room now stored fifteen master tapes, much of the content was old file footage, but there was enough new material to fill a VID.

"We got the best of what's his name's speech at some rally," Karen said. "I haven't seen a crowd act like that since a Michael Jackson concert some blind date dragged me to. I can get it—"

Karen was cut off by the ringing of the secure green line on Garnett's desk.

"Four five one nine three," he answered.

Karen watched Garnett's face turn a little pale as the one-sided conversation continued. In a minute, the call ended. He hesitated for a moment before grabbing his notepad.

"I've got a meeting on the seventh floor."

"When?"

"Now. Make sure those VIDs get out. I'm not sure how long I'll be gone."

"Anything you want me to do?"

"No."

Garnett walked out of his office and through the landscape of the EMB office, which consisted of videotapes, newspapers, and video equipment. As he reached the door, Karen tapped him on the shoulder.

"How many meetings have you been invited to on the seventh floor?"

"In three years, this will make one."

The Intel Officer had been waiting for some sort of response for over a week, but like normal Headquarters pukes, they took their time. When it did arrive, he was the talk of his colleagues in Chicago Station—a rare E (Excellent) report, the first for any case officer in the station in nearly a year.

CHAPTER SIX

Mukhtar tossed his glasses on the overflowing stack of papers, rubbed his eyes, and leaned back from his desk. Out the large window was Tripoli, Libya. He could see the People's Palace overlooking Green Square toward the Al-Saraya Al-Hamra castle, which dominated the Tripoli skyline.

It was only eleven in the morning, but he had been at his desk since dawn. He usually arrived early, after morning prayers, to beat the awful and worsening Tripoli traffic. The quiet gave him a chance to read the international newspapers and watch CNN. Unlike those now controlling the Revolutionary Councils, Mukhtar knew the world's diplomacy was played out on the front pages of the likes of the *New York Times*, *Washington Post*, and, now more than ever, on television. The stack of messages from every major news group in the world awaited him, each asking for an interview. He declined them all.

Let the regular propaganda people worry about that from now on.

Although he held the title of Minister of Foreign Affairs, Mukhtar had been seeing his real power within the government rapidly decrease for many months. He had built and rebuilt Libya's relations around the world. And despite the current external and internal pressures, he would not lessen his commitment to his country. Someone in his government had to stand for something more than him or herself.

It was hard with a foreign policy based on national sovereignty and ridding the world of the "Zionist Imperialists." The Europeans tried to ingratiate themselves, especially the Italians, as they had the most to lose. It didn't work; he was tough on them. The United States was a special target, since they supported Israel. He didn't even complain when the Leader went out of his way to support every extremist and militant group. Every violent PLO splinter group. IRA. Red Brigades. Black September. The list went on. The regime had helped create Abu Nidal, the most wanted terrorist in the world, and allowed him freedom to train in special camps. It was a policy of subversion, tension, and terror Mukhtar could no longer assist. The Leader's most recent dismissal of his political risk and impact analyses, if the man had even seen them, was the final indicator of his own future.

He looked forward to peace that would come from being rid of this burden, and the extra time with Marwa.

The people of Libya were in serious trouble. The numbers were indisputable. Libya, the country he loved with the heart of a lion, was broke, and there was nothing he could do. The price for a barrel of Libyan oil had dropped from thirty to ten dollars in the last year. This reality was in contrast to the fact that the cost of extracting, selling, and transporting the oil had remained constant at five dollars. By his calculations, the country would be $2 billion in debt by the end of the year. Despite promises from their Arab allies, no one was going to help.

The Leader had made it a point of national pride to waste billions of those oil dollars purchasing obsolete T-55 and T-72 tanks, MIG-23 fighters, and SA-2, SA-3, and SAM-5 antiaircraft weapons from the Soviet Union, Eastern Europe, and other friends. Not to mention the millions of dollars diverted yearly to the "Special Friends Accounts," supporting revolutionary camps in Libya, the Bakaa Valley of Lebanon, and hundreds of other locations around the world.

Mukhtar would admit that the overall daily life of the population was better since the revolution, and he had to concede that the Leader remained as popular as ever. But now the austerity measures were resulting in empty shelves and a hard life made harder.

The door opened, interrupting his thoughts.

Major Abdessalaam al-Megrahi, a powerful, tall man with a chiseled, grooved face accentuated by a head of short, curly dark hair, filled the doorframe. His eyes were his trademark—dark and piercing—magnifying his authoritarian frame. Although they had been a combination of friend and enemy for over twenty years, only one person made Mukhtar fear for his life. That person was the man standing

three feet in front of him—dressed in his simple, unmarked fatigues—
the number two man in the country, but assuredly the most dangerous.

Megrahi had been top of his class at the Benghazi Military Academy.
In 1969, he supported his younger, more charismatic classmate,
Captain Muammar Qadhafi, in the formation of the Free Officers
Movement. Together, they led a dozen other officers in a military coup
against King Idris. Megrahi was astute enough to show his satisfaction
with being second-in-command—he was marginally more reform-
minded than the now self-promoted Colonel Qadhafi. His pragmatic
advice and leadership of the Revolutionary Command Councils had
protected him during the times when Qadhafi was eliminating former
colleagues and concentrating his power.

As Qadhafi eliminated any rivals to his leadership, he gave Megrahi
latitude to operate the functions of the country. It was an open secret
and a source of amusement on the street that he was the only person
who could speak frankly to the Leader to his face.

"Yes?" Mukhtar looked up with weary eyes.

"Our Brother Leader has asked for a report on the impact of
actions the American president has taken against him and what other
foolishness he will take. Contrary to the world press, he feels nothing else will happen except worthless sanctions. You should write that,
nothing else."

"And the Italians, Germans, and the rest of Europe?"

"You know they will not take any actions. He says not to fear them.
They will side with America's senile president—and their people will
wonder why the price of oil has doubled."

"I don't think we should underestimate the resolve of the Europeans
in supporting the Americans this time."

Megrahi looked at Mukhtar with cold eyes. "Please just write the
report as I have asked and have it to me this evening." The door closed
with a thud.

Mukhtar sat calmly. He had seen the look in those empty eyes
many times before. A close friendship developed during the coup,
when Megrahi enlisted the aid of the young progressive diplomat to
establish the new government. Power and time had taken a toll. At

some point, Megrahi had radicalized in his views, deciding which in his own inner circle were disposable—many were no longer alive or spoken of. Mukhtar knew their history together, his stature in the West, and perhaps the recent tragedy—*To Allah we belong, and to him we will return*—kept Megrahi from making him vanish also.

The sound of the noon chimes interrupted his thoughts. Gabbing his trademark walking stick, one he kept for both image and utility, he slowly stood. It was time. He was pleased that the weather was clear and the *khamsin*, the hot Sahara winds that sweep across the arid deserts, had not arrived.

He had walked the streets of Arous Albahr Almotawasit, "the Jewel of the Mediterranean," thousands of times. His daily walk through the streets of Tripoli was a routine he had begun years ago for the health of his heart, knee, and now his mind dealing with his sorrow. *Tareq.*

The walkways and streets were congested with traffic and peasants seeking work. His driver dropped Mukhtar at Green Square, Tripoli's commercial center, where he started his walk at the castle of the old walled city of Medina, where the bazaars and shops stood mostly silent and empty. Fewer tourists came to purchase the rare artifacts from his country's rich culture and history.

The route became less congested as he limped along Sharah Omar Mukhtar, named for the national hero who ousted the Turks from Libya—a distant relative. Keeping his pace even through the modern business district, he turned at the gigantic Tripoli Fair building and made his way to Sharah Mohammed Magarief. Angling toward Maidan Al-Jazair, crossing this part of the city confirmed that the modern Libya he had had a significant role in shaping was in decay. The Sharah Jamahiriya district—once a crowded, busy stretch of shops with activity that rivaled the greatest shopping areas of London or New York—was now an area as desolate as the desert.

Mukhtar ventured into Souk el-Magamah, one of the massive state-run supermarkets. The gala grand opening ceremony of the giant concrete structure had just been three years ago, with the Leader and Yasser Arafat, head of the Palestinian Liberation Organization (PLO), as guests of honor. Mukhtar remembered shelves overflowing with food and the Leader lauding the "people's store" as an example of the continued prosperity of the Jamahiriyah, or "Gathering of the Masses," his new name for the country.

Now, the shelves in front of him were almost empty. There was no meat, fish, or bread. He could see only a few large bags of coffee from Cuba, some tea from China, spoiled tomatoes, salt, insect repellent, and boxes of shoes. As he stood for a moment to rest his leg, a man with a cart loaded with boxes marked "Bananas—From the People of Nicaragua" stopped at the storefront. Instantly, Mukhtar sensed a change in mood. The few shoppers suddenly swelled to over one hundred. Mukhtar was pushed to the wall as the people clawed and shoved their way to try to grab some of the rare imported fruit. Screams of elderly women and young children echoed in his ears. The youngest and fittest shoppers, mostly males, made their way to the front to gobble up handfuls of bananas, peeling and eating as they grabbed for more.

Chaos exploded before him. Children screamed as the mob separated them from their mothers. Bloodied women wailed, searching for their children, all the while still trying to get a hand on a piece of precious fruit. The victorious rioters threw fists at anyone trying to take their treasure. One woman stumbled out of the battle clutching four battered bananas to her chest. A thug hit her in the face as hard as he could, and blood shot from her nose like a burst water balloon. As she collapsed to the floor, the rioter grabbed for her fruit. Screeching through her blood-filled mouth, she tried to fight him off with her free hand. She was not successful. Another attacker grabbed her fruit and ran to the exit.

A man hyperventilating with rage spotted Mukhtar hiding against the wall and ran wildly toward him, but he was stopped in his tracks—a sharp metal point stuck him in his throat. At the end of it was eighteen inches of steel and Mukhtar, glaring. The man froze, then turned and ran. By the time Mukhtar replaced the blade into his walking stick, the woman was gone, probably thinking he wanted her prize. In the blink of an eye, the quiet returned to the store. A pile of debris and small spots of blood covered the floor. He was surprised he did not feel scared, or even pride in himself. He felt sick.

During the remainder of his walk and afternoon prayers, he could think only of the chaos he had seen. He needed to complete the last task the Leader had given him and the other he had promised in the memory of Tareq.

CHAPTER SEVEN

The US Sixth Fleet was one of the most powerful military armadas ever assembled. It consisted of three aircraft carriers—the USS *America*, USS *Saratoga*, and USS *Coral Sea*; five cruisers, eighteen destroyers, 250 aircraft, and twenty-seven thousand military personnel. Already in the Mediterranean because of the *Achille Lauro* hijacking a few months earlier, the Sixth Fleet was now conducting Operation Attain Document, a series of freedom of navigation exercises in the Gulf of Sidra—a direct response to the Rome and Vienna airport attacks.

Libya, in an effort to flex international muscle, was claiming a two-hundred-mile territorial water, something the US administration was not going to allow for any reason. In response, President Reagan ordered US military aircraft to cross Qadhafi's self-proclaimed "line of death" at 32 degrees, 30 minutes north latitude.

Aboard the *America*, the Admiral had specific orders from the secretary of state to keep the international sea-lanes open and ensure that US forces could conduct naval and air operations anywhere in the world in international waters. Despite the firepower of his force, that this was a dangerous exercise. They had clashed once before with Libya, back in 1981, when US Navy fighters shot down two Libyan jets. So his pilots were on edge and ready to shoot. Not a bad position to be in when conflict was near, but he wanted to avoid any mistakes.

His biggest concern was missiles. Recent intelligence reports speculated on the possibility of Libya possessing French Exocet missiles. He was not going to have pictures of a burning aircraft carrier splashed across the world media. The world fully expected an attack on Libya by the United States. In fact, his staff was already working out the contingencies of any possible "joint" interservice mission. Air force officers were already onboard, coordinating specifics with navy aviators and support systems.

So far, the operation was running smoothly. As he watched his command peacefully gliding across the smooth waters of the Gulf, he wasn't sure how long that would last.

Hidden along the George Washington Parkway on 260 acres of land in Langley, Virginia, the CIA Headquarters building is seven stories tall and laid out like a big H, with each arm designated by a floor number and letter of the alphabet. New employees needed time to know which part of the H was which, causing many rookies to arrive late for meetings, to the scorn of senior officers.

Garnett had made it a point to memorize the floor plan early in this career. He had been on the seventh floor several times, but only to deliver video materials. As Garnett was told when he began his immersion into the strange world of Directorate of Operations activities, "Anyone who gets called to the seventh floor by the DO is either incompetent, getting an assignment too impossible to comprehend, or being fired—and no one ever gets fired here."

Garnett was a little disappointed for feeling nervous. He tried to relax by running the corridor letters in his head to calculate the best route to make it on time. When the elevator opened, he turned right into the 7D corridor.

All the deputy directors who ran the four directorates of the Agency—Science and Technology, Administration, Intelligence, and Operations—had offices on this floor. They needed to be close to one of the most powerful men in the country, if not the world: Director of the Central Intelligence (DCI), William J. Casey.

Garnett cursed himself for his decision to wear his blue sport coat, remembering that during his training, one of the senior case officers told him that he should always wear a suit to work. *Sport coats are too causal. Espionage is a serious business, not sport.* He was joking, or an idiot, and Garnett had never really given it much thought—until now.

When he found the right conference room, he was glad to find the lights down to cover his sport coat mistake.

"Sit here, son," said a voice from the dimness at the far side of the table.

"Sure, yes."

He took a seat in an empty chair next to the voice. The only things resembling decorations in the room were an American flag, a plastic plant, and rows of framed black-and-white pictures of mostly old, bald men with suits and ties, hung on paneled walls. To Garnett, each looked like a college professor.

Seriousness hung in the air.

Garnett found himself sitting next to Wes Henslow, Chief/Counter-Terrorism Center (C/CTC). Henslow was one of the originals. Fierce. A legend. Flamboyant, even in his midsixties. A "dinosaur," as the new MBA-style, Casey-hired officers would disparagingly describe him. When it came to intelligence operations, Henslow knew he was right—that was all there was to it. And to the displeasure of those who didn't care for him or his style, after an over-thirty-year career, he normally was. A visceral love of America fueled him, which placed terrorism as the latest enemy to the driving doctrine of his CIA existence: "We're America. Fuck them."

Garnett first met Henslow soon after he had joined the DO covert action team, when he briefed the CTC on his new propaganda media program. Garnett was sure he was being tested when Henslow commissioned him to create a series of important clandestine Arabic language antiterrorist videos for the Egyptian Intelligence Service. He must have passed, as several requests followed.

Garnett found him a funny-looking man, given his job—short, thin, a crew cut; skin, eyeballs, and nails all having the same look of chewed Juicy Fruit gum. And he had a habit of calling him "son," which annoyed Garnett to no end. But Garnett knew that one of the citations on his wall was a result of Henslow's appreciation of the work of EMB.

"I've been informed by the DCI..." Henslow started slowly with a nasal, slight New England accent. He was glancing toward the woman sitting across the table, a green-striped visitor badge hanging from her lapel. "...that tomorrow, the administration is going to sign a finding authorizing covert means to stop Libya's support for international terrorism and other actions against the government of Libya. Concurrently, State will publicly announce sanctions freezing all Libyan assets in the United States and halting all business transactions with the country."

"Does that mean—" someone started to ask.

"Not what you are thinking. We can't kill him directly, unfortunately. But I expect the administration won't shed too many tears if he is removed as collateral damage."

"Didn't anyone read our analysis?" the same man asked, drumming his sausage fingers on the table. "Confrontation is the wrong approach with Qadhafi. If we back him into a corner, we only force him to target US personnel and installations."

"Well, now, perhaps you can summarize the report for everyone," Henslow said, looking the man in the eyes.

Garnett looked at the Analyst in awe—a representation of the foundation of the CIA. Anywhere the Agency was active, diverse experts like this Analyst, case officers, and professional staff of all backgrounds were working, waiting. *They are the unknowns that keep the Intelligence Community humming. Just people. Working hard.*

The Analyst balanced a small pair of rectangular glasses on his nose and flipped open a folder on the table in front of him.

"This was fully laid out in our Special National Intelligence Estimate from March 1985. We concluded that if he is left alone, he is more than likely to focus on the regional issues he has been championing for years. Yes, he poses a threat to the Middle East region, but those attacks are focused mostly on his regional and domestic enemies. He is obsessed with assassinating Libyan dissidents living abroad, the so-called stray dogs. But these are mostly absurd gestures. We should leave him alone."

"Those absurd gestures, as you call them, have claimed over a dozen lives, and it's those assassin teams we are trying to stop from coming to the streets of America. He is a killer. He hangs people, students, every year on the revolution anniversary, just so he can call them spies. He does it in front of schoolchildren, for heaven's sake," a woman said, her voice rising.

"For those not aware, this is Andrea Harper, Deputy Secretary of State for Terrorism," Henslow announced, clearly enunciating each syllable. She was forty, maybe, Garnett guessed, but her deep-blue eyes, oval face, and bright smile easily cut her age in half. Garnett noticed she had taken her time to look perfect. Her form-fitting red business suit accentuated a figure that probably had most men she met speculating on what it would be like to get her into bed.

"Ms. Harper, by treating him overtly as an international enemy, we make him into just that."

"But—" Harper started, but Henslow cut her off.

"What else do the psychologists in Leadership Branch think?" He was going to let the Analyst have his say.

"Our 1982 psychological profile gave him a borderline personality disorder. Recent events have only strengthened our conclusion. He is, therefore, uncontrollable. We determined that the additional notoriety granted to him by the West could only exacerbate his feeling of self-importance and might lead him to attempt more dangerous international ventures. Sources indicate he has exhibited some rather bizarre behavior, including wearing high heels and makeup and carrying a teddy bear. There is some evidence that he might be using excessive amounts of sleeping pills. His disorder makes predicting actions virtually impossible. He had all the camels in Tripoli killed one day because he decided camels are a sign of an old Libya, not the modern society he has in his mind." The Analyst leaned back and took off his glasses. "Not your average Boy Scout, to say the least."

"The president wants him dealt with," Harper responded coldly.

"We should not declare war on this individual simply for his support of terrorism, as ugly as the recent pictures have been. He does not control terrorism. He only supports it. Publicly declaring war on him is out of proportion as a response, given the evidence and options." The Analyst would not yield.

"You can't believe any of that. That is flawed analysis at best." She glanced at Henslow with a face of confused anger. "He has welcome mats out for every terrorist in the world. Carlos the Jackal. Abu Nidal. What we do makes a difference for the families of five dead Americans and the dead citizens of our allies. President Reagan is standing firm on this," she said.

"Fine, but—"

Henslow cut him off. "That was a nice summary, but there is no more time for this. I have to brief the DCI in three hours. Good-bye."

Henslow sat staring at the Analyst who sat and stared back in silence. Garnett, who had watched this all with tense excitement, felt the room grow even more silent than before as Henslow sat like a statue looking at the man. Finally, the Analyst realized he was being asked to leave. Muttering apologies, he gathered up his materials and left the room, closing the door gently behind him.

Henslow pulled out a long, orange legal-sized folder from under the papers in front of him. It was a 201 file. A naming convention left over from the old Office of Strategic Services military numbering system, a 201 file contained biographic, operational, and intelligence information specific to an individual Agency source. Each individual recruited to support the CIA's clandestine operations was assigned a 201 number.

"What do you know of Abdallah Mukhtar?" Henslow asked, turning toward Garnett.

"He's the Libyan foreign minister. Around fifty, maybe, very clean, looks like an accountant. Distinguished." They looked at Garnett in amazement. "Sorry, can't help it. I remember everything. Got me through college, plus he has been on some news shows." He smiled at them. Henslow managed a slight appreciative smirk back.

"We had regular communications with him for years. Some intel came our way on foreign-policy intentions, oil, etc. Whenever we probed on terror or the military, we got nothing. Either he didn't know, which I doubt, or was too stubborn, or scared to let it go. That just pissed me off. How could he not know? He had been out of communication for over a year for no apparent reason until a meeting with a source out of Chicago. He volunteered that he is frustrated with the situation in Libya. Even more, tired of the leadership. He is sending out signals. He might be quitting."

"What does that mean?" Garnett asked.

"I don't know exactly, but he is smart. Crafty. It's a signal," Henslow added.

"What do you want me to do?"

"The White House is eager to move against the terrorist situation by any means possible," Harper warned.

Henslow looked at Harper, then at Garnett.

"We need to finally get him fully working on our side now, and fast. None of his quitting bullshit. I've—we've been trying for years to get him set up as a fully recruited asset. Every traditional approach. Every trick. Every pitch. He has ignored it. But now he knows it is going to hit the fan there. I want to make certain he stays put, and more importantly, says goddamn yes this time. I need something new, a different angle. That's where you come in. So here it is. You have till the end of the week to give me a plan."

Henslow slid the 201 over to Garnett. It was labeled HJSHIELD.

Garnett sat in a silence. He had supported Henslow's covert operations a few times since he had come to the Agency. Nothing like this. The entire operation, its execution, its success, was his. He thought back to his sophomore acting class at Iowa, when the instructor was going around the room asking each student his or her major. When Garnett answered politics and communications, he remembered the teacher stopping and saying, "You are the most dangerous person in this room." Garnett had thought it funny at the time. Now he found it prophetic.

"How much time do I have?"

"Eight weeks, tops. Six is better. Any problems with that?"

"No problem," he lied.

"Then we're done. Keep me briefed, and remember, this is 'need to know.' That is it." Harper and Henslow stared at him in silence.

Garnett stood up and left the conference room without being asked, 201 tucked under his arm. *Brief in a few days, maybe six weeks to complete.* He had no idea what he was going to do. Not even a place to start. He was sure of only one thing.

He was certain he had just categorically promised to create a covert op for one of the most powerful men in the entire CIA, acting on orders from the Director of Central Intelligence William Casey and the President of the United States Ronald Reagan.

CHAPTER EIGHT

By this time of the afternoon, the office would normally have been empty, allowing for a rendezvous between husband and wife, lovers, or any particular combination thereof. But on this day, the Managing Director of the Rome office decided to call his yearly staff meeting.

While the others showed their annoyance by mumbling among themselves, the man was certain the Managing Director would speed things along, as one of his favorite mistresses was waiting at the Hotel Michelangelo. The NOC also had an appointment with a young American art student who had proven to him the night before that she loved everything Italian.

Ostensibly a businessman, in actuality he was a deep cover CIA agent known as a NOC (nonofficial cover—sounds like "knock"). He had no diplomatic cover or immunity. If an unfriendly, or even friendly, intelligence service caught a NOC, he could expect no help from the United States. If a NOC operation went bad, he would either end up in jail or be executed for espionage.

The NOC watched his colleagues squeeze into the small but nicely decorated offices of International Resource Consultants. Many were older than his thirty years by decades but were willing to accept their young colleague, as his success since his arrival had increased their bonuses. Although he was the newest consultant in the office, he was good at his job, and in his eighteen months, he had landed the top three foreign worker labor contracts of the year, bringing in over $80 million. This made the Rome office the IRC Branch of the Year. The Managing Director was assured a healthy bonus and bragging rights with his peers.

The NOC could tell by the red checks and sweat he kept wiping from his forehead with a silk handkerchief that the Managing Director had something more important to say than announcing the yearly sales quotas, pep talk, bonus percentages, or firings. After clearing his throat, adjusting his tie, and wiping his brow, the Managing Director launched into a review of past years' results. The NOC's mind started to drift; he only smiled and nodded when hearing his name as the Managing Director singled him out for his loyalty and efforts under his mentoring.

After fifteen minutes, the Managing Director looked at his watch, and, realizing he wouldn't get his afternoon exercise if he continued, decided that he had better come to the point. He cleared his throat again.

"Recent events in Libya have come to the attention of the home office," he began. "Soon, it is quite possible that many, if not all, American oil-field technicians and maintenance workers will be forced to leave. Their departure presents an opportunity for us to supply contract labor to Libya to keep its important operations functioning."

The NOC sat motionless in his chair, hiding his pleasure. He had anticipated this for weeks and had already examined the political angles and worked the mathematics. If the West continued the boycotts and sanctions against Libya, perhaps it would stop supporting international terrorism as the oil receipts declined and dwindled.

Oil was Libya's major source of hard currency. But this would require European Common Market cooperation that just didn't seem to exist. By his latest estimates, there were almost forty thousand Western Europeans and fifty thousand Eastern Europeans keeping the oil fields running. Italy was Libya's largest trading partner and the largest importer of Libyan oil, with over fifteen thousand Italian citizens in Libya working in every sector of the economy. Agip, Italy's largest oil company, was helping West Germany and France to pump one-third of Libya's oil out of the ground.

Although the number of Americans was small, fewer than two thousand, they represented the highest skilled labor in forty or so service companies. These workers were critical to keeping the massive oil fields across Libya, such as Nassar, Waha, and dozens of others, operational. If they left and were not replaced, Libya could lose close to $2 billion of its oil revenues, the NOC had concluded. Surely the Libyans would pay plenty to keep them running, perhaps $200 million to save $2 billion. The NOC liked those numbers. Last year after he arrived, he successfully negotiated the Morocco contract with the Libyans after they expelled forty thousand hardworking Tunisians for no apparent reason, bringing in over $30 million to the Rome office alone. He was named as the lead account representative to Libya.

Most importantly, he had been required to travel into the country each month ever since. Still, the NOC had arranged the "chance" meeting between his superior and the brunette waiting nearby. A little insurance to make certain the Managing Director would pick him to lead the most lucrative projects.

"Signore, it is my decision that you will lead this most important project, under my leadership. The office will issue bonuses of fifty percent to all." He hurriedly rose, grabbed his hat, and made his way out the door to the brunette, certainly naked by now. His colleagues stood, offering *congratulaciones* to him—and also to themselves for the size of the bonuses they all expected. The NOC smiled and hurried out the door.

He still might make his meeting with the young artist after all.

CHAPTER NINE

Even at 6:00 a.m., the commute to Langley on Interstate 66 from the western suburbs of Virginia was white-knuckle stressful. Garnett liked to walk along the path surrounding the building to release some tension. The construction of the New Headquarters Building was well under way with the copper TEMPEST eavesdropping material being added to the exterior. Unfortunately, the new building took up a good portion of the old parking lot, causing all kinds of problems and adding ten minutes to the cold walk. Garnett strode by the statue of Nathan Hale standing guard near the entrance as he climbed the steps to enter through the main CIA doors.

He felt insignificant as he walked across the large marble CIA seal on the floor and by the dozens of memorial stars chiseled into the marble wall, framed on either side by the US and CIA flags. Each star represented an Agency employee killed in the line of duty. *The Book of Honor* was mounted to the wall in a glass case, identifying the names signified by the stars. Less than half were identified; the others would always remain nameless.

Entering the security access station, the guards watched as he inserted his ID into the reader, activating the gate behind him to rise. He punched his security code into the machine, lifting a gate on the other side to let him in. He smiled at the armed Special Police Officer as he made his way to the cramped EMB office.

Garnett had gone home for just a few hours to change clothes and get a glimpse of his sleeping wife and daughter. Karen, dark circles under her eyes, sat at her desk. Files flowed across her desktop and onto the floor. They had spent endless hours during the past week collecting everything they could find on HJSHIELD—news reports, biographies, and most importantly films and video. But Garnett needed more time. With over two days gone, he still had no idea what to do.

"Good morning?" he asked.

"Go to hell. Here are some more." She handed him the top folder in the stack.

"Thanks. Is John ready?"

"Across the hall."

Garnett turned. "Keep up the good work." He meant it.

"Go to hell" echoed through the office as Garnett headed for the theater. She meant it too.

Waiting inside was John Childs, EMB's chief video editor and electronics expert, a tall, California blond with blue, detail-focused eyes. Prior to joining the Agency, John had spent much of his career working for beachwear and suntan oil companies, working the cruise ship circuit, filming programs he liked to call *Miss Almost Nothing On* or *Look, I Have No Tan Lines.* Garnett found John hard to believe when he said that it was a job that had become boring.

Garnett had come to appreciate the quiet but resourceful master of all things classified as "gizmo" during their work on the *Achille Lauro* hijacking. John's lightning-quick hands on the editing board had put a detailed video tour of the exterior and interior of the ship into the hands of the Special Operations gang down the hall within a few hours of its seizure—the first unit citation claimed for EMB.

"Are we ready?" Garnett asked the man slumped across two of the seats.

"I've *been* ready. What about you?"

"Get in your booth and stay there."

John left his seat and went through a door in back leading to the projection booth. Taking his seat in the front row, Garnett flipped open the folder to yet again scan for newspaper clippings and reports, looking for an answer.

As the lights dimmed, the video appeared on the screen. New footage was added to the end of the ever-growing video, but he liked to start from the beginning on the chance that it would stimulate his tired brain. By this point, he could recall the accomplishments of Mukhtar better than he could remember his wedding day. The video started with black-and-white still images of the diminutive man in September 1969, soon after the Qadhafi-led coup that overthrew the King Idris government. He watched him grow older before his eyes as file film moved Mukhtar through his life.

He was a smart, studious, and meticulous man. After his soccer career ended prematurely, he earned his bachelor of arts from the Sorbonne in Paris. He followed that by studying international law at Columbia University in the United States during the early 1960s. His diplomatic service began in 1966 when he accepted a position in the Libyan government—chargé d'affaires of Libya in Paris, followed by consul general of Libya in Geneva.

Fully committed to the new leadership, he was approached by Megrahi to assist in the arena of foreign affairs—a skill they had no proficiency in. He sharpened his expertise in global matters, kept company with renowned scholars and experts, and expanded his already substantial political contacts around the world. With every interaction, he made certain to credit his success to the Brother Leader, who returned this loyalty by appointing Mukhtar foreign minister in 1970. Qadhafi sent him on foreign missions to establish relationships with heads of state and leaders of national liberation movements. His intent was to polish Qadhafi's image as he made himself an influential player in regional and international crises.

Footage of him from this period was plentiful—greeting world leaders, attending international meetings, standing with Qadhafi and Megrahi. His name jumped out early in the diplomatic community for his negotiation of the sensitive relationship with the United States; most importantly, the status of Wheelus Air Field near Tripoli and the review of the oil pricing system, which effectively gave Libya half the revenues from the oil pumped and shipped by US and British companies. This, in turn, raised the standard of living in the country, as wealth was redistributed.

Pretty amazing guy. Boring, but a true statesman.

Karen, coffee mug in hand, walked in just as the title slide filled the screen—*September 1985, Al-Wabia.*

"The new stuff." She collapsed in a chair.

Grainy battle images, like those from World War II recon photos, started to appear, followed by shaky amateur film footage of soldiers in uniform, armed men and civilians running, haphazard and blurry glimpses of airplanes and bombed-out buildings.

"This was the coup last year?"

"Yep." She pulled out and read from a run-of-video sheet. "Thirteen senior air force officers and thirty army officers, many secretly sympathetic to the main opposition group, the Libyan Freedom Front. Qadhafi wanted them to attack Tunisia. Instead, the officers led a mutiny against him, attacking his barracks and causing quite a mess. He only made it out because his personal guards, a bunch of East German goons and some loyal thugs from his tribe, put it down. Nicely timed. It was the sixteenth anniversary of the coup that brought *him* to power."

Minutes later, the lights came up.

"Mukhtar's son, Captain Tareq Mukhtar, was killed there. Supposedly, he wasn't part of the uprising, according to intel sources. Actually was a good soldier trying to stop them. He got blown up in a copter. Kaboom! His body was never found. So it was reported." She set her sheet down and rubbed her eyes.

"So it was reported." Garnett repeated the words deliberately, as if in a trance. Slowly his worn-out brain stirred as the first trimester of an idea started stirring around his head. "The old man was pretty upset over that—his only son dead, no body. Rewind the tape. About five minutes back," he called over his shoulder to the booth.

"Again?" John didn't wait for the normal sarcastic answer from his boss.

The lights quickly dimmed, and a few moments later, the tape ran again, right where Garnett had asked. Garnett knew what to look for.

He sat back in his seat and folded his hands across his chest as the face of Captain Tareq Mukhtar filled the screen. Karen watched him.

"You got something?"

"Maybe." A truth.

CHAPTER TEN

The NOC looked across the table at the blond hair and blue eyes nibbling on her *mazzancole ala griglia* and glancing back at him. *American women.* They loved Italian men, and who was he to stop them from loving him as much as possible? He let her drone on about her art studies, travels through Europe, and how friendly everyone was, while he enjoyed impressing her with his knowledge of art history and staring at her breasts. Savoring the perfectly prepared *rombo e patate al formo* and a second bottle of Vini dei Caetelli, he permitted her to babble and laugh too loud, even for the crowd at Ristorante da Vincenzo. He was hoping she was already his for the night, to avoid having to pay for a third bottle of wine.

By midnight, the NOC decided it was time to leave and get on with the night's other business. He tossed down 150,000 lire, and they headed out into the cold, clear Rome evening. He offered his arm to her, which she gladly grasped with both hands, more to steady herself than to protect her from the cold. As usual, the streets and sidewalks were active.

"Shall we walk? There is too much romance in the air tonight for a taxi." The NOC liked that line.

"Oh, yes, oui," she agreed, grasping his arm tighter. Her breast squeezed up against his elbow—34D, he estimated. He would have to verify that later.

After a winding stroll though the Historic District, they headed toward the Spanish Steps. Despite the winter chill, the Spanish Steps still drew tourists and the usual couples who rested there, enjoying the view of Rome.

"Let's stop," he said, stopping her halfway up the left side.

He turned her toward him, and her eyes widened as he gave her a deep kiss. She opened her mouth willingly as he leaned her against the wall behind, pressing their bodies together. After a minute, they separated. He saw the familiar look in her eyes, pleased that he was right—34D. *Two bottles of wine were enough.* He put his arm around her shoulder, and she nestled into to his body.

"My apartment is nearby," he suggested. She smiled. He smiled back.

They finished climbing the stairs and headed for his apartment and warmth.

He was certain no one would notice the small blue chalk circle he had left on the wall behind her.

The ornate lobby of Tripoli's Al Waddan Hotel was crowded with the remaining American journalists in country. They surrounded the well-dressed Libyan official, grateful that they were finally getting the interview they had been promised weeks before. They had been asked to submit questions in advance, which they had all refused to do. Many of the reporters had decided to leave after getting tired of being sequestered in their hotels for weeks. Those who remained were restricted to quarters, as the Libyan government hoped to make their lives so miserable that there would be no other option but to go also.

Mukhtar sat in a large chair of heavy gold fabric in the center of the lobby. The cameras and lights made a glare on his glasses, which bothered him. He disliked not controlling his appearance, preferring to maintain a calm, emotionless exterior.

"How many of the US workers do you estimate have really left, Mr. Foreign Minister?" asked CNN.

"I do not know," he responded truthfully.

"What impact will the sanctions have?" ABC followed up.

"We have allies assisting, such as our Arab neighbors." *A half-truth.* The Algerians and Iranians had lowered their official contract prices on a barrel of oil by three dollars, and the Soviets had upped their production to about 120,000 barrels a day, but they were drawing down payments on $10 billion of debt owed for military purchases. *What good are tanks when there is no food?*

It was the BBC's turn. "What are the conditions like for the average Libyan citizen?"

"The citizens of Libya fully support the Leader of the Revolution," he lied.

Mukhtar could not forget the images of the riot. Since then, he had driven the streets and seen even fewer shops open. Friends went out daily to the countryside trying to buy any fruits, vegetables, or meats that the farmers might be peddling. *Doesn't anyone else but me see what is happening to the country where the cultures of the Phoenicians, Greeks, Romans, and Egyptians once thrived?*

It had been over a week since he had submitted his report, and he still hoped the sensible would win over the emotional. His assessment spoke in plain numbers of the true political and economic situation in Libya, the bankrupt treasury, the impact of sanctions. Most deadly, he concluded that the American reaction had made the Leader an international pariah. Any support of terrorism, real or imaginary, could not be sustained.

The sudden appearance of security police forcing themselves between Mukhtar and the cameras startled him. The interview was over, but the reporters persisted. "Have you seen Colonel Qadhafi?" "What about the support for terrorism?" The voices came at him like bullets as the camera lights blazed. Mukhtar picked up his cane and struggled to his feet.

They chased him across the lobby—the questions and cameras kept shooting at him. He stopped and collected himself with the experience of the career diplomat that he was.

"Please, most of our people are just trying to feed and clothe their families, friends, and neighbors. That is our main concern, not terrorism."

Quickly turning, he escaped through the front door of the hotel, where his driver waited.

In the People's Palace, the country's second-in-command watched the live broadcast on CNN. Megrahi closely examined the face of the interviewee, noticing the change of expression with each question. He recognized that face. *You cannot hide your thoughts from me, Abdallah. We have been through too much. I can see it.*

On his desk, a neatly typed report lay open to the last page. Picking up the phone, he slowly dialed three digits. Almost instantly, it was answered.

"Come here. I have an assignment."

CHAPTER ELEVEN

Although the Rome office of IRC had been closed for an hour, the NOC was glad for the extra time. He was late this morning, having been surprised by the sexual appetite of the student. But he had a lot of work to do, and he had a standing rule against turning one-night stands into marriage. *Perhaps I could fit her into my schedule later?*

With three hours still before his meeting, he used the time to arrange his journey and meetings in Libya, which, given the headlines, was not going to be as easy as the dozen trips he had made already. There was also the matter of the American Sixth Fleet standing in the way. He hoped to get a direct flight to avoid going through Malta, or worse yet, to Egypt, which would require an overland journey by rented car.

By 2000 hours, it was time to get moving. Putting on his overcoat, he slung a leather bag over his shoulder and headed out into the cold to run his surveillance detection route (SDR). He would have preferred to start in a cab, but they were hard to find at night, and in Rome's congested traffic, walking was just as effective.

Starting southeast along the Tiber River, his numb ears decided it was just too chilly for that, so he diverted the SDR north, then east along Corso Vittorio Emmanuele, mindful to stroll at a natural pace. Crossing the street whenever possible, he turned up narrow, less-busy side streets, then back onto the wider Corso. After a quick dinner and a cappuccino at a pizzeria, he came to the Palazzo Venezia, the former headquarters of Benito Mussolini. Passing by the balcony made famous—or was it infamous—by Il Duce, the NOC turned north toward

Via del Corso, quickening his pace. He sat for a few minutes at the well-lit Trevi Fountain, watching tourists toss coins and take pictures.

All along, he tried to memorize faces—a fundamental tenet of running an SDR. If he saw one of them a second time, he could shrug it off as coincidence. If he saw a face a third time, he would consider himself under surveillance and abort.

So far so good, with less than an hour to go, he thought, avoiding the urge to look at his watch.

As he passed the famous Gucci and Bulgari stores on Via Condotti, he entered the Piazza di Spagna, then turned south again to make his way to Piazza Barberni. No one else would notice the small blue two-door Fiat, with the white index card attached to the turned-down passenger-side sun visor, parked along the road.

Reaching the piazza five minutes before his meeting, he walked once around the square, circling his way toward the lobby of the Bernini Bristol. The NOC looked around, happy to be out of the chill. He exited the elevator on the third floor, turned left, and knocked on the first door on his right. When it opened, he entered.

"Right on time, as usual," said the man as he closed the door and locked it.

"I wouldn't want to waste the CIA's money by having one of its best men sitting around," the NOC responded.

"It's OK; they understand. Coffee?"

"No."

The man from the CIA station in Rome poured a cup for himself, then increased the volume on the television to cover the sounds of their conversation, just in case. He did not know the NOC's real name. On the other hand, the NOC did not know his real name either.

"You must have been reading my mind. I was about to call a meeting when I saw your signal. What's up?"

"I'm heading to Libya again."

"You are always heading to Libya."

"Special project this time. Similar to Morocco. Looks like they are running out of people to work the oil fields."

"What a shame."

The NOC dropped his leather bag onto the bed and released the hidden clasps of the concealment device. The bottom panel gave, allowing just enough space to place two pieces of folded paper without causing an outline in the outer layer. He tossed the handwritten report to the Case Officer, who read the paper carefully, making sure he understood its contents.

He liked the NOC, even if he was a little arrogant like all NOCs.

Born in Rome, the son of a US Air Force major and his Italian wife, the NOC moved at age eleven to the United States when his father was reassigned to the Pentagon. When he graduated from Georgetown University with a degree in international studies at age twenty-two, he was accepted into the CIA's Career Trainee (CT) program. For the next three years, he rotated and trained in the various Agency directorates until he went permanent change of station (PCS) to Rome a year and a half ago. The NOC was assigned to his cover job at IRC to develop sources and collect intelligence on the Middle East, terror, and economics. He was on the young side for a NOC. His quick wit and initiative thinking had been noticed during his year of intensive training.

The American CEO of IRC, no fan of terrorists, personally approved of the NOC's placement after being fully vetted and having signed a secrecy agreement. He was the only person within IRC who knew the NOC's real affiliation. The NOC's CIA contact with the Rome Station was limited to once a month on a varying schedule, or special circumstances, such as today.

"Leaving at the regular time?" the Case Officer asked after finishing reading the paper.

"Probably."

"How long are you staying?"

"Three or four days, I think. I should be able to line this deal up fairly quickly."

"Try a week, maybe two," he responded with a slight smile.

The NOC stood still. "I'm not sure I need to do that. Or want to."

"Make sure you do."

"Why?"

"A letter from home."

The Case Officer reached into his briefcase, pulled out a small note card, and handed it to the NOC. After reading the card, he looked up. His trip had just become a little more interesting.

"Sounds like a big my-ass-is-hanging-out-there trip."

"You want to argue? Send a postcard," the Case Officer said with enough sarcasm to get a laugh out of the NOC.

For the next hour, they covered the normal operational logistics of his travel and what support he could expect. They concluded with the obligatory administrative paperwork, accountings, and receipts. They were done by a quarter past midnight.

The NOC left the hotel and spent the next hour walking through the streets, much as he had done a few hours before. Until this last hour, he had taken his trips for granted. He was annoyed at himself when it crossed his mind that he should avoid the trip altogether, hoping instead that the Headquarters pukes were wrong as usual.

CHAPTER TWELVE

If they do not get better, I will have them all killed.
The Terrorist watched the line of martyrs through his dark reflective sunglasses. Mostly teenage boys fresh out of the camps in Lebanon, barely able to control their AK-47s as they fired at body-shaped cardboard cutouts fifty yards away. Sidi Balal camp was secluded along the Libyan coast, providing his trainers the freedom to teach a curriculum ranging from underwater demolition to bomb making.

He was not satisfied with results of the recent European operations, so he had ordered more weapons training. Certainly his plan had had the desired impact: the condemnation of the traitor Arafat, terror and political problems for the cowards in Europe and the United States, and guaranteed financial backing for him, but there was always room for improvement. Poor shooting and missed targets had been costly in Rome and Vienna. And then there were the faulty grenades. Inferior weapons could not be used in his professionally planned and executed operations. He needed to speak to Megrahi.

It will not happen again.
Actually, things had been going rather well lately. When he was not managing an operation, he was supporting and consulting with colleagues on their plans. His reach had become that much larger and lethal. And most importantly, his current benefactor, Qadhafi, relied on him to execute his terror vision.

Daily he received dispatches of intelligence, courteously provided by his associates at Istikhbarat al Askariya, Libyan Military Intelligence, as well as his own extensive network throughout Europe and the Middle East. At his disposal was more intelligence than most countries in the world, and he used it.

As he strolled across his camp, he stared out across the Gulf of Sidra, knowing the United States Sixth Fleet patrolled less than two hundred miles away. *One well-placed bomb on an aircraft carrier.*

Hundreds of tents ran from one end of the camp to the other, and he entered the only one suitable for his office and quarters. Sitting at his desk was the man he needed to talk to.

"As-salamu alaikum."

"Wa alaikumu s-salam, Major. I am glad you are here. I want to discuss muni—"

"I don't have time for that. We have decided that we need to strike the Americans directly. Make up a plan and let me see it."

"It is not difficult. They are soft, everywhere. Airports—"

"No more airports."

"Do you have any targets in mind?"

"Europe is the most reasonable location. A base. Or a place the soldiers live."

"We have assets in most countries. France, Germany, England."

"Make your selection. It must be dramatic, successful—but it must not be linked to us, of course."

"Of course."

"Ma'assalama," Megrahi said as he rose.

"Allah ysalmak."

Perfect. He wanted somewhere that would cause mass chaos, something to remind the West that while they might think they had tightened security, he could launch his weapons anywhere. It wasn't until he had flipped through the stack of intelligence that he saw his opportunity right before his eyes. In an instant, his mind had made the calculations. It was a simple operation—his landlords would not pass on something so easy.

The Terrorist wrote out his memo and sent his courier on his way to Europe.

US Colonel Oscar J. Trinche, Vice Wing Commander, Forty-Eighth Tactical Fighter Wing, US base, Lakenheath, United Kingdom, received the special-category communication during the first few moments of 1986.

The message from National Command Authority, consisting of the president and his chief military advisers, was simple—make preparations for a possible air strike, code named Operation Prime Pump, on selected targets in Libya. Trinche received the communication and took good notice of the unusual twenty-four-hour turnaround response time.

A career fighter jock, he had risen through the ranks due to his stick skill, smarts, and ability to lead. He had been with the Forty-Eighth for over two years and had earned the admiration of his superiors for his administrative skills and respect from the pilots for his willingness to *strap it on*. The Forty-Eighth was officially designated the Statue of Liberty Wing during World War II, when the new unit was first stationed near Chaumont, France, the village where the Statue of Liberty was created. The unit's main weapon was the General Dynamics F-111 Aardvark, long-range fighter aircraft. Called the Widow Maker during Vietnam for its questionable reliability, the Vark was well suited for air-to-ground combat. Trinche loved the plane.

Even prior to the coded message hitting his desk, Trinche had planned for this contingency the moment he heard about the airport murders. A tour at the Pentagon's Diplomatic Office made him sensitive to the comments out of Washington, which only fueled the world press with the possibility of a military strike. Outside his base, as well as at several other air force bases around the world, television crews packed the road. Requests for press tours had doubled in the last forty-eight hours.

Message in hand, Trinche ordered his planning staff to assemble a list of possible targets, ordinance requirements, refueling issues, support needs, attack plans, scenarios, and possible routes. He sent his first response on Operation Prime Pump less than twelve hours later. The second special-category communication came in a few days, requesting additional details and asking more specific questions.

It took only ten hours for Trinche to respond this time.

CHAPTER THIRTEEN

It took almost a year after they met for them to start the affair, or more correctly, to start sleeping together. His wife was fully aware of her husband's infidelities but was willing to put up with them in return for living in exotic locations where golden antiquities were available for plundering. Harper, on the other hand, was tired of the lovers who treated her like a trophy. It was obvious to her that she was smarter and had more potential than the men in her class. She found much more in common with Henslow, an older, powerful man.

Their lovemaking usually ended with her on top, since toward the end he was almost always exhausted. Plus, it gave him time to concentrate on the day's events and catalog what he needed to do next. Her comments regarding terrorism had stayed with him. He admired her fierce hatred of terrorists, and at the moment, it matched her fierceness as a lover.

Afterward, he watched her stare out the Watergate Hotel window, across the night sky of the District. It was a glorious sight. Harper was one of the rare individuals actually born and raised in Washington, DC—something the transplants from around the rest of country thought was illegal. Her deep appreciation of democracy was born from her parents; both had served every administration since Truman in some capacity. They were a family who got things done and made a difference. She was determined to follow in their footsteps. She was working for a president she loved and wouldn't let him down.

She had risen quickly through the ranks of the male-dominated diplomatic corps of the US. She loved this town, *her* town. She remembered it once as a place of free and easy access, where a flowerpot actually was for decoration and contained flowers.

"Dreaming of the good ol' days again?"

"This whole city is preoccupied with terrorists," she responded, not moving a muscle.

"Drink this; you'll feel better." Henslow handed her the second of the evening's Manhattans. Killing off his third Chivas, he dropped down onto the overstuffed couch behind her, which offered a good view of the city and a better view of the contours of her body.

"It's just frustrating. The suits at State think they can really secure this—all the monuments, the National Mall, the museums. You know this city is more than just the seat of our government. It's a tourist attraction. The president understands, but he is surrounded by a bunch of rank amateurs." He detected the sadness in her voice. "Fix me another of these. I'm going to take a shower."

Henslow took the empty glass and headed toward the small bar set up in the corner of the large apartment. It was more than the normal State employee could afford, but Henslow knew the Harper family name was synonymous with influence, and therefore money, in DC. He was always on the lookout for useful contacts, inside and outside the government. She had proven to be smart, aggressive, well connected, and gorgeous. Her knowledge of both the Middle East and the halls of the State Department was powerful and encyclopedic, two things Henslow found extremely useful.

Her stature grew a few years later, when the Reagan revolution rolled into town in 1980 and she was selected to brief the novice leader on Middle East issues. No one was surprised, or could deny, that she was deserving of her selection as the new assistant secretary position in the Counter-Terrorism office. Henslow's faith was again justified as her influence over the Reagan administration's antiterrorism policy continued to grow.

Harper knew no one would take advantage of her. That would require inequities on one side or the other. She always made certain that she was getting as much as she gave. Few State employees had access across the government as she did. Her part in the current efforts against Libya was an excellent example. Henslow was one of the most powerful and dangerous men in government, the kind you definitely did not want against you. A draw was satisfactory, and to have him on your side at any level was a bonus. She would keep him close, even if that meant sleeping with him.

"Security is only part of it. Terrorism isn't just about killing people. It's theater, violence for the effect it can have on those in the immediate vicinity and those thousands of miles away," he said.

"So we build walls around ourselves and descend into a siege mentality," the voice replied. Henslow looked up to find Harper standing in the doorway to the bathroom in a short white robe loosely tied at the waist.

"I have your drink." He waved it in front of her.

She was correct. Security was part of the solution to the terrorism problem. Barriers and bolts were only one preventative option. It was the normal reaction by a society that had never experienced a consistent threat of international violence by the hands of foreigners. But Americans always become complacent, ignoring the rational threats, returning to the narrow problems of their lives. The only real deterrents to determined terrorists were fear and death—fear that the United States was too formidable an opponent to piss off, and if they did, in thought or actuality, then the result was certain death.

Tugging on the belt on her robe, he decided it was time to interrupt their global analysis with something a little more mindless.

A few hours later, after she fell asleep, he went home. Another night's work completed.

BOOK 2

FEBRUARY 1986

The essence of lying is in deception, not in words.

—*John Ruskin*

CHAPTER FOURTEEN

"*Tasharrafna*, Safrina."

"*Ahln Wasahlen*, sir," replied the front desk clerk, greeting the well-dressed man in an Italian suit standing across the high dark-wood counter. She liked him and always made sure his visit to the Al Waddan Hotel was pleasant.

"Your Arabic is getting much better," she said in hushed English, leaning over the desk so the manager could not hear. The Leader had proclaimed Arabic the official language, but despite this, English remained the underground language in the country for most businesses and the younger generation.

Charming women was both one of his favorite hobbies and an operational necessity. There was not a more powerful position than the front desk worker of a hotel. "And your English is like you were born right in America. This time I must teach you some romantic Italian phrases like *sieta una donna bello*," he said, making her olive skin blush as he signed the guest registry. Her beautiful dark-brown eyes looked away bashfully.

"Three days this time, but perhaps more. Is that a problem?" he asked, looking around a lobby busier with activity than he had expected.

"We are one of the few hotels remaining open to foreigners," she said quietly, noticing his glances, embarrassed at labeling the word *foreigner* on such a handsome man. "The journalists who remain are here. Our restaurant is still serving quite nicely."

"The couscous is always delicious here," he lied, slipping the registry card and two thousand dinars across the counter, more than enough for three nights in advance, but they both knew for whom the overage was meant. The card would soon be copied and find its way into the hands of Internal Security, who would cross-check it for previous visits and the purpose of the current trip.

"Room three twelve, as usual," she said, handing him the key.

"Thank you, Safrina. Oh, almost forgot." He pulled a small package from his leather bag and slid it across the counter. "To help you study."

She grabbed the gift, an Italian dictionary, and hid it. "You are most welcome."

Key and bags in hand, he walked across the lobby, looking for anyone familiar or unfamiliar. Inside the empty elevator he took a moment to relax. Traveling undercover into a denied area was always filled with anxiety. He had decided to take Air Italia directly into Tripoli Airport rather than drive from Tunisia or take the Malta ferry. He might take the ferry back; he liked Valletta, and there was a waitress there he would like to see again, if only for a night. Airport security was much tighter than the last time he had come. At the customs desk, where usually an extra carton of cigarettes found while searching the shoulder bag or a few lire in the passport might make entry for a foreigner easier, the green-uniformed security guards had made a close examination of all his documents, taking the carton with them for good measure.

He had selected room 312 on his first visit over a year ago. It was to the rear of the hotel, off street level but near the stairs and an exit. He threw his over-the-shoulder leather bag on the bed and hung his suit bag in the closet—no wrinkles allowed, even in Libya.

An hour later, after a quick shower and change of shirts, he headed out to his meeting.

The vibrations echoed off the walls of the small office as Henslow rapidly tapped his knuckles on the thick folder.

"I've read this a dozen times now. This is the best you got? A mourning father?"

"Yes. I need a more detailed psych profile to confirm how he might react, but on the surface, I think it would at least provide serious motivation." Garnett hesitated. He had been anticipating his meeting since he sent Henslow the proposal the day before. He had barely eaten or slept.

"Forget that. Do you have enough time?"

"Yes." Garnett hoped he wasn't lying.

"You need help, son."

"That's true. There are a ton of things I don't have answers for. It's all in there." He motioned to the report.

Henslow picked up his phone. "Send him in."

A debonair man with almost-white hair walked in, hand extended. Powerful. Distinguished, clear blue eyes, square jaw.

"This is Gene Carver. No one knows Libya like he does, except me. He has met Mukhtar and put together the opposition there. I think you will find him a useful resource—in many ways."

Rising, he felt the strength as he shook the man's hand. "It's an honor to have you with us." Garnett meant it. Everyone, even newbies like Garnett, knew of Carver. Gene Carver was a legend in the Clandestine Services, was one the Agency's first case officers, dating back to the early 1950s. He had spent most of his career in the Middle East. He was a personal friend with most of the region's leaders through history, from the Shah of Iran to the Kings of Jordan and Saudi Arabia...and the regime in Libya. His knowledge of the target and his access increased the plan's likelihood for success exponentially.

"Glad to help. Wes says good things about you." Carver winked, looking at Henslow. "You got some porn pictures of him or something?"

"Fuck you, Gene."

"You've read the report?"

"I did. It is interesting. He has a point. We—the opposition—have been pretty active," Carver added, giving a look toward Garnett.

"Right," Garnett confirmed. "The last time was the mutiny at Al-Wabia last September, coincidentally the sixteenth anniversary of Qadahfi's coup. It was bloody on both sides. That's when it happened."

Carver listened attentively to Garnett, but Garnett sensed the man was assessing him. The man knew every one of these details and more than Garnett could ever imagine.

"It has to be convincing. Unattributable," Henslow said coolly.

"Yes," Garnett answered confidently.

Henslow looked at Garnett, then Carver. "Do it."

"I have a few ideas. Want to go outside for a walk?" Carver offered to Garnett.

They talked until daylight.

CHAPTER FIFTEEN

We could be meeting in East Berlin, but that is a rather depressing place, worse than Libya. Plus, good restaurants are hard to find there. Brussels will have to do. You can trust Chez Leon to have fresh mussels, even if the month doesn't contain the letter r.

The Terrorist traveled alone—less chance of raising alarms at the CIA, or worse, the KGB. This operation was too sensitive, and there was always the chance the terror camp had been infiltrated by Western intelligence.

As he walked toward the center of the city, the bells from La Grand-Place rang ten times through the darkness of the cool Brussels evening. The overcoat and hat helped hide his appearance from the annoying tourists, or any other eyes, crowding the narrow streets. He arrived an hour early, positioning himself at an outside table with a good view of the entrance to the restaurant. Finally, the man he was waiting for arrived. He sat another fifteen minutes to make sure. He should have waited longer, but he was starving.

Once inside, he went to the table where his connection from the East Berlin Branch of the Libyan People's Bureau was waiting. They greeted each other without ceremony or even handshakes.

"Don't worry; I was not followed," the Associate said with a slight smile. "I am very cautious whenever I meet the world's most wanted terrorist."

They fell silent as the waiter took their order. Mussels and frites.

"You should not be afraid. I am not, especially of the Americans. They cannot harm me, they cannot stop me, they do not know where I am, where I will strike next, or what I even look like. I am invincible to their threats. Their ships are as worthless as footprints on the beach.

Their airports are closed. The tourists stay at home. The Israelis beg them for help. Arafat—I will kill him and all his Fatah. I do not fear them."

The Associate had witnessed his dinner companion's fame and ego grow with every successful operation. Unlike the others he had helped, the Terrorist ran his attacks like a business. He calculated. He planned. The more he planned, the more deadly and infamous he became. He had killed hundreds around the world, creating the most dangerous terrorist operation in the world. To be asked to dinner with him was an honor.

"So, why are you bringing me to Belgium?" the Associate asked.

He laid out his plans and needs. There were few people in the world the Terrorist could trust. By necessity, the Associate was one.

He finished just as the food arrived. The Terrorist could finally savor every delicious bite.

"The Libyan regime does not support independent and fair trials, ignoring the International Covenant on Civil and Political Rights, nor do they even believe in basic principles of the independence of the judiciary as adopted by United Nations Assembly Resolutions, just passed in December. Gross injustices permeate Libyan society, devastating the common Libyan citizens, who are experiencing every day new hardships and oppression, violations at all levels of their human rights.

"Kind ladies and gentlemen, in this time of international tension, when innocent people are killed around the world at the hands of this regime, remember the poor Libyan citizen denied most of the civil rights and fundamental freedoms that are at the root of this great English society. For I have not, and will not, in Allah's name. The courageous members of the LFF thank you, and I thank you. Questions now, please."

The Chairman of the Libyan Freedom Front (LFF) opposition force waited for the applause from the hundreds of spectators jamming a lecture room designed for only half that many. He had given the speech at many fund-raising events over the years, but mostly to crowds one-third this size. Invitations arrived constantly from prestigious London universities, and he accepted them all, especially when his expenses were paid and a generous donation to the LFF was included.

The Chairman had been begging for public support for his opposition movement for nearly five years, ever since he had walked away from his position as Libyan ambassador to France. Of all ironies, the events in the news with the Americans were the reason for full lecture halls. The money had begun pouring into the LFF bank accounts.

"Sir?" He changed his gaze to find a young female, certainly a student, sitting in the front row.

"Yes?"

"I enjoyed your talk. I was wondering, what you think will happen—between the Americans and Libyans, I mean?"

"It is a dangerous time for our people. Not that the Americans pose any immediate threat. After all, the rhetoric out of Washington has been rather clear regarding its condemnation of state-sponsored terrorism. The right of free elections, free press, and all the ideals encompassed by a free, democratic government—that is what the people of Libya, my country, seek."

He watched the people nod their approval.

A young woman jumped to her feet. "I'm with the *Middle East Student Times…*"

Trouble. "Yes?"

"There have been rumors that the LFF is funded by the American CIA, and the attack last fall by the LFF…"

The crowd grew silent. The Chairman smiled at the student, who stared back. Some hissing noises filled the room.

"That is not true," he began without hesitation. "Our aims may be the same, I would imagine—the removal of the Libyan regime and democracy for the people. So I would hazard to guess that they certainly would like to see the brave LFF fighters succeed. I expect it would make their jobs easier."

The crowd laughed and applauded, breaking the tension. The reporter tried to get in another question, but dozens of other hands reached up. The frustrated student gave up.

When it was over, he was pleased to see a long line at the donation table.

CHAPTER SIXTEEN

"Our man is on TV," a voice shouted over Warren Zevon's "Lawyers, Guns and Money" blasting from the jukebox in the corner as a drunken training class of fatigue-clad CTs blew off some stream by singing along. Garnett strained to get a view of the TV suspended from the ceiling over the bar in the Student Recreational Building (SRB), located almost in the center of the Farm's main campus. Consisting of an adequately stocked bar and some broken game tables, the SRB also functioned as a meeting room, classroom, and banquet facility.

The team, which now included two of Henslow's CTC officers, had taken residence the week before at the Farm, the CIA's training facility in rural Virginia. A vast plantation, the Farm looked more like a small college campus, complete with several large classroom buildings, dormitories, cafeteria, athletic and training fields, and recreation buildings. But the only curriculum taught here was the tradecraft of espionage.

Garnett looked at the screen and saw Mukhtar, apparently giving an interview in a hotel lobby. The face look tired. Tense. Defiant. Defeated. All at once. He wished he could hear what was being said, but the music and singing were way too loud. Instead, he watched until the camera no longer followed the man as he limped out of the lobby.

"Looked a little pissed," John shouted, finishing his fifth—or was it sixth?—Rolling Rock.

"I'll get a copy of that down here," John yelled into his ear, then forced himself to his feet.

Garnett finished his latest Diet Coke, hoping the caffeine generated enough consciousness so he could make it to his bed. The day had been full, as they rehearsed his plan for hours inside one of many stark concrete bunkers scattered across the fields. *Time to leave.*

The twilight air was cool and damp as he walked to the Bachelor Officer Quarters (BOQ). It always somewhat annoyed him that the CIA was still run like a military organization. The time and dates were military time, something that had taken him several months to get used to. There were abbreviations for everything—a government-wide problem for sure—but most were military jargon. Many of the Agency leaders were former military, which meant they treated civilians like him as children.

"Tired?" A voice came from the round gazebo halfway to the BOQ. Ice clinked in the glass.

"Didn't know it showed."

Carver took a swallow from his drink as he looked deep into the semidarkness. "I'm watching the deer. This place is loaded with them. They let hunters in every year to thin them out. Not very sporting. It doesn't seem to bother the hunters."

"Bet it bothers the deer," Garnett said as he took a seat next to the man in the shelter.

"I would think it would."

They shared a chuckle. Sip. Silence.

"Does any of this bother you? I've spent a career observing people. You look like someone who still has a conscience," Carver asked.

"I would hope I do."

"So what keeps you in a place that has absolutely no conscience at all?"

Garnett hesitated. It was a good question, one he learned early in his career he needed to suppress, along with the related emotions the answer stirred. Should he tell this man the truth, a half-truth, or just deceive him?

"There was a dinner after I completed my training," he started. "The guest of honor was a Romanian. A big bear of a man with gray hair combed straight back and a bushy moustache. I guess he was a recent retiree after a thirty-year career as a NOC. In that time, he had amassed a fortune, millions, as part of his job. Something in the shipping business, or maybe international trade. He told this story about how when he retired, he handed DCI Casey a check for his entire fortune—down to the penny—he had legally earned it, and was entitled to it. Casey kept saying he could keep it, but the Romanian refused. When Casey finally agreed and took the money, he shook his hand and repeated how proud and honored he was of the man's devotion to the CIA. The Romanian finally told Casey, 'It was my job, and I never considered anything else. It is I who should be thanking you.'

He turned to us and said, 'Remember this, my friends: Some people call us spies. That is wrong. A spy—I do not prefer that word. Everyone in this room, I call a patriot. That is what I prefer, and it is the truth. You are patriots.' I always think about that when this place gets to me. I liked that." He stared at Carver. "We are the patriots."

He had told the truth.

Staring back, Carver nodded, trying to coax more from his now empty glass. The alcohol had taken a loose grip on him.

"Here is my advice. Intelligence is a narcotic. Be careful."

Garnett watched him slowly walk to the door of the BOQ. Suddenly he stopped and turned. "I think it's a good plan. Original. It will work." He went inside. Garnett sat.

"Thanks." Only the darkness heard him.

Mukhtar was certain they were watching him. He had traveled the world enough that the sense of being watched was ingrained in his senses.

The man behind the counter looked the same as he had for decades. Small. Thinner than a dried Libyan date. His hair was sparse and his teeth were sparser. The Shopkeeper made a living selling traditional clothes, carpets, plates, silver, and gold—an impressive assortment of semiprecious artifacts that represented Bedouin life.

The Shopkeeper saw the man approaching and stood. Mukhtar managed to keep a dispassionate face as he neared the shop for the first time in a year.

"Do you have any horses today?" Mukhtar asked at a deliberate pace.

"Yes, we had a request for them last week," the Shopkeeper responded.

The coded signals were completed.

"And how is business today?"

"Slow, now. But with a little help, I expect it to get much better," the Shopkeeper replied with a note of optimism in this voice.

Mukhtar picked up a piece of desert glass.

"Very rare, and a good price."

"Yes, very rare, but the price?" He set it down.

"I have new pieces—necklaces, earrings, bracelets, rings." The Shopkeeper started pulling out merchandise. "You have not visited my shop in many months, if my memory has not yet given up on an old man."

"Yes, a year." He fondled a nice set of silver earrings, a present for Marwa.

"Fifty dinars," the Shopkeeper offered. "But I remember you preferred horses."

"Yes. I would like to collect them again, if possible." Mukhtar said, his voice not betraying any emotion.

"It is still possible."

"It is very important. I need to complete my collection, and you are the only shop I know that carries what I desire."

"It can be done. The man interested in these specific goods still visits occasionally. I will hear from him soon."

"I greatly appreciate your help. I will take these," he said, pocketing the earrings and handing over a few dinars. "I will be back for the horses."

"Yes, that is fine," the Shopkeeper said, pocketing the money. Allah had smiled on him.

Mukhtar walked away, his sweaty palm barely able to hold the metal crown of his cane. The Shopkeeper had remembered him and the recognition sentences as if they had never stopped meeting.

He wished he could have communicated more, but there was no way to know if the correspondence hidden in the money would reach its destination safely. At this point, it was better to be safe…than dead.

What makes this old man worth all this effort? The skills of a professional military intelligence officer are better served anywhere than standing in Green Square.

Following this limping man with the cane was becoming boring, and he still had no idea what to look for. The problem with this type of surveillance was the tendency to get lazy and make a mistake, perhaps a fatal mistake. Sure, he recognized the man, but it told him nothing about why he should spend so much time following him. *Was there a chance the man might not be loyal to the Leader after all these years?* But he had a task to complete, and he would. Perfectly.

With this target, it was always the same: early to the People's Palace, a walk after noon prayers, a drive back home, then little else. He placed and received few phone calls and received hardly any visitors outside of his official duties. He almost felt sorry for the subject. Almost. But Major Megrahi had personally placed this mission in his hands, and the last person he could disappoint was the man who could make him and his family disappear in a blink. Too many friends had, much to the grief of any remaining family. He really didn't need to worry, too much; he had never failed the Leader during his ten years in the Libyan Military Intelligence.

The square was crowded. Proper surveillance technique would require three people, but his orders were not to trust anybody, and he followed orders. The Libyan shadowed the slow-moving man as he approached the Sharah Jamahiriyah shopping district. He didn't seem to be in any hurry, but the subject occasionally checked his watch. *Do you have an appointment?*

A few minutes later, the man stopped at a small kiosk—a peddler selling cheap antiquities. He couldn't stand out in the open or get in front of the kiosk. The Libyan was forced to take a position a good thirty meters away, amid some trees and bushes. *A good spot, one a professional might have picked, out in the open, indicating nothing to hide, but also a place where no one can listen. Why did I not bring my camera today?*

The man exchanged a few words with the peddler, occasionally picking up a small trinket to examine it. The Libyan took out his notepad and logged the place and time of the events and a description of the man. After a few words, he watched the target buy some jewelry and walk away. He resumed following the man as he finished his walk, and the Libyan was relieved when the man returned precisely on time to the palace.

A final observation for the day entered into the notepad.

CHAPTER SEVENTEEN

"SPECAT just arrived, Colonel." The aide handed the message across the desk to Colonel Trinche, turned smartly, and exited the office.

Trinche sat back in the large leather chair of his small office decorated in memorabilia, a collecting passion of his since he was a boy. Wing commanders from around the world still told jokes about Trinche and his "junk" boxes he transported from base to base—*a C-130 load,* they joked. He had stopped defending himself years ago against the charge of buying other people's garbage. They were his good-luck mojo, and he couldn't think about not being surrounded by the walls full of pictures, squadron emblems, intricate airplane models, war souvenirs, and machine parts.

His staff had replied to the last revision of the operation, and he was getting a little anxious regarding the meaning of the silence from NAC. The lack of action had only increased the frenzy of the media. Watching the supposed experts on the nightly US news by satellite was a ritual of the squadron in order to find out the next "secret" strike plan against Libya, Iran, Syria, or other favorite hideout for terrorists.

The humor was lost on Trinche when he returned to the base one evening to find camera crews on the road outside the base because a report indicated that Lakenheath would be the launch point for any raid. *Beautiful.* The base had been on full terrorist alert since then.

He slowly read the special communication and then hit the big button on his intercom. "Beans, get in here."

Within seconds, there was a knock on the door, and Major David "Beans" Franks strode in. Serving as Trinche's Weapons Officer since he started flying the Vark years ago, Beans was tall, his thick, dark hair prematurely graying, and he carried the perpetual look of having just woken up.

"You rang, Trinchie?"

"New orders," he said, flipping the paper across the desk to Beans, who settled into the hardwood guest chair.

"Adjustments to the original plan. Looks like new routes and possible target designations."

"Get the staff together at"—Trinche looked at his watch, pausing—"now."

"Affirmative." Beans looked hard at Trinche. "I know that look. When I see that look, I worry. Then my wife worries, and I worry more about her worrying. What are you worrying about?"

"I don't like changes."

"It's all part of the business. You know that. We've been through it hundreds of times, from Vietnam to Lebanon. It's all the same."

Trinche was not comforted. "This mission requires practice and more practice. Most of these guys have never flown a real combat mission. Not to mention the distance, precise timing, and coordination with the navy it requires. And let's not forget the heavy antiaircraft resistance we can expect. These guys are the best there is, but every mission has limits." Beans stared silently at Trinche. "All right. I'm wing commander, and it's my job to worry. My apologies to your wife."

"Now I'm worried," Beans said as he walked out into the hall.

CHAPTER EIGHTEEN

Looking at his watch, he decided to spend the two hours until his meeting walking around the city.

Locking the door behind him, the Oilman liked his sparse, comfortable, two-room apartment in the foreign-worker area of Tripoli. He kept his life in a suitcase and his travel bag packed and ready to go in case he ever felt his security was threatened. After years working in the oil fields, he owned nothing of sentimental value except his truck, boxes full of cassette tapes, a portable tape recorder, and Jack Daniel's. Alcohol was banned in Libya, though the oil workers knew where to get anything they needed through a local black market. If he got caught, the penalty would be severe. So he drank not to think about it.

He figured he could be out in less than a day. The foreign workers supporting the oil industry had a clear idea of the international tensions that were mounting and took great pains not to talk about it, especially to their Libyan employers. The possibility of reprisals against them was not insignificant when the motivating element of money was involved. Of course, he probably was the only one whose income was supplemented by the CIA.

"Would you be willing to supply information you receive to the US government?" a young man had asked him in Saudi Arabia years ago.

"What's in it for me?"

"If you agree, you receive a thousand dollars a month from us for your troubles."

"How did you get my name?"

"I can't tell you."

"OK," he replied. *A thousand bucks!*

The Oilman had never intended to spy for the CIA. Of course, he had never discounted it either. He loved the United States for the opportunity it provided his family. He was officially Venezuelan by birth and citizenship but hadn't been there since he was fourteen, when his parents immigrated to the United States in the early 1960s. His father had a job for an oil company in Houston, and the son had followed the tradition.

He was allergic to a having a wife or children.

He earned his CIA-augmented salary many times by working around the world for most of the big oil firms—Mobil, Occidental Petroleum, Conoco, Grace, as well as the larger European firms. As the years passed and Libya became more relevant, his importance increased, as did his monthly salary. For the last three years, he had been assisting Libya's National Oil Company maintain its dilapidated oil production facilities, which still produced the 1.3 million barrels a day required for export. Libya needed his specialty, as its aging oil infrastructure was getting harder to maintain under the weight of international sanctions.

Even better, it gave him ample time to drive his custom Toyota pickup truck across the vast deserts. It was the only thing he really loved, and treated it better than he had any woman he had met—it had never let him down. The Toyota was also his sanctuary. A functional "cabin on wheels" was added in the truck bed, large enough for a relatively comfortable bed, a little stove, and an actual working refrigerator.

Monthly, the Oilman meandered from the large Al-Hamra oil fields in the west, to the giant Waha and Nasser fields in the north region, and to the east and the huge facilities at Sarir, an area covering almost a thousand kilometers of desert and oil.

The long hours of driving provided the solitude to savor the marvels along the desert's remote roads. He knew them all, as well as some that weren't quite as well known, better than the Bedouins who had wandered there for over two thousand years. The souk owners and Bedouins he met during his journey were his family. It helped that his Venezuelan heritage kept him from looking like a "regular" American.

On the main road from Tripoli to Benghazi, he would see huge eucalyptus trees and stop and wait for herds of camels and goats to cross the road while dodging the traffic speeding along the coast road—barely roadworthy transport trucks hauling wood, hay, oil drums, or propane tanks. At Marsa el-Burayqah, the Oilman would sometimes see workers up from the fields to the south. They were loud men, living it up on lamb and couscous in the local cafes that lined the dusty, fly-infested streets, ignoring the country's restrictions on alcohol and sexual contact with the local girls.

The area was a history and geography lesson. World War II battle sites near Tripoli, Benghazi, and Tobruk surrounded him. Little towns and markets were mostly mountains of metal junk strewn between handwoven silks, saffron, jasmine, olive-oil soaps, copper pots, and fruits.

At the end of his month-long treks, he would return to a small office in the National Oil Company headquarters to piece together his status reports on oil production, refinery capacity, and internal atmospherics. He would do the same for his CIA employers, with added details.

Then, like most foreign workers, whether Koreans, Algerians, Egyptians, or Americans, he often would get out of the country. The Libyans had made this pretty easy for the Americans since the president had ordered all citizens out of the country in 1981. Rather than stamping passports, Libyan immigration stamped a slip of paper that was returned at the border, leaving no evidence they had left the country. Egypt and Malta were the favorites, his preference being Malta, where he would drink for ten straight days. He sometimes had to remind himself to remain sober long enough to dutifully hand over the information to his CIA contact.

Today, he took his usual circuitous route through Tripoli, spending an hour zigzagging through the streets. He never detected any surveillance, but he wasn't going to be notified he was wrong by being locked into prison or worse, shot. The Shopkeeper smiled the same wide grin as he approached, as he would any prospective customer.

"Do you have any horses today?"

"Yes, we had a request for them recently."

The answer froze him. *Holy shit!* It had been over a year since he had heard the affirmative response from the Shopkeeper. When the messages suddenly stopped, they had developed a simple ritual. The Oilman would ask once a month, the man would say no, and the Oilman would leave after fumbling with a few items.

"Would you like to see one?" He reached under the table, his eyes scanning the area imperceptibly. He produced a small, elegantly carved white horse. "It dates to the Romans. Very rare."

"Yes, I see." The Oilman knew it was actually a hollow piece of plaster, made valuable only by the message hidden inside. But he handled the object with the utmost care.

"Very reasonable. Only one hundred dinars."

"Twenty," the Oilman countered.

"Seventy-five."

"Thirty."

"Thirty! For my own sacred mother! Fifty."

"Deal."

"Done." The Shopkeeper took the statue, wrapped it in cloth, and placed it in a rough paper bag.

"Thank you, my friend! I may have more. Come back next month, perhaps?"

"Perhaps."

The Oilman knew he had to concentrate. Rushing back to his apartment would be too suspicious in the unlikely event he was being followed, so he stopped at more shops to cover his movements and blend into the crowd.

Over a year. What's inside this horse?

CHAPTER NINETEEN

Brian Shay walked along Sunset Boulevard trying to match the address on the slip of paper in his hand with the endless line of stores and doors lining the busy street. After three blocks, he stopped outside the one that matched. Hollywood Art and Beauty. He tried the door, but it was locked. Not finding a doorbell, he pounded on the window, shading his eyes as he tried to peer into the dark office. After a few minutes, he heard the latch click, and the door swung open.

"Can I help you?"

Brian was looking directly at a set of gorgeous dark eyes and olive skin standing in the doorway. He paused, too long, in stunned silence.

"Well?"

"I'm Brian...Brian from back east. Garnett sent me," he finally stammered. A red-haired freckle-faced health nut sporting a thick Boston accent, Brian was fanatically loyal to Garnett, who had rescued him from a tour scraping the barnacles off Agency boats somewhere in Florida. Although he didn't possess any particular propaganda skills, Garnett recognized he was sneaky smart, with a strong desire to learn and work. He had proved to be quick on his feet and personable, which made him the perfect scrounger. And for this operation, Garnett thought he was about the perfect size.

"Oh. Come in." Shaking his hand, the Artist made room for him to enter, closing and locking the door behind him. "I'm working in back."

She led him through another door to a neat but overcrowded greenhouse-shaped work studio. High, opaque windows lined the walls on both sides. Classic movie posters of *Frankenstein, Lawrence of Arabia,* and *Blazing Saddles* filled the remaining space. The room was full of paint supplies, Styrofoam heads, masks, and things he didn't recognize. He followed her to a table—a lump was covered with a clean white cloth.

"This is you." The Artist pulled off a cloth, revealing a full-head rubber mask of a man, maybe in his late twenties, with a dark wig and mustache. "It's almost done. The chin is wrong, and I can't get the hair right." She took a magnifying glass to photographs lining the table. "I just can't see them clearly."

"I need a break. I'm thirsty. How about a soda?"

"Sure. Anything you want." *Anything you want.*

She took him into a small kitchen off the studio littered with coffee cups and half-eaten donuts. Taking some Cokes out of the refrigerator, she collapsed her five-foot frame onto a broken-down easy chair in the corner, stuffing one leg under her.

"So, Brian from Back East, tell me your story."

"Not much to tell. Been with you-know-who for almost two years, right out of school. Been working for the team a few months. I'm from Boston originally," he added.

The Artist laughed. "No shit, Sherlock. Like it? The job, not Boston."

"Sure, real interesting."

"Interesting is one word for it. Wars, communists, terrorists, and drug lords are good for business." She gulped her last drop of soda. Brian realized he hadn't started his yet. He was too busy staring.

"What about you?"

She smiled. "Pretty simple. I was born and raised in LA. Movies were in my blood. My father was a bit actor; my mother did costumes and makeup. So I followed in her footsteps. I could have worked for the studios, but I decided to free-lance. I do some theater, commercial work. But I like makeup. I'm in control."

"And this place?" Brian waved his hands in the air.

"Why not?" She shrugged. "Seemed like the thing to do—you know, apple pie and stuff. Like you said, real interesting. Meet different kinds of people doing really weird shit. Plus, it pays well." She got up, tossing her soda can toward the garbage. She missed. "Now let's see if we can't go fix our friend."

He followed her back to the mask. Brian could tell she wasn't happy with it yet.

"It looks almost exactly like him," he offered.

"Believe me, it's not. A pro could tell. I'm not going to let that happen. I've got a reputation in this business. I'll make it right in time. What do I have? A week?"

"Four days. The team should be here then, I think. We're looking for the right location now. We need a few props. I'll be here till then."

"Then we had better make sure our pal is ready by then, hadn't we?" the Artist said, smiling.

CHAPTER TWENTY

An enormous network of friends willing to provide the occasional favor was the reward for a lifetime of work within the government.

Handing the fax to the clerk, the daughter of a former colleague, Mukhtar knew she would not log the transmission into the record. He would know soon if the Istikhbarat Al Askariya was interested in him—they would intercept the fax, arrest him, jail him, kill him, or both. His life would end like so many nameless others in the basement of Abu Salim prison. But he had to take that chance.

She programmed the phone number and set the paper in the machine. After a moment, the paper was fed through the machine; a dial tone followed by a series of squeals, then a high-pitched whine signaled the transmission was on its way. She handed him the original note, which he folded and concealed in his pocket for destruction later. After a moment, a confirmation notice was received from the Swedish bank, confirming the amounts in his personal bank accounts and transfers to two other accounts in Paris and London.

Putting the paper next to the other, he thanked the young woman, picked up his cane and limped out of the office.

"Hello, Abdallah. Follow me."

Mukhtar was shocked to find Megrahi in the corridor waiting for him. He followed the man into his opulent office. It smelled of cigarettes.

"Sit." Megrahi pointed to a chair.

"I am tired of sitting, if you do not mind." His knee ached, and he had forgotten to bring any aspirin, but he wouldn't obey the command in spite of it.

"Yes, your famous leg. As you wish." Shuffling a few papers from one side of his enormous mahogany desktop to the other, he ignored his visitor.

"I am—" Mukhtar finally started to say, but was cut off.

"You are making a mistake. Why did you think I wouldn't know what you were doing? I want to tell you that you should stop."

Mukhtar did not react.

"May I go?"

"No. Sit. Please." For a moment, they sounded like the words of an old colleague, not a command. He sat.

"We have been through much. And I know your heart, Abdallah. You cannot hide it from me. I want you to understand that I share your concerns. The Leader is losing his senses. I cannot tolerate his abuses, the corruption, the dictatorial behaviors. The revolution we fought and many died for is failing. Our position of power with our Arab brothers has been squandered. We cannot motivate our armies to fight, let alone train them. He worries they will rise up against him, as last year when Tareq was so tragically killed defending his country from rebels."

"It is only the Leader to blame?" It was his turn to interrupt. He didn't want to relive any more than needed.

"Yes, I have supported him. Is that what you want me to say? We have all supported his ambitions. But the goals we set to improve— schools, health care, roads—we accomplished that. You and I brought the oil wealth to the people. Remember?" Megrahi lit a cigarette. "Now we buy missiles and tanks that do not work and have nothing but debt to show for it. He is fixated on the Americans."

Mukhtar could not believe his ears.

"I know your heart also. What of our people? All of our shops have empty shelves. What about the jails full of enemies?" Mukhtar countered. "Murderers and torturers receive money that should be feeding our people. You were once leading the advances; now you lead us to be a terrorist state. If you want to be a martyr, stop the violence."

"We are all suffering. Does our situation need to improve, as we promised years ago? It does. I want to live too and want to stop the deaths. I have tried to stop it. There is little I can do. Perhaps the Americans have it right. Perhaps the country would be better off."

The questions poured into his brain like water from a faucet. *Does he expect me to believe this? That he is just a pawn like the other members of the Revolutionary Councils and General Assembly? What does he want me to believe?*

"I want to see him."

Megrahi paused. "Why?"

"To tell him since he no longer values my advice or consul, I will resign. Call me when the meeting is set." He moved to the door, and Megrahi followed him, grabbing his arm as he reached for the knob.

"It is too late for that. He will make me kill you, whatever you do, wherever you are. That is certain."

Mukhtar looked at him and then his arm, firmly in the grasp of the powerful man, then back up to look directly into the man's eyes. There was something in those eyes he could not interpret. His arm was released, and he walked into the waiting room. A dark-haired man, oddly wearing dark sunglasses, waited impatiently inside the dim room. He looked vaguely familiar, but Mukhtar dropped the thought, replacing it with the urge to go home and hug Marwa.

CHAPTER TWENTY-ONE

The Oilman approached at dusk. Nothing on his survival instinct radar blinked red; he was of no interest to the Libyans, but carelessness was not normally his way. Early on in their relationship, he would get brief espionage training at every meeting. Surveillance. Secret Writing. Disguise. *Right.*

Getting trained during any of his trips to Malta made sense to him, but the CIA rejected it. *Your own safety. This whole process seems more dangerous than simply handing over a report accompanied by a meal and bottle of wine in a fine Maltese restaurant.*

After maneuvering through roads that hugged the seaside, he came to the small park. It was bordered on three sides by narrow roads. The high, brown wall of some trade school completed the fourth side of the square. Covering less than half a block, the park was landscaped with short, thick palms, blocking most of the view from the empty streets. The Oilman entered the empty park and followed the gravel path that angled to the center, where a large, unmarked statue of a uniformed man rose from a stone block.

Keeping his pace, he passed the monument without notice. It would have taken trained eyes to see him drop the small object out of his right hand. The oval-shaped flat rock rolled to a stop at the base of a palm, blending in with the stones and gravel that the CIA had sampled and copied years before. He left and continued to the center of town, never looking back. After a good meal, he taxied back to his apartment and finished his task that evening with a few good scotches.

Blocks away, the NOC started his evening at the only restaurant serving anything that resembled Italian food. There was no urgency—

it would be waiting for him in the park. It always was. And he would leave his, as usual.

His primary mission was to service a dead-drop location by retrieving a concealment device, in this instance a rock, at a small park, and replace it with an identical "rock." It came from someone he had never met, or even seen. If he had any messages for his anonymous colleague, it would be in the rock he left behind. A clandestine fortune cookie. *As it should be.* An hour after dusk, the NOC entered the park. He stopped to tie the shoelace he had loosened before he left.

The concealment device could have been difficult to locate if it had not been placed in the exact same spot every month. *If I ever meet him, I'll kiss him.* The NOC hated the moment when he had to reach in the extra pocket of his jacket to get his rock and retrieve the other. From that moment, he was vulnerable until the time he returned to his hotel room and secured the content in the concealment area of his suitcase.

With one last glance to the left and right, the NOC finished tying his shoelace, grabbed the rock, secured it in his jacket, and left his duplicate. The whole operation had taken a few seconds. He needed to burn some adrenaline, but the lack of nightclubs, liquor, and women made that as difficult as the operation he had just completed.

When he arrived in his room back at the Al Waddan Hotel, he hoped it wouldn't happen, but it was inevitable. He couldn't stop it any more than he could stop the sun from rising. He had developed the habit during his training at the Farm after any stressful course. One of his instructors told him it was unprofessional and to get over it. But he couldn't. His hands started to violently shake and the nausea attacked his stomach. Almost everyone in the Agency had a hidden weakness. Alcoholism and divorce were statistics that the CIA hierarchy couldn't deny.

By the glow of a small penlight, he applied pressure to both ends of the rock with his fingers and twisted counterclockwise. The rock split along an almost-invisible seam, and tightly folded pieces of paper fell to the floor. The NOC could not decipher the code, which appeared as small random holes across the paper. Only a one-time decoding pad in the Rome station could be used to extract the contents of the paper. It was an old, yet still effective, method of secret writing. This afforded him a small level of protection if he was ever caught.

The NOC officially completed his business for the IRC within a few days then left Libya immediately after securing the preliminary contract to supply workers to the emptying oil fields. The communication was delivered a few hours after he landed in Rome. Not long after that, he was enjoying the feeling of an attractive brunette rolling on top of him.

The Oilman later picked up the rock and decoded it without a problem at his apartment. The note was self-explanatory. Still, the Oilman read it over several times before he burned it. *Please now check weekly at shop (not monthly) for any signals at location. Pick up and deliver immediately upon receipt.*

Something was up, but in the end, he really didn't care. He needed to figure out how to rearrange his work schedule with his Libyan employers. Some critical problem with his truck was always a good excuse. No one questioned him on that in a place like Libya, if they even cared.

CHAPTER TWENTY-TWO

"**F**or ten thousand dollars cash, we rent your house for the week. You scoot. We shoot our documentary without interruptions. We won't damage or mess with your house in any way except what we have already discussed. So, we have an agreement?" John asked the suntanned man sitting across the glass-topped dining-room table. On the other side of the large picture window was the exclusive Bel Air section of Los Angeles.

"Let me think." The man flipped open a notebook.

John had already decided he disliked the homeowner, and if he didn't answer soon, he was sure he would hate him. Brian had found the location, pulling off the impressive feat in less than two days. John was willing to admit that the kid sitting next to him was a pretty good scrounger.

The homeowner bought their cover story after John and Brian explained that they were representatives from an independent documentary company producing a film on the history of terrorism. *Could we rent your house for a week? It's perfect. Of course you will get credit. Perhaps $3,000 for the trouble. $10,000 for the week? Agreed? Is cash OK with you?*

The house matched all their requirements: a single-story ranch, over thirty years old, under renovation, with an Italian exterior decor. The owner gave them the grand tour for over an hour, providing in detail all the remodeling underway and its costs. John took special note of the large patio in back.

"Could we possibly get those palm trees moved? We need to roll a car back here," John had asked.

"Well, they were just planted. I'm not sure. Why do you need a car?" the man said hesitantly.

"It's a prop. Would an extra $500 cover it?"

"Per tree?"

"Of course." John pulled out an envelope and counted out fifty one-hundred-dollar bills. "We'll have the rest when we arrive to shoot. If you need to reach me, you can call me at the number on this card."

The owner took John's business card and stuck it in the pocket of his tennis shorts. If he got itchy and decided to call the number on the card, he would get an answering service somewhere in Maryland that would have the cover story ready, just in case.

"Right. It's a deal. Glad to be of help. I don't think I'll need to call."

They shook hands, and John and Brian left through the double-size front doorway.

"What a dick," John said, walking down the winding stone sidewalk.

"It's amazing what people believe if you hand them a business card and act like an ass. The sunglasses were a nice touch."

"Hollywood. I love it. Come on, we have a date with the RV dealer and car guy."

"This one's for you, Ricochet," said the Chief of Station/Cairo, handing the cable to the junior CIA case officer.

"Really?" was all he asked after the reading the short cable.

"Ours is not to reason why, especially when Langley asks. Get it done right away."

"Yes, sir," he said as the COS left. He read it again.

IMMEDIATE
TO: COS/CAIRO
FROM: HEADQUARTERS
SUBJ: SEE BELOW REGARDING POUCH OF VIDEOTAPE
REF: NONE

1. PLEASE PURCHASE ARABIC-LANGUAGE MOVIE ON ONE-HALF-INCH VIDEOTAPE, PAL FORMAT, PRE-1983 RELEASE DATE, LENGTH OVER TWO HOURS. POUCH IMMEDIATE TO DO/PO/EMB. THX.

"This is a bunch of crap," Ricochet said to no one after he read the short cable.

Still a junior field officer, he had impressed the COS with a few minor recruitments of support assets, safe-house keepers, and mail handlers. He was constantly busy, having to work his full-time cover job stamping passports in the embassy visa office every day and his real occupation at night and on weekends. Ricochet had gotten his nickname from his two-six-packs-a-day sugar addiction to Coca-Cola, a cache replenished every few months by understanding in-laws back in Indiana. A stack of empty cans lined the edges of his desk like the Great Wall of China.

He could do without some crazy-ass request that sometimes came in from the pukes back in Langley. But the boss had asked him to take care of it personally, so he grabbed his coat and a handful of Egyptian pounds from his cashbox and headed out of the embassy to the market on the corner, where he hoped they had videos. They didn't. He spent the rest of the day looking for a tape meeting the cable's strict requirements.

Hours later, it was securely wrapped, waiting to go out in the next diplomatic pouch.

CHAPTER TWENTY-THREE

"How long will you be gone this time?" her quiet voice rumbled through the darkness of the bedroom.

"A week, maybe a few days longer. It depends," Garnett lied. It would be longer, but he couldn't stand the pain associated with the truth of how long he would really be gone.

"What time do you leave?"

"Six a.m."

"OK."

He could hear her tears.

When he met Elizabeth in college, he never intended to be a "spy." He was all set to do the conventional thing—college, wife, law degree, good firm, kids, suburbs, and all the trappings of life after that. When the CIA recruited on campus, it felt like the right thing to do. After a year of applications, interviews, paperwork, and background checks, he was in.

It was not the life Elizabeth had dreamed of, and she had made sacrifices to live his undercover life. He loved her for it. There was a time when he almost had her convinced that a life overseas as a spouse of a case officer wasn't so bad. There were promises of a nice house. Drivers. Maid. Exotic locations. But when they said she shouldn't worry about her first child being born in the "American hospital compound in Delhi," all bets were off.

In a few minutes, she rolled over, pressing her body close to his. Her arm wrapped tight around his shoulder; the sniffles turned to heavy breathing. They didn't even have the conversation anymore; rather, he just packed his bag and set it by the door for the flight. He watched the clock on the VCR blink 12:00, almost in rhythm to her

breathing. *A media professional who doesn't have time to set his own VCR.*
Finally, he got up, hoping the antique bed wouldn't creak. It did.

Maneuvering through the darkness, shadows, and toy minefield of
the townhouse to his daughter's room was quite a trick. The destruc-
tive power of a toddler was simply overwhelming and something he
had not been prepared for. He looked in her room and saw the stuffed
white bunny clutched securely in the arms of his unconditionally loving three-year-old.

"Daddies always come back," he whispered into her ear before
every trip. When, his insomnia took full effect, he went down to the living room to think. Husband. Father. Mission. Team. Carver. Henslow.
Mukhtar. In the morning, once again, he would take some of those
lives into his hands one way or another.

She woke briefly for a light kiss and hug when he left for Dulles
Airport a few hours later. He would call her when he arrived in Los
Angeles and every evening after that while he was away. Garnett really
didn't like to be away himself, but it was part of the job.

"Tight security," Karen said as he joined her in the security line at the
main terminal entrance of Dulles International Airport forty minutes
later.

"The results of living in a free society."

"Free? Eighteen bucks for long-term parking ain't free."

"Keep your receipts for your accounting. You'll get reimbursed."

She was right, though. Security at Dulles International Airport was
tighter than Garnett had ever experienced. Extra police cars made
their presence known as they lined up along the side of the Dulles
Access Road and outside the departure and arrival concourses. Inside
the terminal, security guards walked German shepherds through the
main concourse. Many of the entrances to the large, curved airport
terminal were closed, forcing passengers and guests to funnel through
the few open doors where airport security personnel searched everyone and everything that entered. *If there was ever a place to see the impact
of even the specter of terrorism on the American way of life, it's at an airport and
the restrictions on freedom of movement.*

The amazing thing to Garnett was how the people took it all in stride and showed little fear. Terrorism was a problem "over there," so these were just precautions. It could never happen in America.

"Where's the old man?" Karen said, her head quickly scanning the terminal.

"He said he would meet us in LA."

"He's probably taking a nap."

Garnett had picked Los Angeles for several reasons. Most importantly, it was at about the same latitude as Tripoli, making weather replication an easy matter. Since Italian architecture was important, LA had enough homes in the area to find a decent location, no matter the $10,000 price tag in John's recent note. The only detail was the angle of the sun. They had to account for a taping date several months different from the actual event, so they needed a variety of lights to ensure the shadows were the right length and could pass scrutiny. Garnett knew the little details would make the show, and he was not going to miss any.

When they landed at LAX, John and Brian were waiting for them with two rental vans large enough to transport the metal boxes that carried the cameras, tripods, and other equipment they needed. Anything they didn't bring with them, they would purchase locally.

Across the city, brushing the hair one more time, the Artist stepped back to look at her creation. First from the right profile, then the left, then straight on. She loved the feeling, something akin to what she would assume a new mother looking at her child for the first time feels. But in her case, she didn't have to endure the pain of delivery.

"Perfect."

She carefully lifted the base of the head and carried it to the special security vault built into an interior wall of the shop. The area was specially designed for the right temperature and humidity to make sure the mask retained its color and shape. The Artist placed the head on a shelf next to a dozen other of her creations and checked out the clothes hanging from a hook in the vault. A perfect replica of a Libyan captain's uniform, complete with exact military decorations, insignia, and the right amount of fading and wear estimated from the last pictures she had available of her subject. A Libyan major's uniform hung next to it.

She locked the vault door, spinning the combination lock three times in each direction. A false wall covered the front. She picked up the phone and dialed.

"Brian, it's me. I'm done and ready to celebrate. Don't you think you should buy me a margarita?"

CHAPTER TWENTY-FOUR

"That is *all* you require?" asked the Chairman of the Libyan Freedom Front.

"Yes, for the moment," Carver replied.

"And for the efforts of the LFF, what should I expect?"

"Two hundred thousand dollars will be transferred to your escrow accounts in Switzerland. All of them." They both knew what that meant. Everyone would benefit from this operation in some way.

The Chairman sipped his coffee and pondered the offer. Nothing was ever as simple as it seemed, and this seemed too simple. Of course, the LFF could use the money, although the bank accounts, both business and personal, were getting quite full. He did not need the American money as much as he had when he began the LFF. With the attention focused on Libya, neighbors like Egypt, Chad, and Tunisia had suddenly been very supportive of his organization. Still, he needed the training and tactical support of that portion of the American government the man sitting across from him represented.

"When will this take place?"

"Within the month. You have to be ready."

"Of course. That is not your concern. When have we let you down, my friend? More of a concern to me is the LFF. We must, as you know, preserve our reputation. The reporters ask questions."

"You can handle them; I'm not worried." *You ungrateful son of a bitch. The price is set. Who saved your ass after you defected? Who funded your precious reputation and position as the leading opposition group? Me.*

Carver didn't have to like his assets, just control them. He had recruited and vetted the Chairman after his defection years ago. Carver had been running the LFF account since, directing the dissident groups inside the Libyan military and leadership. They had spent the better part of a decade constructing a viable opposition to the Libyan regime. Piece by piece, he had pushed, shoved, and prodded the Chairman through a global public-relations campaign aided by the powerful machine of the CIA. He was uncertain whether he was any closer to success, since previous destabilization attempts, such as the 1985 revolt, had been marginally successful.

After a lifetime of crawling through the back streets of Delhi, Beirut, Tehran, and Tripoli, Carver knew never to underestimate the chance of success, however slight, or of failure, which was more probable. This had to succeed, or he would make the Chairman feel his disappointment.

"Then it is settled. I will be back in contact soon."

"Yes. I can see this is very important. Again, the LFF always appreciates your support. "

"Yes, many things are important. Many things."

"Mike Garnett. I have an appointment," he announced, pushing the intercom button in the small antechamber. Staring into the security camera hanging from the ceiling, certainly someone on the inside was staring back, giving him a good look. Within a few seconds, a buzzer sounded, and he opened the heavy wooden unmarked door opposite the one he had come through.

"Please follow me," an elderly secretary greeted him.

Besides the security at the door, nothing would identify the office as anything more than a business that took security seriously. Only a few local officials knew the office was actually the CIA station in Los Angeles, one of the few plum Agency jobs in the United States. Most of the offices were empty, he noticed as he was ushered into a large, ornate office. Sitting behind the desk, wearing the slight, bespectacled look of a college professor, sat the all-powerful Chief of Station/Los Angeles.

"Mike, thanks for stopping by." He shook Garnett's hand like an old friend, although they were meeting for the first time.

"My pleasure."

"Please, sit down," the COS said, offering a place on a rich brown-leather couch in the corner as he sat on a matching leather love seat across a glass coffee table.

Although they were both in the Directorate of Operations, tensions ran high between divisions. Many times it was a turf battle, or funding, but mostly it was based on the perceived relative importance between operations and collection. Domestic collection officers thought overseas field ops officers were cowboy assholes who got the best training and promotions, since the recruitment of an asset was valued in many cases more than the actual intelligence received from the source.

On the other hand, most overseas case officers thought domestic collection was for case officers who couldn't make the grade as recruiters. They spent their time going to fancy business lunches, driving nice government-provided vehicles, writing a few reports, and making enough contacts to wiggle a lucrative job on the outside.

Garnett was a third type. He was a "Headquarters puke."

"So, your cable stated you have an operation in the area," the COS said, reading deliberately from the communication Garnett had sent a few days ago. "Is that correct?"

Garnett had sent out the courtesy cable informing the COS of the operation and requesting the assistance. He had intentionally failed to mention that Brian would be in the area, just in case the COS got too nosy too early.

"Yes, we are doing some filming in support of an operation. We should be done this week," Garnett responded, offering as little information as possible.

"Well, I'm not too sure about this," the COS said, titling his head back and then rotating it around in a circle.

"Well, it has been approved by Casey." Garnett stared at him. He wasn't going to let this guy get in the way, COS or not. Although they worked for the same organization and directorate, there was a "need to know" principle involved.

"Fine. If there are any complications that might require our assistance, please let us know where and when. We don't need any blowback coming our way from any city officials getting calls from angry constituents. I don't want to have to clean up your mess."

"That should not be a problem. We are totally undercover and untraceable."

"I'm glad. I believe you also pouched some materials here." The COS rose and hit an intercom button. "Please get those materials we've been storing for our visitor." The COS retrieved a small gold case from his pocket and handed Garnett a business card. "If I can help in any way, please call. Here is my home number and office secure line if needed."

"Thank you. I will, and thanks for storing the pouch."

Garnett took the card and followed the COS toward the reception area. Waiting at the door was a long rectangular box wrapped in paper and heavily taped.

"The forecast is for rain. Hope that does not present a problem."

"Good-bye, and thank you again," Garnett said, holding in his annoyance.

"You're welcome. Call if you need assistance."

"I will."

A few minutes later, the heavy box was loaded into the back of the van. Garnett pulled out of the parking garage and drove carefully to ensure he was not stopped for speeding by some zealous LA cop. If the police opened it, he would certainly use the business card for his call from jail.

BOOK 3

MARCH 1986

Why is propaganda so much more successful when it stirs
up hatred than when it tries to stir up friendly feeling?

—*Bertrand Russell*

CHAPTER TWENTY-FIVE

This section of East Berlin had never been one of the Associate's favorites. Tall concrete buildings, *plattenbrau*, some only a few years old, sat crumbling from a combination of substandard materials and poor workmanship. Many had been turned into vacant lots. Personal safety was never his concern—the automatic pistol in his coat pocket was there only if needed. Some criminal stealing his Mercedes was his number one concern. Pulling the car into a small space next to a row of lower high-rise apartments, each exactly like the others except for the differing numbers carved on the outside.

Radiating "I will kill you" from his eyes to anyone who might be watching in the dim early morning, as he stood for a moment next to the Mercedes. Inside building number 1153, he rode the creaky elevator up to the eighth floor and knocked on the door of number 814. A young man opened it within a few seconds. He looked surprised but happy to see the visitor. A woman standing behind him looked anxiously over the man's shoulder.

"*Sabah El Kheer.*"

The Associate greeted them as he made his way into the apartment. It was a small space whose faded decorations and furnishings tried to hide the room's poor condition. It smelled sanitized—scrubbed from top to bottom, with bright curtains and plants to add color. "Your apartment is very nice."

"*Shukran.*" The young woman tried to hide her smile.

"Do not thank me. It is Allah's law that I provide deeds of charity to my fellow man. I promised myself I would help refugees from Palestine to make a life for them, as I was once helped myself," he lied, moving the orange curtain back from the window overlooking the street and his car.

As part of his job, he needed a broad network of helpers, so he spent time looking for anyone who could assist him. The Brother and Sister came to his attention several months ago from another source at the immigration center. Seizing the opportunity, the Associate set them up in their apartment and helped the Brother get a handyman job in the West on the chance they might prove useful someday. That day had arrived quicker than he anticipated.

"But without your generosity, we would certainly be suffering, or sent back home," the Brother replied as the Sister handed the man a cup of dark tea.

""You have surely shown charity to us many, many times. Money, food, clothes, this apartment, a job…" the Sister said, her emotions getting the better of her.

"All in the past. We must think of the future. And how do you like your work in the Western Sector?" He sipped the tea that he had long ago decided he hated.

"It is going well, very well. I help to fix things and clean. I get to practice my English. I am glad to work hard," the Brother said proudly. The Sister nodded agreement, taking the empty cup to refill it.

"No problems traveling to the West?"

"No. We have not been bothered at all on the subway."

"That is all good news." His comment completed his reason for being there—almost.

"Why am I here, besides this delicious tea?" He took another cup. "I need your help."

"Please tell us."

The Associate watched their eyes get bigger as they looked at each other and smiled. "The bureau has received many threats the past months from the Americans." He could see concern enter their eyes. "Do not worry. We get them all the time from people who hate us. Many of these threats we do not take seriously. But I need help to protect our cause. I can't do it alone."

Their eyes turned to sympathy.

"So I asked for permission from my superiors to seek help in protecting my colleagues. I thought of you."

Sympathy turned to pride.

"It would greatly help me if, for the next few weeks, you could keep a closer eye on where you work, the people who come and go, the buses, the taxis. It is not hard. Just take note of what you see. Of course this will require extra money, and I certainly would not ask you spend your hard-earned income just to help me."

They were shocked as he pulled an inch-thick stack of West German deutsche marks out of his jacket.

"Can you help me?"

"Of course, of course we will help," they both said, heads bobbing up and down, talking over each other.

"Very good. We must move quickly, but do not call me or try to contact me. We can never be sure when our enemies are listening. I will call you when we are ready." He walked to the door.

"Go without fear," the Brother said, holding the door open for their benefactor.

"So long, until the next time."

Outside, the morning sun was up, and the streets were getting busier. His car was not touched. His friend in Libya would welcome the positive news that the project was going well.

The day had started very well.

CHAPTER TWENTY-SIX

"**H**e should walk slower. After all, he is probably in pretty bad shape and may know he is about to die. I would take my time." Carver was feeling his age in his jet-lagged body, but he was a pro and watched with a critical eye to detail. Garnett appreciated that.

"I agree with Gene, and we could use the extra few seconds establishing the face shot." Garnett watched him take a few steps back and then limp forward slowly across the patio behind the Bel Air home.

"Like this?" Brian asked.

"Count two extra beats, then tilt your head to the left at the step."

Garnett looked at the monitor of the security camera apparatus he was using making sure it was framed. Brian walked into the shot, titled his head, and then limped into the back of the house. With him stood the two CTC staff, recruited to play the role of guards. They had been squatting over some plates, pantomiming eating until they walked out of the shot and then "escorted" Brian back and through the door.

"Good. Gene, this is where you will appear. Let's rehearse, if you don't mind."

"Sure, it's your show." Carver tried to hide his fatigue as he walked into the shot and through the door, making sure his face was never exposed to the camera. "How was that?"

"Fine, just like that." It was his show, but he wasn't going to critique a legend. "Let's go one more time from the top."

"You want the mask and costumes this time?" the Artist asked. She had been sitting patiently, looking for something to do. Since they hadn't rehearsed in full costume yet, she was bored hours ago.

"No. We'll save that," Garnett replied. *She's a pro.*

They had already spent four days rehearsing each shot, which would amount to no more than a few seconds of tape. A myriad of details surrounded the operation, each critical to gain the maximum impact for those few brief moments. Each step was marked exactly, each detail accounted for: shadows, time of day, architecture. The difficulty was making something as totally fabricated as those seconds look absolutely real, eliminating suspicion—or worse, scrutiny.

He had gathered meteorological reports on the weather around Tripoli for the date they had randomly chosen to display on the tape— a month after Tareq was killed in the helicopter crash. The day had been warm and sunny. No rain. Not a drop.

Garnett had been checking the weather for the Los Angeles area for over two weeks. He could control everything about the shoot—the length, subjects, quality, even the time, day, and angle of the sun. But he could not control the weather.

The rain had hit LA the morning after they arrived and hadn't let up for two straight days.

Garnett tried not to let the anxiety of the waiting show. To relieve the boredom and avoid mistakes, he had rented one of the meeting rooms of the Marriott to get in some practice. Still, he could already see impatience in his team. You can only practice so long. Like golf— the driving range is no substitute for a tough eighteen holes. This team was ready.

Sensing the team needed to relax, Garnett had made reservations for dinner the night before. They sat at a table that would have had a nice view of the ocean if it weren't for the clouds and rain. They masked their stress through the consumption of California Napa Valley Burgundy and Chardonnay, and, for Carver, a seemingly bottomless glass of Chivas on the rocks with a twist. Karen was happy with her Budweiser.

"We do all this work, and we never know what happens. Nicaragua, Afghanistan, all the rest. We toss our tapes over the transom, and we never know if it has an impact," Karen slurred, leaning over to Garnett.

"You can't measure what we do. We are dealing with people's emotions. Subtle inferences, maybe the occasional blow to the head. There aren't any Nielsen ratings for propaganda. You know that," Garnett replied.

"I understand, but don't you wonder sometimes about just what's the point?"

"The point?"

It was Carver. For most of the evening he sat silently, putting down one scotch after another. Garnett had wondered about that. Most lifetime case officers were dying to tell you their war stories about how great the CIA had been back in the good old days. They were driven to share their exploits about some long-forgotten, once-in-a-lifetime recruitment or how real tradecraft wasn't practiced anymore. Not Carver. Carver was unusually silent.

"Let me say this." He was slurring his words slightly, not talking to anyone in particular, as he killed off another Chivas. "I graduated from the JOT class—junior officer trainee, for those too young to remember…a long time ago. That's a long time ago, my friends, and I have seen and done a lot. The point is to be part something that is pretty damned important, at some point, in a place where you never really know what the point is."

He poured another drink. "I will say categorically that this is one of the more creative operations I have worked on. Unique. Out of the box, as they like to say."

Gene patted Garnett on the arm. He took a swallow from this glass and sat silent for a moment.

"The point? It was 1954. Iran. Mohammed Shah Pahlavi had just overthrown the government to become the Shah of Iran. We all were hanging around Tehran, to put it delicately, and even though we had established sources within the government, we were always assessing, looking for a good agent. I spotted WUZANY as he was entering the Interior Ministry as a low-level bureaucrat. Young kid, bright, eager, full of vinegar. Must have been twenty-one, maybe twenty-two at the time."

Garnett watched Carver's mind journey back to his youth.

"Small guy, but with smart eyes and a nice smile. Just gotten married, beautiful girl. What was her name?"

Carver drifted to the past, just for a moment, while the team waited.

"He was looking to make a career in the new government. After I met ZANY, it didn't take long to recruit him. It was rather simple for him. He liked America and what we stood for. He had some access to personnel files and details on security issues—little shit, nothing we couldn't get any other way, but ZANY had potential to move up in the world, so we kept him. Twenty bucks a month—that was all it cost to buy him. And that was dumped into an offshore account. Time passed, and ZANY moved up the ladder, gaining better access to better shit.

"By 1960, he was getting up in rank, undersecretary level, and started to pass some pretty valuable stuff on dissent groups and what-not. I was meeting him still at that time, and he was making fifteen hundred dollars a month. He had three kids and could use it. But he never spent it to avoid drawing attention and getting caught. The years passed, and I was sort of moving in and out of country. I didn't see him as much. But occasionally, I'd check on WUZANY to make sure he was treated right and see how his career was doing. He was getting handed off from one case officer to another, but I tried to see him whenever I could.

"By 1979, he had become deputy interior minister with a hand in controlling the internal Islamic fundamentalist movements. He was earning $5,000 a month and still dedicated to the cause. I started see-ing him again pretty often when I returned to the country as liaison with SAVAK internal security. When the Ayatollah's thugs overthrew the Shah, I warned WUZANY to leave. Chances were he was a marked man, but he stayed. After we left, I found out he had been tried and sent to prison. He was executed in 1981."

He paused for a moment, listening to the emotion of his own words. Garnett could tell that Carver had never told this story before. This was a man looking back on his life—and wondering.

"I didn't hear anything about his wife and children for years. Occasionally I ran a trace, but I only had a few minor sources left in country. Then I got word that the wife and daughter had managed to get to Paris. The sons, I guess, didn't make it. I went to see her. I found them living in a small one-room apartment in the Paris suburbs.

When I knocked on the door, ZANY's wife looked small, frail, nothing like the woman I had met three decades before. I just handed her his escrow account info and how to get access. Twenty-six years of salary plus interest, and a bonus—nearly a million dollars—he had never touched. She took it without hesitating and then looked at me and said, 'He always told me that his friends would take care of me if anything happened to him. Thank you.' And she shut the door."

Carver raised his glass. "WUZANY." He drained the remaining Chivas.

"WUZANY," the team responded, drinks raised.

Later that evening, alone in his hotel room, Garnett called his wife and daughter to tell them that he loved them. He would have called them anyway—he always did when he traveled—but tonight, for some reason, it just felt better.

CHAPTER TWENTY-SEVEN

In the darkness of the Mediterranean night, Trinche felt comfortably alone in the cockpit of his F-111 Aardvark, even though Beans was right next to him looking for the familiar lights in the night sky. He also knew his wing of F-111 aircraft was close by, and a few hundred feet above him was a McDonnell Douglas KC-10 Extender tanker waiting for him to get the F-111 in position for his turn to hook up.

Although the mission plans were not yet finalized, Trinche needed to get in some training while they waited to keep the reflexes of his pilots sharp and relieve nervous energy. He had arranged a series of five joint attack exercises with the naval forces in the Med, knowing that refueling was a critical part of any long-distance operation. Plans called for up to six aerial refueling hookups, so he managed to scrape up a few KC-10s in Europe for some practice runs. If he used more than a couple of tankers, it would tip off the eager press, who had now become experts on the capabilities of US Air Force squadrons stationed in Europe. In the final exercise in the series, Trinche was grateful, if not a little surprised, that there had not been any news leaks.

Trinche was very familiar with the lights and positioning cues of the KC-10, so he easily maneuvered the Vark behind and under the tanker to his designated position. With the lights of the KC-10 above him, Trinche concentrated on keeping the stick smooth. In a few seconds, he heard a metal-on-metal clank behind his head as the long refueling arm locked into position. Five minutes later, he gracefully pulled away from the tanker and returned to the lead of his wing.

By the time they returned to Lakenheath, six hours later, and after the standard debriefing of his pilots, they were ready whenever, and wherever, needed.

As his driver maneuvered the car through the dark streets toward the People's Palace, his passenger had trouble keeping his eyes open. Mukhtar had hardly slept since his visit to the Shopkeeper. He had never thought he would do that again.

Since Tareq's death, he had considered all his options—the thought of leaving the country had crossed his mind many times. He had to admit he was tempted, but he had never seriously considered it, or given into the opportunities. His travel out of the country over the last few months had included OPEC meetings, diplomatic negotiations in Europe, and even the United Nations General Assembly meeting in the United States. They never had refused him. Finances were not a problem, as he had made sure the accounts in Geneva were full, untraceable, and untouchable. Even for a man as ethical as he was, it was hard to avoid the temptation that came with an education and constant interaction in the West. As it was, he could honestly debate that his fortune was well earned.

Staying would allow him the chance to effect policy for the better of the people. He hoped he still had status with the Leader, but it had been months since he had spoken to him directly. Mukhtar was actually relieved now that he had made his decision, with Megrahi's help.

It is time to go.

The car slowed. Traffic was getting worse in Tripoli.

But what of Marwa? The question weighed on him. Sadly, but now fortunately, they no longer had a child to complicate the matter. That had been Allah's will. It had been hard on her—both of them, for that matter—but they managed to live and love, their mutual grief left mostly unspoken.

Being a practical man, he had examined all the possible alternatives from a purely logical framework. Even though they had been married for decades, he had no idea what was best for her. Could he just leave her? Abandon her, really—without even a good-bye? This could protect her from any revenge against him, as the family name still held power among many of Libya's tribes. He could tell her. Her reaction would be complete shock, but she knew better than to try to talk him out of his decision.

His analysis had determined that the best viable option afforded them the highest degree of safety. It was simple. He would orchestrate travel out of the country, taking her with him. Then, safely out of the country and immediate danger at least, he would tell her he was not going back. Her options would be limited, but she wouldn't mind. She had shown her strength of character countless times. She would stay with him to help him lead his crusade against the evil that had taken over their country. They had been inseparable for decades, and only death, or the Leader, could change that now.

By the time he arrived at his office door, how to control his own future was still uncertain.

"Abdallah, you are late this morning." Megrahi sat behind Mukhtar's desk, moving papers randomly on the desktop, messing the neat stacks.

"Traffic is worse."

"The price for our country's progress. You look tired; how is your leg?"

"Fine, thank you."

"Your reports on the current situation were very well received by the Brother Leader." He paused. "I know these months have been difficult for you." Megrahi remained seated. Mukhtar sat in the guest chair, resting his cane on his desk.

"Difficult, yes, but I am glad I have been of service to the country," he lied.

"And you have been. And you are still needed here. The American fleet is violating our territorial waters, and I expect an incident shortly. The Brother Leader has decided your presence here is very important. Do not plan any travel outside the country for the foreseeable future." Megrahi watched the man rise to his feet and leave. *You do not seem pleased, Abdallah. Not at all. The Leader might be also. But he knows nothing.*

"I did request a chance to speak—" was all he said.

"I know." And he left.

Mukhtar sat, knowing his best option had just been removed from the equation. His country was likely to be attacked, and control of his—and Marwa's—future was quickly slipping away.

He was glad he left the message at the market now—he hoped it was delivered.

CHAPTER TWENTY-EIGHT

"**H**ow many twenty-foot Winnebago RVs and beat-up Mazdas pull into a driveway in fashionable Bel Air on a Saturday morning?" John whispered.

"Not many, I bet. I'm sure the neighbors and the local security have noticed," Garnett answered. Still, one of the reasons he liked the house was that the grounds were protected from nosy neighbors by huge hedges and entry gates. He was really not worried. The cover story was solid, but smaller things had blown operations.

"Yeah," was all the blurry-eyed man wearing a bathrobe could muster as he opened the door.

"Mike with Docu-Films," Garnett said, smiling and holding out his hand to the man in the bathrobe. Garnett had called several times over the last few days to remind the man that the film crew would be there when the weather changed. They were impatient and ready to get going. *Any problems from this guy now, and I'll give him a rectal heart massage.*

"Oh. Yes. Come in." The man hesitated momentarily.

"Let's look around," said Garnett.

They walked through the house to the patio in back. Karen was already out of the Winnebago getting things organized. Garnett took a moment to survey the area. The Italian patio was nearly finished. The tree had been moved as requested and paid for. Everything else looked as ordered. Only a wire hung from the wall, wanting a light fixture. In the middle off the wall, across the patio, was the plain, arched door.

"Nice work. I like the wire. Good effect," John observed as he looked over the angles to the door.

"Get Gene out of the RV. The rest come out only to shoot." Garnett looked to the sky. It was going to be sunny and warm, finally.

"Any problems?" the man asked, still in his robe.

"No, just fine, thank you."

The owner stood, staring at the Winnebago and beat-up Mazda sitting in his driveway.

"The house is locked except for the patio door. Please keep them off the grass. It is a new lawn."

Garnett took a white business envelope from this pocket. "Here's the remainder of what we owe you. Thanks for the use of your home. Really beautiful place."

"Great. Say, will this show be on PBS, or something? I'd like to see it."

"Well, we hope so. We'll let you know. Good-bye, and thanks again."

"Take care of my house." The man vanished inside. A few moments later, Garnett watched a black BMW 325i pull out of the driveway and disappear down the street. John and Brian started carrying equipment immediately. The two CTC staffers, called the Extras by the team, exited the RV dressed in the same type of green fatigues worn by the Libyan army, carrying a long, wide box.

Garnett liked to watch his EMB team in action. They had done productions on Afghanistan, Nicaragua, Cambodia, Angola, and a dozen other locations. Propaganda operations on narcotics, terrorism, and the Soviet Union occupied the rest of their time. They rarely knew the purpose of their efforts—*need to know*—which had an impact on their morale. Garnett tried to make sure they at least received some letter of appreciation from a senior official. Each could double his or her salary in the private sector, but they stayed. They were pros and loyal.

They decided to set the camera date/time display to 1315 hours, close enough to the sun's highest point, to minimize shadows. Even if anyone took the time to analyze the tape, which he doubted would happen, there were numerous variables of orientation, location, and terrain that could potentially moot the shadow issue. Although not sure of the worthiness of the actual camera equipment in Libya, they had decided to take their chances by not distorting the picture quality in fear of losing sharpness on the more important facial images. Garnett had John buy Minolta cameras, since they were popular and used in country. They were placed at right angles to the arched Italian-style door dominating the middle of the tan wall across the tiled patio. Small monitors were attached to the cameras.

The Artist came out of the RV and walked up to Garnett.

"We need another half an hour, maybe a little more. Now this is a SoCal day," she said, looking up at the blue sky.

Garnett followed her glance upward. A washout today would mean they had only one left. It should only take a few hours, but simple things could become complex, and he wanted that extra time. If they had to, they could wait all day and hope there would not be that many puddles to contend with. *A complex and life-threatening worldwide covert operation canceled due to puddles.*

"How are we doing?" Garnett shouted to John.

"Ready to roll, anytime."

The Extras were on the patio, sitting on top of the box. They looked at Garnett, who gave them the thumbs-up sign. With the help of a crowbar, they pried the lid off. They reached in, pulled out two heavily used AK-47 machine guns, and slung them over their shoulders. One took his position next to the patio door. The other leaned against a late-model 1970s Mazda they had pushed around side of the house and onto the patio. A used-car dealer had had one that was a reasonable duplicate of one that would be found in Tripoli in 1986. To account for some body-style inconsistencies, Garnett had Brian rip off the bumper and some chrome. Period-correct license plates were attached, and the camera was angled to catch a glimpse with every pass.

Garnett walked over to the RV, swung open the door, and stepped into the cold, dual air-conditioned interior.

"Damn, it's cold in here," he said.

"Gets hot under that makeup. Don't want to lose our boy," the Artist said. She was combing the hair of a man dressed in the worn uniform of a Libyan captain, a man Garnett was certain was Tareq Mukhtar. Quietly sitting next to him was Carver, dressed in a plain set of fatigues and holding a cap with a wig of curly black theatrical hair attached to the inside.

"How you doing under there, Brian?" Garnett asked.

"Fine. I'm ready when you are."

"Ready?" Garnett looked at Carver.

"Affirmative."

"Let's go," the Artist said, taking Brian by the arm and leading him out the door. Immediately upon exiting the Winnebago, Brian took on the persona of his character. *He takes direction well.*

On the black-and-white monitors for endless minutes, the camera slowly panned left and right across the patio. In the shot, the Extras went about mundane activities—mostly standing by a barren wall, apparently guarding the door behind them, casually holding their AK-47s, doing nothing. Occasionally they would squat and talk or prepare some food. It was boring—just what Garnett wanted. At a few seconds over the randomly chosen mark, the two armed Libyan army soldiers left the screen as the camera continued its boring path across the patio. A random amount of time later, Captain Tareq Mukhtar (a.k.a. Brian Shay) walked into the frame from right to left, escorted by the guards. They walked across the patio and stepped through the door. Following them by a few seconds was a man dressed in simple green fatigues, dark hair protruding from under his officer's hat. He never turned his face to the camera as he entered the door.

The addition of the unknown officer (a.k.a. Gene Carver) was a suggestion from Henslow. Garnett considered it a decent addition, giving the death an additional sense of authenticity and conspiracy. Plus, Henslow seemed to want it.

Waiting inside, the Artist applied new effects to the makeup on the Tareq mask.

Outside, the camera panned the empty space of the patio once more. Five minutes passed before the soldiers emerged. One had his hands under the shoulders, and the other carried the feet of the now limp body of Captain Mukhtar. His head fell to the side toward the camera to give a good look at the makeup-applied bullet hole in the side of his head, dripping good amounts of theatrical blood. The group walked out of the frame from left to right. Garnett gave the signal to John, who switched off the power. The camera stopped.

Perhaps it was practice, nerves, or the fact that they didn't want to waste what was turning out to be a picture-perfect southern California day, but the actual final take went so smoothly that it almost bothered Garnett. He ran them through the routine two more times as security against something happening to any of the tapes. Before they tore down the sct, they reviewed the tapes, searching for any errors they might have overlooked. They couldn't find any.

"It looks good, boss," John said.

"Yes. It does," the Artist said with a smile on her face.

"That's it. That's a wrap," Garnett said in his best Hollywood director's voice.

Garnett watched Carver, who had been waiting for the signal to exit the door.

"Well done," he said.

In minutes, the equipment was stored, makeup removed, and costumes and props packed. The bulk of the team would leave that night. Brian would stay behind to return the RV and drop the repacked AK-47s at the LA station for shipment back east.

That night, Garnett looked out the window of the airplane as it headed home, with a bag of videotapes securely placed under the seat in front of him, his foot resting on them. He was proud of the effort and knew they had done a good job so far. They had executed a very difficult plan almost flawlessly.

Now, if Henslow did his part as promised, the *real* spy shit would begin.

"Flash cable from Rome," his secretary said, placing the folder on the desk.

Henslow was slightly surprised. He had been expecting it, but not this soon. His eyes scanned down to the short cable.

SUBJECT: HJSHIELD CONTACT

TEXT: HJSHIELD MSG RECEIVED BY IN-COUNTRY ASSET DEAD DROP.

1. (BEGIN MSG) IN THE NAME OF ALLAH, THE MERCIFUL, WE MUST ALL STRIVE TO END THE TERROR AND VIOLENCE AGAINST THE INNOCENT PEOPLE OF THE WORLD AND MY COUNTRYMEN. I AM LEAVING. PLEASE BE READY. (END MSG)

2. PLS ADVISE GUIDANCE TO ROME STATION RE FURTHER CONTACT.

He picked up his secure phone and punched Harper's numbers. "I am a genius."

"You heard from him. What did he say?"

"It's a little vague—but he is doing something, like we figured. Get your ass over here."

"Screw you. On my way."

"I am leaving. Please be ready." What the fuck does that mean? Henslow started to bang out his reply to Rome.

This operation is going too well. Something has to go wrong; it always does.

CHAPTER TWENTY-NINE

"This is it? You should have more." He tossed the papers on the large oak desk.

"I had hoped you would find it very interesting—what is there." The Libyan's response was designed to avoid directly contradicting the second-most powerful man in all of Libya.

"Yes, interesting, perhaps. What of this man you spotted?" Megrahi tested him.

"We have our people checking. He works for the oil industry"

Is there any better way to hide than to be our friend? So, Abdallah, what is this? Are you returning to your old ways? Or did you think you were leaving?

It was not much of a shock. After they had taken power decades ago, it was normal to have contact with useful foreign intelligence services. They helped assist the new officials in many ways, not least of which was in the strange arena of diplomatic and international relationships. They had a vested interest in the early success of the new State of the Masses—and provided a means of escape in the event the help didn't work out as planned. Megrahi knew Mukhtar still had intelligence friends who were in a position to help. It was somewhat ironic that Mukhtar trusted the American intelligence more than his own people. Megrahi knew many of the same Americans, but he was always more comfortable with the Israeli Mossad. They were more ruthless and didn't publically debate the moral issues when it came to killing. They just killed.

The phone rang. He listened carefully, then hung up.

"I need more before I take this to the Leader. Continue your work and report to me daily."

"I will," the Libyan said, rising.

Sometimes opportunities just fell from the sky, as if by the will of Allah. When they did, Megrahi was never slow to make use of them. The oil revenues had started to make life better. Schools, hospitals, and roads—they had supported it all, even the terrorism. The oil money had leveled the field, and the requests came from around the world from every group with a cause that felt it needed a few dollars. Megrahi found many of the groups they supported useful, as they helped him build his security apparatus and gather information on friends and enemies worldwide.

Mukhtar had seen it coming first. The creation of the Jamahiriyah—the People's Republic, the brainchild of the Brother Leader—was a way for an inexperienced leadership cadre to run a country without any of the bureaucracy, they would explain. Mukhtar did not interfere as Megrahi started the trickle of money to support the terrorists and meddle in foreign lands. It then became a flood, straight from the Libyan Central Bank. When Mukhtar began to question the project, Megrahi grew more distant from him.

Megrahi would counter Mukhtar's objections by arguing that a sign of a powerful country was its relationships overseas and its strength at home. And during it all, the Leader seemed oblivious. The structure of the People's Government had started to break down, resulting in chaos within every facet of the Libyan citizen's life. It just seemed to infuse more vigor into the creation of the personality cult that fed his ego. His behavior became erratic, and the day-to-day management of the country fell more and more to Megrahi. The downward spiral had to stop, and it could—someday—by a revolt by the people.

Megrahi knew that would take years. It was time for a change. The Terrorist had the plan moving, and soon everything would come together. The Leader had to go, one way or another.

1400 hours: "*Yorktown*, this is Yankee-4. I read two SAMs launched, over."

"Roger, Yankee-4, we copy," answered the Operations Officer inside the windowless combat information center of the Aegis cruiser

USS *Yorktown*. He had been tracking the progress of the F-14 Tomcat of *America*'s VF-102.

The Admiral had received his orders and wasn't going to waste time. With his F-14 flying combat air patrol, the USS *Ticonderoga*, the guided-missile cruiser USS *Scott*, and the destroyer USS *Caron*, each part of Cruiser-Destroyer Group 8 crossed the "line of death" during the early morning hours. For days, navy aircraft had flown into the 150-mile-wide mouth of the Gulf of Sidra, challenging the Libyan government's claims on that area of the Med in the latest Freedom of Navigation operation.

Yankee-4 saw the markers grow steadily brighter on his radar screen. The whining of the electronic detection system, which had been growing louder in his earphones, turned to a scream. Yankee-4 began a series of tight turns to force the slower-moving SAM-5 missiles to mimic the difficult maneuvers. The nearby Grumman EA-6B Prowler aircraft, fitted with five underwing jamming devices, began busily mimicking the radar signatures of the US aircraft. Dozens of false targets attacked the missiles' radar guidance system, creating images a safe distance from the planes and warships.

Yorktown's four twelve-foot-high phased-array SPY-1 radars were pumping out six megawatts of power looking for enemy aircraft. They were constantly monitoring the activities of the SAM-5 missile site after intercepting Libyan communications ordering missiles fired at any US aircraft that came within seventy kilometers at Sirte, 450 kilometers east of Tripoli. Until 1970, the site had been the location of America's Wheelus Air Force Base.

Yankee-4 completed his maneuver in time to watch the missiles fall harmlessly into the gulf waters below him.

1600 hours: The Libyan pilots of the Soviet-built MiG-23s were given clear orders: intercept and shoot down the invading US planes. When they took off from Benina Airbase, an E-2C Hawkeye AWACS plane immediately detected the Libyans and sent an update to the *Yorktown*. Two F-14s intercepted the MiGs, and the MiGs began a series of aggressive head-on maneuvers, trying to get into firing positions on the two F-14s.

"*America*, Yankee-1, I have excessive hostile actions and intentions."

"Yankee-1. Be advised you are warning yellow, weapons-hold condition." The Admiral had just signaled the F-14s could open fire in self-defense. The F-14s moved into a position behind the hostile MiGs, locked on to them with radar and acquired Sidewinder tones, which meant they were ready to shoot the Libyans down. The MiGs moved off.

For the next several hours, more SAM-5s roared from the mobile transport launcher at Sirte. The Missile Operator received his orders directly from the Libyan military commanders, which suited him just fine. He was tired of taking directions from the Soviets, who, since January, had been at Sirte installing the launchers. He laughed as the Soviets retreated to their technicians' trailer when the missiles were launched. *Cowards.*

Despite this, the Missile Operator was happy to have his new SAM-5 capability, with their 120-kilometer reach, much better than recently discarded SAM-2's twenty-five-kilometer range. He was eager to use the new weapons against the Americans, or on the Israelis. He did not care. He just wanted to see them fly.

It was tense inside the carrier *Saratoga* as the Admiral monitored the situation in the darkened combat information center. Officers and sailors peered at the radar blips and lines, a pale red glow on their faces. The Grumman Prowlers still flew inside Libyan radar coverage, picking up the changing radar frequencies made by the Libyan missile operations. This information was fed back to the Aegis cruisers and the three carriers in the Gulf. Weapons Officers, flying Vought A-7 Corsair attack aircraft, were receiving the data and feeding it into their High-Speed Anti-Radiation Missiles (HARM).

The missiles' targets were flying at the very outer range of the rockets. The Admiral knew that his high-speed, low-flying jets were armed with the latest electronic countermeasure equipment and therefore not in any danger. The pilots constantly turned their aircraft, reducing their radar profile to avoid showing their tail pipes to any heat-seeking missiles. Some pilots actually enjoyed watching the pretty missile launch arc on their radar. It almost made them forget that rocketing toward them was a telephone-pole-size tube of high explosives.

The Admiral had all the data he needed as he watched the large screens in the *Saratoga*'s command center. He was glad. His patience had just worn out.

CHAPTER THIRTY

"I am sorry; she no longer works in this department," the receptionist replied.

"Where is she now?" Mukhtar asked in a diplomatically calm manner as he glanced at the fax machine.

"I do not know. She was summoned yesterday afternoon and did not return. Her desk—she is no longer in our department; that is all I know," said the attendant, pretending to return to her work as she held back tears.

"Thank you." Her disappearance was not a coincidence, of course. No one vanishing in Libya was an accident. The surveillance on him had gotten tighter. For her innocent favor, she was certainly suffering, as was her family. *Poor girl.*

"Excuse me, Mr. Foreign Minister. You are to accompany me immediately on the order of Major Megrahi."

"For what reason?"

"I do not know, sir. But I think there is trouble with the Americans. Please follow me."

He arrived in the military command post under the People's Palace to find Megrahi speaking on the telephone. The staff ran from one post to another as the sounds of warning alarms and static radio communications filled the air.

"Yes, we shall counter their aggression," the Megrahi said quietly over the phone, looking at Mukhtar almost hopelessly.

"Yes, he is here now. You are right…yes, Brother Leader…yes…we must not allow the intruders…yes, it is a violation of our territory." He hung up. The phone started to ring almost immediately. He ignored it.

"You sent for me." It was a statement.

"It has begun in the Gulf, between our forces and the Americans. The Americans will win, of course. You know as well our resistance is impossible." Mukhtar was puzzled by Megrahi's reaction. He looked sincere with concern. "Our ships are not seaworthy. We cannibalize parts from one to another. After so much spent, our radar is controlled by the Soviets, but the technician on site assured me that it is ready—most likely to be destroyed."

The phone was still ringing.

"So why continue? You should stop this."

"What am I to do? The time for diplomacy has passed; we know that—it will not help stop their navy. It is too late for that."

Megrahi finally answered and listened. There was a long pause, as if the person on the other end was distracted. He rolled his eyes at Mukhtar. It could only be one person.

"Yes, I have informed the navy to set sail at once...yes, Brother Leader, very good." He replaced the phone with more force than necessary. "We shouldn't be surprised at his reaction, which at the moment could best be described as obsessed. He has decided tonight is the time to test the capabilities of our Soviet-purchased equipment and the skill of our navy once again. He is a mumbling idiot."

"We have known that for years. They will certainly die; he must know that." Mukhtar spoke as if it was a fact.

"Yes, he does, but we will have to deal with him later. We have a country to defend now. After another humiliating defeat in a few hours, it will be your job as foreign minister to defend the Jamahiriyah to the world. You must prepare."

The phone started to ring again.

Mukhtar listened emotionlessly. It all sounded confusingly familiar, like the many crises they had faced over the decades when the pair had fought for a better country for the masses. However, there was a sense of relief. Despite everything he hated about what was happening and how much he wanted out of it, he did have a duty to the people.

"For the people."

"Yes, of course. Do not look so bleak, my friend. We will have our own success soon; you will see."

He waved his hand like a teacher dismissing students and picked up the phone. Mukhtar could tell it was another one-sided conversation. Mukhtar was tired, and it was time to return home for the few hours he had. Limping slowly through the building, he pulled half a dozen aspirin from his pocket and swallowed them, his third handful of the day.

Across Tripoli, the Libyan was leaving Abu Salim prison. His work was complete. He had professionally extracted the relevant information hours ago. He could have stopped, but she was such a beautiful girl— dark eyes, olive skin, and raven hair. It would be a pity to waste such a desirable opportunity. *And such a shame.* She really did not know much, just doing a favor for an old man. He had to make sure she learned her lesson. *Well, sometimes favors can be big mistakes. Too bad it's the last lesson she will ever learn.*

CHAPTER THIRTY-ONE

2000 *hours:* "November-3, this is *America.* Two surface vessels approaching one hundred ten degrees, range sixty miles. Proceed on target."

"Roger, *America.* Proceeding as ordered."

November-3 checked his digital attack computer system. All system indicators were green. The low-flying A-6 Intruder attack bomber launched its Harpoon antiship missiles at the French-built Combattante fast-attack boat that was approaching from a Libyan port on the western end of the Gulf of Sidra. Two fourteen-foot McDonnell Douglas all-weather cruise missiles released from under the wing of the streaking A-6. The radar-guided missiles, carrying five hundred pounds of explosives each, skimmed just above the waves of the Gulf toward the ship over thirty kilometers away.

Aboard the Combattante, the captain had no idea what was approaching his ship and his crew of twenty-seven men. His weapons-control teams were preparing their surface-to-air missiles to strike at the American planes. He was busy receiving telemetry from the four friendly Soviet ships shadowing the American fleet. With any luck, he thought, he was certain he could maneuver in close under radar cover and release several missiles at the planes. He would not have that chance.

After gaining altitude to increase its angle of penetration to the hull, the Harpoon missile hit the stern of the Libyan attack boat at approximately six hundred miles per hour. The explosion tore the back end of the ship off, but it did not sink. He was thrown through the door of the bridge on impact, breaking his legs on the rail. Dazed and screaming in pain, he watched the fire spread along the deck as the surviving members of his crew jumped into the dark waters. Before he died, he sensed the sea and his ship being hit with rocks, and he thought it was most unusual for this area of the Gulf.

The Rockeye cluster bomb dropped by November-3 spread its 247 small warheads in a devastating pattern, penetrating the armor of the burning ship. The dark waters of the Gulf quickly extinguished the fires.

"*America*, November-3, scratch one ship, dead and sunk."

2230 hours: "*Saratoga*, this is Sierra-11. We have radar contact, over. Request permission to proceed."

"Roger, Sierra-11, you are authorized to proceed on specified targets as directed, over."

"Copy, *Saratoga*."

"Sierra-12, you copy?"

"Roger, Sierra-11, let's go."

The two Corsair A-7s, accompanied by F-14 Tomcats and F/A-18 Hornets, sliced through the dark Mediterranean sky, releasing from their perimeter patrol points. The electronic sensors were picking up the radar from the Libyan missile-launching site, more than forty kilometers away. Circling above, an E-2C Hawkeye radar plane used its six tons of electronic jamming equipment to protect the aircraft.

A HARM attached under a wing of each plane came to life as programmed at about twenty-five kilometers from the target. Detaching from the wings, the missiles' jet engines accelerated to 760 miles per hour, locked on to the radar emissions from Sirte, and rode the signals toward their destination. Within a minute, the 146 pounds of explosives in each warhead slammed into the SAM missile radar arrays.

The Missile Operator heard the distant rumble turn into a roar and tried to yell at his crew. It was too late. The impact threw him across the launcher as a bright orange flash blinded his eyes. The heat seared his skin. It took him a few moments to get his eyes focused on the burning radar. His ears were out of commission, registering only the sound of rushing air. As his head cleared, he saw the launchers themselves were not damaged, only the radar. As he struggled to his feet, he had to admit the Soviet technicians had been right in insisting they place the equipment at opposite ends of the complex. Although the radar was effectively blinded and inoperable, his crew could get the site operational in a few hours.

"Sir, the Soviets are remaining outside the target area."

"Thank you," responded the *Yorktown*'s Operations Officer, looking at the white, diamond-shaped mark that represented the Soviet Bear airplane circling safely several hundred miles away. The symbol contrasted well against the blue background of one of the four glowing forty-two-inch square screens. The screens were alive with dozens of symbols that indicated the courses and speeds of hostile ships, submarines, aircraft, and flying missiles, in addition to friendly ships and aircraft.

The Soviet planes were providing data to the Libyan ship he was tracking, but the Operations Officer did not have authority to shoot the inviting Soviet targets down, as much as he would have liked to.

An E-2C Hawkeye continued to feed the *Yorktown*'s Sperry computer system through secure satellite links. A few moments later, two A-6 aircraft fired at the Libyan Nanuchka II-class corvette attack boat from Benghazi moving toward the American vessels. The Libyan sailors decided to return to port.

CHAPTER THIRTY-TWO

"**W**hat is happening, Abdallah?" Marwa said, entering the study. He was sitting at his desk, leaning back in his chair, staring out to the dark gulf waters beyond. Moments of sanctuary at home were few tonight—he needed to return to write the predictable statements for the Leader.

"There is fighting with the American fleet. What is there for Libya to gain? What is he up to? Diplomacy..." his voice trailed off.

"That is not what I mean. What is the trouble? Tell me now," Marwa said, a request just shy of a demand.

"There is noth..." he started.

He had never lied to her. Not in thirty years. The truth was their bond, and it was impossible to start lying to her now. Besides, she would see right through him. His silence had given him away.

"Sit down, Marwa."

He told her of his despair at the state of the country internally. The fear he saw in the eyes of the people. The empty shelves. The human rights abuses he could no longer tolerate or defend. The terrorism. The Leader whom he had not seen, or Megrahi, whose motives he could not understand, or know which side he was on.

"There is more." She waited, knowing; her voice was calming.

"I sent them a note—as insurance, but we may need it now..."

She listened to it all silently. He could tell she was trying to make certain her face did not betray her emotions when he mentioned his approach to the Americans. She was always confident and self-assured. Friends would joke to him at diplomatic receptions that she should be the foreign minister, not him. He would watch her move about the room, saying the right thing, laughing at the precise moment, or greeting guests and making sure everyone had a good time. Many times, she was more knowledgeable of current events than he was. Now, it hurt him to see how he had hurt her.

Over the years, Marwa had been more than a supportive wife for her up-and-coming political husband. She had almost completed her training as a nurse when she met the young Abdallah in the hospital. His knee was terribly damaged. He was somewhat of a celebrity, and she had heard stories of him—his soccer skills matching his quiet charm. When they talked, she could tell he was in pain, despite the medications, but he never showed it.

After they married, she moved with him as he completed his studies. She loved Europe. Adored the United States. She relished the opportunity her position as his spouse provided—to touch the lives of the needy inside her country. She raised her one child to do the right thing, and for him, that started with serving his country. For her, it became a nightmare. She had felt this way only once before: when they received news of Tareq's death during the rebellion. She needed to be strong once again.

Her most precious possession was a small silver frame with a picture of them together, all of them smiling happily on a family vacation sailing in the Mediterranean. Their last picture together.

"Abdallah, I have known of your discontent for many, many months. I was worried for you…before Tareq…and since, I…do as you must. I am with you."

He smiled.

The pounding on the door frightened them out of an embrace they were silently sharing. With more pounding, harder the second time, Marwa got up to see who it was. Mukhtar heard voices, Marwa's and a lower, darker sound. Marwa returned. She didn't say a word.

"I must go. If I do not come back—you remember the emergency plan." She nodded. "Repeat it."

"Ferry to Malta, or drive to the border at Ras el-Jedir. I will wait for you."

"No, you won't."

She patted him on his shoulder and smiled. "You are needed. Go."

0020 hours: "You will return to sea immediately and attack the American ships," Megrahi said calmly into the phone.

"But—" the commander of the Nanuchka tried to respond.

"The Leader is watching you. You will be destroyed at sea, return a hero, or he will order you shot on the spot." Megrahi hung up. It had been a long night, and he wasn't as young as he used to be.

The missile boat commander decided to take his chances at sea and left Benghazi harbor at full speed. His missile had a range of twenty kilometers, and he hoped he could get close, launch quickly, and then retreat under cover of the shore-based missile.

Only a few miles out of Benghazi harbor, he realized his plan was not going to succeed.

The two A-6 Intruders, one from the *Saratoga*, the other from the *Coral Sea*, had launched their Harpoon missiles at the approaching ship. The radar-guided missiles flew at wave-top levels until they neared their targets. This time, each missile shed its protective covering to reveal a torpedo carrying five hundred pounds of explosives, which dove into the water.

The torpedoes struck the cruiser amidships, raising it completely out of the water. The commander did not see them coming and had not taken any defensive maneuvers. Even if he had, there was no escape. Death was instantaneous. The surviving crew were thrown into the oil-covered water, where they would soon drown. The ship lay dead and burning in the water.

0047 hours: As promised, the SAM-5 installation was up and running in just four hours. His crew had to roll the smoldering debris of the destroyed radar array out of the way and replace it with new sensors. The Soviet technicians even helped to reconnect the launch cables before they returned to their trailer. The Missile Operator picked up the phone to inform the command center.

"This is the SAM Missile Complex, Sirte. Please be informed that the radar is again operational, and we await your instructions," the Missile Operator said with authority and pride.

"Very good. You have served the Jamahiriyah well," Megrahi replied smartly. "Please commence firing as soon as possible. Communicate all events back to me directly."

"Yes, sir." The Missile Operator hung up the phone. He ordered the radar switched on, and the technicians began to scan the screens for the best targets.

Two waiting A-7s from the *Saratoga* retraced the steps taken a few hours before by their colleagues. And as before, the HARMs skimmed above the water until they reached their target.

This time, the Missile Operator did not hear them coming, his eardrums damaged as a by-product of the previous explosion. When the first missile slammed into the newly installed radar array, his first thought was that they did not have any more spare parts to fix the sensors. He had no time left to think when the second missile hit the radar fire control system where he was standing.

The frightened Soviet technicians watched from their trailer as the missile complex burned.

The Admiral sat back in his command center chair reviewing the events of the last sixteen hours. At least six missiles had been fired at his aircraft, with no damage to his fleet. There were no American casualties. They had disabled at least two Libyan patrol boats and knocked out the radar at Sirte twice. *It was a first-rate job.* With the number of aircraft launching and flying around the clock and no incidents, he couldn't ask for anything better.

The Terrorist knew the Americans were coming. Being a prudent man, he thought it best to leave his camp, since their final objective might be broader than testing his host's defense of the waters off Libya. It was not in his plans to find a team of US Special Forces showing up at his door to take him to some surely unpleasant CIA interrogation center. It was a good opportunity to brief Megrahi personally in one of the safest locations in the country.

"We have identified some targets. I like the location in Berlin. The Americans are creatures of habit. They congregate socially at a few specific locations. Very desirable and easy target. Additionally, we have people there," the Terrorist offered.

"When can you be ready?"

"Less than a week."

"Very good." Megrahi looked at the Terrorist. "You may remain in here until the hostilities have ceased."

The Terrorist nodded and left Megrahi alone.

The night had gone better than expected, both for his country and for him. A few minutes later, Megrahi sent a cable to the People's Bureaus in Paris, Rome, Madrid, and East Berlin, informing them of the day's events and telling them to be prepared.

Sitting in the communications center buried deep inside the USS *Coral Sea*, the radio specialist listened to the static of the encoded radio signals emanating from the Libyan government center. Following standing orders, the seaman recorded the signals in their original coded transmission and then immediately began relaying them through one of the dozen Defense Satellite Communications Systems satellites.

In a large, square, glass building thousands of miles away in Fort Meade, Maryland, America's code breakers at the National Security Agency began their tasks. Simultaneously, the message was sent to the NSA employees located at the United Kingdom's Government Communications Headquarters in Cheltenham.

The intercept was fed into a series of Cray supercomputers, where they were attacked by the world's most advanced descrambling algorithms. On the orders of the NSA, "ferret" satellites capable of listening to long-distance and other radio traffic were tasked to monitor and validate any further Libyan communications. Within a few seconds, the meaningless signals were transformed into comprehensible English sentences.

A few minutes later, they were sent to the other US government security agencies and the fleet at sea.

CHAPTER THIRTY-THREE

"**W**here do you want it?" John asked.

"Somewhere around the middle, but not exactly in the middle; you know what I mean?" Garnett smiled as he stared at the monitor. Only the glare of the TVs and the colored lights of the electronic equipment filling the racks along the walls illuminated the cold, air-conditioned room. This was an important moment.

John rolled his eyes at Garnett as he flipped the dial on his editing board, moving the images at four times the normal speed. The whining sound was as familiar and pleasant to Garnett now as the midnight screams of his daughter.

"How about here?"

"A little more," Garnett said.

His eyes glazed over as the images sped along. He was suffering from a dangerous exhaustion cocktail. The trip to LA was catching up with him. The good night's sleep he had hoped for had been interrupted by his obsession with watching President Reagan's speech and the news coverage of the attacks in Libya. This was cured when his wife decided it was a good night to start working on the next child. He crawled into work an hour late. *They don't need to know all the reasons.*

In response to his request, a pouch from Cairo containing a VHS tape was waiting for Garnett when he arrived at Headquarters. According to the attached note, the movie was called *Shay Min Al-Khawf—A Touch of Fear*—which supposedly was a pretty famous movie in Egypt. The cable described it as an allegory to the Nasser regime, but it looked like a Western to Garnett. No matter, it seemed like a good choice. The content of the tape was important, but the physical nature was of paramount importance. Tapes in North America were coded with a *T* followed normally by the length of the tape in minutes (T-10, T-120, etc.). European tapes were marked with an *E* followed by the tape length. If the recipient knew this difference in coding and saw an American *T*, the operation was blown.

"That's enough," Garnett told John as the counter on the editor passed the fifty-minute mark of the 116-minute film. He handed John the master tape containing the assassination footage shot over the weekend.

"Whatever you say," John said.

"Ready?"

"Just watch."

John ejected the movie from the machine and followed Garnett through the narrow darkness of the Tech Room to a rack of VCRs. John put the movie in one VCR and the original Tareq tape in another.

"I patched the VCRs and wound through the movie a few dozen times to give it some stretch. Should be enough wear and tear. I'm about to crash edit the footage in one after another, really shitty-like." Garnett watched John hit play on both VCRs. "As a highly trained professional, this hurts."

On the left monitor was the movie. On the right was the familiar black-and-white image of a fake Libyan location. John hit record on one VCR, and the left monitor blinked and rolled. An almost imperceptible rainbow of color washed across the screen from the right corner down to the left, and suddenly both VCRs showed black-and-white. Garnett, his eyes fighting fatigue within the darkened room, watched the living Tareq Mukhtar again. John hit stop and the screen again blinked, rolled, and turned rainbow colors as the movie reappeared.

"One more time," he said and repeated the process for the second segment. This time Mukhtar was dead.

The tape was genuine, at least technically. The belief in the content was more problematic and required a reliable cover story and a mind-set willing to believe, which for Garnett was Henslow's problem.

"Here you go, one top-secret CIA operation, caught on tape," John said after the tape rewound. He handed the movie and footage back to Garnett, who felt the pressure lifting with the completion of his part of the covert operation.

"Let's see if you pass the test."

"I'm not worried. Especially when the DI is involved." Directorate rivalries ruled the Agency.

"Yes you are," Garnett said as he swung open the door and stepped out into the bright lights and warmer temperatures of the hallway. He almost ran over Brian coming out from EMB.

"Sorry, I should signal before I turn."

"Yes, you got the cover?" Garnett asked.

"Right here. Spent an hour on it."

The plastic case was covered in Arabic, with a picture of an ugly-looking guy terrorizing some innocent-looking person. The box was far from the pristine look it had had when it arrived in the pouch. On the outside, some corners were bent; the plastic edges were just slightly frayed in one, maybe two places. Just enough wear to make it look like a tape that had not just jumped off the shelf.

"Nice."

"We aim to please." Brian smiled and walked away. The pressure was certainly off for some of them.

Garnett put the tape in the case and clutched it to his chest as he headed across the building, down to the first floor, and past the credit union, and finally entered the recently renamed Directorate of Intelligence Library. The library had its own video production branch aimed mostly at training videos, but Garnett had made sure that the relationship between the different offices was close. He never knew when he might need their help, such as now when he entered the office of the Branch Chief.

"Mind if I borrow you guys for a moment?" Garnett asked the gray-haired woman, who looked as if she had a perpetual smile on her face.

"Hey, Mike. Good to see you. Sure. What do you have?" The Branch Chief jumped from her chair and grasped Garnett's arm.

"We got this tape in from overseas, and our guys have looked at it. I just want to get a second opinion." Garnett didn't like deceiving her. The Branch Chief was one of the few people in the CIA he really liked. Plus, she was one of the other few true believers in the power of video. On top of that, she was just a decent and nice person who had worked in the CIA her entire life, as had her husband and two children. Nepotism ran big in the Agency. It was easier to trace and trust family members. Garnett couldn't imagine a nicer family.

"Sure, let's go in back. So, you keeping busy? We sure are with this Libya stuff."

"We have our moments," Garnett responded.

They walked through the desks to the back part of the L-shaped office, where the technicians sat in a dark work area staring at monitors and punching buttons. The Branch Chief approached a man wearing headphones and watching a tape and tapped him on the shoulder.

"Could you look at something here?"

"No problem," the bearded man said. He tossed down his headphones and stopped the tape.

"We want to see if there is anything screwy from a technical point of view on this tape. John has an opinion, but I want to make sure. There is something around the fifty-minute mark." Garnett handed it to him. Then panic set in. The prerecorded VHS movie had the tab that allows recording removed. John worked around this by covering the hole with tape so he could make the edit. Garnett could not remember if he had removed the tape.

A single careless moment could ruin all their work. *Holy shit! Did I screw this up?*

As the man jammed the tape into the machine, Garnett tried not to make it obvious as he shifted to see if the piece of tape was covering the hole. It wasn't. His lungs started to function again.

"Well, it's a European tape. You can tell by the marking here on the side. E-120. That means Europe and one hundred twenty minutes long. Looks like a Middle East movie. Minute fifty, you said?" He pushed fast forward on the machine, as John had done less than an hour before. The black-and-white images appeared. "Well, it was dubbed from two machines hooked together, not through an editing system. You can tell by the rolling and rainbow effect." The taped rolled on to the second segment. "Again, same thing. The oscilloscope spikes when the edit hits too. Not much more beyond that. Real enough, in my opinion. Looks like a bad day for that guy."

"John agrees with you," Garnett said.

"Of course, he's DO."

"Thanks. That was a big help," Garnett said, shaking his hand.

"Anytime, Mike, anytime."

Garnett held the tape so that no wandering eyes in the hallway could get a good look at what he was carrying.

Garnett had delivered the fuel. It was time for Henslow to light the fire.

CHAPTER THIRTY-FOUR

H e was in his element, rallying and chanting with the masses. It is natural to feel a swell of nationalistic fervor after being attacked by a stronger foreign power. Mukhtar was certainly feeling a combination of emotions. The Leader was making this first public statement on the attacks. He was taking full advantage for the international press assembled, and many of the world's TV networks were broadcasting the event live.

Mukhtar watched on television like the rest of the world, delighted he wasn't standing for hours on that stage having his mind assaulted by gibberish. His leg ached just to think about it. As much as he wanted to see the Leader, that wasn't the place, and this wasn't the time. He had spent a long night in his office, so resting was a priority. Megrahi was eager to get the statement to the Leader. His interruptions every few minutes asking if it was finished did not help Mukhtar's progress.

"It is not as difficult as you are making it. Just do it," he would say as his patience waned.

He had struggled formulating the wording and tone. They had suffered a defeat they could not acknowledge, but they would look foolish if they denied it. He compromised on sincerity—a statement that focused on the people, their commitment to their country. It was as good as could be done in a situation that demanded restraint. When Megrahi read it, he said nothing and left, the crafted speech stuffed in his pocket.

Mukhtar sat forward as the Leader ended the hyperbole portion and reached the substance of his speech. *The Libyan air force shot down three US fighters...no patrol boats were destroyed...Arab holy war against the United States...cause maximum casualties to US citizens and other Western people.* His well-crafted phrases were nowhere to be heard. The crowd roared its approval. Mukhtar just sat shaking his head, mindlessly rubbing his cane between his fingers.

Behind the Leader, Mukhtar could see Megrahi clapping and shaking his fist in the air—looking pleased and content.

This area of East Berlin was a little better. The construction in preparation for the eight hundredth anniversary of Berlin had made some areas of the Eastern side more like the West, but only slightly. The skyline surrounding the Associate was still a series of bland apartment buildings. East Berlin was a drab place, and the Associate missed the greens and browns of Libya.

He walked through the ordinary middle-class neighborhood, passing through imposing gates toward a massive office complex on Normannenstrasse. Crossing a courtyard, he approached the seven-story building at the heart of the grim concrete forty-one-building complex. The nondescript buildings were the headquarters of East Germany's dreaded Ministry for State Security—Staatsicherheit—or Stasi.

The Associate had worked with the Stasi for years and found the sophisticated espionage organization well deserving of its infamous reputation. Centered in these buildings, over thirty thousand officers ran over three dozen departments aimed at espionage, subversion, terrorism, propaganda, and counterintelligence. Thousands of other employees worked around the clock reading mail forwarded from post offices. At Stasi regional locations, another five thousand agents were assigned to surveillance of suspects. Another six thousand agents were required to listen in on the telephone conversations of private citizens.

For an East German citizen, this was the most frightening ground in the country. The Associate felt himself among friends. The previous year, he and the Terrorist had been the guests of Club Stasi, the area in the woods just outside of East Berlin. Called the Forest House by the Stream by his Stasi counterparts, it supported an athletic field and other delightful amenities. His friend had brought some of his more promising pupils there for special training. They had delighted at the successful results over the past six months—a massacre at a synagogue in Istanbul, an airplane hijacking, and the destruction at the Rome and Vienna airports. Now he was back looking for help once again.

He showed his special pass to a series of guards and took the elevator to the fifth floor. The dimly lit hallway could not hide the 1960s-era "modern" decor. He walked through a door, one of ten thousand in the complex, simply marked Department 23. The air inside the building was as oppressive as the reputation of the occupants.

"Erich," he said to the pale receptionist who sat among a dozen other pale receptionists. It wasn't the real name of his Stasi contact, but every time, it was enough for her to push a security lock, allowing him to walk though a door into a cluttered office barely larger than the elevator he had just ridden on.

"*Guten morgen*," the powerful-looking man said, rising and extending a hand.

"Good morning, sir," the Associate said, trying to avoid wincing at the firmness of the handshake.

"Please, sit. Coffee, *bitte*," the Stasi Officer said, pouring a cup of dark coffee from an instant coffee maker sitting on the corner of his desk. "It is Colombian."

"Thank you. And thank you for seeing me."

The man stifled a smile. "How can we help you?" He only marginally tolerated his visitor. He was competent, so that was a positive, and he had proven useful supporting a few previous operations. After that, he was just another in a long line of underachievers deriving their power from others who were also using him for their own objectives. It was his terrorist companion and support by the crazy man in Libya that he feared most. Better to work with them than have them turn their attention to his country.

"By the order of my Brother Leader, we plan on promoting an incident in the Western Sector. We hope to show the Americans they are not safe anywhere. My superior in Libya has chosen the target and plan. He has sent our colleague to make the device, but we are in need of some material and logistical support."

"And where and when are you planning this incident to occur?"

"Recent events in the Gulf of Sidra have pushed our timetable up slightly, but it should not be a problem. We are looking at one of these five locations," he said, pulling a list from his pocket and sliding it across the desk. He provided the list as a professional courtesy. The reason was sound. The Stasi might be interested in assisting the operation. If not, they at least would want to know its location to protect any espionage activities running or to make certain their people didn't end up getting hurt.

"We have surveillance on the locations now. Target number one seems the most likely. Perhaps a few weeks, early April."

The list looked safe to the Stasi contact. Military installations mostly, cargo depots, supply areas, clubs, but he had to check it with other departments. His people had tacitly monitored the movement of the visas from East to West, but the order was that they should pass unchallenged. Although he did not have the details of the exact operation, there was no reason to doubt the professional terrorist sitting across from him. *If they want to blow up a few Americans on the other side of Berlin, fine.*

"What materials do you need?"

"Very little," he said, handing over a second short list of required items.

"I shall have to get the proper signatures, but it should not be a problem. I will call in a few days. Anything the Stasi can do to help you, you must let us know," he said, appearing sincere, raising and extending his hand.

"On behalf of the Great Leader, we appreciate your hospitality," he said, and with another painful shake of the hand, the business transaction was complete.

CHAPTER THIRTY-FIVE

Garnett watched Harper's reaction as she stared at the TV, feeling proud of what they had created. Horror filled her eyes. Henslow saw it too. He smiled.

"This isn't real, right?" she asked, turning to face away from the screen.

"About as real as a fucking space alien." Henslow beamed. "Good work, son."

"Thanks."

"It is very good." She directed this comment toward Garnett and then turned to Henslow. "What's next?"

"Well—" Garnett started.

"You and Carver are making a quick trip to London," Henslow interrupted. "Right, son?"

Garnett looked at Henslow.

"Right." *Elizabeth is going to kill me.*

They always enjoyed walking through the neighborhoods of Friedenau, when the signs of spring started to pierce Germany's drab winter days. Dozens of Berliners took pleasure in sitting at cafés, drinking their morning coffee—even if it was a little chilly—looking at the pink flowers sprouting on the trees. Occasionally, as they walked along a narrow sidewalk, they would pass an American soldier. They had been told to be afraid of the soldiers, but they found it difficult to believe that these laughing, smiling faces were any real threat.

As they strolled past the building, a delivery truck sat outside the closed club. In the evening, it would be a different environment altogether. Hundreds of US servicemen would stream into the disco looking for beautiful German girls, who themselves were looking for husbands. By midnight, people crowded the sidewalk waiting to get in.

They caught the U-Bahn through West Berlin to Friedrichstrasse in the East. The border guards never really noticed the innocent-looking couple and waved them through without checking their bags. From there, they caught a taxi to complete the twenty-minute ride to the small park. The whole journey had taken less than an hour, and it was near dusk by the time they arrived and walked to the center, which had only a few visitors. They took a seat on a secluded bench to wait. In fifteen minutes, the Associate walked up to them, knowing he had lost any surveillance.

"Do you have something for me?"

The Brother retrieved the folded sheets of paper buried deep in the pocket of his overcoat and handed them to the man, who quickly placed them in this pocket.

"We have all the details and times. I even have drawn a map—"

"Yes, fine, I appreciate your conscientiousness. I am sure it is fine. Now I need you to listen carefully. Sometime soon, a man will come to your apartment. He will stay a few days in your spare room. Leave him alone. Do not speak to him or interrupt him in any way. When he leaves, he will hand you a package. You must not open it. Do not touch it. Do not look into it. Do not unwrap it. Do what he says. Understand?"

"Yes," they replied in unison, startled at his uncharacteristic firmness.

In the next few minutes, he outlined the rest of the details.

"Should we keep watching the building?" the Brother asked.

"Yes, but only look for anything that is dramatically different from what you have observed already. If something strikes you as unusual, then you can call me at my number, but only if it is really important. No other time. Remember, it must be important, and remember what I have told you. Do not write anything down. This is for you."

The Associate pulled out another envelope, exactly like the one he had handed to them during their last meeting. This time he took it and put it in his pocket without looking.

"Thank you. But—"

"Your efforts are appreciated, and they deserve a reward." He faked a smile. "Now I must go."

He got up and walked away.

That night they returned home to open the envelope. As the thousands of marks fell out onto the kitchen table, they grabbed each other in happiness, muffling their shouts of joy.

"The F-111, the main weapon of the Forty-Eighth Tactical Fighter Squadron, weighs forty-five tons and is powered by two Pratt & Whitney TF-30P-100 afterburning turbofan engines. Maximum speed is Mach 2.5 at an altitude of 53,450 feet. The F-111 carries a crew of two: the pilot and a weapons systems operator—WSO, or, as we call them, wizzos—seated side by side in an air-conditioned, pressurized cockpit."

The base Press Officer purposefully droned the mind-numbing details as he escorted the team of reporters closer to an Aardvark parked in an open hanger inside Lakenheath. The reporters, representing a pool of international print and television journalists, were the lucky winners, having their names pulled out of a hat to represent their numerous counterparts who had hoped to get inside and get a story. The rules of the briefing were presented with military precision and firmness. *No photographs of any kind without approval. No television cameras allowed on the base. No names can be used. Brief Q&A. Still photos from an approved press packet will be made available.*

"The aircraft is equipped with an automatic terrain-following radar system that flies the aircraft at a constant altitude, following the contours of the land or water. It allows the F-111 to fly in valleys and over mountains, day or night, regardless of weather conditions."

In a briefing room, Trinche watched the group shuffle toward him through a newly unrestricted area of the base. He likened the mass to a herd of sheep, the reporters bleating their way through the tour, asking questions they knew would only receive a no comment.

The Press Officer, a young kid compared to most in attendance, was acting on Trinches' direct orders. *Bore the reporters to sleep.*

Speculation remained red hot that Lakenheath was the location for the United States to launch any air strikes against Libya. Since the thrashing the navy had handed out in the Gulf, the pressure had become more intense. Washington had ordered the base commander to hold one briefing to relieve some pressure.

"We are privileged," he announced from the podium, "to have one of the senior base commanders here to answer questions for us today. I'd like to introduce Colonel Oscar J. Trinche, Vice Wing Commander, Forty-Eighth Tactical Fighter Wing."

"Thank you. Welcome to Lakenheath. I'm sure our fascinating tour of the inside has been much more pleasant for you than your endless tour sitting on the road outside our gate." Laughter. "Questions?"

"Has the squadron received any notification to be prepared to move in the event of any other terrorist incidents or fighting with Libya?" a reporter asked.

"No comment" was the reply. "We do not discuss deployments or operations of any kind. Next?" Trinche knew this was a ridiculous answer. The press was well aware of the increase in training exercises over the last four months. Even the British TV show *Spitting Image* was making fun of the potential attack.

"What are the air force's views on Libya and our response in the Gulf?" another reported parried.

"We are pleased and proud that all of the navy aircraft and pilots carried out their missions and returned safely." He paused. "I will not answer questions on our readiness and tactical plans, if any. I can only state that if or when the pilots of the Forty-Eighth TFW are called upon, we will successfully carry out any mission with professionalism and honor. Thank you for coming."

After several more probing questions were followed by vague responses, Trinche left the podium and walked out the door.

Trinche thought it ironic that a military sworn to defend and secure the American way of life, most importantly freedom of speech, found itself at greater risk because of the right they were protecting. But that was how it should be, as any alternative was incomprehensible to him.

The mission plan, target, and rules of engagement were locked in a safe in his office, approved and ready for execution.

CHAPTER THIRTY-SIX

He was exhausted.

Traveling internationally always gave Garnett a headache, especially when you leave at night and arrive when it's morning—and you have trouble sleeping on a plane. Garnett's mind and body were doing everything they could to put him to sleep. The night before was sleepless as he talked through leaving Elizabeth with a child sick with a horrible cough. He wished he could tell her details about the project. Maybe it would have helped. But he couldn't, so he did all he could—hold her in the silent darkness.

To his annoyance, Carver slept soundly for the entire trip. When the plane landed at London's Heathrow Airport, he was ready to get going.

Reaching the baggage claim, Garnett noticed more security than normal milling about. The world was braced for more terrorist attacks after the recent fighting in the Gulf, and security agencies, already pressed to the limit, were near the breaking point. Even the customs officials, normally the epitome of British friendliness and cheery character, were stoic and businesslike. Passengers did not stop and loiter in the terminals. The threat of terrorism had not stopped international travel, but it certainly made it less attractive. Airline revenues had dropped 60 percent worldwide since Rome and Vienna.

Garnett carried his blue-covered tourist passport and his black-covered US diplomatic passport. Being identified as an American diplomat would not be good if the plane was hijacked, so a rubber band was wrapped around his tourist passport to quickly distinguish it in a pocket if some hijacker was anxiously waving a gun in his face. Garnett had to admit he was happy when the plane landed and would be happier when he was out of the airport and in a cab heading to downtown London. Perhaps he could even close his eyes for a few moments.

"Are we checking in with the station?" Garnett asked Carver.

"No."

"That is quite impressive. Quite a work of fiction. It is fiction, I assume," the LFF opposition leader commented after the videotape stopped.

"We have one more step, which requires your network, as we discussed," Carver said, leaving the answer to the question hanging.

"It is all arranged. The courier is awaiting his instructions."

"Good. I'll have my colleague explain the details."

They were in a private room at 106 Pall Mall, the prestigious Travellers Club, the exclusive members-only domain of the rich, the distinguished, and the diplomats. He was surprised he had even been asked to attend this meeting. Compartmentalization of sources and methods should have separated Garnett from such a high-value asset as the leader of an opposition group. He questioned the reasoning, but it had to be one of three possibilities: He was being rewarded with a trip to London for a job well done. He was needed to explain the cover story and answer any technical issues. He was there in case the op blew up and would be used as a scapegoat.

The man was polite but so far had said nothing directly to Garnett, but now it was his turn to tell the story.

"It is important that he fully understand this is real. It came from a guard at the location where Captain Mukhtar was being held after his capture last September. He was not killed in a crash as reported. He was held. Interrogated, killed. A security guard befriended him. He liked him. He was nice. When he saw what happened, he was very upset and wanted to let the family know, since the name Mukhtar is very respected, etc. So he decided to steal a security tape and made a copy to smuggle out. He sent it out of Libya through a friend who hoped that somehow it would get to the right hands. After that, the less said the better."

"I understand. I would say it certainly looks most authentic to me."
Is this what really happened? "I knew Tareq, and this is a sad thing to see.
Most sad."

Carver took the tape out of the machine and handed it to the
Chairman, handling the plastic case as if it were fine china.

"We appreciate your assistance, as usual," Carver said with an
infusion of sarcasm they recognized, causing a slight smile on the
Chairman's face. Garnett had no clue.

"It will take a few days. Perhaps a week."

"No longer. Let us know when it is delivered."

The Chairman looked at the videotape in his hand, impressed
with his American friends. The young man had something to do with
this—his face gave away the look of pride. *Such a work of art, and the
execution—well done.* The Chairman would do as they asked, naturally.
It would not help him, or his cause, to upset his sponsors. It was always
best to have people like his visitors owe him a favor.

Getting the tape to Mukhtar presented many risks, but none
that couldn't be overcome. The Chairman personally wrote the note
before he wrapped the tape securely in several sheets of plain brown
paper. Within a day, the tape was in the hands of an LFF courier on a
flight to Cairo where the LFF had a well-established network infiltrat-
ing the border into the eastern section of Libya. From Cairo, it would
head west, crossing into Libya at the chaotic Musaid-El Salloum border crossing. It would be driven over 1,500 kilometers across northern
Libya through Tobruk, Benghazi, Misurata—passed along by a series
of couriers all the way to Tripoli—none aware of what they were transporting. The final delivery in Tripoli would be much more dangerous.
Monitoring Mukhtar's movements verified he was under constant surveillance by the intelligence service. The Chairman would have to pick
the right time and select an expendable follower for the final leg of
the package's journey.

No matter the outcome, the Chairman knew that if caught, the
cost to the LFF would be slight in the short term, but a bonus in the
future.

BOOK 4

APRIL 1–15, 1986

Terrorism and deception are weapons not
of the strong, but of the weak.

—*Mahatma Gandhi*

CHAPTER THIRTY-SEVEN

Sitting in the terminal in East Berlin's Schoenefeld Airport, the Associate was nervous—this was no ordinary visitor. The tickets, with a variety of alias names, were routing the passenger through Athens, Rome, Paris, Madrid, and finally Berlin. The passenger was known to terrorist organizations by the code name Specter. International law enforcement and intelligence organizations knew him as the world's most dangerous explosives expert. Specter made a living traveling from country to country, selling his services to the highest bidder. Terrorism experts attributed a majority of the successful bombings around the world to Specter, either through his own hand or others he mentored.

Getting him was a coup. This must be big, for his friend in Libya to pay for him.

A man emerged from the crowd and walked up to the Associate. He was small, with a look better suited for a librarian than an expert bomb maker. They made no sign of greeting except a handshake, and they did not speak. Only when they were safely in the Mercedes and maneuvering through traffic did they talk.

"The materials are in a safe in my office. I have a safe house where you can work. The couple there will not bother you."

"Very good." He had worked with the Libyan before and knew him to be a professional's professional who had helped enlarge Specter's bank accounts many times. They were top notch and always paid on time. Still, he liked to work alone.

"May I see the target, if it is not too much trouble?"

"Yes, of course."

In silence, the Associate drove to Friedrichstrasse, the location of one of the four crossing points between East and West Berlin, known to the world as Checkpoint Charlie. The area was under construction, an effort by President Erich Honecker to make the border look more like crossing a frontier. He drove the car quickly through the guard stations on the strength of the diplomatic license plates provided by the Communist East German government. To maintain the perception that Berlin was a free city, not divided by *Die Mauer*, the Western allies responsible for security in West Berlin—the United States, Britain, and France—refused to conduct international border controls to their sector, making the Associate's escort of Specter through the infamous wall that much easier.

Specter barely glanced at the building when the Associate drove by.

"Any questions?"

"No."

Forty-five minutes later, they arrived at the block of apartments in the Eastern Sector. He pulled the car around the corner into a small alley and handed the man a white note card.

"Here is the address. It is just around this corner. I shall not see you again. When you are ready, call the number on the card. If…" Specter looked at him. "When they are completed, you may go, with your many friends', Allah's, and the Leader's greatest appreciation." They got out of the car. The Associate took the bag out of the trunk and handed it to Specter.

"Yes?"

Specter stood and admired the beautiful dark-eyed woman staring at him for a moment. *How did such an innocent-looking girl get involved with this? It takes all kinds to fight and win the struggle. It is amazing, the kinds of soldiers in our battle. Too bad they do not know their future.* Without speaking, he entered. Confused, she reacted not in fear but by closing the door behind him.

"May I help you?" the Sister asked.

"I would like to see my room, please," was all he said. A man stood up from a small couch and turned toward him.

Specter saw confidence in his eyes, but they also betrayed their fear.

"Yes, certainly. We have kept it ready for you," the Brother said, slamming his shin into the coffee table as he rushed to direct the visitor to the guest room. He limped down the short hallway, trying to ignore the pain shooting up his leg. Opening the door, he let the man enter the small room. Inside were a single bed, a desk, and a floor lamp. Specter set his bags on the bed and then walked to the window overlooking the street. He closed the curtains, blocking the view from the apartments a few meters away.

"If it is not too much trouble, I eat once a day at seven in the evening. Three eggs, poached, two cups of black tea with my meal. Four slices of bread, wheat only, buttered heavily. Just set it outside the door. If it is not too much trouble, I am not to be interrupted. I shall like to start my work now; please excuse me."

He watched them leave with puzzled looks on their faces.

"The packages have been picked up and delivered," the Associate said over the secure line an hour later. On the other end, the Terrorist had received and understood the simple message.

CHAPTER THIRTY-EIGHT

"We are being watched—by them."

"Yes," Mukhtar said to his wife. "It is the way it will be until this—how it will be for now."

She was doing her best. After all, she had not been certain she would see him again when he left home the night of the battle in the Gulf. That had been over a week ago, and she had barely left the house since. Mostly, she spent her time looking out the windows toward the Gulf waters, praying. It was important to keep up his work schedule— he had a duty to respond to the world's requests and criticisms. He had faith that things would work out in the end.

His faith had remained firm throughout his life. Allah provided him a standard to live by even as his own moral fiber was badly shaken or confused. He had found comfort in the knowledge that God provided limitless paths of moral resolve and humanity. Faced with a society that violated the basic tenets of Islam that human blood is sacred and oppression is not permissible—he was certain his own individual soul must remain firm and unshaken in all circumstances. As the Koran reads: *And God loves those who are firm and steadfast.*

It comforted him to know that on his Day of Judgment, Allah, the Sustainer and the Merciful, would record his generosity and reward him. Until then, he waited in his beloved home, a house he had taken from the Americans when he and Megrahi forced them out many years ago.

So he worked and waited. For what, he was not sure.

He was also a practical man. Days before, he had called Marwa aside, in the garden of his house, where he hoped any listening devices could not overhear his conversation.

"In case something happens to me, you need to leave, find the Americans—more likely they will find you—no matter; there is information that must be shared with them and the world. First, there are the terror camps and how we fund them." The rest of the evening and into the early morning, he told her the only remaining secrets he had purposely concealed from her. The financing of terror networks. The unpublicized erratic actions of the Leader to obtain nuclear and biological weapons. The weapons-smuggling program to support his latest terrorist pet project. Assassinations of opposition overseas. The torture at Abu Salim prison, beatings, hangings, mass killings, and worse.

His relationship with Megrahi was much more difficult to explain. It just wasn't consistent with what he thought. Was he for or against the Leader? Was he supporting the terrorists just to kill, or just using them for some larger reason Mukhtar couldn't ascertain? Had he manipulated the defense forces during the attack in the Gulf? Was he a friend or a psychopathic enemy? Was it possible to be both?

Marwa listened intently, as if she were back studying for her nursing degree. She let her husband tell her the facts and express his opinions of what they meant. By the time he had completed the narrative, she was stoic, understanding the pressure that was on her husband and her country. Much she had already known, or had surmised, but in the context of the manic goals and behavior of the Leader, the situation had been illuminated. The actions of Megrahi, whom she had considered a friend for decades, were more disconcerting. It was best to stay out of his way, for now, if possible.

"You must remember it all. I believe it will be important." Whether a premonition or just hope, he felt much better now that he had spoken to her.

"I also believe, Abdallah. I believe our country will survive this—as will we. In the Name of Allah, Most Gracious, Most Merciful. We have lost Tareq, but we will be rewarded."

A tapping sound surprised them. If someone was at the door, it was very early for visitors. Their small group of friends had stopped contacting them at the first indication that something was wrong in their circle. Also, the guard at the security entrance to the community would have alerted them to a visitor. Finally, the driver waiting outside would have stopped anyone as a last line of defense.

Mukhtar stood near their front door, listening. The tapping started again, but more rapidly, from the rear of the house. As he slowly approached the door to the outside sitting area, the tapping grew louder. He loosened the knob of his cane and slid the blade a few inches out of its hiding place.

"Who is there?" he shouted in his most threatening voice. The rapid tapping stopped, and he could clearly make out the form of a person outside turn and run away. He quickly opened the door. No one was there. A package wrapped in plain brown paper was at his feet.

"What is it?" Marwa asked as he carefully carried the package into the room.

He slowly tore the paper away from one corner, attempting to peer beyond the outer cover. Finally, he summoned the courage to just rip the wrapping away. He stood holding a VHS tape in his hand, alternately looking inquisitively between it and Marwa.

"It is a video cassette. A movie. There is a something else here," he told her, pulling the note out of the case. "It is from the leader of the opposition," he whispered with a tone of impending doom.

She saw his face turn white as he read the note.

"He says it was smuggled to him through soldiers who support us. It says it is very disturbing, but he felt obligated to get it to us no matter the difficulty and risk to them."

"What could it be?" she asked.

He rose slowly from his chair and walked across the study to the mahogany bookshelf that held his Sony television and Mitsubishi videotape machine. He could tell the tape had been played and was almost halfway through. He started the movie and sat in his chair. Marwa stood behind him, her hands gripping the leather near his head.

After a few minutes had passed, he grew impatient, but he would not turn it off. *He sent it for a reason.* Then the film seemed to break, and black-and-white images appeared.

"Tareq!" Marwa screamed, her hand making a sharp slapping sound as she covered her mouth. She started to sob as the familiar figure on the screen was carried out a door and across a courtyard. Then, just as quickly, the segments ended, and the movie started again. They were both weeping.

Mukhtar sat on the edge of his chair letting the movie run. His felt as if he were suddenly on fire. Logic took over as his brain categorized everything he had seen. *The man. The note explained how the tape was smuggled out of the country. It looked like his son. It was his son. The soldiers. The uniforms. The date. The blood. Who was that man? It looked like—it couldn't have been. Why would he? Why would he lie?* The TV screen exploded into a black-and-white cloud of static as the tape ended.

He rose, relying on his cane, as his knee had stiffened after his muscle convulsed in terror. Marwa stood motionless, her hand still to her mouth, the other clutching the priceless family picture to her chest over her heart.

He picked up the phone, his shaking hand barely able to dial. He cleared his throat and took a deep breath.

"Major Megrahi, please. This is Minister Mukhtar." The shaking from his hand ran up his arm and took over the rest of his body. He forced calm to his voice. "I need to see you. Immediately."

CHAPTER THIRTY-NINE

It was a simple process, but he gained great satisfaction doing it well—better than anyone else in the world, according to the Western intelligence services. All he needed were a few kilos of plastic explosives, a timing device, a fuse, and usually some additional material for extra deadly effectiveness. Many expert bomb makers had come before him. Many died at the hands of their own creations. *Poor technique.* An explosives expert who dies from poor workmanship deserves his fate, his mentor, the legendary inventor of the suitcase bomb, Abu Ibrahim, would tell him.

When Abu Ibrahim went into retirement in Baghdad, it was Specter who ascended to the throne of the lead terror bomb maker. The teachings of Abu Ibrahim were relevant for many practical and new bombing applications helping Specter learn his trade, always tinkering with new methods.

Cold, detached, random, and deadly effectiveness was Specter's trademark. The more people he killed or wounded, the larger his reputation became to both terror groups and intelligence organizations worldwide. He delighted in the notoriety when his activities forced him to go underground, where he took his carefully chosen code name, Specter. *An invisible, terrifying spirit.*

Now, seated in a small apartment in Germany, he methodically pieced together his latest creation. Men from the Libyan Bureau had delivered ten pounds of Semtex explosives and other materials. The malleable, easy-to-use Czechoslovakian explosive was his favorite, and the favorite of many colleagues in his trade, as friendly nations stocked a significant supply for resale. It was often overlooked by newer bomb-detecting X-ray machines and electronic chemical "sniffers," as he understood they were called, currently being tested at airports around the world. Only trained dogs seemed to have any luck in detecting its weak odor, and there were few of those around to really cause him any major concern.

Like its American cousin, C-4, Semtex was easy to handle. The risk of accidentally blowing yourself to tiny bits was small. A blasting cap or piece of detonating cord was required to take the materials from benign lump to killer mass. For a timer, he preferred a Swiss clock—very precise and reliable—randomly using the inner workings from different models, again to make tracing the origin difficult. The timer attached to the explosives with a common blasting cap and he made certain the contacts lined up cleanly, one of his signatures. Experimentation proved that canvas shredded better than most materials so he used a small black canvas bag filled with roofing nails and tacks.

He sealed the bag and placed it next to the two others he had completed earlier. All three were then enclosed in a larger faded green duffel bag purchased from a US military surplus store days before. The connecting wires from each small package were attached to the next. The remaining space was filled with the last of the nails before he tightly zipped the bag closed and pried the small metal tag off, making it virtually impossible to open by hand. The first phase of the mission was completed.

"Come here, please," he asked the tenants on the other side of the wall.

The Sister watched as her brother quickly entered the room. The door closed behind him. In less than a minute, it opened again. The small man exited, and she was relieved to see her brother behind him, nervous but alive. The bag remained in the room as the man left the apartment without a word.

In the dim morning light, the man strolled through the streets of East Berlin. He always liked to walk after he was done, a habit he found useful to wash away the fatigue that came from concentrating on his craft. At a corner pay phone, chosen randomly, he dialed the number on the card. After two dozens rings, it was answered.

"I am done," he said into the mouthpiece, disappointed that he had consciously lowered his voice in a veiled attempt at disguise.

"God be with you," was all the voice on the other end said before the receiver clicked dead.

The Associate rose from his desk in the People's Bureau, noting it had taken Specter little more than two days to construct his packages. It was slightly past six on Friday morning, which he calculated gave them plenty of time to set the plan in motion by that evening. Friday nights assured the operation its best chance to kill.

He walked down the dingy corridor into the even dingier communications room, where the Commo Officer, not used to evening interruptions of his boredom, jumped out of his swivel chair in surprise.

"I have a priority message to send of the utmost urgency and secrecy." He wrote a few words on a pad of paper and handed it to the young officer. "Do not discuss this." The Commo Officer quickly turned to his machine and began encoding the short message into the sophisticated machines purchased from the world's leading encryption companies.

Within a few minutes, the intercepted message was sent FLASH to the White House Situation Room, the CIA, the Pentagon, the commander of NATO, and the US embassy in Germany, as well as other members of the defense and intelligence systems. The special intelligence from East Berlin to Tripoli, captured and decoded by the NSA, was vague, but it indicated that a terrorist event aimed at US servicemen in Berlin was imminent.

At the camp in Libya, a few hours later, not knowing that it had been intercepted, the Libyan Intelligence Service gave it to the Terrorist, who happily read the same short message ending with the menacing boast: *You will be happy when you see the headlines tomorrow.*

"Any news?"

Garnett looked up as John set his tray down at the table. His plate was covered with fried chicken, mashed potatoes, and gravy. No vegetables. A slice of pie filled the remaining space.

"No. How's the diet?" Garnett said, taking in a forkful of salad as he watched John's feeding frenzy begin.

"Hey, when death comes knocking, I ain't going to be thinking, what was the point of skipping that pie? Well, he should have seen it by now. Any chance we will get some feedback on what happens?"

"I'll have to check, but don't hold your breath. I'm sure they are as anxious as we are."

"Just would like to know, right?" A heaping mound of potatoes disappeared into his mouth.

The cafeteria was small and filled quickly around noon, so Garnett made it a point to eat early, or late, if at all. The Agency actually had two cafeterias—a large one for employees not undercover and visitors, and another for personnel who needed to protect their connections to their actual employer, like Garnett. Despite its secure perimeter, the building was crowded with nongovernment employees essential to keep the building operating.

"This seat taken?" Carver asked.

"No, of course not," Garnett replied, slightly shocked. He hadn't known the man before the operation, but for some reason, it just didn't register to Garnett that Carver would eat in the cafeteria like everybody else.

"We were just wondering how it was going. You heard anything?" John asked, already halfway through his pie.

"No, I haven't heard."

"He must have seen it by now. Wonder how he took it. I'd go nuts."

"They expect him to stay in country and work in place. No revenge or anything like that, according to Henslow," Garnett said reassuringly.

Carver paused and then finished his last spoonful of soup. He shrugged his shoulders as he sat back in his chair.

"Can't argue with the logic, except I think that it is bullshit."

"What do you mean?" Garnett asked, shocked.

"I would suggest an alternative scenario. Think about it. For your entire career, you have dedicated yourself to the betterment of your country. Not the easiest position to be in under normal circumstances. You are a smart man, and you look at the books and you see falling oil prices, poverty in a legitimately wealthy country. You know that millions are being siphoned off to fund terrorism, something you vehemently oppose. You have a history of supporting human rights, even defending political prisoners. Your country is seen as an international pariah. You have the USA at your doorstep pounding you with bombs and sanctions. Even your reliable European and Soviet allies are giving you the international equivalent of the finger. But, being a loyal diplomat of some standing, you carry on."

"I don't see the bullshit yet," John said.

"The bullshit arrives when your son, whom you dearly love, dies—or at least you think he died. So, what happens one day when you find out that the people you have been working with most of your life killed your only son? Islamic law and tradition are filled with the concept of revenge. One chronic fault of this organization is that we analyze issues in a *Western* context. Too many Georgetown graduates around here who only understand events though cable traffic or the occasional cocktail party. Henslow knows what is going through that man's mind right now. Thanks for the company." Carver left as suddenly as he had appeared.

Garnett was stunned. In all the exchanges with Henslow, the idea that Mukhtar might resort to violence had never come up. He had read his psychological profile but had never looked for that aspect of his personality.

He had never asked.

CHAPTER FORTY

"**A**t this moment, he is the winner," the Chairman replied to the reporter listening on the other end of the phone call. "What the Americans do not fully comprehend is they have rallied the people to Qadhafi even more. The man is shrewd. He portrays himself as standing up against armed aggression. For him, it is a victory, not a defeat. The Americans do not understand this. Algeria, Syria, Iran, Malta, even Jordan and Saudi have joined in support of Qadhafi. Mubarak in Egypt must be nervous." *It never hurts to publically chastise the hand that feeds you for the sake of cover.*

"So, what are the opposition and human groups planning to do now?" asked the AP bureau chief in London.

"We will do what is necessary to free the people of the country trapped in the grip of tyranny."

It played well to the audience so he did his best to end every conversation with that quote. After a few more questions, he interrupted a reporter, faking a busy schedule and another interview waiting. It had been well over a week since the Americans had taught the regime a bloody message in the Gulf of Sidra. He was beginning to think the press had forgotten him. A few weeks before, he had been the darling of the media, and they all came to him, wanting his insights and opinions. *How quickly they have forgotten my place among the defenders of human rights.*

The news of the successful delivery of the package was a pleasant surprise. They would be happy, guaranteeing even more American money would fill the LFF and his personal account in Geneva.

The larger plan was already in motion.

His CIA-supported camps in Chad were filling with defecting Libyan soldiers ready to fight for him. The LFF cells inside the country had amassed enough arms and logistical support to mount the first effective strike at the Leader's security apparatus. When that was eliminated, it would just be matter of time. The military units—those not already totally subverted by the LFF—would quickly fall in line with the opposition and make the regime change swift and complete.

The Chairman was prepared to return to his native land and, through popular mandate, assume his rightful position as president. At that point, he would no longer need the misguided assistance of his associates at the American embassy. He would be appreciative of their support, but it was time for the people of Libya to lead themselves, he would say.

As his Americans friends often said, *it will be a whole new ball game.*

The NOC forced himself to sit on the edge of his bed. Keeping his eyes shut was not decreasing the pounding in his ears from the hypnotic disco music reverberating deep within his skull. Stretching his arms to the ceiling, he hoped to relieve the developing pain in his lower back—a result of his libido and too many worn mattresses. The squeak of the springs woke the brunette, so he took the opportunity to watch her as she flipped over, exposing her entertaining breasts from under the sheets. For a moment, the NOC thought he might just give into temptation to explore them for the fifth—*sixth?*—time since he had brought her back a few hours ago. There was way too much to do and he wished there was more time to prepare. *Boom! Boom! Boom!* wasn't helping, and neither were those breasts.

His mind couldn't recall much about the nightclubs and the women, one of whom was in the bed now. *Her name is—it starts with an A, doesn't it?* His eyes rolled in his head and he squeezed his lids tighter in their sockets to focus and concentrate. *Antoinette? Annabelle?* They had hit it off, especially after he kept the red wine flowing and ran his hands over her body at the crowded bar. They had walked back and started their night of lovemaking, if he recollected correctly, near the

Trevi Fountain. The second time was on the Spanish Steps before they made it back to his room. *Angelica?*

He forced himself to his feet and staggered to the bathroom. Leaning against the wall, he looked at his reflection coming from the medicine cabinet. His face looked like ten miles of bad road attached to a body that had felt better days. *I used to party for days and never felt it. It must be stress.*

"*Dar-ling?*" a soft voice called from the other room.

"I'm in here, A..." he stuttered.

"Come here."

He didn't want to seem ungrateful, but he really needed her to leave. His meeting the previous morning was unusual, if not unnerving. He could tell something was different immediately.

"So you are hot shit," the Case Officer had declared when the NOC arrived at their rendezvous.

"Oh?"

"I hold in my hand a cable direct from C/CTC himself, Mr. Wes Henslow." He waved a piece of folded paper in the air as if it were a golden ticket.

"Oh, shit." The NOC could feel the shaking start under his skin.

"Yes. Seems the last message from your dead drop got, shall we say, a significant amount of attention. So significant they have some directions specifically for you. You may not like them." This was what the Case Officer had been waiting for. It didn't hurt that he was now running a very important NOC in what had to be an operation of national importance. The station chief had even taken time to stick his nose into the office to see how it was going. A first.

The key words stuck in the NOC's head: "RETURN LIBYA IMMEDIATELY... MAKE CONTACT WITH HJSHIELD...ASCERTAIN STATUS AND PLANS. USE OWN INTITATIVE. SERVICE DEAD DROP AS SCHEDULED." This was a quick turnaround. Something was up, and he figured he was in it deep, so deep they were compromising his operational security to get whatever they were looking for. It was a risk they were willing to take—with his life. The Case Officer could provide little additional information, but if Wes Henslow was involved, then whatever they wanted was much more valuable than his ass. *So why not one more brunette before exile to Libya?*

"I am waiting," the voice beckoned. He went back into the bedroom, where she lay on her side, head propped in her hand, smiling at him. He needed to get back to the office to finalize the logistics

What the hell? You never can predict the future. What IS her name?

CHAPTER FORTY-ONE

The Analyst was eating lunch at a desk covered with multicolored files, in a room crammed with files. The smell of medicines filled the air from the nearby examination area of the CIA's Office of Medical Services.

"Hi. I'm Mike Garnett, from Propaganda Operations. We met a few months ago regarding Libya," he said, standing in the doorway.

"Yes, I know. Come in. Sit down. Banana?" the Analyst offered, pulling the fruit out of a brown paper bag.

"No, thanks. I just had lunch." There was a moment of silence.

"I know I'm not supposed to ask, need to know and all, but did Henslow and Harper go ahead with anything against Libya?" He took a big bite out of the banana.

He was right. He didn't have a need to know, but Garnett did.

"Yes. There is an operation going on now," he answered in a vague truthfulness. "I wanted to ask about something related to that. I was wondering, is there anything in Mukhtar's profile about violence?"

"Well, I'm not sure. I'll have to check." The Analyst, stuffing the rest of the fruit into his mouth, began to rummage through the files on his desk. He reached into one of the stacks and pulled out a half-inch-thick folder. "Pretty solid guy. Wonder why they decided to pick on him. Here it is."

He turned each page slowly until he found the right section.

"It's raised as a remote possibility of his character, rated as less than ten percent. That pretty much means used only in self-defense or extreme provocation."

"So he could be provoked?"

"He is a diplomat by profession, therefore almost a pacifist. It defines his total character. Steady. Contemplative. Astute. Under stress, he has never exhibited any violent tendencies, preferring negotiation and objective alternatives instead. Never served in the military. Has openly spoken on human rights and against torture. Education is a factor against random acts of violence, as well as his years in the diplomat corps. It would take something catastrophically extreme before he would resort to violence."

"But you aren't sure. Ten percent chance, maybe?"

"That is true. This isn't a perfect science. There are always possibilities—or, as you say, a chance."

"Thanks." Garnett got up to leave.

"Funny, that's the same question Henslow asked me too. I gave him the same answer. I had totally forgotten till you asked."

Garnett tried not to react. "Henslow asked?"

"Yes. Ms. Harper too."

He left.

The OMS door exited into an exhibition hallway where rotating displays, each on the history of some aspect of intelligence, were normally on display. Garnett stood for a moment, looking at the pictures retelling the story of Office of Special Services, the OSS, the World War II precursor to the CIA. *Their mission was clear: kill or piss off the enemy, knowing right away whether they were successful.*

He was not sure what to make of the thoughts in his head, most of which carried the classification *none of your business,* but others gnawed at his sense of finality. He had played a significant part in a major operation. The need for some clarification was gnawing at him. Staring at the exhibits, Garnett knew he needed to do something but was not sure what. He nervously took the elevator to the Counter-Terrorism Center office.

"Got a minute?"

"Sure, son. My wife says I shouldn't eat at my desk. Not good for my health." The Chief of the Counter-Terrorism Center held up a half-eaten jumbo burrito.

"I was wondering about our friend. Any news? The team was wondering—too."

"We have some indication the package was delivered. The rest is progressing. I think you can tell them that."

"That's good. You know I've been wondering about the video and Mukhtar's reaction." *Trying to coax an answer.*

"What do you mean?" Henslow asked matter-of-factly, taking a big bite of the burrito.

"Well, the profile speaks of a possibility of retaliation, if provoked. So it really isn't totally ruled out, as I read it."

"Anything is possible, son, so what does it mean? Look, you did a marvelous job with the video. It was a professional job. Top notch. You should be proud. We have several assets in the field working on it now. Leave it at that. When I can give you more, I will. Till then, don't ask."

Henslow finished the burrito in a bite. He looked a little agitated. Garnett could feel it and decided he couldn't get out of there fast enough.

"You're right. We just don't get a lot of feedback where we are." A painful truth.

"Anytime, son. Hey, I do have a question for you."

Garnett stopped quickly—just out the door.

"My granddaughter wants a bunny for her birthday next month. Know anybody who has one?" Garnett shook his head. "Damn! Thought maybe I'd get lucky, but not today."

That was his cue to leave, and he took it. Garnett wasn't exactly sure what to make of it all. Even implicitly questioning a man like Henslow was not a wise career option. After all, it was the OSS and guys like Henslow who were fighting the Cold War long before Garnett was even born. The "Old Boy Network" was real, it was successful, and Henslow was a charter member.

CHAPTER FORTY-TWO

After the FLASH message regarding the intercepted communication reached the National Command Authority, alerts were quickly sent to all American bases in Europe with a special warning for the 250,000 US soldiers stationed in West Germany. The NATO command center and Commander/US Army/Europe sent special alerts to the over six thousand soldiers of the Berlin Brigade and their families. West Berlin police authorities were contacted and asked to inform the bars, restaurants, and nightclubs frequented by the US soldiers of the alert. The police kept a file on the hundreds of these establishments.

The problem was enormous. It was impossible to locate and put extra security precautions in place in so short a time. After a frantic call from the superintendent, the clerk who was on duty removed the list of establishments from the filing cabinet in police headquarters, sat down at the telephone, and began dialing.

No covert sources had any information on an impending terrorist event.

By April 4, the trail was cold.

The Mercedes pulled up in front of the apartment in East Berlin at 2345 hours. Just as the wheels stopped rolling, the Sister slid into the backseat, placing the bag next to her. The car pulled away and headed to the Western Sector. The traffic in the West was heavy, even for late on a Friday night. Not a word was spoken as the Associate watched the Sister check her watch constantly. The car arrived exactly an hour later and parked along a side street a few blocks away from La Belle Discotheque, located at Hauptstrasse 78 in the Friedenau subdistrict.

"I will be here waiting for you. Do exactly as instructed. Put the bag near the bar, by the music area. Here." The man pointed to the map. "Remember this: you must leave immediately. Be quick. We are late. Understand?"

She nodded in reply, carefully grabbed the duffel bag, and headed toward the building.

The Brother was already inside, standing by the bar between a mass of drunken servicemen who were busy talking to equally drunk servicewomen. The disco was a combination of noise, heat, and bodies—lights flashed and bodies slammed into him in a type of motion he would not call dancing. Sweat drenched his body, a mixture of nervousness and the tremendous heat that was inside the room. He checked the time, trying to remember what he had been told to do. *See if there is anything unusual. Security. Police. Do not look nervous; it is crowded, and no one is interested in you.*

Remembering the conversation made him shudder. It was 0130. She was late.

Finally he saw her, fighting through the crowd, trying to protect the bag with her body from the gyrating bodies. She struggled toward him, shoving her way toward the disc jockey area, where stacks of records and empty glasses surrounded the young, sweating people enjoying the music. It seemed that there were people everywhere, perhaps five hundred of them, and he could not see how she could place a bag without being seen.

Outside, the Associate made a call from a pay phone to a secure number in the People's Bureau telling them to relay a message to the HQ of the Libyan Intelligence Service.

The message: "Happening now."

0140. She had no time to think as she dropped the bag along the back wall between the DJ and the bar. She turned immediately for the door. Moving quickly, he fought to meet her. The cool air felt like the Arctic when it hit his sweat-soaked clothes and skin, and his ears kept ringing to the music. The chill sent shock waves through his body, and he began to shake uncontrollably as he crossed the street. In a few steps, the car pulled up beside him, and they got in.

173

JOE GOLDBERG

"Is it done?"

"Yes," was all she could reply, her teeth shaking too hard to form a sentence.

"Go, now," he commanded the driver. The car pulled away.

It was 0145, Saturday, April 5.

At 0148, the dance floor of the disco was packed with over five hundred US soldiers dancing and drinking the night away as they did every Friday night.

At 0149, while the music was playing a new hip-hop song, two kilos of Semtex, surrounded by pounds of metal fragments, exploded. A roomful of horror was the result.

The force of the explosion blew the club's DJ into the air, then down through a new huge hole in the floor. A small fire started, and panic filled the room, already a picture of horror from the fallen ceiling and the broken walls, windows, bricks, and pieces of shattered records that were transformed into deadly flying projectiles. Limbs stuck out of the debris. Wounded soldiers walked around in shock as others ran shouting and screaming out the front door.

An hour later in East Berlin, after dropping the couple at the train, the Associate monitored the emergency radio frequencies with a simple scanner he had bought at an electronics store nearby. It sounded too good to be true. On the television, the late-night movie was interrupted to report an incident at a nightclub in the West: "Many are believed hurt, but there are no further details." Members of sympathetic and supportive terror groups were ready to make calls to take the credit for the blast, a move to confuse the police.

His desk phone started to ring with the call he was impatiently expecting.

"Yes?" he answered.

"I am looking for Eter," the shaken voice said before the line went dead.

The call signaled the Brother and Sister had made it to their apartment safely.

He was a professional, so tasks needed to be completed before he could celebrate the victory. The first was to send a cable to the

174

Terrorist, who had masterminded this operation, that it was a success. Stasi needed to be thanked. The coverage in the local press needed monitoring and summarized in a report for Tripoli. Then there were the Brother and Sister. There were several options there, but he just couldn't focus on them. He needed some rest now. As he laid his head on his pillow back at his apartment an hour later, his eyes closed almost immediately.

It was his first restful sleep in weeks.

CHAPTER FORTY-THREE

"**S**omething is happening," she said from the kitchen when he came through the front door.

Garnett's first reaction was that there was something wrong with their child. But he saw his daughter sitting on the floor playing with a toy. He joined Elizabeth, who was staring at the TV. He followed her eyes as a CNN special report flashed on the screen, projecting images of some sort of disaster scene.

"Bomb" was all she said.

"Reports are still sketchy, but German authorities believe the bomb was planted in the rear of the disco," the anchor said in his most serious tone.

The shot was an exterior, from across the street—as close as the police would let the journalists get, Garnett figured. Close enough. The video showed the collapsed exterior of a building, its ceiling covering most of what must have been the front. Hoses poured water into the hole, and smoke poured out. The familiar yellow tape was stretched across the street. Ambulances were coming and going, protected by heavy security—Garnett recognized the special antiterrorist unit GSG9, which was the model for most Western special forces. As the camera panned, it showed dozens of people, covered in blankets and dirt, standing, still in a state of shock.

"The discotheque is a favorite hangout of US military personnel in Berlin. Early indications are that several hundred people were injured, with at least two dead. John, what do you make of this?" The news anchor turned to the man next to him, the obligatory terrorism expert on retainer and always on call.

"I expect that a dozen or so groups will call in to take credit for the bombing. Many names will be new, others familiar. Let's not forget that there are several indigenous terrorist organizations in Germany, such as the Red Army Faction or the Holger Meins Commando. However, the timing does lead investigators to believe that Libya may be behind the attack. It comes just a week after the naval actions in the Gulf of Sidra. However, it will take some time before they can come to any conclusions."

Video was coming in unedited, and CNN was relaying the feed directly to the air, Garnett noticed, *just in time for evening news.* He was too much of a cynic to believe that the timing was accidental. Terrorists were adding adept skills at public relations and propaganda to their already potent arsenal of violence and fear.

Garnett had breezed through his international politics classes at Iowa. They were easy: US vs. USSR. Structure and orderly world conflict. The frightening difference between terrorism and Cold War was the terrorists' seemingly total lack of compassion or rational thought. The reason the world had not glowed nuclear hues since World War II was the belief that the person on the other end of the hot line was a rational human being who did not want to destroy civilization. Terrorists, Berlin was proving, couldn't care less. The images on television were the proof playing out before his eyes.

Gone were the days of repetitious, standardized, manageable, mutually assured destruction. They were being replaced by irrational, unorthodox, suicidal terrorism. The world's intelligence organizations and internal security systems would have to adapt. Garnett could see no other viable defense.

"We have the CNN Berlin bureau chief on the phone," the anchor continued. "Can you give us any details?"

"Not really," he said over a crackling phone line. "Authorities really don't have much to say. The bomb went off just before two a.m. local time. There was an explosion and fire, causing the structure to partially collapse. Hundreds are injured, perhaps thirty seriously. Many of the injured are US military personnel. Some are being transported to the US Army's Regional Medical Center in Landstuhl. Others are being treated at the local Schoeneburg District Hospital, among others. Unconfirmed reports have at least two dead, but that could go up. Reports are that several groups have already called in to take credit for the blast, but nothing is confirmed."

They were repeating themselves now. They didn't have anything new to say, so they were just going to continue saying the same thing in different ways and show the same pictures, like Rome and Vienna a few months before. The phone connected to Garnett's unlisted ops line rang.

"You see this?" asked the voice.

"Yes. Are we getting it taped?" Garnett asked John.

"Questions like that put you on this week's cover of *DUH Magazine.* Of course. I've already had calls from CTC, EUR, and Security."

"Give them what they want."

"I'm copying tapes now."

"You need me to come in?"

Elizabeth looked at him. One of the benefits of a CIA job, if there were any, was that it was hard to take work home. It wasn't as if he could take a briefcase of classified documents or video materials home. He had gotten into the habit of not even talking about work and leaving it behind him when he walked through the front door. She was protective of their time together.

"Why? You and the wife have a fight? I was planning on working late anyway. Just remember this at bonus time."

"OK. I'll be in early. And the CIA doesn't give bonuses."

"Bye."

Garnett turned off the television. He witnessed enough destruction during his normal workday; he didn't need to watch any more tonight.

"Does this have an impact on what you are working on?"

"Good question," he answered honestly.

Tomorrow, he would see the scenes over and over again. He gave Elizabeth the tightest hug she could handle.

At the Watergate Hotel, Henslow almost missed the news. His meeting had been canceled, so he decided to pay Harper a visit. As he lay in bed, he thought he might actually have a moment to relax. But then the phone rang.

"Berlin" was all she said. She swung around to see the images, just breaking on CNN. Sitting up, she focused her attention on the screen. "Bastards."

"We expected something. Berlin. Berlin is as good a choice as any."

Harper got up and threw a dress over her head. Henslow noticed she hadn't put on any underwear. After running a brush through her hair and another on her teeth, she came out of the bathroom.

He was already at the door.

"Is it going to work? People are dying again," she said, her emotions rising as she closed the door behind them.

"Perhaps. There is still time."

With this explosion, he had little time left, as the inevitable US response would be fast and violent. It was time to stop waiting.

The CIA was energized, as if they had all eaten a bag of sugar. But the mood was also sad, uneasy, and angry, like waiting in line at a wake to pay condolences to the grieving family.

The heavily entrenched CIA military background was shaken by the attack in Germany. Everyone, former military or not, was affected. Groups huddled in the halls and cafeterias, where words such as *murderers, revenge,* and *air strike* were overheard. Garnett figured it must be the group mentality that strikes police when one of their own is shot and killed. *If a trained, armed professional is not safe, then what of the general population?* The CIA was supposed to be leading this battle, along with their counterparts overseas.

By the time he reached the office at 5:00 a.m., WTOP news radio had given him the latest headlines on the bombing. Now his team needed to take care of the pictures.

"VID's almost ready," Karen told him, her eyes burning with emotion. On his desk were the review tapes with TV news reports from around the world. He pushed it into the VCR and punched play. "There was some good video from ZDF and RAI in Italy. There are interviews with Kohl and Ambassador Burt in Germany. He's blaming Libya, pure and simple. Kohl looks pretty pissed."

"He should be. What else?"

"Actually, Europe is rallying on this one. France has already expelled some diplomats, two Libyans, accusing them of plotting anti-American attacks. Germany's expected to do the same. Probably Spain too."

"Spain?"

"They have US bases. They're scared. Plus, I'm hearing from my NSA friends that there might be some evidence linking this to Libya directly. Wouldn't that be nice?"

She was a valuable piece of work. He mentally noted to make sure she got a good bump at the next pay cycle.

In less than an hour, the tape was on its way to the White House.

CHAPTER FORTY-FOUR

They didn't waste any time.

Surveillance was always present against East German Libyan People's Bureau personnel, but it was pervasive when tensions were high and the Western intelligence officers needed to put on a good show for their superiors. He noticed the car following him as he drove through the center of town, and it conspicuously stopped and watched him as he sat with Erich in a café along the Unter den Linder.

"Congratulations," the Stasi Officer said without the slight sense of meaning it.

"Thank you. Is something wrong?"

"President Honecker called this time. Those above me are not happy," the Stasi Officer said, despair and frustration mixing in his voice. "Times are changing for us. He is craving attention from the West; he needs their money to rebuild our place in history, the prewar glory days of Frederick the Great. Unofficially, of course."

The Stasi Officer had seen some improvements, but he wanted out. He was tired of being cramped between the Baltic, Czechoslovakia, Poland, and the West. Socialism had determined his destiny—a permanent sentence to a life of monotonous deception and voyeurism within a culture based on mediocrity. No, he was trapped, spying on his own people and meeting the disgusting likes of the man celebrating with a cigarette across the table from him.

Sipping his coffee and puffing a cigarette, the Associate contemplated the moment. The future of the man's country was a problem for them, but as long as he could get what he needed, it didn't matter if he was right.

"You have been a great help. I did not intend to place you in a bad situation. You do not want to become too much like the West. Americans and the other followers want us to obey their rules. Rules, as they say, were meant to be broken," the Associate replied with a smile.

When the Associate reached the People's Bureau, congratulatory messages from Megrahi and the Terrorist were waiting for him. They respected his abilities, and he was valuable. The Leader also offered his appreciation, with brief platitudes about his support for the Great Cause and how he would be rewarded. He burned the notes.

There was a knock on the door, and the young man entered. He could see the look of pure anger on the Associate's face.

"May I interrupt you, sir?" he started timidly.

"Why would you be here?" The Associate was furious.

The Brother looked exhausted, with bags under his eyes, unshaved, wearing the same clothes as the day before. Coming here compromised everything they had done. It was unacceptable and would have to be dealt with.

"I have never done anything like last ni...never. It is that I am against...I did not—"

"Control yourself. You did what was right, and what you were asked to do. You promised to help, and you did." The Associate was a little disappointed but not surprised. The Sister might still have value, but cowards attract cowards.

"I liked them. They were nice to me."

"You did well last night. You should be proud. This is for you, for your great efforts."

The Associate opened the middle drawer of his desk, removed an envelope, and held it out to the shaken young man. As he started to reach for it, he hesitated, stopped, then put his hand back in his lap.

What they had done was wrong, but if they had not kept their promise he feared the worse for him and his sister. The Associate would harm them; he was certain of it. The distant sound of the explosion still echoed in his ears. The faces, young and strong, were burned into his eyes. No, he was not a terrorist, despite what he had done. There was a choice to be made, which required him to live through the day. He had just a few seconds to decide his fate. He took the envelope.

"Good. I am glad. Now I want you to go home and rest. Do not come to visit me for a while, and do not call, as we agreed. Understand?"

"Yes. Thank you."

When the door closed, the Associate let out a sigh as he picked up the phone.

When will my life stop being so complicated?

CHAPTER FORTY-FIVE

The feeling of euphoria swept through the halls of the People's Palace. There were no official pronouncements. Everyone just knew. A new sense of confidence covered the faces of people who were in the know, or had figured it out—a confidence shattered after the Gulf of Sidra.

When Megrahi finally called to set up their meeting, Mukhtar was already on his way to the ministry, deciding it was time to at least act the part of a foreign minister. He had finally managed to control his grief and fury as Megrahi continually delayed a meeting. Many days had passed since the bombing, and his country needed him for the brief moments he surely had left. With this meeting now arranged, he loaded his courage with the memory of Tareq and said good-bye to Marwa. She would know what to do if he didn't call her as planned.

His other important reason for coming back to work was personal. He had made one last stop to visit the Shopkeeper. One last message needed to get out—for Marwa. Hopefully, it would be delivered. *I will never know.*

Calls poured in from his diplomatic colleagues and the world's media. Another round of messages waited on his desk after the bombing in Berlin. It was the type of work that no longer held any interest to him. *A pathetic weapon against armies of violence and hate.*

Mustering all his strength for the task ahead, he separated the messages into three piles—friends he may call, familiar names or organizations he might call, and those who would call a dozen times before they realized he would never call. With as much mental energy he could spare, he crafted answers in the language of diplomacy, always evasive but never condescending. Conciliatory but strong.

Mukhtar was aware of the speculation growing within the community regarding his suddenly more muted voice. They would soon all understand and be even more surprised. They would talk among themselves at the lounges of the United Nations about what had happened to Abdallah, never saying exactly what they were really thinking or wanted to say. *True diplomats.*

Quickly and with a barrage of negative news, his name would be removed from their lips altogether, and then, like a distant relative, he would be forgotten forever, only to be brought up by the elder statesmen of the diplomatic corps as an example to the younger generation of what could happen when one really cared too much. It was a certainty; he had done the same thing himself when he was young, for men long forgotten, names he could no longer remember.

Now, he was in the right place. He just needed the opportunity. He needed the courage.

The phone ringing startled him.

"Fifteen minutes." The line went dead.

Mukhtar gathered himself, pulled the VHS tape from his bag, grasped his cane firmly in his hands, and slowly stood. Looking around his office, the place where he had spent more time over the years than his own home, he was certain it would be for the last time. He did not have a soldier's mentality, or nerve, so preparing for this type of stress was foreign to him. The palace seemed more drab and deteriorated than normal as he made his way through the endless hallways to Megrahi's office. As he turned down the last hall, the door to his destination was just ahead. *Was this how Tareq felt as he approached the door? What was he thinking? Did he know he was also going to his death?* His anger returned as well as his focus. He clutched the tape tighter in his sweating hands.

Planting his cane hard on the marble floor with each step, he strode with authority directly past security into Megrahi's office. He worried that if he hesitated, he might lose his momentarily obtained courage. Megrahi was sitting behind a desk covered with newspapers. A television tuned to BBC flickered in the corner of the ornate room.

"Abdallah, I am sorry for taking so long. We both have been busy, I am sure. I was about—."

"Do you know why I am here?" he asked, still standing.

"You want to see him. I assume you are not happy that your speech was not used, and your position with the Leader. We have discussed that. I share your concerns and fears. Something has to be done before he destroys our country. If we don't, the people cannot be contained forever. They will find him and rip his limbs and head from his body. Ours too."

What is he talking about? The shield of self-control and willpower he had inserted between his emotions and action dissolved in an instant.

"You know why I am here. You know what has happened!" he shouted. He raised the tape over his head like a club, and it shook violently as the unleashed river of anger flowed to his arm.

Megrahi was shocked by his normally placid colleague's sudden outburst. This was a man whose reputation was built on order and control. The shaking, sweating person standing in front of him now was not the Abdallah Mukhtar he had known for decades. Something serious was happening to him.

"What are you talking about? What is that?"

"Don't pretend you are innocent. It was you. I saw." VHS still waving in the air.

"I am guilty of many things, but whatever it is that has you in such a rage, please tell me. Show me what is on that tape."

"Do not insult my son! He is dead. He is dead because of you. Why did you take him? Was it *his* orders to get back at me? Why? Why murder him?"

In his fury, he had forgotten he needed a free hand to unscrew the knob of the cane to release the weapon. Fumbling between the tape and cane, Mukhtar struggled to get a firm grip on the knob, his hands wet with sweat.

Megrahi watched as Mukhtar twisted to move the cane under his arm. His military instincts alerted him that the situation was becoming deadly and he needed to prepare. In an instant, Megrahi opened his desk drawer, pulled out a .45 revolver, and placed it in his lap.

"Murder? Have you gone insane also?"

"I know what I saw. He was a prisoner in one of your camps. He was shot, and then I saw you." Finally, the knob of the cane rotated and came free. Mukhtar started to pull the sword out, but a metallic sound distracted him. He looked up to see a pistol pointed directly at his head. The sound was the hammer being cocked by Megrahi, a look of bewilderment on his face.

"Now, please get control of yourself. I would never harm Tareq, you, or Marwa. If you believe I did, then it is a grievous mistake."

Time stood still, as did Mukhtar. He ignored the pistol. His senses focused on the face and the voice of the man he had come to kill. There was nothing the man could say to defend himself, but it was the sound of his voice and look on his face. *I have heard that voice before. The tone. The face. His eyes sometimes provide a look beyond the cold. Is he REALLY telling the truth? Who would do such a thing to Tareq? Who would make it look as if the second-most powerful man in the country killed him? Who would make that tape and send it…?*

The answer was obvious now. He slowly slid the blade back to its home and screwed the knob tight. Simultaneously, Megrahi lowered his weapon, placing it on the desk. Still cocked and pointed in his friend's direction.

"Arrange a meeting with him. Please."

"As I was about to tell you before…this incident, I have arranged a meeting for you tonight, at the residence. Go there and wait."

Mukhtar clutched the tape to his chest as his body started to shake from the chills of the drying sweat covering him from head to toe.

"Did you hear me, Abdallah?"

"Yes. I am going. I am going for Tareq." He walked out the door as if the events of the last few minutes were forgotten, or perhaps had never happened.

Megrahi smiled as the returned the .45 to his drawer.

"Good luck," he whispered to the empty room.

CHAPTER FORTY-SIX

The Brother waited impatiently. He couldn't help it. He was nervous. Trying to control his emotions, he grabbed handfuls of seed from the little white paper bag he held in his hands, scattering dinner to the pigeons cooing at his feet. It didn't work. He started pacing back and forth, looking anxiously at his watch. The big decision had been made and he could not make it go away. The appointment with the official from the American embassy was set.

It had taken him hours to build up enough courage to finish dialing the embassy number. A dozen times he would start, only to hang up before anyone answered. Finally, in a moment of courage, he had let it go through.

They didn't understand him at first. His accent and rapid, breathless retelling of the story made it hard for them to comprehend. The call bounced around to several officials, each impatiently listened to a few sentences as he stammered, trying to retell his story about the bombing at the disco. When he finally mentioned that he worked for the Libyan Bureau in East Berlin, a fact he had tried to hide, a meeting was arranged.

The Brother wanted to meet in the East, in an area familiar to him. The voice tried to pick the location, but the Brother remained firm. So now he waited in the park at dusk, looking for a man about two meters tall, with dark hair and blue eyes, carrying a copy of *Bildzeitung* rolled up in his left hand. The Brother held his bag of seed and waited in the center of the park scanning the faces and hands of every man. None carried the recognition signal.

He never noticed him. The .22-caliber bullet entered the Brother's skull above the right ear at point-blank range, The discharge made very little noise—nothing more than a child's cap pistol. The special hand-packed cartridge did not have enough powder to create the force required to exit the skull, which would have opened a large exit wound on the left side, sending blood and debris flying for all to see. Instead, it remained nicely lodged inside the brain—a trick the Associate had copied from the Terrorist, who had learned it from the Israeli Mossad. The Brother collapsed in a heap, scattering the pigeons momentarily before they returned to finish off the birdseed that was spread around the body.

The Associate did not look back at the man. He felt no emotion toward him. After all, the Sister was already dead at their apartment. Her Brother had nothing left to live for.

The gun was dropped in a garbage can nearby, as he walked to the train station, happy to get back to some real work.

The hottest selling items in the Green Book Shop of Tripoli Airport, as far as the NOC could tell, were posters of the Leader and signs with political commentaries, containing quotes from the man himself. The rest of the shelves of the duty-free shop were virtually empty except for copies of *The Green Book* and a German-language political book comparing the Leader with the nineteenth-century German philosopher Georg Hegel.

His stomach was flipping like a gymnast as he quickly translated the airport signs, which were mandated to be written in only Arabic. The only English in the airport, or anywhere else, for that matter, were quotes from *The Green Book* that seemed to be everywhere: "No Democracy Without Popular Congresses and Committees Everywhere." "Partners, Not Wage Earners."

Paranoia was a national pastime in Libya and he wasn't immune when he visited. Being careful was his operational imperative, without looking as if he was trying to be careful to avoid any security patrolling the airport. Because of Libya's semiautonomous People's Committees, a half dozen different police forces claimed responsibility for airport security, each independent of the others.

If he was arrested, it might take days before anyone could determine which element held him and could get him released. He expected some sort of surveillance; usually they had at least one person checking out new arrivals on Libyan Air. The "All Libyans are Qadhafi" slogan sprawled across the cover of his ticket envelope was a good reminder.

Outside, he found a dingy Fiat that doubled as a taxi, a "beater" in the States. The NOC sized up the driver. The man was older, weather-beaten. The eyes looking back at him from the dangling rearview mirror were not threatening, just tired. *Not a member of the intelligence agencies. Just an informant. They were all told to be.*

It had been less than forty-eight hours since he had serviced the dead drop and returned to Italy. It was obvious this operation had reached a new level of importance since the head of the Agency's Counter-Terror Center had sent the cable directly to him. "Make DIRECT CONTACT with target and/or spouse immediately. Assess and assist."

Henslow knew what he was asking of him. *He must.* Otherwise, it was a total betrayal of tradecraft in an extremely dangerous operation that was now obviously worth risking his life. Instead of the comparative safety of an anonymous dead drop, he was being asked to meet the Libyan official directly, who was certainly under surveillance, without breaking cover, in the equivalent of a warzone. Until the Case Officer told him Henslow had approved sharing all information, he wasn't even aware of the true name and position of the source.

How did Henslow so kindly put it in the cable? Use your own initiative.

The taxi rounded the corner near the Al Waddan Hotel. Soldiers were clustered around something outside the building. The NOC knew a Soviet-built antiaircraft battery when he saw one.

"What is going on?" he asked.

"Trouble coming," the Driver replied stoically.

For weeks, the saber rattling had continued between the United States and Libya. The NOC was not sure if his mission played any part in the bigger arena of international tensions, but he did care that he was in the country at this moment—a place he didn't want to be at all. Given a choice, this was not the place to be.

"I'd like to see the city; please, just drive," the NOC said, changing plans as he handed the Driver several thousand lira sandwiched between a few American twenty-dollar bills. "OK?"

"Yes." The Driver took the bills, and his eyes blinked for a moment, sitting up a little straighter behind the wheel.

They started moving through the streets in no apparent pattern. In fact, about everything he saw was green—the shutters on the closed shops, the flag, the license plates on the cars, and more omnipresent green-and-white posters. "In Need, Freedom Is Latent." "An Armed People Can Overcome Any Obstacle." On almost every street corner were more soldiers.

The world press was stating categorically that an American attack on Libya was imminent since the bombing in Berlin. *They would have to be totally dumb, deaf, and blind not to be ready.*

Looking out the window, he saw a city not as grand as many North Africa capitals, but Tripoli still had charm. Not many cities could say they were 2,700 years old. How many could say that the Phoenicians, Greeks, Romans, Egyptians, Vandals, Byzantines, Turks, Italians, indigenous tribes, and Berbers all had conquered and settled there? These were the shores of Tripoli made famous in the "Marines' Hymn." America's first battle fought over seas. *Still fighting.*

It was at sunset when the beauty of Tripoli became apparent. The castle glittered against the darkening sky.

The NOC knew the Libyan people as decent and friendly. They possessed a belief—one they were told to believe, true or not—that they were unjustly victims of the US president. They rose to the defense of their Brother Leader, and despite the situation, they still filled the congested streets. Understandable, but the NOC also sensed they just wanted it all to stop.

"I'd like to visit a certain area. I have a friend who used to live in Tripoli who asked me to take a look at his neighborhood," the NOC said after twenty minutes of sight-seeing chitchat.

The NOC gave the Driver an address he had memorized from the file. It was in the old American residential area, near Bin Ashur. The excuse was awful, and the NOC knew it. If the Driver knew it, he really didn't care. Within a few minutes, the cab arrived at the address. It was in a more affluent residential area, surrounded by a wall and guarded by hired security.

"Slowly." The NOC stuck his head out the window, trying to get a glimpse beyond the security gate, through the trees, and over a wall. It was dark, mostly. A light was on somewhere, but it was too hard to see. "Pull in."

"But the guard—"

"I have faith," the NOC said reassuringly, stuffing a few more twenty-dollar bills into the Driver's hand.

The Driver pulled the taxi up to the gate, where an annoyed guard slung his taped and tattered AK-47 over his shoulder and tapped on the window. For the next few minutes, the NOC watched an animated conversation in Arabic as the Driver told some story, and the guard would have nothing of it. He kept looking and pointing to the NOC in the backseat. Hands waved and voices rose, and his stomach was just about at its breaking point when finally the Driver looked over his shoulder.

"Excuse me, sir. I apologize." The NOC tensed, ready. Pause. "Do you have sixty more American dollars?"

He laughed a little as he handed over the bribe. The gate opened, and they drove through.

"He wanted much more money. Very greedy man."

Jumping out of the taxi, he formulated a plan as he walked up to the house. *This is stupid and dangerous. Screw tradecraft.* He knocked on the door. No answer. He knocked louder, too loud for the quiet of the night. A dog started to bark. Finally the door opened, slightly.

When she opened the door, his first thought was that his career, as he had enjoyed and planned it, was at an abrupt end. When he saw the woman's red face, with tear-swollen eyes looking back at him through the crack in the door, there was no turning back. If he lived, he would certainly be sent back where his identity would have to be washed for at least two years, forced to stay on the Farm for months, undergoing "new training." The possibility of ever returning to his beloved Italy was remote. True or not, his superiors would assume his cover was blown. They would construct some false cover story to explain to the IRC why he had to leave so abruptly.

She clutched a tissue to her chest. She was frightened.

"May I—"

"I'm sorry to bother you. Is your husband at home?"

Her dark eyes grew wider as the foreigner spoke. She looked over his shoulder, scanning the area behind him.

"Come in." Inside, she closed the door behind him, making sure she didn't let him go more than a few feet into the entry. "I am sorry; he is at the ministry. He has a meeting. I do not know when he will return."

This sounded more like a plea than a statement of fact to the NOC. A meeting. Good or bad? He did not have enough information to know. From the look on the face of the woman, it didn't look promising.

"Please let him know that I am in town and wish to see him at his convenience. I'm at the Al Waddan Hotel. I should be here for a few days. Could you let him know, please?" He handed her his card.

"Who are you?"

"I'm here to help. Thank you for speaking with me."

She looked at him, then at the card, then spoke in total control of her emotions. "Thank you."

As the cab pulled away, he wondered why she had said that. Why thank him? It would make sense if Mukhtar had told her. Anyway, it really wouldn't make a difference until he got the opportunity to talk to him. If she did know about him and decided to send internal security after him, he figured he would find out when he arrived back at the hotel.

As the cab neared the Al Waddan, his anxiety took hold, and he pulled a pack of antacids from his pocket and popped a few into his mouth. Time to use his own initiative again.

"Can I ask you to pick me up tomorrow morning? Around nine?"

"Yes, glad, yes," he replied, happy to have a well-paying fare.

"Thank you. Go without fear," he said as he stepped out of the cab. The Driver nodded and drove away.

When he reached his room, the tension had wound his body tight. He sat in a chair and waited for the door to be broken down. After the events of the last few weeks, Libyan Internal Security would be looking for a media show. *Show off the spy.* At least that was what he would do. Ten minutes passed. He checked the hallway. It was empty. Outside his window, everything looked normal.

He sighed, went into the bathroom, threw up, and then went to bed.

CHAPTER FORTY-SEVEN

"That was goosey," Trinche said as he pulled away after the second high-speed refueling of Remit-1. The 40-ton F-111 was hard enough to handle, but a refueling at night, fully loaded with thousands of pounds of bombs, was almost more than the underpowered fighter could handle.

To keep up the airspeed and make contact with the refueling boom from the KC-10 overhead, Trinche had to "stoke the burner"—use his afterburners to give the craft small, precise blasts of extra power as the weight from the fuel was added. When he did that, it was hard to handle. This was all done within fifty feet of a tanker carrying thousands of pounds of fuel and three fully armed fighters a few yards off his wings.

"Blame the French, Trinchie," Beans responded from his WSO seat to Trinche's right.

They had been sitting shoulder to shoulder for over four hours, only briefly communicating through their facemask microphones. Normally, his pilot was a talkative guy, but as the hours ticked away on this mission, he had grown more silent.

The day before, Trinche had stood behind a podium at Lakenheath to give the final briefing to the twenty-four pilots and their crews. Ninety percent of the faces staring back at him were flying their first combat mission. This time, they sensed the briefing was the real deal—the room was full of air force brass.

Behind him, a large back-and-white satellite image appeared. Numbered and colored-coded shapes and arrows indicated targets. Trinche held a long wooden pointer up to the map. He briefed it one more time.

"The mission is code named El Dorado Canyon. Due to operational changes from EUCOM, we have had to amend the original flight profile. The three original small tactical strikes are now being joined as one larger simultaneous strike. Targets and radio call signs are as follows: Remit, Elton, Karma—the Al-Azziziyah Barracks command-and-control center military and staff headquarters, which is also the residence of the country's leader. Six F-111s, Puffy, Lujac, on the military facilities at Tripoli airport. Three F-111s are on Jewel, the Sidi Balal terrorist training camp. Simultaneously, A-6s from the aircraft carriers *America* and *Coral Sea* will strike the Jamahiriyah military barracks in Benghazi and the Benina air base southeast of Benghazi."

He paused for a moment to let it sink in.

"To attain the required tactical surprise, we will hit all five targets at once at night. The complexity and scope of this mission have been increased, as we have just been informed that the French government has refused to grant us overfly authority. This will add 1,300 nautical miles each way, adding six to seven hours of flight time and four additional air refuelings.

"Command and control for air force resources will be maintained by a KC-10, which will serve as an airborne coordination center to integrate our force with the navy. Actual target-strike responsibilities will be divided between the KC-10 for Tripoli and the carrier *America* for the navy missions on the Benghazi area. E-2C Hawkeyes will provide early warning, air-control vector, and operations. Total time over the strike area is estimated at five to six minutes, depending on wind."

He paused again, putting down the wooden stick.

Trinche remembered the smattering of whistles and mumbling that filled the room. "Questions?"

"ROE?" a voice asked.

"The rules of engagement are simple: no Vark, repeat, no fighter goes to the strike area unless all systems are green and fully operational. Point blank. No collateral damage."

"Will Qadhafi be at home?" one pilot asked.

"If he is there today, with all we are throwing at him, he had better not be there tomorrow," one of the brass replied.

They all knew what he meant.

The changes had left little time for the pilots to prepare, especially the twelve additional fighters who had not been expecting to be part of the mission. Of all the targets, Azziziyah was the most difficult. Located in a residential area, it was heavily defended, making the ROE requirement a tough assignment.

At about 1930, on April 14, 1986, Trinche lumbered his khaki-and-green-colored fighter down the runway, leading the first US combat mission to originate from Lakenheath, UK, since World War II.

"The Brother Leader of the Revolution is not available. You are to wait," a guard had said as she ushered him into the room when he arrived at 5:00 p.m. Looking at his watch, he saw that it was now past 10:00. Mukhtar had been sitting quietly for hours, trying to forget the images, but still thinking of Tareq. He prayed, cane clutched firmly between his legs, and replayed the drama in Megrahi's office many times. *Was he really telling the truth?* Mukhtar could not shake the feeling that someone somewhere was manipulating him. Occasionally, he slowly rose to stretch, leaning on the cane to steady his aching muscles. This time it would complete its task.

It had been several months since he had sat in this waiting room, which served as the portal to the Leader's residence and administrative offices, Bab El-Azziziyah Barracks—the Splendid Gate. Just to get to this point had taken an hour of scrutiny by the Leader's East German security force, including a through search and examination of all his clothes. He had been here many times, and he could not remember an instance when the Leader had been on time to any meeting. So he waited in the most secure area in the country, where the Brother Leader of the Revolution was forced to live after seven assassination attempts.

West Germans had built the barracks, mostly. They had demolished the inside of a medieval Tripoli fortress and the surrounding area to construct a mile-long, almost oval-shaped complex of buildings two miles from downtown Tripoli. It included bunkers able to withstand nuclear attacks. Mukhtar was reminded how formidable the complex was. High-security walls were constantly scanned with cameras, sensors, and alarms monitored by a state-of-the-art security nerve center. A Soviet tank was a permanent fixture just inside the gate, positioned to prevent a ground assault. Heavily armed guards walked the perimeter as armored personnel carriers moved up and down the access roads. Barricades blocked access to the gates for any possible suicide bombers. In the center of the complex, a one-hundred-foot-high antenna, signifying the use of the residence as a military command-and-control center, towered over everything. A battery of Crotale missiles scanned the sky for aerial defense.

Mukhtar wondered whom the Leader feared most: external threats or his own people.

Once inside Azziziyah, he was reminded that the residence was actually quite nice. Two tennis courts and a gymnasium were available, as was a soccer field. About two hundred meters away was the famous Bedouin tent the Leader used to meet most of his guests. When he approached the two-story blue-and-white building next to the tent—the residence of the Leader and his family—Mukhtar heard camels grunting, completing the desert Bedouin illusion.

Every minute he was forced to wait was torture. The hours gave him a chance to think through what he was going to say and how to say it. *The country needs to move forward. We must be ruled by more than oil. Stop wasting our wealth on ego-building purchases of arms and financing of terrorism. Political and human rights abuses must stop. Then there was Tareq.*

Instead of hearing his pleas, he expected the man would listen for only a few seconds and then drone into some unintelligible ranting, the kind he had seen so many times before, the kind that brought the young crowds to their feet and confounded the West. He would sit and listen, but the result of the conversation seemed inevitable. His last words—"You killed my son"—would complete his task.

As for Marwa, his heart broke when he left her at home. He had tried his best to protect, if possible. They had discussed it, as they had done as a couple for decades. Their agreement frightened as well as calmed him. He was not a martyr, but she needed him to have hope, as hollow as it would be. She needed a plan, and he provided it to her even if they both knew it was a lie.

If he did make it home, she would be waiting in the car. They would drive all night to the Tunisian border at Ras el-Jedir. With some luck, they could be across by daylight—then Europe, France, and then perhaps the United States. If he was not able to make it home, she was to follow the same plan on her own and hope somehow his foreign friends would come for her.

Either way, the Leader would no longer be in control, and Tareq would be avenged.

CHAPTER FORTY-EIGHT

They flew over the English Channel, refueling off the Bay of Biscay, and then though the Straits of Gibraltar. Trinche tried to see how many groups of three had made the last refueling, to determine whether any fighters were heading back because of malfunctions.

"Did anyone ever consider that the poor bastards at the end of the attack formation are up shit creek?" Beans said without warning. Their minds were thinking alike.

"Don't remind me." The cockpit went silent again.

Remit-1 flew just over five hundred feet above the Med, using its terrain-following guidance system as they closed in on the Libyan coast. Trinche's hand rested just behind the stick, in case a quick climb was needed. In the darkness behind him were seventeen other F-111s. They were flying "comm out," in total radio silence. Each pilot had turned off his IFF (Identification Friend or Foe) electronic equipment and was proceeding unmonitored under the international airspace. If any aircraft experienced a malfunction, it had to turn back.

The extra mission parameters had added another dimension.

"We're behind schedule, maybe ten minutes."

"What do we do?"

"Speed up. Shorten our course."

"That takes us pretty close to Algeria and Tunisia," the WSO said.

"We don't have a choice. We need to make our drop time. If the navy hits Benghazi too soon before we hit Tripoli, it might get a little dicey, and we lose surprise and defense suppression." Ninety minutes later, Remit-1 made its last refueling west of Sicily, back on schedule.

"Make final checks. Let's see how lost we are."

Trinche checked his radar, seeking the predetermined offset aim points monitoring the terrain and man-made objects that helped update Remit-1's position on the inertial guidance system. During a trip this long, the normal small guidance errors could be magnified, forcing them into missing their target altogether, something he was not going to allow to happen.

"Fence check," Trinche said. "Attack radar, defensive systems, Pave Tack FLIR, laser designator, weapons release panel."

"All systems show green. Good jet," Beans responded.

"Roger."

All systems registered as fully functional. The remaining craft in the formation were also checking their systems, praying that no minor malfunction would force them to abort now so many hours into the flight. He turned off his external lights and armed his bombs.

"Getting tickled," Beans said, reading brief radar energy hitting the craft. "Probably from Sirte. The SAM-5s are operational again."

"We're too far away, but let's drop just to make sure. Changing altitude two zero zero."

The fighter accelerated. They were eighty thousand feet from the target, approaching the Libyan coast and the lights of the Libyan capital at nearly six hundred miles per hour. Fatigue from hours strapped into the cockpit was replaced by the addictive adrenaline rush of combat. *Time for the training to pay off.*

All of the crews behind him were feeling this for the first time. He and Beans had been there many times before in what seemed like a lifetime ago in Vietnam. But this mission was nothing like then. They were using precision "smart bombs," not the mostly dumb gravity bombs used in Southeast Asia.

"Look at that," Beans said, looking up from his scope. "We're first. Those guys behind us—"

"The guys behind us are in for it."

"So you are still here. Good." The noise of the door swinging open and the voice both startled and terrified him. Mukhtar felt frightened for the first time. It was always Megrahi. "I wanted to make sure he was here tonight. They said he would be, but you know how he is. I demanded they not cancel. After this afternoon's...after our conversation, I could tell this was very important. I also wanted to wish you good luck tonight."

"Luck?" His feeling of calm disappeared.

"I know this meeting is very important to you."

"Is it important to you?"

He started for the door. "Please come to tell me how it goes," he said, smiling. "Allah is with you, Abdallah."

"What could possibly happen in this country that you do not know about?"

He paused, still smiling, leaving Mukhtar alone again in the waiting room.

Outside, Megrahi stretched, enjoying the cool air as he began a leisurely stroll through the maze of buildings. The stop under a group of palms seemed random, but it was an area that could not be monitored. He reached into a pocket and pulled out a small secure radio. Flipping a switch, he raised it to his mouth.

"Confirmed," he whispered and nonchalantly hid the device back in his pocket.

On a rooftop nearby, Israeli Mossad agents received the message and instantly relayed the confirmation that the Libyan leader would be in his residence for the next hour to the Mossad Tel Aviv operations center, which bounced it just as quickly to their American intelligence and military counterparts.

Someone grabbing his shoulder and shaking him startled Mukhtar from a quick nap. He opened his eyes to see a beautiful young woman standing over him, a stern look on her face, a red beret on her head.

The dream was of his younger days. Of him and Marwa. Tareq as a baby. A family vacation sailing. Time had been kind and cruel to them.

"The Leader is ready," she declared without a drop of kindness.

The guard stepped back as he rose to his feet as quickly as he could, which was not quick enough for her. He had dealt with the Leader's East German–trained female personal bodyguards many times—the man liked to be surrounded by women. As he started toward the door, she put her hand on his chest, stopping him. His heart raced as she took his cane, gave it a quick examination, and then set it against the wall.

"Arms out, please," she added, although the sleepy old man in front of her did not appear to be a real threat, despite her instructors' lectures that she should trust no one. She ran her hands over his body, checking for weapons.

"You are only doing your job, my dear."

Then she pulled a video cassette from the pocket of his jacket.

"What is this?" she snapped, looking at one side and then the other.

"It is why I am here. I need to discuss the contents with the Brother Leader. It is of critical diplomatic importance."

He took the cassette from her hand, retrieved his cane, nodding and smiling as he moved toward the door, before she could respond. He glanced at his watch. *A little after one in the morning. Marwa is certainly worried now.*

With each step, he felt fear drain from his nerves, being replaced with courage. Often he would wonder, for some unknown reason, what it would be like to be walking to one's death. What would a person be thinking, knowing that they were about to die? That any sights they were seeing, any sounds they were hearing, were the last ones? Images not even long enough to make a memory. Today he had felt it twice.

What was it like for Tareq? Did he know? I could see he was courageous.

He walked silently through a long tunnel and then up some more steps. He gripped the head of his cane tighter as his hands became wet and his mouth became dry. At the top of the steps was another guard. She stood watch at a door. The escort guard stopped.

"You go through here. The Leader will be in soon," the new guard told him as the door automatically opened.

Stepping through, Mukhtar found himself outside, in the cool night air. Directly in front of him, no more than ten feet away, was the Bedouin tent. He went through the brightly colored opening to find the air filled with the overwhelming smell of aftershave. The walls were covered with sayings from *The Green Book*. The rest of the tent was simply decorated with pillows, mats, low coffee tables, a small bed, and bookshelves. The only concessions to modern life were a television and a VCR on an entertainment center tucked away in a corner. He was not sure what to do—sit, stand, or pace.

CHAPTER FORTY-NINE

Even Trinche was surprised by the amount of Soviet ZSU-23 mm antiaircraft fire rising behind them from the coastal defenses. His concentration drifted for a moment to watch the tracers arch harmlessly above and behind. *You're late. You forgot to account for our altitude and speed, dumb SOBs.*

Flares shot up from boats in the harbor, turning night into day. He was first in line, and he should have had more of an element of surprise on his side. No matter; he had enough. *Focus.* Downtown Tripoli was now at his twelve o'clock, level, six miles beyond his windshield. Their headsets were alive with a series of beeps, telling them they were being hit by radar and warning them they were flying too low.

The aircraft behind him were on their own now, checking their positions to their assigned targets, trying to ignore the radar-guided Triple-A and missiles trying to blow them out of the sky. With Libya's supply of Soviet-purchased surface-to-air missiles, and recent addition of the French-built Crotales, Tripoli was one of the most heavily defended cities in the world.

Mukhtar had not felt this tired since life as a soccer star. It was the feeling when one had crossed the point of mental fatigue that hours of concentration and exhaustion could bring. He had reached the moment of the unexpected when one just wants to get whatever might come over with. The moment was close, but as he stood staring at the flap of the tent at the slightly overcast evening, he was not entirely certain what he was actually going to do. This brought on more panic, and he began to shake.

As the minutes passed, his whole body was trembling. Each emotion played on the next, making the previous tremor seem like a mild shake. He took deep breaths through his mouth and nose, exhaling slowly to calm himself. *Is this what is to become of my life?*

In an instant, laughter and scampering feet filled the tent as half a dozen young children rushed in, dodging his legs on both sides. They jumped into the air, doing belly flops on the big, soft cushions. Behind them came the Leader's wife, dressed in colorful robes. She smiled at him, perhaps not remembering who he was, or even caring. Affairs of state were not her concern.

Another tall, attractive, well-armed guard stood by the entrance, observed the situation, and then positioned herself just outside, ten meters away. The Leader strode in ignoring Mukhtar's presence. His fate was sealed shut, and with that realization, calm overtook him. For a few minutes, he watched the Leader play with his children, stroking their hair, laughing, and displaying all the characteristics of a loving, devoted father.

"It has been a long time, my friend." The Leader, smiling, dressed in brown silk pajamas, walked to him and grasped both hands in his and shook them.

Is this the mastermind behind the world's terrorists who have the Americans irrational with fear?

"Much time, since…" the Leader said, collapsing on some cushions.

Mukhtar stared at the face— tired, with deep lines cutting across it like scars. The eyes were distant, cold, and narrow. Which man would be talking tonight? Would it be the charismatic soldier who led a revolution at age twenty-seven with a soft smile and bright ideas, or the moody, brooding figure leading 3.5 million citizens of the country? The paranoid dictator? Or both?

"You see. I am a man. I have a family," was his next random utterance. Then he playfully grabbed one of his daughters and pulled her laughing into his lap. She struggled free and raced across the tent to join her brothers and sisters.

"I have never heard anyone doubt your love of family and faith," Mukhtar replied, watching her run, surprising himself with his truthful compliment. *Focus.*

The Leader stared over to the corner, where the television, its sound turned down, replayed an old rally from early in the regime. Young Revolutionary Council members, leading chants and waving huge posters covered with photos of a man in more photogenic times—then the tired person sitting in front of him now.

"I expect tricks. I am willing to talk directly. I will go to see Reagan. Personally. Tonight. The people of America, or Britain—I have no quarrel with them. I want to teach them *The Green Book.* They will understand me and love me, as do our people. The people of Africa. I am their King."

Mukhtar did not feel sorry for him. Or any other emotion except hatred. He had come this far. He was in the same room, less than three meters away. The time had come, and time was running out.

A twist of the top of his cane released the blade from the shaft.

"There goes one! Good to see the CAP force is around," Beans said as a Shrike missile, probably fired from an A-7 flying combat air patrol above, slammed into one of the SAM sites below, setting off an impressive fireworks show. More antiaircraft fire rose to meet them, their aim getting closer to the F-111.

"They're shooting for the afterburners. We're lighting the sky up ourselves," Beans said. Small-arms fire joined the Triple-A aiming for his fighter.

"Ready?" Trinche asked, the Aardvark still approaching at low altitude and high speed.

Semirecessed inside the internal weapons bay of Remit-1 was the Pave Tack—a Ford AVQ-26 laser designator and forward-looking radar (FLIR) that gave pinpoint accuracy for the two-thousand-pound GBU-10 Paveway-2 laser-guided bombs it carried. The FLIR was bore sighted into the WSO's cockpit avionics display and weapons-aiming systems, allowing for magnified images of the targets.

Beans, his face firmly positioned in his scope, continually updated the inertial guidance systems to locate the radar offset points. He was having trouble locating the right points; the photographs didn't match the heat pictures he was seeing through his scope at night—especially in a fighter traveling at nine hundred feet per second. In a desperate, panic-filled moment, he acquired the positions, and, training the cross hairs of the radar system on the correct locations, punched the computerized navigation system.

The fighter now knew exactly where it was.

"I'm getting fly-ups, paddling off," Trinche told Beans as he moved the safety interrupt switch on his stick to release the malfunctioning terrain guidance system of Remit-1 to manual. Trinche tried to monitor the warfare instruments, but with the guidance system off, he had to concentrate on the bomb release and the thickening antiaircraft fire exploding around them. He had to hold the course steady for another twenty or thirty seconds.

"Roger. Keep it steady. Ready. Looking good."

"Range?" Trinche asked.

"OK. Twenty-six thousand feet…twenty-five thousand…" Beans counted down the distance to the target. Through his scope, he got his first clear view of the tent and buildings of the Azziziyah complex. "Switching from radar to FLIR. Target direct. Lighting target." He struggled to keep the cross hairs of the laser directed on the target. He punched another button, and a laser beam emanating from the Pave Tack pod hit the Azziziyah Barracks.

"Ready. Pull," Beans shouted.

Trinche quickly nosed the fighter up into a 4-G, thirty-degree climb. The bombs released from the weapons bay, lobbing forward toward the target as Trinche continued the pull-up maneuver to avoid flying through the impact area. The GBU-10s picked up the laser hot spot reflection, locked onto it with their nose-mounted "seeker" sensors, and began riding the beam to the target, making midcourse corrections with their small movable fins.

"Laser on?" he asked, the blood rushing from this head.

"Laser on and on target...keep it steady; I'm losing acquisition... come on, baby...in three, two, one...impact." Through the scope, Beans watched a cloud rise from the area of the tent, obstructing the view as they pulled away.

"Going down," Trinche said as he brought the fighter back to the safety of low altitude and over the waters of the Gulf.

"I think we hit the basket...but I'm not sure...I was getting jitter from the pod, damn it! I might have lost it at the last second."

"Let's get out of here," Trinche said, increasing speed as the water rushed a few hundred feet below them. The entire bombing run had taken less than forty-five seconds.

"Roger that. One pass, haul ass."

"I have suffering. They have tricks. Excuses and explanations. Things should be clear, after all." The rambling nonsense continued from his mouth.

Mukhtar was not listening, or more accurately, was simply in a hate-filled rage that did not want to comprehend the jumbled words. Stepping forward, he clutched the top in his right hand while his left held the shaft halfway down. This morning had been a dress rehearsal. He would not make the same mistake with his weapon when it was time to strike. *Now is the time.*

"You have ruined Libya—our precious oil wealth spent on weapons. We send more millions to support murderers across the world who have no interest in the people. All the while, our stores are empty. They fight for food," he said louder than he wanted. The guard had not moved. The children and their mother played on the other side of the tent, ignoring them. He started to pull the blade from its sheath.

"Walk with me. The killing...a means to an end." He rose, walking out without waiting for an answer. Shocked, Mukhtar pushed the blade back and followed the man out of tent, toward the door to the office building he had come through a few minutes before.

He hasn't heard a word. This is the time; it must be.

Mukhtar stayed as close to the man as he could, limping with every step. The guard opened the door he had walked through earlier. Before she could follow, he pushed the Leader through the door, grabbed the doorknob, and slammed it shut behind him, sliding a large bolt into place. The guard screamed and beat on the door with her fists.

"This is for my son—Tareq—whom you murdered," he shouted, drawing the sword from its hiding place.

"You—What?" the Leader sputtered, his eyes registering confusion, ignorance, and terror.

They didn't hear the planes until they were right above them.

Explosions followed the screaming jet engines almost immediately. The walls, windows, and ground shook. They froze in place, only inches separating the blade from his chest.

Neither man, nor the guard on the other side still pounding on the bolted door, had time to react when a bomb landed less than fifty yards from them. The door blew off its hinges, knocking him, the door, and the now dead guard down the stairs into the tunnel. The Leader tumbled over them, debris missing his head by an inch.

The precious video was tossed from Mukhtar's pocket, across the floor, landing in falling debris. Smashed. The sword followed the same path. Unused.

"What the hell?" Beans said. A huge flash and fireball exploded in the air a few miles behind them. It could only be one thing.

"I think it's one of us."

Determination plus concentration were needed for the grueling flight back to Lakenheath. He felt sick. *Have we really lost pilots? Who were they?* His mission complete, survival became the main mission parameter as he tried to find the rendezvous point with the tankers, his fuel running dangerously low. He was hungry and tired, and he needed to pee; the rubberized bottle he had been using since he had left was getting too uncomfortable to use. He wanted out of the cockpit, but knew he had five more hours to go as they retraced their path. He tried to avoid taking a pep pill to stay awake.

"Tranquil tiger," Trinche said into the microphone a minute later, the first authorized communication of the mission since they had left. The navy command plane noted the call for a successful mission.

In a dim office at CIA Headquarters, Henslow waited with the DCI and a few other key officials for reports on the attack. To relieve the tension, they had drinks in hand. When the calls came that the attack was a success, they had no idea whether the prime objective had been achieved. Henslow sipped the Chivas.

This is going to be a long night.

CHAPTER FIFTY

"This just in to NBC News. Reports are that within the last hour, US forces have bombed the Libyan capital of Tripoli."

"Turn that up," Garnett told Elizabeth, who was standing closer to the television. Having a TV in their kitchen was a bad habit from childhood, Garnett had to admit, and one he would have to break someday, when the kids were older, he told himself. Now, it was part of the job.

The news anchor continued. "Sources at the Pentagon have confirmed that Tripoli has been attacked. A statement from the White House is expected shortly."

"Great."

"Bad news?" she asked.

"Good news, unless I wanted a peaceful night at home."

The phone rang.

"I'm watching," he said immediately into the receiver, knowing it was Karen on the other end.

"We have received word that President Reagan is about to speak," the TV interrupted.

"Let me call you back." Garnett hung up without an answer.

For the next twenty minutes, he watched President Reagan address the nation on the raid. He used all the right phrases: "Evidence was direct, it is precise, it is irrefutable...nerve centers...we bear the people of Libya no ill will...if their government continues...we will strike again." It was a masterful piece of communications, supported by enough truth that the actions seemed like an imperative, not a matter of foreign policy.

"Fun day ahead, huh?" Elizabeth smirked.

"Should keep us busy for a while."

The moment Reagan was done, the phone rang again.

"How long do we have?" he spoke into the phone, again without waiting.

"We can rip the Europeans, BBC, ZDF, RAI, the French right away. Maybe Israel. We will have something in an hour. Bye, I'm busy."

"I'm going in."

She handed him a sack with his dinner wrapped inside. "I figured."

By the time he arrived at his office, Brian had all the TV monitors on different news channels. The images were all the same.

"Anyone know if he is dead?"

"No word," Brian relayed without moving his eyes from the screen. For the relatively new Agency employee, this was exciting. "It's too early for the experts to say much, but they seem to be able to analyze the information they don't have pretty damned well. All the networks are covering the secretaries of state and defense. They're outlining the mission. The chairman of the Joint Chiefs of Staff is with them."

Brian took a remote and turned the sound up on one of the TV monitors.

"Planes from the US Navy task force in the Mediterranean and US Air Force F-111s stationed in England were used in this strike. All embassies and military installations around the world are on full alert."

Long way to go to drop bombs. No one was sure where he was, but of course, he could not be the target, as assassination is illegal.

"You know what to do. Everything to the CTC right away."

"Yes, sir."

"I'll be in my office."

Garnett sat back in his chair and switched the channels on the TV in his office at an almost rhythmic click. Not to his surprise, the experts were divided over the effect and reasoning of the raid.

"The raids are counterproductive to the American efforts to support a viable opposition in Libya. We cannot pick the next leader of Libya for the people of that country," a professor from Georgetown declared.

Moron. Click.

"Why do we think Libya will change its tune because the West finally decided, after months of inaction and passive responses, to take action? The people of Libya, as discouraged as they are, are not suddenly going to mount a coup just because a few bombs were dropped on them," an old guy with a head like Charlie Brown spewed.

Idiot. Click.

"The foundation of his revolution is crumbling as oil prices fall. The military does not support him. Tribal tensions are running high. He could be in jeopardy. At the least, it was a move by America—at least the administration hopes it is viewed this way—to show our resolve against terrorism."

A voice of some reason?

The video started to roll, repeating the images of bombed-out homes and buildings. Dazed people wandered the streets in the pre-dawn hours, some crying, looking and pointing at the rubble.

"I want this edited to a master tape in real time," he said on the intercom to Brian.

"Right."

Garnett waited for more video.

"Several Western reporters made their way to the damaged Bin Ashur residential area, an area inhabited by many foreigners and devastated last night by several bombs that supposedly went astray."

The video under the narration caught the destruction in all its fury.

"In addition, the Azziziyah Barracks is believed to have sustained heavy damage. The whereabouts and health of the country's leader is a subject of some speculation at the moment. The exact nature of the damage to military targets at the Tripoli airport as well as those in Benghazi is not currently known. Nether is the status of strikes against the terrorist base at Sidi Balal, ten miles West of Tripoli."

Hope we got him.

As dawn broke, the Terrorist looked over what was left of his camp. In a series of flashes, everything, including the young soldiers, had disappeared from the earth. They were replaced with burning debris and rubble. He had managed to come out alive. *Only through the Mercy of Allah.*

Remit-1 broke through the low overcast above Lakenheath, landed with a thud on the runway, and taxied to the aircraft shelter. The path was lined with hundreds of base personnel holding up signs congratulating them on their mission. One read: "L.I.B.Y.A.—Lakenheath Is Bombing Your Ass."

The emotion Trinche had been suppressing for fourteen hours rose inside him. He began to shake as he fought back the tears. Behind him, more Varks were making their descent.

"You did it, Colonel," was all Beans could say.

Exhausted, Trinche was helped from his cockpit, struggling to regain use of his numb legs. A beer was thrust into one hand and a donut into the other. Devouring the pastry, he tried to shake the hands reaching out in front of him.

His fight against terrorism was over—for the day.

The briefings with the DCI went through the night and most of the next day. No one could answer the only question worth asking. The SR-71 reconnaissance flight confirmed the compound and other designated targets had been hit hard, but privately, Henslow knew the bastard had somehow survived. The intel chatter just wasn't right if he had been blown to little bits. Henslow had factored in that if he lived, it wouldn't be long before Libya exploited the attempt.

Sitting for a moment, eyes closed, in the sanctuary of his CTC office, he allowed his mind to consider briefly the status of Mukhtar. There was no mention of him in the thick stack of cables in front of him he had just read. Nothing from the NOC. Nothing from the Mossad assets in Tripoli. The LFF opposition. The Brits. Zero. The Foreign Minister of Libya had vanished.

The rest of the cables dealt with worldwide reaction. It was the tough duty of CTC—the planning, the destruction, and the killing. Terrorism was his turf, and he needed to make certain CTC was ahead of any retaliation. It was his burden to organize a systematic program to fight worldwide terror. Emotional. Deadly. Impossible. So it had to be done.

Cable traffic and public statements showed that every Arab nation condemned the attack in some fashion. Syria was calling for political and economic sanctions against the United States. It was the same for Iran and the radical portions of the PLO. All called for retaliation.

The moderates, if there really was such a thing in this world— Jordan, Saudi, Egypt, and Tunisia—appeared lukewarm or offered no comment.

The allies were as predictable as the enemies. France was against. *The bastards.* West Germany. Not really. The rest were basically taking the diplomatic line against violence of any type. Some were calling for a United Nations Security Council meeting and resolution.

The Soviets condemned the aggression on the surface, but Henslow didn't care about the normal communist ranting.

When he heard the knock, Henslow looked up. Rather than annoyance, his face registered surprise and relief. He waved Garnett in.

"Latest update. Thought I would deliver it this time," Garnett said, handing over the cassette.

"Keep them coming, son. Anything I should worry about?"

"Small stuff—smashed windows and flag burnings at the US embassies to protests and riots to bomb scares worldwide. Nothing original."

"Stay alert. I might need you again soon."

"Yes, sir." Garnett stood for a moment, his mouth opening as if to start to say something. "See you later" came out.

Henslow let him leave. He had to work on the next step, if in actuality; both the Mukhtar op and the bombs had failed. There wouldn't be a second chance for a military strike. It would take longer, but the next option was something the CIA had been doing successfully for years: regime change.

Terrorism was going to be a global problem for a long time.

CHAPTER FIFTY-ONE

"Where were you?"

It had become the question of the day for everyone the next morning. Sharing the experience helped them get through difficult hours when all was clear. And from what he was seeing, the hours after the raid were difficult.

The NOC had been in his hotel room, lying in bed, trying to decide what to do about Mukhtar, his wife, the mission, and his life. She appeared to be a strong woman. Her husband was certainly dead. She would be next if she didn't get out soon.

His windows started to shake and the sounds of jet engines were so close it seemed they were screaming into his room. Outside, white flashes and red tracers lit up the black sky. Childish excitement overtook him, screaming like a cowboy, and pogoing around his room.

It had lasted only a few minutes, but it had seemed like a day. Hundreds of people swarmed to the streets shouting and honking car horns. On the radio, an excited announcer was speaking fast, spewing out words he understood as "barbaric" and "treacherous." Running down to the lobby, he saw reporters screaming at the terrified desk clerk, trying desperately to find working telephones to file their stories.

Deciding it was best to stay away from the chaos, he went back to his room to get a few hours of sleep, but gave up to spend the rest of the night staring out the window at the fire and smoke. He was in the right place at the right time. The intel reports were there for the taking. He just had to collect them and get the hell out of the country.

As long as my country doesn't drop any bombs on me.

That morning, the NOC was shocked and pleased to find the beat-up Renault taxi sitting outside the hotel exactly at nine.

"I want to see the bomb damage," he told the Driver as they pulled away.

"There is damage, I hear. The security people. They are anxious."

"I'm just curious."

They drove the streets of Tripoli looking at the aftermath, which, given the noise and chaos of just a few hours ago, was not very evident. Word on the street was that the Leader's home was the target, and rumors were on everyone's lips about whether he had survived.

"More attacks, they will come again," the Driver said nervously.

"Why do you think so?"

The Driver checked every direction out his windows, as if to confirm no one could overhear him in the moving cab. "I heard that he survived. I hope they will come again for him. Maybe next time." The Driver took his thumb and drew it slowly across his throat.

"I thought he was popular," the NOC elicited, trying to keep the promising conversation going.

There wasn't an answer.

The cab crawled through the streets, crowded with military vehicles. Frustrated, he pulled the Renault off the main street and maneuvered through the less-crowded narrow back streets until a jeep surrounded by four heavily armed, green-uniformed soldiers blocked their path. The Driver stomped on his brakes, the worn pads making a loud metal-on-metal screech.

"Do not worry."

He bolted out of the car and ran shouting toward the soldiers, who shouted back, aiming their machine guns from the Driver to the cab and back. After five minutes, the Driver finally sat behind the steering wheel again. Throwing the car into gear, they drove pass the sentries, waving politely as they moved down the street out of their sight.

"What was it?" the NOC asked nervously.

"They did not want to let us through. I told them you were a visiting doctor here to help the wounded. They still did not want to let us through. I explained you had permission from the government, and that it would not be good for them to delay your humanitarian work. They decided it was best to let us pass."

"But what if they check your story?"

"Them? They are not looking for more work. They are lazy."

He may be nervous, but this guy is one cool cat. Out the window, signs of the aftermath of the raid became more evident. Shattered windows mostly. Debris still in the streets.

"Bab al-Azziziyah." He pointed ahead.

The NOC saw nothing but military vehicles parked in the street. There was some foot traffic—curious people, like him—doing what they could to mange their fear. Even the Driver could sense danger.

"The road is blocked. You should walk from here. There is a road on the right side. I will meet you there." The taxi stopped at the corner, and the NOC got out.

"I'll be there in about fifteen minutes."

"Yes, I'll wait." The Driver pulled the taxi around and disappeared back down the road.

The NOC began his walk, trying not to give the dozens of soldiers patrolling the street a reason to pay any attention to him. The more he tried to hide, the more he felt unnatural. His stomach was telling him to make quick observations then get back to his hotel room as soon as possible.

The walls of the barracks and the buildings across the street were demolished or riddled with shell fragments, huge stones scattered randomly. He stopped. Looking. Memorizing. Beyond the wall a two-story blue-and-white house was virtually destroyed, its facade torn away. Outside were mounds of rubble, burned and broken furniture, twisted metal that looked as if it had once been a railing for a stairway, and huge chunks of plaster.

The images stored in his head, the NOC knew his safety depended on getting out of the country as soon as possible, but as a CIA officer on a mission, he had things to do first.

BOOK 5

APRIL 16–30, 1986

Propaganda is that branch of the art of lying which consists in nearly deceiving your friends without quite deceiving your enemies.

—*F.M. Cornford*

CHAPTER FIFTY-TWO

"**W**ake up. Wake up. Wake up!" The shouts were more emphatic each time.

He heard the voice and felt the shaking, but both felt as if they were happening someplace else, as if he were watching it happen at a safe distance, in a dream. Hoping if he held onto the vision of the dream it would become just that, the pain that shot through his body when the club struck him across the right kneecap brought that hope to an end. Nausea attacked his body and he tried to vomit, but his stomach had long since emptied down his chest and into his lap, the aftermath of hours of beating.

He opened his left eye as far as the swelling permitted, giving him a blurred view of the dim room. The right eye was swollen shut, which he actually thought a blessing, as it denied his mind a clear picture of the hell he was in.

"Good morning, Mr. Foreign Minister. Did you sleep well?" the Libyan asked. A sharp slap went across his face when Mukhtar did not answer.

"What shall we talk about today? Your murderous attack on our leader? Your contact with the American spies? Perhaps your role in the killing of the innocent people of Libya with bombs?"

The Libyan started to walk around the man, who was bound to a chair in the middle of a bare room. *This is pathetic. Not even a challenge.* But Megrahi had specifically picked him for this work. Tormenting this man was more enjoyable than wandering the streets after him like a mongrel dog.

"I have had the pleasure of meeting many types of people in this room. Businessmen. Mothers. Wives. A few generals, who are really cowards, if I am honest. I have even had a secretary once or twice. What was that last one's name? Tabrina? Yes, that was it. I think you knew her. A nice girl, very fresh. I will miss her. But you are my first foreign minister—and not just any foreign minister. You are a murdering traitor minister. Nothing quick for you. No sudden heart attack or bullet in the head. I am grateful for the opportunity. For that I thank you. You give me purpose. For trying to murder the Leader, I give you this."

The Libyan took his cigarette and stuck the lit end into the man's scarred neck as he passed behind him. The man moaned and tried to get away, but his straps held him tight.

Mukhtar groaned as the pain shocked his system.

If it was possible, he was actually getting used to it. Mukhtar's body was so numb he could not imagine any pain that could penetrate enough to make much of a difference to him. His mind, in a defense against the horror his body was receiving, had split, separated rational thought from the terrible reality of his situation—it considered his body dead. Through the blur, he saw a purplish-green swollen mass the size of a large melon where his knee should have been.

Time had stopped and he remembered little about how he had gotten there. It was darkness, mostly—and pain. *Shouting. Guards kicking and voices screaming through sounds of explosions.* Thrown into the trunk of a car, and a wild ride. Then the beatings when his interrogator appeared, endlessly beating the soles of his feet with clubs, then more endless hours of pain.

Until a few moments ago, he had not even been asked a question. Still, he was able to understand where he was. *The smell of filth. The sounds of torture. The scurrying feet of rats.*

He was in the interrogation and torture chambers of Abu Salim, the prison for the Internal Security Service.

It was time to take one more huge gamble with his life. He gave the address to his new friend, who didn't seem too happy about going somewhere else, but he agreed, for double the fare.

They drove in silence through the city again.

"Any news about the airport?" the NOC asked.

"Closed."

The cab pulled onto a tree-lined boulevard. At the right spot, he brought the car to a halt. A twisted pile of metal replaced the security gate where he had spent anxious minutes the previous night. The NOC could see a bulldozer moving a mound of debris that had replaced the beautiful home.

"Whoever lived here is dead," the Driver said nervously, pulling the car away.

"What do you mean?"

"The house, they have destroyed it. They do that to the houses of people who oppose too much, to show what happens to anyone if they do the same. If there is family of any generation, they will be sent to prison, or if they are lucky, they will be killed. Horribly. You did not choose your friends wisely."

At times like these, fully immersed in a dangerous operation with no office colleagues to depend on, the NOC would always remind himself of one thing to find focus. Despite it all, his job was to help in the collection of foreign intelligence so the foreign policy makers back in Washington could make informed decisions about the future of the United States of America. It sounded stupid, but in the end, that was what it was all about. It kept him going.

The Driver stopped the car in front of the Al Waddan. The NOC reached into his pocket and took out another stack of lira, dollars, and dinars.

"Here, my friend, with greatest thanks."

"I cannot. It is too much," the Driver said trying to refuse, but the NOC pushed the money into his hand and jumped out of the taxi.

Inside the Al Waddan, the lobby was busy with reporters milling about with little else to do.

"You *are* here."

The voice was familiar. The woman appeared from nowhere. She clung tightly to a large bag, its strap digging deeply into her shoulder. Taking her elbow, he quickly escorted her around a corner out of sight.

"Let's go to my room." Safely locked in 312, she tried to hide her exhaustion as she sat as dignified as possible, sitting on the edge of the bed, a bag at her feet.

"Mrs. Mukhtar, can I get you some water?" He offered her a glass.

"Yes, thank you."

"Why are you here?"

"My husband. You know him."

"I have never met him." He wasn't lying.

"Then you know of him, and you are trying to help him."

"Why have you come to me?" He was going to protect his cover story. *She doesn't know anything.*

"My husband told me recently about his friends. He thought I didn't know, but he is bad at keeping secrets from me. I cannot trust anyone."

She knows everything. The NOC had underestimated this woman. She was strong.

"Where is your husband?"

Her eyes started to fill with tears, but she stopped them, sitting up even straighter. "They came to tear down my house. The soldiers said he had tried to kill…they told me he was in Abu Salim. They made me watch as they destroyed my home."

"This may sound inappropriate at this time, but why are you still alive?"

"They had orders to let me go."

"Orders? Whose orders?"

"Major Megrahi."

The NOC was trying to piece it together, but little was making sense. There were too many questions and too many possible answers, and none of them seemed to fit. It was time to get out of the country.

"And he is alive?"

"I pray that he is."

"You need to get out of the country."

She stiffened. "I will not leave Abdallah."

"If you want to save him, then you must leave. Now. I just don't know how to get out of here. The airport is closed, and who knows when it will open up?"

Marwa did not have the strength to argue. She was willing to put herself in his hands for the time being. If it turned out to be a mistake, then she would have to decide what to do, or pay for her mistake. She assumed he was connected with American spies. So for now, she would follow him.

"I have a car."

"You have a car?" He looked at her with a smile on his face.

"Yes. We had a plan…if he didn't return."

"Plan? Where is your car?" *I could kiss her.*

"Across the avenue."

"Let's go." He packed his suitcase, and they headed to the lobby.

"I will meet you at your car," he said as they reached the bottom of the steps. "I'll be right there."

He walked across the lobby and approached the front desk. She was there.

"Are you leaving us?"

"Yes. Sorry, I need to settle my accounts. My company wants me to leave. They are afraid of the bombs."

"Yes, it was terrible. I was at home."

"The airports are closed. I heard that there is a ferry to Malta."

"Yes, it is still on schedule. It leaves today—in a few hours," she replied, nodding.

"I will try it. I thank you." He settled the account, with extra dinars for her help. She blushed as she pocketed the money. If Internal Security asked her where he was, they would be looking in the wrong place.

He found Marwa sitting on the passenger side of a well-maintained Mazda, right where she had said she would meet him. In her hands he noticed a small picture frame, the image hidden from view.

"You must drive. It will look suspicious if a woman drives a man," she said, placing the frame in her bag.

"Good idea." He tossed his suitcase in the trunk. "We have one stop to make."

The car went west, toward the setting sun.

CHAPTER FIFTY-THREE

"**W**ould you like a drink? I imagine you are thirsty," the Libyan offered as he raised a glass of water to his own lips. The Libyan took long gulps, the overflow running out of the corners of his mouth onto this uniform, until the glass was empty.

Mukhtar watched, his dry mouth and throat begging for a drop. He had not had food or water for as long as he had been in the room. *How long? One day? Two days? A week?*

"Sorry. All gone. Maybe tomorrow."

Death felt near, but until the end, as long as he could, he would show the man circling around him honor and courage. He would confess to nothing.

"We went to your home looking for your wife. We thought she might like to visit you. She wasn't there. Too bad. I'd like to meet her. But don't worry; we will find her," the Libyan said, smiling, running his hand over his crotch so the bound man could see his intentions.

No sound escaped his swollen throat. Only fractured thoughts of Marwa were possible and whether she had taken his advice and escaped. Hope was slipping, but he had to believe to survive his ordeal.

"So, tell me. How did you plan to escape after your murderous plot?"

Silence.

"No more!" Mukhtar felt the numbness strike his body before it started to convulse as the man applied electrodes to Mukhtar's naked chest. His head snapped back then sagged forward, his chin on his chest.

"Enough."

"Yes, sir," the Libyan said, obeying the command and releasing the probes from the scorched flesh. Megrahi entered unnoticed. Disappointed, he stopped his session.

"How is he?"

"A stubborn man, but I believe he was just about to confess his guilt."

"Is that right, Abdallah?" Megrahi said, moving close to the sobbing man in the chair. "Oh, come now, Abdallah. What did you expect me to do?" He turned to the Libyan. "Leave."

"Yes, sir."

Megrahi closed the door behind him, waited for a moment, making certain he heard the man walk away.

"Can you keep a secret? I don't like him—an awful man. But he does what I need done. You do not look too good, Abdallah. Look at that leg. Terrible. That might have to come off. Here, let me help you. Would you like that?"

Mukhtar nodded feebly.

"Good." Megrahi took a filthy rag from a bucket in the corner and started to wipe the vomit and blood from Mukhtar's face. "You bit through your lip. What have you done to yourself?" He sat.

"Tareq." Mukhtar choked the word as he felt the blood from the gash in his lip running down his throat.

"You are still talking about that? Tareq died defending the country. He is a hero. Whatever—or whoever—gave you the idea that we killed him?"

"Murdered. I saw..." Words choked out with what little strength remained.

"I would have liked to see it, but it was lost in the rubble. No doubt you believe what you saw. Please believe me. I would not do anything to harm you, or Marwa." Megrahi sat back in his chair, ignoring the irony of that comment. "Maybe it is real. He may have been caught and killed—for what, I am not sure. Perhaps this is a deception. Was this done to you on purpose?"

The words hit harder than the abuse from the torturer. Mukhtar used his remaining energy to focus his brain. *A fake?*

"Who?" was all he could mange.

"Who? I do not know. Our lunatic leader? Very possible, but as you said once, nothing happens in my country unless I know. Still, he is a powerful, devious, and deceitful being. He could have done something. Maybe Tareq was killed as a lesson to you and others. Or the Israelis? Your American friends? Would they deceive you like this? Did they want you to kill me, or the Leader? An interesting thought... let me tell you a little secret." He leaned forward and whispered in the man's ear. "I would not have shed a tear for him if you had succeeded."

He stood and started to walk in circles around the chair.

"I could see it in your eyes. Maybe the Brother Idiot saw it too. You have a heart, Abdallah. You care. But in this world, you cannot afford to care. We adapt. I had to, or I would have been eliminated like our deceased friends. I swayed in the shifting moods and rants of our leader. Yes. I have had to be as inhuman as he is to make it to the next day. I have murdered and ordered many killed. You have witnessed it. What about you? You did little."

Megrahi was still circling.

"Human rights, freedom, diplomacy. He has no concept of that. The law. His law. Death. If you had succeeded, I would be in control and could rule the Jamahiriyah as I saw fit. Not the vision of the sociopath we have today. It was not meant to be."

Mukhtar had listened to it all but was having trouble comprehending the meaning. Why was Megrahi saying this? Nothing about Tareq? Was he just playing more tricks? It slowly started to make twisted sense somehow, but he could not keep the thoughts organized as his brain had been trained. His pain, fatigue, and malnutrition had caught up to him. He was ready for it to end.

Megrahi stopped his patter and started to laugh.

"You should have seen him, Abdallah. I am not sure what he was more frightened of: you with your little sword or the bombs raining down on him from the sky. The alleged mastermind of the terrorist world, the soulless clown the Americans want the world to believe is single-handedly in command of every act of violence. Shaking like a child. He survived, yes—but for how long?" These words shocked him. He was thinking out loud, mostly to himself. "It might be many years before there is another chance like we had these past few days. Years. Many people will suffer for our failure."

"Kill me…if…burden."

"I can't. I know it pains you. It does me as well. Since he did not die, by your sword or the American bombs, he must see I am still loyal." He paused and then momentarily spoke with a morsel of sincerity. "You cannot die. I am still your friend. I am. I need you. I want you to know I let Marwa go."

Mukhtar forced his head up enough to look at the man to see whether he was deceiving him or being sincere. If she was safe, then he would fight for life so he could see her again.

Megrahi opened the door to leave and immediately the Libyan was dragged into the cell by a large, snarling dog with ugly patches of dirty fur caked to its body. It took all his strength to hold onto the chain. The animal leaped immediately at Mukhtar, who screamed, head back in terror. The Libyan jerked the chain hard around the dog's neck just in time to keep it from biting into Mukhtar's swollen leg. It barely noticed and tried again and again to sink its fangs into his flesh.

"You are done. Give him some water and food. Do not touch him again in any way. Understand?" Avoiding the snapping teeth of the beast, Megrahi looked at the Libyan so he could see the "no accidents" expression glaring at him.

"Yes," he said, disappointment registering in his voice.

"I will be back tomorrow. We can talk again. Have a good night."

Peering from his position down the dirty concrete-and-metal hall, he tried not to look too interested. Security Police were everywhere, and they spent their time looking for traitors, real or imaginary. The man with the hideous animal was with him—in the notorious Room 4, the torture room. The dozens of unlucky people he witnessed entering the room came out dead after they were paid a visit. Every time he wanted to help the people he had been ordered to only watch and report. The helpless man was dragged past him. *Still alive? Barely.* It was hard to tell under the bruises, blood, and filth.

The battered body was tossed into a cell he knew to be nothing more than a windowless concrete closet. They kicked the purplish, bloated feet into the space so the door could be closed. *If he is not dead yet, he soon will be, and better for him—the martyr is beloved by Allah.*

After his shift, he would pass the information up the chain of command to the shadow opposition force he supported, happy to have something to report.

CHAPTER FIFTY-FOUR

T he ringing phone surprised him. For a moment, he stared at it before he put the receiver to his ear.

"Hello?"

"Yes, I was wondering how much it is to rent your apartment," inquired an unfamiliar voice.

The Oilman's heart jumped right to his throat. He almost couldn't get the sounds out. "It's not for rent."

"I understood that it was. So I can't see it today?"

"No. But perhaps soon," the Oilman replied, signaling he had understood the message, noting a slight Italian accent from the caller.

"I must have been misinformed. I apologize," the NOC said, hanging up the pay phone. He closed the Casio electronic organizer, shutting down the encrypted files in the secure area of the device.

The attack had not really frightened the Oilman, since he had recognized the sound of the jets right away. From the direction of the explosions, he could tell the planes were attacking the airport and downtown, and he still felt stupid that he rolled under his bed. *If a bomb decided to drop on my apartment, the mattress would provide little protection.*

The phone call meant danger, but there was no way to determine the exact meaning. No matter, he had to follow instructions, and do it quickly. Within seconds of receiving the message, he grabbed his passport and suitcase and moved toward the door. Not certain whether he would ever return, he stopped long enough to stuff a few of his favorite music tapes into his pocket.

The emergency contact call required him to leave the country within twenty-four hours through the established escape route, which was by ferry to Malta. Before he had arrived in country, he was given an open ticket good for passage without reservation, an arrangement made with the ferry line at a level far above him. Frequent vacations to Malta aboard the ferry established a thin relationship with the crew in case the "magic ticket" failed in his time of need.

Foreign workers trying to get out of harm's way jammed the ferry terminal. Walking by the ticket line, the Oilman moved into the next line at the customs and immigration checkpoint.

"Passport," a weary man in a drab uniform said without looking up. He complied. "Ticket." A cursory glance, and the man waved him through. *Easy. Too easy?*

When he reached the gangway to the ferry, the security officials standing on either side took his pass. Prepared for the worst, he was pleased it hadn't arrived, so far. Bored security guards let him pass as easily as at the first checkpoint. He was one of the regulars on this run, and the extra five hundred dinars in the passport was always an added bonus. A private room, not much larger than his suitcase, awaited him aboard the two-tiered ferry. It was much better than sitting in the lounge areas for the entire twelve-hour trip to Valletta.

In an hour, he was at sea.

The NOC had to admit that as despised as their ruler was by the West, he had made certain that the country had nicely paved roads. They had encountered few checkpoints on their journey, and the guards at the barricades didn't seem to care about them.

Few words were exchanged as he navigated the car the one hundred kilometers from Tripoli to the Tunisian border at Ras El-Jefir. The questions and their answers were so enormous that they both silently agreed to avoid talking at all. When they arrived at the border crossing station, it was almost dark. Only one lane to cross the border was open. Cars and trucks lined the side of the road waiting to begin the tedious, time-consuming crossing process. The border post was the only official crossing point between the countries—a mixture of two-story buildings and a few ten-meter-tall trees lining dusty crossroads separated by guard huts and crossing gates.

Disorganized queues of vehicles, many taking goods to be sold at the "Libyan Market" in Ben Guerdane thirty-three kilometers over the arid Tunisian border, waited daily to cross the frontier. For ordinary travelers, the procedures were time consuming, requiring at least half a day to get to the other side. Many of the owners pushed their cars, saving on gasoline. Despite the delays, the officials at the border on both sides rarely caused any problems unless they were provoked.

The NOC pulled the Mazda off the road behind an oil tanker, turned off the engine, and waited. Marwa was asleep. She awoke to the sound of engines revving. The line started to crawl forward.

"I was dreaming," she said, her voice weary.

"About what?"

He saw her wipe a tear from her eyes, trying to get control.

"That Abdallah had managed to escape. I could feel the relief and hope clinging to me, and as you drove me away, Abdallah was following in another car. And Tareq was in a car behind him. But we couldn't stop, and they could not catch up."

"Sad dream." Her life had changed permanently, and only for the worse. Perhaps it was a result of the spiritual bond that develops between two people who have been together for so long, sharing experiences. No matter. He wondered if he would ever have emotions for someone like what she was feeling.

"But the more we drove away, the more powerful the feeling became that I would see him again," she continued.

"And you will. If I have anything to do about it."

Only a few cars stood between them and the border, but the guards took their time checking each vehicle.

She looked at her new friend closely for the first time. He was younger than she had first thought, about the same age as Tareq before…there was a similar look of sensitivity in their eyes, a caring. He was cautious, but a young man certain of his actions. Like her son, he talked to her gently, with an honest quality—asking if she needed to rest and apologizing for the length of the journey, as if it were within his control.

"My husband was a spy?"

"No." Since they had been together, the NOC had never broken his cover story with the wife of HJSHIELD.

They reached the front of the line.

"If there is trouble, I might run the gates. Be prepared," he warned.

"Yes." She braced herself against the car door.

The crossing consisted of nothing more than two small buildings on either side of the road flying green flags, with a barricade arm that swung up and down to allow traffic to pass. The soldiers on duty, dressed in green uniforms, had their guns out and were pointing at their car as he pulled up. They yelled and screamed, waving their weapons in a motion for them to stop. The NOC pushed hard on the brakes. The car slid to a stop, almost crushing the foot of one of the soldiers running toward them. The four circled the vehicle, pushing the AK-47s and rifles through her windows.

"Out!" one screamed.

The NOC tensed, but before he could open the door, he felt her hand on his arm.

"Stay," she said confidently, getting out of the car. She walked around to the driver's side so the NOC could hear.

She had been a diplomat's wife for many years, which meant she must remain calm and control the situation to her benefit. If they were waiting for her, there was little she could do. She could be dead in a minute or returned to Tripoli to face a slower death. *Perhaps then he would try to run the car through the gate. No, he would come to my defense and die also.*

"Is a there a problem?" she asked. "I need to get to Tunis—to see family. Here is my identification and passport."

The soldier took her documents and looked at them.

"You are the wife of Foreign Minister Mukhtar?"

"Yes." The name was famous in Libya, and if the soldiers had not yet heard of the trouble in Tripoli, they had a chance.

"Proceed."

"Thank you." Taking her papers, she returned to the car as the gate went up.

"Shall we go?" She asked him.

"Absolutely."

He put the Mazda in gear, headed across the frontier then stopped at the first telephone he could find. She waited, knowing that she was leaving her homeland, perhaps forever.

CHAPTER FIFTY-FIVE

Everything was happening quickly. Panic mode set in as they worked on the material Henslow had requested during a middle-of-the-night call.

"How much longer?" Garnett asked, not realizing it was for the second time that minute.

"Twenty minutes to edit and an hour for dubs," John replied tersely.

"That's cutting it pretty close."

"Go away."

"You're right," Garnett admitted, knowing he had to get off John's back and let him do his work. To meet the 9:00 a.m. deadline, they had been working all night.

Garnett was surprised that they had found anything at all. When Henslow called, Garnett's first response was to doubt that they had any footage of Abu Salim. His branch, by virtue of having a secure and climate-controlled vault to store film and video, had become a repository for most film, video, and still images the Agency had collected over the years. At some point, Garnett's librarians, who had been in the department for more years than anyone could recall, had indexed this mass of stored media. He was always amazed at what they could find—the proverbial needle in a haystack—using their almost photographic memories to recall the tiniest fragment of any image.

In 1984, upon completion of the massive white-wall structure, a sufficient number of stories hailing the opening were aired. Ninety minutes of Abu Salim footage were scattered through the files, including one detailed segment about its construction by an independent film crew out of Europe. The librarians scavenged a small stack of photographs out of the massive files.

Abu Salim was a complex of many buildings in a relatively small area inside Tripoli. It revealed imposing walls topped with razor wire. Huge courtyards gave way to long, narrow corridors lined with green metal doors, each leading to a sparse cell. The name Abu Salim had become synonymous with torture and murder.

Tensions mounted in the EMB office as the deadline neared. Secluded in the small editing room with no rest for hours, Garnett needed the space as well. When Henslow called him, it was not unlike any other past impossible task his office had been asked to perform, except it had come directly from the C/CTC at two in the morning.

When he arrived at Henslow's office in the middle-of-the-night, the old man looked tired.

"What happened?" Garnett asked the only question on his mind.

"Don't worry about it, son," Henslow said in the same kind of voice, which really meant leave me alone.

"I'm curious about what is happening, especially if it deals with you know who."

"Maybe, but right now we need the information on Abu Salim prison in Tripoli. I want pictures, film, everything and every angle you can find. It's all the help I need right now." He looked at his watch. "It's after two now. I need it by nine, no later."

Something is really wrong. Mukhtar was in trouble, something not expected. Perhaps out of even Henslow's considerable control.

"He tried to kill him, didn't he?"

"You are a perceptive fucking person, Mike Garnett." Henslow leaned back, momentarily allowing a smile to slip onto his lips. "Tried to skewer him with a sword, according to sources. Can you believe it? I love him."

"What happened to his nonviolent profile?"

"You did a hell of a job. Leave it at that."

"Was that always the goal?"

"Who cares? Would I cry a river if he had succeeded? Absolutely not. I'm not in the caring business. Are you?"

The words shocked Garnett. He had been asked almost the same question the day he started as Chief/Propaganda Ops: "Do you have any moral or ethical problems with what you will do here?" Garnett really hadn't thought about it since, and he knew why. He really *didn't* have any moral or ethical problems with propaganda. In fact, he enjoyed it. Had he started to care? Had he crossed his own line? *If I cared too much, my judgment would become impaired, and I would be unable to make the right decisions.* Deception was his sword. Control was his target. That was key. But this time, for the first time, the lies were not targeting a faceless population, or even a small group of bad guys. This was directed at one individual with a face, a family, and a life.

"Don't try to bullshit me, or yourself, that you didn't think it was possible. You aren't that naïve. You didn't object when I asked to add the other officer lookalike. Because you knew. You knew Mukhtar needed something, someone, to blame to get him to act, and it worked. Megrahi. Qadhafi. Didn't matter. The fact he didn't act the way you thought he might is no reason to get moralistic. The choice was his. He tried to kill a very bad guy."

"I'm done."

Garnett flinched, startled from the memory replay by a voice behind him. John wearily handed Garnett the finished tapes, then collapsed on the office couch.

"I'm done," he repeated.

"Good. I'll take it up. Want to come along?" John deserved some credit for his work.

"No. I'm going home to see if I still have a family. Today is our anniversary. Guess I should stop by Safeway and grab some flowers and a card."

"Get the hell out of here. You should have told me."

"I would have…but would it have made a difference?" John said with a tired half smile as he struggled to his feet and headed out the door.

"No."

Inside Henslow's office a few minutes later, Garnett handed over the tapes. It was 8:30 a.m. Thirty minutes early.

"About time."

Henslow appeared as if he hadn't moved in the hours since Garnett had left him. He took the tape and slammed it into a VCR next to his desk. Titles and images started to move across the screen of the small Sony color monitor. Garnett watched as Henslow, arms folded across his chest, stared in a trance at the gray stone walls, roads, and interiors.

"Dismal place."

"Hard to think of him in there."

"Won't be for long. If he is alive," Henslow replied, his lips barely moving. "Oh, get video guy and grab your crap. Tomorrow we're going to Italy."

CHAPTER FIFTY-SIX

Moving was almost impossible. Even if he wanted to, the size of the cell and the stiffness and pain in his joints limited any movement. It was just as agonizing to lie curled in a ball as it was to do anything else in the oppressive heat. He was semiconscious, and the remaining area of his brain that refused to give in to the pain kept a small one-way conversation of rational thought moving in his head.

His mind took him on a journey to his home, in the living room richly furnished in traditional Arabic style. Oriental carpets on the floors. Crystal vase and glasses decorated with revolutionary slogans from *The Green Book* displayed on the mantel. Next to those were the memories of a life and career: antique lantern, a silver statue of a camel, a gilt-edge Koran, and a framed picture of the Leader.

When his mind tired, the reality of his situation caved in on him.

It was time to die.

"We don't expect revolts and uprisings. In fact, the attack certainly delayed indefinitely any serious internal threats to him. Much of the army remains loyal, as do the People's Army and the Revolutionary Guards. There isn't popular support, and they would be defeated. The main army units have been restricted to quarters. The Revolutionary Guards control the streets—Megrahi's boys. There are reports of sporadic fighting near the Jamahiriyah Benghazi Barracks." Henslow relayed the latest intel to his longtime friend.

"We missed him," the DCI stated.

"He is one lucky bastard," Henslow admitted.

"State agrees," Harper added, disappointedly. "He's doing TV interviews from his barracks. We may have killed his daughter, if reports are accurate. That could cause some image problems for us, if true."

"It's a bunch of propaganda bullshit."

"True or not, it's something the president would have liked to avoid." Harper glared at Henslow.

"What's Megrahi's position?" the DCI asked.

"His grand plan to take over is blown to fucking hell. Sources indicate he is forming a junta of the remaining members of the 1969 coup, the jokers who have de facto been running the country anyway. But that shit Qadhafi is still there, alive and kicking."

It was Harper's turn. "I anticipate Qadhafi will use this to strengthen himself diplomatically. He may go to the UN. There are protests around the world against us. If he plays it right, he retains control and reasserts his leadership."

They sat waiting for the man's mind to catalog and analyze all the data he had at his disposal.

"So he tried to assassinate Qadhafi?"

"It would seem that way," Henslow answered honestly.

"It would have been nice, but not if the United States Congress—or worse, the press—ever found out that the United States government sanctioned the assassination of a foreign leader. It would be a problem for the administration." Harper warned.

"For Christ's sake, we just dropped bombs on him. The Congress, the people—hell, the entire world—knows exactly what was going on. And we weren't targeting *him.*"

"Where is he now?" the DCI asked with the slightest trace of amusement in his voice.

"Abu Salim, if he is still alive."

The DCI waited again before he spoke. "Then maybe we should get him out." That signaled the end of the meeting.

Outside in the hallway, Harper cornered Henslow before he could get away.

"Can you do it? Get him out?" she asked.

"We can do anything. We are America. Fuck them." He brushed past her and disappeared through the stairway door.

Inside his office, Henslow personally fired off a series of urgent cables to stations in London, Rome, Malta, and Tunis. His felt energized as his fingers flew across his keyboard, the capital letters scrawling across his glowing green screen. The operation had taken shape in his mind hours before he called Garnett. Now he had the approval to move ahead.

There was nothing else he would rather be doing and no place else he would rather be.

"Have you heard anything more about Mukhtar?" Carver asked the Chairman.

He had, but he didn't want to make the American's job too easy. The Chairman was pleased that although his opposition force was not yet strong enough or organized to mount a successful coup, the force he had created was viewed as a valuable weapon. It ensured his personal value and a monetary annuity for the foreseeable future with his surrogate sponsors. So he provided information that was verifiable—some things more easy to validate than others. They played the game, stealthily he had to admit, so the opposition leader waited for the real reason for this visit.

"Yes. My people have been monitoring his condition since we first located him. As of this morning, he was alive."

"So we know exactly where he is?" Henslow had dispatched him to London immediately after the bombing, anticipating the LFF might be needed. The cable that had arrived an hour before was no surprise, and any delay in getting what he needed could prove fatal.

"Yes, at the moment."

"We are getting him out."

The Chairman contemplated the decree with a moment of silence.

"That could be challenging."

"The plan is in motion. We want to get him out of there, right now. Your assets are in position and we expect them to assist. Timing will be crucial, so we can't afford fuck-ups."

"If you are asking for an assault on the prison, it is too heavily defended, and we could not amass enough people in Tripoli to be effective."

"That's not a problem. This operation requires a few key people and Swiss-accuracy timing. We need to get this into motion right now. We want him alive." Carver directed trying not to get agitated.

"We need to get this into motion right now. Forty-eight hours is too late. We want him alive." Carver was getting agitated.

"Abdallah is a great man, but given the obstacles we face, is he worth the effort?"

"If you are not interested in helping, then stop wasting my time. I will inform Langley, and we can say good-bye." Carver was now in no mood to play.

"I must check with my people inside." Message received.

"We don't have time. I need a yes or no."

"It is very dangerous for my people. Even if it is successful. Our base in Tunis needs more supplies, as you know."

"Everyone will get what they deserve." They both knew what that meant. The cash would flow.

"That is very nice; thank you. The LFF is happy to assist in any manner possible."

"Get started." Carver rose. There was no time to write a cable. Within another hour, he was on the STU-III secure phone briefing Henslow.

CHAPTER FIFTY-SEVEN

"They died for the revolution, for the Jamahiriyah."

The cheer echoed against the stone markers each time the Brother Leader of the Revolution spoke. He stood on a platform near the small, white mosque among the other mourners, dressed immaculately in his best green military uniform and bright-red beret, sweating under a blistering sun near the entrance to the Martyr of Al-Hanni cemetery. In front of him, twenty caskets were ready to be buried, neatly arranged in a graveyard littered with broken tombstones. Just a few feet behind him, Megrahi looked on with contempt, loathing, and admiration. He wondered how the crowd would react if he were to take out his knife and slit the man's throat from ear to ear right in front of them. It would not shock him if they kept on chanting, this time with real happiness and delight.

Anti-American slogans rose in unison from the masses as Megrahi feigned the appropriate emotions—enthusiasm, hatred, mass hysteria, loyalty—as the caskets with military flags and wreaths of flowers with company insignias, a couple of sailors, and a few antiaircraft gunners, were mourned. *Lucky. At least they died somewhat in the honor of battle.* Survival now depended on taking measures against the more conservative military, the ones who had run from their posts or had not returned fire. The more he could purge the regular military now, actions that would meet with little resistance, the less dissent the more radical Revolutionary Guard forces would have when he maneuvered into a position of even greater control and power.

Families, who arrived after the day's prayers, cried sincere tears of grief as their martyred relatives were buried. If it weren't for the fortuitous attack by the Americans creating chaos and photo opportunities for the press, both of which helped his personal cause, he would feel some sympathy for them.

"Unity, unity," he shouted to the throng as their numbers continued to swell at the entrance.

Thousands of Libyans crowded before him. Most had been paid to be there or had been bused in from outside the city, and they screamed back at him with fists raised in unison. The young gangs of armed Revolutionary Committees had done well to get the masses out. Those he counted as members of his surreptitious followers were scattered in the throngs, some wearing civilian clothes, but most conspicuous in their green fatigue jackets, white belts, and shoulder straps, each carrying a machine gun. On the roof of the mosque behind him, more military police watched, hands tightly gripping their AK-47s.

To one side, sympathetic ambassadors from nonaligned countries accompanied by his Middle East brethren forced their way through the crowd. Most importantly, the dozens of foreign journalists received positions in the best area to view the ceremony and hear the speeches, no matter how rambling. By the end of the day, the world would see the faces of the crying mourners, the coffins, and the anger—all brought on by the hands of the West.

The power of world public opinion will be on our side, if it wasn't already.

Inside Libya, while many accused the Leader of causing the bombs to fall on their heads, they knew if they voiced an opinion, even if whispered, they would end up at Abu Salim. To strengthen the point, Megrahi made sure that every night since the attack, the air raid sirens blared and the antiaircraft batteries fired their artillery into the air, sending the bright-red tracers across the sky. *How could the people believe the problems of their country were caused by anything other than unprovoked American aggression?*

Megrahi watched as the coffins were lowered into the small concrete-block tombs and then covered with tiles and cement. A military guard fired AK-47s into the air for their fallen colleagues, the spent rounds showering down on the heads of the mourners.

"There is no internal unrest in this country. You saw it today at the cemetery, where our innocent citizens and brave soldiers were buried.

You love me. Direct your hate toward the Americans. Those who say they are against me—I am sorry to have to say those are stupid people." The crowd went into a frenzy.

A few hours after the ceremony, assuming the role left vacant by the "currently unavailable" foreign minister, Megrahi sat in his air-conditioned office behind a row of microphones to address the world's press, who swarmed his office like hungry sharks. The television cameramen crowded toward him, pushing one another to clear their view, the rapid click of the still cameras filled the space as he prepared to give his speech. As he spoke, every word was copied and recorded.

Thousands of miles away, sitting in the departure lounge of Dulles Airport, Henslow, Garnett, and John stared at a television watching the news conference being broadcast live on CNN.

"He's a movie star," John said.

"Impressive. Nicely done," Garnett observed.

"There have been calls for people to rise against the Americans," a BBC reporter addressed to Megrahi.

"The Brother Leader supports the struggles of oppressed people and liberation movements around the world."

"There are rumors of consolidation of power between you and other remaining military officers from the 1969 coup. Is this true?" The BBC reporter was relentless.

Henslow noticed Megrahi's eyes narrow to slits. *Now, that pissed him off.*

"The establishment of the Jamahiriyah was not a coup, but a people's revolution. Our Leader, the Brother Leader of the Revolution, commands the Revolutionary Council. It takes its direction from his wishes. The Revolutionary Committees are the Leader's. An attack on them is an attack on him."

This is going very well. I must personally congratulate the staff in the Information Ministry for their work releasing false statements and quotes by the Leader, which I can now slightly contradict. The order to attack the NATO base on the island of Lampadusa with one of the patrol boats followed by his statement ceasing the hostilities provided the desired moderate view he was trying to establish. Now it was time to twist the knife.

"We are looking at many alternatives to protect our people from more death at the hands of the Americans."

"Are you talking about the Soviets, sir?" asked a young journalist he recognized from American television.

Actually, the Soviets had been a total disappointment. Megrahi had little use for them. Their weapons had proved to be inferior and not worth the billions of dollars spent every year to procure them. They were worthless as partners, and the chatter among his Soviet satellite connections indicated the once world power was on its final chapter.

At least the Americans, as impulsive as they tend to act and react, have some sense of honor.

"They have been helpful."

"He's lying through his teeth," Henslow said. "The Soviets let him down, big-time. He'd rather kiss Reagan than let them have a permanent base in Libya. On top of that, the Soviets don't like Qadhafi either. They think he is weird."

Their attention was drawn back to the interview.

"We have heard that certain opposition figures are being detained. Particularly, we have heard that Foreign Minister Abdallah Mukhtar has been jailed. Do you have any comments on this, sir?" someone from the back of the room shouted.

"Finally," Garnett said.

Megrahi sat for a brief moment of stunned silence. When he started to answer, he realized he had waited too long and cursed himself.

"That is a lie. The foreign minister, my friend, was present at the Azziziyah Barracks meeting with the Brother Leader on matters of high state importance when he was severely injured by American bombs. His wounds are critical, and we do not know if he will survive them. We pray for him and Marwa—such tragedy in his family. Thank you."

The room exploded with shouts, yelling, and motion as the reporters responded to the bombshell news. The nation's second-in-command ignored the pleas for more information as he exited the room with the composure of a man in full control of everything.

"Looks like that pissed him off," John said.

"Was that reporter one of ours?"

"Yes," Garnett answered.

John looked closely at Garnett. "Nice."

"What he said was basically true."

"At least we know he is alive," Henslow said.

"We do?" John asked.

"Absolutely," he replied. "It's time to get on that plane. Let's go."

They followed Henslow on their journey to save the man they never had met but who deserved a chance to survive.

CHAPTER FIFTY-EIGHT

"**H**ello, son," Henslow said, extending his hand.

"Hello, sir."

"Well done getting her out."

"Thank you, sir," the NOC replied.

Garnett and John struggled to carry four large suitcases through the front door of the large secluded villa somewhere in the suburbs of Rome.

"In there." Henslow pointed toward a set of doors.

"Any help? I didn't think so," John said as they disappeared into the room.

"So she showed up at your hotel?" Henslow asked.

It was the question that the NOC had been expecting, causing his stomach to flip. He had thought over the various responses since they had left. Although he had been mostly candid in his cable, he had decided to leave a few incidents out—not the least of which was his unorthodox taxi ride and conversation with the wife of Mukhtar the night of the bombing. In a world of deception, sometimes telling the truth was the only logical course of action.

"Your instructions were pretty open, other than to make contact. I went to their house, but he wasn't there. She told me he was at a meeting at the barracks, so I gave her my card. She showed up at my hotel the next day, after they destroyed her house."

"This wasn't in your cable," Henslow said, staring at the NOC, who felt it right between his eyes.

"I didn't want to get my ass chewed out and find myself stationed in the North Pole. I didn't think she would make it—if she did, I doubted she would contact me, a stranger. If she did knock on my door, I figured we

didn't have much of a chance, but then she said there was a way to get out."
More honesty, even if he had only thought of it a few moments before.

Pause.

"She trusts you."

"I guess."

Pause. *She likes the kid. Tareq was about his age.*

"I have something for you to do." He followed Henslow along the route John and Garnett had struggled through moments before. They entered a small library with walls lined with old red-and-brown books. The smell of aged leather and coffee filled the room. A ceramic tray piled with a mountain of cookies and fruit sat on a table next to a pair of large chairs occupying the limited space in the middle of the room.

Garnett felt a jealous spike shoot through the depths of his brain as he observed the way Henslow treated the other CIA employee. A force existed between them that was barely perceptible to Garnett, but he could sense it as he had many times before. He likened it to being a member of a secret club, one in which the membership was confined to a small clique whose inconspicuous members shared one trait in common. They were case officers of the CIA running real intelligence operations. Garnett could get close to them, maybe even get temporarily invited into the club to glimpse what "real" intel officers did, such as this operation, but permanent membership—that was out of his reach.

"I'm Mike. This is John. We're here to take some video." Handshakes were cordial and genuine.

They started to set up the equipment.

A tired but stately woman sat in one of the comfortable chairs, drinking some tea and nibbling on an orange. Garnett knew the impressive biography of the wife of the famous Libyan diplomat. She was a remarkable person whose life he had disrupted. *Confident. Intelligent. Determined. This is a person who has made the choice to seek out American help.* Despite the fatigue that covered her like a shroud, she commanded the respect of a person who normally obtained what she sought.

"Hello, Mrs. Mukhtar. It is a pleasure to meet you. We're here to record your story. Is there anything you need?" Garnett asked.

"No, fine, thank you," she responded with little emotion.

"You must have had some trip getting here. Would you mind telling us about it?"

"You are interested?"

"Many people will take strength in your story. And others in the world want to hear of the situation you left behind."

John turned on lights and set the camera and microphone.

They listened intently to Marwa as she told of her husband's work... the death of their only son and the mysterious video...her last conversations with Abdallah...the journey across Libya to Tunisia...crossing at Ras El-Jedir, then their long drive to Tunis. Garnett mostly let John handle the shots, but occasionally he would point to something of interest he wanted captured. It was hard not to see her gripping tightly to a small picture she held in her lap.

"Tell me about the picture, can you?" he asked.

She stiffened at the question, momentarily hiding it in her closed palms, then smiled. Taking a long look at her son, she let out a sigh. "It is my son, Tareq. His last picture. The video...I told you..."

"I am sorry to hear that," Garnett said, keeping his face as calm as he could. "We're done."

Her story was incredible. *This was one strong woman.* Her life could easily be made into a TV movie, if not an actual feature film. It had passion, drama, political intrigue, and espionage. He would have no problems making some powerful propaganda with these tapes.

"My husband. He is in prison. Abu Salim...I know he is alive...he must be rescued...you...your people, they can help get him out."

"You are certain he is still alive?" Henslow asked from the corner. He had been stoic the entire time, sitting in the darkness absorbing the silence.

The first real uncontrolled emotion rose to her face. This was the women whom the NOC had seen standing alone and unsure at a door a few days before—the face that had made him hand over his card.

"He is alive. I can feel it."

"We need to get him out," Henslow said to her directly, but the rest understood it was a direct command.

"He was helping you," she said softly.

Normally, Henslow would play the control game and play it hard, guaranteeing she did what he wanted, when, and where.

But not this time.

"Consider this your temporary home. It is safe. Anything you want, just ask. I will be back as soon as I can."

Henslow left the room. The rest followed.

"Get to Malta now, today. I want it started now," he said to the NOC. "You have the exfiltration plan details. You." He pointed to Garnett. "Do that shit you do. Now."

The terrorism chief disappeared out the door into the darkness.

John edited the materials on their portable machines within a few hours. Garnett passed the materials to a journalist recruited by Rome Station.

Within a day, RAI television news ran a story on the heroic escape of the wife of the foreign minister of Libya. ZDF in West Germany followed. Then BBC. Her tears and words were soon rebroadcast around the world. Her ordeal, and the unknown fate of her husband, instantly became an international sensation.

"I want him kept alive."

"He is too far gone," the Libyan said into the phone.

"Alive. Do you understand?" Megrahi said sternly. The line went dead.

The Libyan hung up slowly. He looked at the man lying on the dirty concrete floor of the closet-size cell, hands and feet still bound tight.

"You are a stubborn man," he commented to the unconscious victim.

He must understand that I am not a magician.

"I'm a friend of Alan's. He sends his regards from Atlanta. He wants you to know that the Yellow Jackets are having a good season."

The words were spoken efficiently over the phone. *Clear. Precise, but with an Italian accent. It's him.*

"I hope they have a winning season for a change," he replied.

The whole thing sounded stupid and ridiculous now that he had heard it out loud. The Oilman had to respond with a sentence that would sound natural to anyone who might overhear the conversation. They were the right recognition signals.

As much as he hated the seclusion in a hotel, the Oilman had spent two straight days in his Valletta, Malta, room waiting for some instructions on his status. The Oilman had made it a habit during his vacation travel to Malta to first get drunk, and then, if he had the strength, find a girl who liked older men to fill his ten days.

This time, his only companions were several bottles of beer and the satellite television. On the third day, he decided to take a risk and visit the famous National Museum of Archeology, to see the antiquities, to smell history, and to stretch his mind and muscles.

Malta's St. John's Co-Cathedral and Museum was his favorite, with its austere facade and impressive baroque interior. The Knights of Malta had built it over four hundred years ago, and he marveled at a mosaic of tombstones commemorating knights who would crusade no more. Flemish tapestries and masterpiece paintings surrounded him, acting like a shield against the worries outside the thick stone walls. As he strolled past the tapestries and frescoes in the Palace of the Grand Masters, the paranoia entered his head—filling it with questions for which he had no answer. Every face, seemingly studying the works, appeared to be looking at him.

"Are you hungry? Can I buy you dinner?" the voice asked over the phone, bringing him back to the present.

"Absolutely."

"I'll pick you up in five minutes out front."

Exactly five minutes later, a small coupe came around the corner from the narrow streets and stopped in front of the imposing Harbor Grand Hotel. The door swung open, and the Oilman got in.

"Pappagall, OK?"

"Absolutely."

The Oilman stared at the man sitting behind the wheel. He was young, maybe half the Oilman's age, but he presented himself well. He looked tired.

"Don't worry," the NOC said, not taking his eyes off the traffic.

"I wasn't worried."

"If anyone asks, we just met on the ferry. We decided to have dinner because we don't know anyone else in town. OK?"

"Sure."

They silently made the rest of their way to Pappagall, a restaurant the Oilman had eaten at several times before. The jovial Maltese atmosphere filled the small, bustling room as usual.

"This is my first time. I hear they have good food," the NOC said.

"Very good. Traditional Maltese."

They ordered *ministra* soup with *hobz biz-zejt* (bread, olive oil, and tomatoes). The Oilman helped his companion with the rest of the menu, suggesting stewed rabbit, while he ordered his favorite, *torta tal-lampuki* (dorado fish pie). For himself, the Oilman completed the meal with a bottle of the local wine. The NOC ordered a Hop Leaf, a popular beer. As the meal progressed and the wine took effect, the Oilman felt his tension ease.

"The worst thing about living in Libya isn't the government, the lack of alcohol or female companionship, or even…well, you know… working two jobs," the Oilman said softly, taking a gulp of wine. "It's finding something to eat. I spend most of my time looking for a decent chicken, or anything else that appears edible."

"Yes, I have heard that. But it seems you are doing well so far, and I would guess you are making up for any shortages," the NOC smiled back.

"I make the best use of my time." He was waiting for his silent partner to come to the point.

"Working in a denied area, all alone, can be difficult."

"No complaints at all. I enjoy being alone," the Oilman said. "I am surrounded by history. Libya is a very historic country, if you are not aware. Very much so. The Provincia Tripolitania, the Land of Three

Cities—Tripoli, Leptis Magna, and Sabratah, each spectacular in its own way, although Tripoli has seen better days."

There was a silence as the Oilman watched the man play with his food.

"You need to go back right away, on the morning ferry."

"Why?"

"Jailbreak."

The Oilman's head jerked back slightly in surprise. For the next thirty minutes, the NOC explained in excruciating detail the same operational plans Henslow had made him commit to memory in Rome the day before. The NOC went slowly, covering all the different pieces of the operation, making sure he let the Oilman ask as many questions as he needed. He needed to make certain the Oilman understood the locations, timing, and signals that would make the plan possible. If he missed something, the most likely outcome was getting caught or killed.

The NOC tutored on the details until he felt confident the Oilman had memorized every last bit of information. Thirty minutes and a third bottle of Marsovin wine later, he was satisfied everything was locked in the Oilman's head. They sat in silence.

Their lives literally had depended on a ghost; now the ghost had come to life. They worked together, separately, each understanding the other's role in the clandestine relationship. Now that they had met, it was over. Each knew the other was feeling the same emotions—fear mixed with trust—they didn't know how to express them.

"I want to thank you for calling."

"You're welcome. It's what I am supposed to do, to be operational about it."

They spent the rest of the dinner on idle conversation. An hour later, the NOC dropped the Oilman at his hotel.

"See you again, someday, I hope" the Oilman said as he got out of the car, half asking, and half wishing.

"Take care of yourself."

That night, the Oilman couldn't sleep. He thought of the young man and the many varied journeys that had led them to this point in history—to meet in historic Malta, of all places. Small steps in time, taken in the shadows of Auberge de Castille, once a palace for Spanish and Portuguese divisions of the Order of St. John. They were crossing paths with Ulysses's stay at Calypso's Isle and the Apostle Paul, ship-wrecked here in 60 AD. The coincidences occupied his mind until morning.

At 6:00 a.m., the Oilman was standing on the dock, rehashing the details from the briefing. The queue was getting long, filling with other oil workers and foreigners returning to Libya. He walked by the crowd and showed the guards his ticket for a stateroom, hands sweating against the leather handle of his suitcase. The guards let him board without a glance.

After a rough eight-hour ride across the Mediterranean, he disembarked in Tripoli and returned to his apartment in just enough time to wash some clothes and gas and oil the truck before he had to leave.

His suitcase fit perfectly behind the seat of the Toyota.

CHAPTER FIFTY-NINE

The unmarked, canvas-covered military truck stopped at the entrance to the prison as the sun turned to red on a pleasant spring evening. Only the Tripoli citizens who worked within the now infamous white walls and metal bars used this particular entrance. Still, it was a better-than-average-paying job, no matter what was happening to their countrymen inside. It was bad, but better someone else than someone they knew—that was the common, unspoken way of life among the workforce.

"Over here," said the Guard.

While motioning the truck driver to stop, he opened the heavy wooden gate at an entrance normally patrolled by two sentries. Just a generous bribe or some favor at the going exchange rate—food, medicine—was needed to make eyes turn away and divert suspicion. When the LFF leaders contacted him less than twelve hours ago, luck would need to be on his side, with so little time to understand the mission.

The duty guards were friends of his, and the price tonight for their lack of attention was reasonable—a few cartons of American cigarettes. He was certain he could get inside; he was less certain of the success of the operation. Tonight, that would be measured by two related criteria—saving a life and taking a life.

He had joined the opposition two years before, after some fellow officers in his infantry unit had told him of the freedom movement. They spoke courageously of the plans to rid the country of the Leader and save the military from destruction. They assured him the transfer to work in the prison would be vital someday, which made his decision to join the secret group only slightly easier. After a year of horrible duties, the prediction had finally come true. Lying was easy when you had a chance to kill those you hated.

When the truck stopped in the shadows next to the high stone walls, four men dressed in unmarked olive-drab clothes, each carrying a large, heavy canvas bag, hopped out. They walked along the wall into the shadows, then through the door. The Guard had never met these four colleagues before, but they were members of the LFF like him, professional soldiers who had lost their ranks to the Leader's new "army of the masses," the same army that found many of its members imprisoned and tortured in this very building. Tonight was a chance to strike back at all of them.

"Come quickly," he beckoned to the squad of men.

Sentries watched in towers and on foot. The Guard saw the silhouettes of a few coworkers walking along the tops of the buildings. His LFF team jogged the fifty meters across one of a number of large courtyards attached to the enormous, high-walled cellblocks. In the shadows, they continued along one of several large stone cellblocks radiating out from a central administrative building, and across a common area between each wing. Inside, thousands of prisoners, including the one they sought, were cramped into overcrowded space intended for only a few hundred.

None of the alarms sounded as the Guard led the men through an unlocked security door, down some metal stairs, and into a dimly lit corridor. He let them pass to make sure the door closed quietly behind them as he checked his watch. *Behind schedule.*

Moving down the corridor, they made several turns toward the sound of voices, which grew louder as they stopped at the barred door at the end of a long hallway. The Guard removed a large ring full of long brass keys. Carefully he checked each one until he found the right key and then slowly slipped it into the lock, listening for any sentries. Time was limited to bribe everyone, so he hoped tonight would be a repeat of the last few, when many of his colleagues had been pulled from their guard duty and put on patrol in the streets and outside government buildings. As a result of this, the prison would be lightly defended.

Each man passed through the door. They were between a set of barred gates ten feet apart. Again, the Guard found the key, opened the access door, and waved the men and their bags through. The sounds and smells of the cellblock hung thick in the air. The Guard took the lead one more time for the remaining ten feet to the last metal door. On the other side were the men who, unknown to them, would help carry out his plan.

"Bring him here," he said, turning his head as the stench hit him when the cell opened.

The two men in uniform grabbed the old man off the floor with little effort and followed their superior down the hall into Room 4. They sat him in a chair, but he fell to the floor like a doll. They tried again, with the same result.

"Leave him. Wait outside," the Libyan said to the men.

Alone in the room, he stood over the unconscious man for brief moment. *Pathetic. Admirable, but pathetic.* Almost everything about the human lying before him was black. His hair, skin, clothes, hands, fingernails, bare feet and toes—everything was black from bruises and filth. He took a pitcher of water off the desk behind him and slowly poured it in the face of his victim. At first there was no response, so he poured the remaining water faster, striking with greater force. The man shook and coughed weakly, barely moving his head out of the stream. His eyelid opened slightly. His head rose slightly off the ground and then fell back again.

"Hello, Mr. Foreign Minister. Sorry to wake you. I received a call from our friend Major Megrahi. If you are not aware, and I doubt you are, people are wondering where you are. Seems you remain an important person. Most important for you, he has commanded me to keep you alive."

The Libyan could tell that his words were being understood, and the dark, blackened eye stared at him, the fog and confusion disappearing.

"Do not get your hopes up. Sorry, in reality there is no hope for you. If anyone should ask, you will die as a result of being a traitor. You are an assassin leading a coup against the Leader and the people of the Jamahiriyah. The reason will not be important. I really do not believe he would mind if I were to kill you immediately."

He saw the hope in the eye leave. But it was not replaced with fear, as he had expected. He looked at the Libyan with pity. He took his pistol from the holster strapped around his waist. He started to pace, playing with the weapon in his hands.

"I must confess I will miss our meetings. You are a brave and strong man. A survivor. That is more than I have seen in the many military officers and other self-proclaimed brave men who have visited me. It is a shame it had to end like this. You deserve some recognition for character and your will to live."

He paused above the old man, who had closed his eye again. He gave the man a gentle kick in his side, which forced his eye open slightly.

"But not too much credit. After all, I do have a reputation. You wouldn't want it ruined, would you? Your death will help both of us, Mr. Foreign Minister. This is our last visit."

The Guard peered through the window into the cellblock, cursing his luck as two sentries, neither sympathetic to the cause of the LFF, were still on station—one patrolled the open area between the cells; the other sat in a wire cage at the far end of the room, thirty meters away, sleeping. The lack of preparation and time had made it impossible for him to cover all the work assignments for that night. He could not respond to all the details and questions he had been asked, so he sent in the answers they wanted to hear and hoped all would work out in the end. Now he would have to improvise.

Signally the men to wait, he unlocked the metal door and walked into the cellblock. It was a large room, three stories or so, with small cells on either side built for one occupant; most had at least six. Between the rows was a narrow common area where the prisoners could gather for the brief moments when they were allowed out of confinement. The noise rose from a constant murmur to a dull roar as he entered the area, echoing in the room and signaling to his colleagues that someone had entered. The man inside the cage looked up and waved to him.

The Guard quickly approached the sentry on patrol, stopping him about halfway down between the walls.

"Hello," the sentry said.

Reaching to his belt, the Guard pulled out his knife, and plunged it into the chest of the unsuspecting man. Prison noise covered the screams as the Guard twisted the knife even as the sentry fell to the floor. The man in the cage jumped up out of his sleep. The Guard continued toward the cage.

Not fully realizing what had happened, the second sentry watched him approach. When he saw his colleague lying on the floor with a knife sticking out of his chest, he hesitated, looking for a prisoner who might be loose. He did not see the Guard pull his pistol from his belt and aim it at him. When he reached the cage, the Guard fired three shots into the chest of the trapped man, who registered a look of disbelief as he flew back against the wall before he fell to the floor. The sound coming off the thick stone walls was deafening in the enclosed space. Cheers rose from the cells.

The four men ran into the cellblock and dropped their bags in the middle of the room. The Guard opened the door to the cage, knelt over the dead man, and rolled him over on his back. Around the neck of the corpse was a large leather strap with two huge keys attached. He pulled the keys from the body and stuck them into large openings in the wall, spinning them as quickly as he could. Behind him, the doors of the cells unlatched and slowly slid open with a piercing, metal-on-metal grinding. Simultaneously, his four colleagues opened the canvas bags and pulled out an assortment of weapons. They tossed machine guns, old rifles, and pistols onto the floor, along with generous amounts of ammunition.

"Fight. Fight for your lives. The LFF has set you free!" they shouted, waving the weapons above their heads.

Before the Guard could leave the cage, the room erupted into a frenzy of motion as the newly freed men armed themselves. The Guard took out his ring of keys and unlocked the doors to the next cellblock. A line of bodies streamed through the door; the look of freedom, hope, and revenge glowed from their faces.

It took two minutes for the Guard and his team to fight their way through the riot. The Guard rushed back down the corridor and hurtled down several flights of stairs as the riot sirens began their deafening wail. When they reached the bottom floor, they turned down the corridor to come face-to-face with two more guards. At point-blank range, his team opened fire. The sentries collapsed, dead before they hit the floor, with a dozen red spots on their uniforms. Leaping over the bodies, the attack squad raced toward a room another ten meters away. Before they could cover the remaining distance, the door swung open, and a figure familiar to the Guard jumped out, pistol up, firing calmly.

The Guard heard the bullets whiz by his head and strike flesh and bone behind him. Throwing his body against the wall, he opened fire with his AK-47. The Libyan dropped and rolled, trying to position himself on his stomach to return fire in the narrow hall. Streams of LFF bullets were in the air, splintering the walls, sending concrete and plaster rocketing in every direction. The Libyan fired twice more, with less accuracy this time. Blood began to pool under the man he hated; the man who had brought terror and pain to so many but now was motionless. *It was not as agonizing a death as this one deserves. He died too much like a soldier. It is not fair, but it is done.*

He fired twice more into the body as he passed.

The Guard hurried into Room 4, certain their target was dead as he saw a pile of blackness motionless on the floor. His heart sank like a stone in the Mediterranean as he approached slowly, convinced he had failed the LFF and the man he had promised to rescue. Kneeling over the body, he started to pray, until he was shocked by a moan. That was followed by short gasps for air.

"Come. Help me," he ordered.

One man picked Mukhtar up by the shoulders as the other grabbed him by the legs and feet. It took almost ten minutes to retrace the route back to the door to the outside.

When they reached the courtyard, the riot was in full force. Shouts of chaos. Fires burning. The riot provided exactly the kind of cover they needed if they were going to escape. They crossed the open area and went through the door to the waiting truck without being noticed. The Guard was relieved to see that the driver was waiting for them, pistol drawn, pacing back and forth. He had been told to wait, but the Guard did not know what courage this man possessed.

They placed their passenger on the floor in the back of the truck. The LFF men, panting with fatigue and fear, placed boxes across the cargo area, blocking it to anyone who might want to look or shoot in. One man took out a medical kit and flashlight and started to examine the man. After closing and securing the truck gate, the Guard climbed into the passenger seat next to the nervous driver.

"Leave, now. But not too fast."

"Where are we going?" the driver asked.

The Guard had kept the location secret, just in case.

"Leptis Magna."

The driver tossed the truck into gear. In less than a hundred meters, the Guard saw the approaching police and security vehicles. He did not have to say a word to the driver, who saw them at the same time. He turned the truck sharply left down a narrow side street, throwing the tired LFF men and their patient against one another as they struck the side of the truck. Mukhtar's moans grew louder as the driver turned rapidly down the narrow streets. The men threw themselves on top of their patient, trying to hold him still.

In twenty minutes, the wild ride ended as the truck exited onto the coast highway, heading east, toward the twilight—and the rendezvous point.

"Golden Sunset," the Guard shouted into a handheld radio.

CHAPTER SIXTY

The voice was distant. It grew louder, like an approaching train. *"Sir...wake...save..."* was all he could make out at first. A face and a pistol. The look of death. A voice praying that Allah would end the misery. Let Allah accept him. *More words. Pain in my side. But more confusion. Louder sounds. Gunfire and shouting. What is happening? A new face. Or is it familiar? More caring.*

It took several minutes for Mukhtar's body to register what was really happening. He was no longer in the small room, as the cool air against his damaged skin registered the temperature change. *Arms under my shoulders. Sitting. Falling. Sitting again. Falling again. One last time falling—then rest.*

His body lifted, moving quickly, painfully, as his senses faded in and out of usefulness. *The pain is different. Not harmful. Apologetic.* The sounds grew louder as he felt hands around his feet and arms grow tighter. *Cooler air. Outside? The sounds of a truck followed by wild, painful bumps. Words of apology and compassion. Forgive us. We are almost there. Then darkness again.*

"How are you feeling?" the voice asked. He could open his eye enough to the dim yellow light. Just beyond was a young face.

"Agh..." He tried to respond. His mouth moved, but only a noise came out, less like a human—more like the grunt of camel.

"You do not need to answer. You neck is swollen very badly with infection and bruises. It will make it hard for you to talk for quite a while. I am giving you morphine for the pain and have started an IV to give you fluids. You are very dehydrated."

The LFF man, a trained medic, opened up some more bandages as he applied antiseptic to the numerous wounds on the body of his patient. His condition was appalling. Bruises. Burns. Animal bites. Malnutrition. The fact that he was alive was a miracle.

"You have many cuts, and I am putting medicine on them to help them heal. I apologize that this might be painful. The morphine will help soon," the Medic said as he spread the cream onto a deep cut along his thigh. Mukhtar groaned slightly as the healing ointment stung his flesh.

"Who?" he managed to get through his throat.

"I am with the Freedom Front. We were sent to rescue you. You are a very important person, and many are looking for you. You are very brave," the Medic answered. "I am covering your eye. It is badly swollen. This will help."

Mukhtar could not feel anything this time, as the medicine numbed battered sections of his body, he could feel others start their healing processes. The faint smell of the eucalyptus lining the road and the saltwater in the distance stimulated his mind. *The familiar smells of home.* Then fear and panic.

"Marwa?" he moaned, trying to raise his head

"I do not know anything of your wife. I am sorry. You should rest now. I need to look at your leg. It is very bad. This will help you sleep." The Medic took a hypodermic needle and squeezed some medicines into the IV. In a few seconds, the Medic saw the eye of his patient close and his body relax.

Megrahi looked down at the dead, bloodied body of his former chief interrogator. It would not be easy to quickly replace him. He felt a little betrayed as he looked at the lifeless eyes. He had no doubt as to who and what had been behind the riot.

Riots by dissatisfied prisoners often complaining about food, overcrowding, or sanitation were becoming more frequent, but not this time. He was certain Mukhtar's American friends would be interested in saving him. The bags of weapons told it all. They must be feeling very pleased with themselves. Actually, he had to be impressed with the directness and speed of the attack. Libya had not spent hundreds of millions of dollars over the years constructing an overpowering internal security apparatus so that the CIA was able to ignore it as it wished.

"I want all military regional and local forces put on alert," he commanded to the Security Chief, standing inside the torture room. "All roads should be blocked in both directions along the main highways, and triple the guards at the border crossings immediately. All ships leaving any port within the next forty-eight hours are to be detained and searched. Report to me hourly."

Abdallah, I let you live, but I can't let you go.

"So, he's free?"

"Not yet. We managed to clear the first obstacle," Henslow confirmed to Garnett, who felt he was in an audition as a bit player for a blockbuster movie in the making. Everything Garnett was experiencing was new to him at an operational level. Immediately upon their arrival at London's Heathrow Airport that morning, waiting cars took them to an enormous Victorian-style CIA safe house situated in the Highgate suburb of North London. A safe-house keeper ushered all but John—who vanished to one of the suites to sleep—into the radio communications room in the massive lower area of the estate.

When the "Golden Sunset" all-clear signal reached them, Henslow allowed himself a very brief moment of internal congratulations. After years of constructing complex clandestine operations, maintaining his emotions and letting events evolve without interference was ingrained in his DNA.

"What's next?" Garnett asked, hoping the double meaning—for the operation and for his role—was not lost on the man in deep concentration.

"We have done well, so far," said the Chairman, who sat, arms folded across his chest, with a slight, pride-filled smile on his lips. "As I promised."

"Promise has nothing to do with it. We have a long way to go before promises are kept. Until he is safely out, nothing has changed."

The smile on the Chairman's face vanished as Henslow turned back to the radio operator and the static-filled transmissions filling the room in the basement of the mansion.

CHAPTER SIXTY-ONE

"In the third century AD, Leptis had a child, whom he named Septimius Severus. Many years later, in 193 AD, to be exact, as the Roman emperor, Severus, eager to display his power and wealth in the city and land of his birth, built this magnificent city, Leptis Magna. Embellished with huge arches of marble, public baths, and grand buildings, Leptis Magna boasted an immense glory of architecture housing over a hundred thousand people. If you follow me, we will visit the swimming pool." The voice of the guide trailed away from the Oilman as he stood in the ruins on the warm evening. He had been to the site several times, strictly as a tourist.

Today it was different; he couldn't enjoy the history lesson he already knew and could recite better than the current guide. In the trade of espionage, he had learned that his visit was called *cover for action*—a reason to be where you were without question or causing attention to yourself.

He was not sure what to think, since he had never been asked to tackle this level of operational task. It had taken several moments for his mind to grasp what the NOC was talking about. The instructions were complex and dangerous. Borderline impossible. *Meet with the opposition—a group I was told to stay away from? Drive to Benghazi—an eight-to-ten-hour drive in the middle of the night? Get to the Port of Benghazi. Find the right pier. Meet the opposition.*

The Oilman checked his well-worn country map, an indispensable guide and a rare find at any State of the Masses store. As he ran his finger along the line signifying the main coast road, the only way to get from Tripoli to Benghazi, the sites he had passed many times in the last year took on new significance. This was a quiet location, a place so isolated that they would never be seen unless the entire military and secret police were looking for them—which seemed likely. It was not far from the main highway, at the crossroads of two hard strips of desert that passed for roads. Quiet.

As he waited by the ancient ruins, he realized he was afraid. He could have said no; after all, it was not what he had agreed to do when he had started to help. *What if they find me? Arrest? Death? Let the real spies handle this.*

The Oilman left the tour group and headed back to his truck, pausing briefly by the grand auditorium, lined with its famous light-pink stone, to listen for the sound of the distant sea echoing in the calm of the ancient arena. Not this time. He finished walking to his truck. The meeting location was five minutes away, but he wanted to get there. *Thirty minutes until they arrive.*

Leptis Magna was lightly guarded, a few local militia on a regular day keeping tourists from taking any souvenirs and vandals from introducing spray paint to the Roman ruins. The only regular military appearing tonight would be an accident of timing, but given the current situation, the Oilman doubted soldiers were being released from their posts for sightseeing these days.

It was a beautiful evening as the dim rays of the setting sun streaked the sky with reds, turning the desert a deep purple. The Oilman felt the cool of the desert night coming through his window as he pulled his truck off the main road north of the area known as Old Bath, a small series of Leptis ruins well off the tourist path. He had only been there once himself, alone among the history.

The area was deserted as he swung the Toyota off the bumpy road and turned it around to see anything that might approach. The area was small—a few walls; the colorful marble that once covered the rock was long gone. A depression in the ground and a few timeworn steps covered with an arch marked where the bath area had once resided. Now overgrown with brush and a haven for seagulls, it was obvious the area was not well kept by the curators—no one would visit this area— no vendors, no profit. He parked behind a crumbling, ancient wall, which slightly hid the truck from view.

The only disturbances were the screeching gulls and a light breeze blowing from the sea over the sands and rubble, across the brush and off into the desert. Checking to make certain there were no visitors, he reached across the seat, flipped the passenger-side visor down, took a large white index card, the type used by college students for notes, and attached it securely to the visor with a rubber band.

He slid a cassette tape into the player, and the low voice of Frank Sinatra filled the ancient Old Bath area of Leptis Magna.

"Why are you bothering me? What is this?" the Regional Commander of the Ajdabiya Revolutionary Council demanded, after opening the door.

"Orders. A communication from headquarters," the junior officer responded. Night duty was the worst shift, twelve boring hours of sitting in the dim, barren command center, with nothing to do but hope the phone would not ring. If it did, it was usually only bad news or extra work, like after the attack on Tripoli. Now he had the task of taking the communication to the Regional Commander—and he did not ever like to be disturbed, ever.

The man ripped the note from his hand, made a face as he read it, and reached for the phone.

"You are to block the main road. There was a prison escape in Tripoli," he shouted into the receiver. Pause. "That is not my concern. You are the local militia, and I am telling you to go block the road." Pause. "Anywhere." Pause. "They are not sure. A car. A truck. It says several prisoners—one will be injured. That is it." Frustration. "NOW!"

The Regional Commander slammed the phone down and looked at the junior officer, who stood there trying to be invisible.

"If there is anything else, give it to me in the morning. I want to sleep." He did not ask whether the junior officer understood.

"Yes, sir." With relief, the junior officer left knowing that any information arriving between now and the end of his shift would be the problem of someone else. So if the radio crackled later from the militia command manning the roadblock, he was happy to save it for the 0600 shift.

"Do you see it? Do you know where it is?" the Guard asked. "We are late."

"A few kilometers," the Soldier replied. He did not like his passenger. *An officer.*

"I don't see it."

The Soldier kept his speed steady. The road appeared suddenly and then passed, taking him by surprise. He turned the wheel sharply to the left, forcing the passengers hard to the right, the wheels kicking up rocks and dust as he struggled to make the turn. It swayed back and forth as it continued in the new direction without his foot ever nearing the brake.

"Stop this!" a voice shouted from the back.

"What are you trying to do, you idiot? Kill us all? We have been through too much tonight for you to kill us now. Get us back on the road."

The Soldier ignored the screams, concentrating on avoiding a row of trees and boulders that had appeared in the headlights. The truck bounced up and down like a toy in a bathtub. He managed to maneuver the truck back onto the main road in time to make the right turn north in the direction of the Old Baths. The Guard, his hands dug deeply into the hard metal dashboard, glared. In back, the Medic pulled his patient back onto his cot. He grabbed some gauze and applied immediate pressure to the freshly bleeding wound caused by the intravenous line ripping out of the man's arm.

"There he is," the Soldier said flatly.

The Guard looked out the window and saw a truck a few hundred meters ahead. Dusk was approaching, making it hard to locate the signal he hoped for, even as they slowed to less than ten kilometers an hour.

The Oilman nervously watched the big truck move down the rocky road toward him. The rendezvous time had already passed, which only let his imagination work, spending the last twenty minutes going through his options—*stay or leave?* He had decided on the former, speculating that they were just late. The alternative, he also speculated, was that they had been captured, leaving open the possibility that they were coming for him. The thought of capture made his legs tremble slightly, as his adventure in this operation, whatever it was, was soon to begin. *What are you waiting for? I'm right here. Can you see me?* Flipping on his dome light, he took the risk that these were the men he was supposed to find. The truck continued its slow approach. The Oilman checked to make sure the card was secure as the truck pulled off the road, swung around, and stopped a few feet from his Toyota. The Oilman ejected Frank from his cassette deck. No one moved. The Oilman tried to look inside the cab of the truck, but it was higher than his Toyota.

"Turn off your light."

The Oilman heard the voice and paused briefly before he switched it off. The Oilman watched a man jump out, and then a few more appeared in his rearview mirror. Nervously, he got out to meet them.

"You should not have had your light on," the Guard complained, shaking the Oilman's hand, his tension releasing. "I apologize for being late; it could not be helped," he said in a softer voice, looking over his shoulder toward the Soldier.

"I wasn't too worried," the Oilman lied, noticing the drying blood on his uniform reflecting in the light of dusk. "You have him?"

"Yes. We rescued him. He is in poor condition." The Guard was certain this was all in vain. The man in the back would soon die from his wounds. The man in front of him was not impressive for a CIA spy, and assuredly he was not a warrior prepared to risk his life for a cause. Despite his observations, he would complete his part of the mission in a few minutes and pray for the best.

The Oilman did not recognize the battered and bandaged face as the opposition men carefully removed a stretcher from the back of the truck. Medicine bottles and tubes were tucked all around him. Another man held the man's arm, checking his pulse.

"Wait a moment," the Oilman said. He unlocked and climbed through the door of the cabin secured within the bed of the Toyota. The men raised the stretcher as the Oilman grabbed the other end and tried to pull it through the door. The handles of the stretcher struck the side of the enclosure a full two inches on either side of the door. The man lay motionless.

"Try angling it," Oilman said, his engineer mind calculating the dimensions. The men struggled to hold the stretcher near level as two more tries still proved unsuccessful.

"You almost dropped him," the Medic said.

"Get him in now. This is taking too long," the Guard ordered.

"Let's try. Once more. One, two, three." The Oilman grunted as he pulled the handles with all his strength, pushing back with his legs like a frog hopping backward.

He tilted the stretcher well past a forty-five-degree angle, and the men on the other side followed this twisting motion. The unconscious passenger started to roll off his bed. The Medic shrieked, throwing his arms around his patient to keep him from falling. The stretcher scraped through the door and dropped on the floor with less than an inch to spare from being too long. The Oilman carefully stepped around the man to jump out of the Toyota. The cool air gave him a chill as it struck his sweat-soaked shirt. Immediately, the Medic jumped in.

"He is all right," a voice said from inside after the examination.

"Anything else? I need to get to Benghazi," the Oilman said after a few moments of silence.

"The doctor will accompany you. He is from Benghazi and can direct you to where you need to go. You do not have much time. We must go." The Guard shook the man's hand, holding it for a moment longer than was normally comfortable and then releasing it.

"Allah be with you."

"And you too."

The men boarded their truck. The roar of the diesel engine startled the gulls wandering nearby, causing them to squawk and fly a few feet farther away.

When the truck's lights disappeared in the distance, the area was again peaceful. The Oilman stood watching the last streaks of light turn dark, thinking about the situation. He was in a foreign, hostile country, working for American intelligence, on a mission for which he had little training, meeting with the opposition in a secluded desert location, transporting a man of international significance, being hunted by the entire Libyan army, about to drive five hundred kilometers across the desert at night to meet more opposition members. The nausea of inadequacy leaped to his throat.

"Hurry. We should be going." The young man emerged from the cabin. He stood silently next the Oilman, looking at the man whom he assumed was an American intelligence officer.

"How is your patient?"

"He is asleep. I have given him morphine to stop the pain and to help him rest."

"Are you a doctor?"

"A medical technician. Trained by the army."

"So you want to be a doctor when you leave the army?"

"Perhaps. My father works in a hotel, as does my mother. I am not sure."

The Oilman smiled. "Why are you doing this?"

"For my country, and because I was ordered to the LFF. And you?"

The man paused. "The same."

"Then we should go. They are certainly searching for us."

"Yes."

The Oilman settled behind the wheel, thinking about why he should continue with the near-hopeless job he was assigned. *For a grand cause like freedom? The CIA? Libya? The poor human whose life had been placed into his hands? Or simply his own survival?* Whatever the answer was, it depended on successfully getting this man to Benghazi before morning.

In a few minutes, he turned the truck east, onto the main road toward Benghazi.

CHAPTER SIXTY-TWO

Hours passed calmly, and then he spotted the series of small lights in the distance. He had pushed his—their—luck, as the lights signaled danger, and luck had run out. Crossing hundred of kilometers, he had not seen anything resembling a military vehicle. Early traces of dawn were rising in front of him, leaving the fear of the night behind.

The Oilman turned off his lights and pulled over to the side of the road, estimating there were two more kilometers to go. If he was lucky, they had not seen him. If they had, he hoped they would assume he was behind a hill and his lights would reappear in a few seconds. That was just enough time to decide what to do.

"What is it? Why have we stopped?" a sleepy voice mumbled through a small window from the back.

"Lights ahead. Looks like a roadblock."

"What are you going to do?"

He had already passed the main road to the Fazzen region and the oil facilities to the south hours ago. He looked at his map and determined that they had just passed Marsa al-Burayqah, in the Ajdabiya Region, where the road started its bend to the north around the Gulf toward Benghazi. *Well over two-thirds of the way.* The huge oil fields of Waha were south of him, beautiful scenery during a normal trip, but now there was nothing to look at but the roadblock ahead. His hands gripped tight around the steering wheel. Time was up. He flipped on the Toyota's beams, stepped on the accelerator, and got back on the road, heading directly toward the danger.

"What are you doing?"

"Get in back and get down. Cover yourself with anything you can find. Stay quiet."

"They will find us. Go back!"

"Trust me."

Knowing he needed to remain calm and relax, he loosened his death grip on the steering wheel. As the lights grew larger, the Oilman saw two jeeps, one on each side of the road. A silhouetted figured appeared raising a hand halfheartedly for him to stop. The Oilman brought his truck to a stop in the middle of the road. Before the man approached, the Oilman opened his door and stepped out.

"Back in your vehicle."

The Oilman ignored the command. Reaching his hands above his head, he stretched, long and loud, completing the motion with a shake of his body.

"That is a long ride."

"Back in your truck," the man said again as two other uniformed men joined him. The Oilman could tell by their makeshift uniforms that they were local militia.

"Sorry, it's been a long night," he said, ignoring the warning for a second time. "What is the matter? I usually don't get many visitors during my drives."

"What are you doing on this road at night?"

The Oilman could see their rifles clearly now—pointed at him. "I work for the oil company, National Oil. I monitor production."

"Why did you stop on the road?," the Militiaman asked with an edge in his voice.

"I saw the lights and thought you might be thieves. I'm not looking for trouble. I was happy to see you were army. I am a lucky man."

"Militia, not army." It was an important distinction for the part-time soldier. "What are you doing here?"

"What has happened? Was there another attack?" he said, with nervousness more real than fake.

"We are looking for escaped prisoners from Tripoli."

"Tripoli? Am I in danger?" Real fear in the Oilman's voice.

"Where are you going?"

"As I said, I monitor oil production and refining facilities. I have permission. Here, let me show you."

The Oilman went into the shadows around the back of the truck, the Militiamen closely following him. The Oilman reached into the cab of this truck and pulled out some wrinkled papers.

"Here are my papers and authorization."

He handed the soldiers his official documentation letter from the National Oil Company, a piece of paper that stated only that he was employed by them and could enter certain properties, and a worn picture ID, the lamination fraying from age. The man took the materials and walked back toward the light. He handed them to the others. Each looked at them in turn until they ended up back in the hands of the leader. They looked at one another, confused. As two of the men huddled, one strolled around the Toyota, shining a flashlight into the cab, peering into the window.

"That's where I sleep when I'm on the road. Here, take a look. I will warn you, it smells a bit." The Oilman reached toward the back doorknob, then paused.

"I haven't been near Tripoli. I'm heading to Waha. I have to be there in a few hours. A heavy crude facility needs some work. I can't be late, or there is a boot up my ass, if you know what I mean. I really need to get going." He walked up to the Militiaman, took the paper and card from his hands, turned, and headed back to the front of the truck.

"Wait!"

The Oilman took two more steps and put his hand on the door. He turned.

"Go on," the Militiaman said after a moment.

The Oilman did a quick bow, a sign of relief rather than respect, got in his truck, and started it. They did not stop him. As the Toyota started to roll forward, he stopped and leaned out his window. "Excuse me. Am I going to have trouble ahead? I can't afford many more stops."

"That is not our concern. Go."

"Thank you," the Oilman said for no reason as he stepped on the accelerator.

The drops of sweat started immediately, and the shakes set in within the first mile. He gripped the wheel to concentrate and steady himself.

"You saved us. You were brave, very, very brave," a voice said from the darkness behind him.

He did not answer as he wiped the sweat from his eyes.

The Militiaman picked up the radio. He was a science teacher by education, a man dedicated to details, equations, and theorems. Although he had seen only one man, he had taken in every detail. He had recorded the name of the man; his supposed profession; the make, model, and registration of the vehicle; everything. His report would be concise but thorough, the mark of a proud academic. In a few minutes, the details were radioed to the Regional Commander, where as instructed, it waited for him to wake up.

Although Libya was drowning in an inept, overburdened bureaucracy as deep as the desert, occasionally things worked, given time. The morning replacement was late as usual, knowing the night officer could not leave until relieved, no matter what time the next shift arrived. Their ranks were the same, but the day job was considered much more important. Day-shift militiamen were senior officers and felt entitled and superior, forcing the "lower-class" officers to remain silent when they arrived late at their post every day.

"The Regional Commander needs to see this," the night officer said as he handed his replacement a report on a vehicle stopped several hours before on the road to Benghazi.

The day-shift officer handed the note to the Regional Revolutionary Council leader thirty minutes later, who, when he read it, had the information transmitted to the Central Revolutionary Council Command located in the People's Palace in Tripoli within another fifteen minutes. The Central Command, having orders to forward all roadblock details to the Security Chief, made three copies of the communication before moving it up the chain. A clerk walked the report three floors up to deliver the message directly to the office of Major Megrahi, where he handed the note to one of the guards standing by the door.

The guard stayed at his post and gave it to a secretary, who arrived ten minutes later from a quick breakfast, to deliver it to its final destination.

It had been hours since the last radio communication, which, given the circumstances, was positive. He had no means to follow their progress, if any, so the frustrating alternative for Henslow was to sit and wait. The Chairman was not as versed in patience as the professional intelligence officer, resorting instead to an annoying pattern of sitting, standing, sitting, standing, and, worse for the CIA men, small talk—which went unanswered.

Henslow had calculated the time it should take for the asset to be driven across the northern Libya frontier. The radio should come to life soon, or the mission was a failure, the man was dead, he had lost a CIA employee working in place, a NOC might have blown cover, and he had let down the DCI. While not ideal, he accepted the risks, as did everyone else involved. Intel reports confirmed an alert had been sent out, but they contained no specific reference to their case officer, his vehicle, or destination. It was a shame to lose a productive Agency asset already in place, even though the Mossad and the Europeans had been cooperative, providing intel.

If those reports remained unchanged, he preferred to keep the man there. The division chief objected, citing the real threat to his safety, but Henslow had personally briefed the DCI, who approved his request.

CHAPTER SIXTY-THREE

"**S**low here and turn to the left at the next intersection," the Medic said from the back of the truck through an opening near the Oilman's head.

They entered the backstreets of Benghazi at dawn, having made excellent time. The Oilman turned the Toyota as instructed, too tired to do more than react. He had almost fallen asleep at the wheel several times—even Sinatra and his big band years couldn't keep him going. As this phase of the journey neared completion, the adrenalin started to flow again as greater uncertainties and danger pulled closer.

The Medic hid when a car suddenly swerved into the path of Toyota, blocking the street. The Oilman's first thought was to step on the gas and turn the truck quickly to get around the vehicle, but the street was too narrow. He braked and the truck slid, slamming into the front end of the car. A loud thump and moan came from the back.

"Stop!" a voice shouted from somewhere.

The Oilman threw the gear into reverse. In his mirror, he saw a second car approaching from behind, blocking his escape. Instantly, he found his truck surrounded by a half dozen men with a variety of weapons pointed at him. He sat, hands raised in the air, waiting for one of the young faces around him to fire and end his mission. Instead he received blank stares. He heard noises from behind but decided against looking, although no one had said a single word to him yet.

"I said stop. Why did you not listen?" The Medic now stood outside at the Oilman's door holding a bloody cloth to his head. "These men are with us. They will help us the rest of the way. Follow them."

The Oilman, shocked into silence, watched the Medic speak to the driver of the car, who was more interested in pointing at the now shattered front left headlight. The Medic, fully back in control, removed the cloth to reveal a small cut in his forehead before returning to his patient in the back of the Toyota.

The car moved, and the Oilman followed. In another fifteen minutes, the Toyota, sandwiched between the opposition cars, arrived at the Port of Benghazi, a scenic harbor filled with rusty cargo ships. They followed the car along a road that wound its way through the endless rows of low warehouses and cargo storage buildings. Near the end of the road, at the water's edge, the lead car pulled into a dilapidated building seemingly no different from the others. The Toyota followed, and as soon as the car behind him cleared the door, it slid shut. The interior was a mess of old crates and debris, proof that this port was not the international shipping destination it once might have been.

The waters of Benghazi harbor were relatively active, as several rusting ships lined the docks or sat just off the shore at pumping stations. The grinding of diesel engines and gearboxes was a constant reminder that the huge freight loaders were decades beyond their normal life-span. It seemed that rust was the official color of the Libyan shipping industry.

The Oilman finally eased his stiff body out. *I am done...when can I sleep? Everyone else seems to know what to do.* He leaned wearily against the hot hood as the LFF fighters carefully removed the stretcher from the back of the truck. Moving as if they were carrying fragile pottery, they handed the stretcher to a waiting CIA team, who completed the final steps to an area set up with a collection of medical equipment.

"We have him, sir," one of them said. The Medic, head wrapped in a bloodstained bandage, looked worried as he continued to hold the hand of the patient, who, in the Oilman's untrained medical opinion, looked dead. "You did a marvelous job getting him to us, doctor. Please."

Finally, he released his grip on his patient to allow the new team a chance.

"I'm Gene."

The Oilman was startled as the man silently approached him from behind. "You have done a fantastic job." He shook the Oilman's hand. "I'm here to finish the operation."

"Now what?" The Oilman stared at him.

"We have an exfiltration plan already under way. We have used it before, to great success."

The Oilman wasn't sure what to do as he scanned the activity in the warehouse, looking for an answer.

"May I see him? I'd like to say goodbye," the Oilman said.

"No need, and I don't think that is a good idea. We're on a pretty tight schedule. The man didn't look very good, so I am sure they are busy with preparations. Anyway, I'm sure you need to rest before you go back."

"What do you mean?"

"Langley wants you to return to your cover job."

The adrenaline started to rush, and the Oilman shifted instantly from exhaustion to wide awake. "Are you sure it isn't too dangerous to stay, with all that has happened?"

"Your situation has been monitored," Carver said, paraphrasing the brief Henslow gave him before he left. "There is no indication that they are aware of your presence."

"We were stopped on the road on the way here. You didn't know that."

"Well, listen, you don't have to stay if you feel you are in danger, but the request came from Henslow, with approval from the DCI." The info that he had been stopped was news, but Carver figured the man needed to know the truth; it was his life, even if total control of it was slipping away.

"I am not particularly interested in who gave this order. They don't know the situation here. Hell, I don't understand the situation in Libya, and I'm living it," he said, his emotions fueled by fatigue.

"I understand. We are both in the field, and we know Headquarters doesn't know what we're doing out here in the real world. But I have a hard time believing that they would intentionally put any officer in harm's way. I'm with you; I'd want out too. We have arranged a safe house for you in Benghazi. You are to stay there for at least two weeks. No commo. We will be in touch. Tell your employers you are taking a vacation."

He handed the man the address.

It sounded good, but something felt wrong. But he was also exhausted and decided he could use some sleep. "OK, safe house first, then I'll go back. But tell them I don't like it."

"Also, even though there isn't any intel on them identifying you, we suggest you change vehicles. That Toyota of yours could have a 'Look at me' sign all over it. We have a clean van for you, all registered and legal."

"I like the Toyota. We go way back."

Carver went into statue mode, making it clear this was not a suggestion. The message was received but not accepted. Rather than fight it now, he gave the answer the stranger wanted.

"Understood."

Wearily, he got into the new van, armed with the address and directions to his safe house. He hesitated for a moment before backing away, looking over his beloved Toyota once, then at Carver, and then out the warehouse cargo doors.

A few minutes later, from his position on the ship's deck, Carver watched "the package" being loaded into the hold of the two-hundred-ton oil tanker *Mediterranean Gold*, another rusting ship flying an Italian flag from its stern. Within the hour, it would be navigating Benghazi harbor heading for Naples, with the special cargo in the hold, under the close care of an expert CIA med team. Carver raised a radio identical to the one the LFF man had used hours ago. He delivered a simple message.

"Golden Sunrise."

CHAPTER SIXTY-FOUR

"We have not found them...yet," the Security Chief told Megrahi, who knew that already.

"Why not?"

The Security Chief understood that there was no answer. Pervious bad experiences had taught him it was better to remain silent and look foolish than open his mouth to Megrahi's questions and prove it. He was impressed by the man's stamina. He could not remember the last time he had seen Megrahi rest.

"Why not?" Megrahi asked again. "Because you are not thinking. They have a plan. You need to think better and find them."

It was a few minutes past eight in the morning, and none of his internal security forces had reported. The lower echelons of the military were trying to be more responsive since the raid, as the blame had to fall somewhere, and it certainly wasn't going to be at the top. He expected news of the capture right away. As the hours passed, there was still nothing, but there was no need to panic. They were playing in his country, with no restrictions—giving up control was not going to happen. The roads were blocked; the border crossings and ports were on alert, all at his command. They could not escape.

If they were heading west toward Tunisia, they would have been there by now, and we would have caught them. They could have returned to Tripoli, but their only way out then would be the airport, or the ferry, which they know will be watched and dangerous. He traced his finger to the south. They could go south into the desert, but with a man in his condition, he would not last long. There was only one direction to go. East. All he needed was one piece of news.

His only real concern was the Western press.

They would certainly have heard about the riot, which would fuel their annoying badgering and questioning of the Leader's human rights policies. He was not in the mood to offer answers after his last experience. That was the now missing foreign minister's job. He dictated the statement to his staff for distribution—"riot of anger over the Western attacks and boycotts." The world would read it soon in *JANA* and the other "official press" outlets. Although most internal affairs were now in his control, Megrahi did not want to have the Brother Leader getting involved. He would have to hear the news like everyone else. Time to consider politely asking the media to leave.

There was a knock on the door.

"Yes."

A secretary entered, handed a note to Megrahi, and left without saying a word.

The Security Chief watched Megrahi's eyes widen as he walked to the map of the country taped to the wall.

"This has to be him." He moved his finger to the left, slowly tracing a line across the coast. "A vehicle was stopped hours ago, along the road to Benghazi."

"They have been arrested?"

"No. They were released." *Someone will pay for this mistake.*

"Where are they now?"

Megrahi's finger stopped and tapped hard on the wall. "Benghazi. The opposition is stronger there. Find that truck. Immediately!"

"Yes." The Security Chief took the dispatch and hurried toward the door.

As he watched the man leave, Megrahi felt rejuvenated, fueled by anger that a spy had been working inside his country. A new hate-driven motivation to apprehend the spy, anyone who was helping him, and, of course, Mukhtar materialized.

Where are you? He surveyed the map as if the more he stared, the greater the chance he would actually be able to see the truck moving. *They have to get him out of the country—if not, he will die soon of his wounds. The borders are closing. Helicopters from Egypt, perhaps, or a warship, but hard to conceal. The harbor…the sea…*

In a few minutes, vehicle registration logs had identified the owner of the truck. Internal Security broadcast the information to hundreds of Revolutionary Councils, militias, and security services under "high alert, urgent, and immediate" channels, the same they had used the night of the American bombing. The orders were specific: *Stop and detain. Do not allow the truck to escape under any circumstance. Anyone failing to follow these orders will be immediately and severely punished.*

The message had the desired effect, as all units reported back almost immediately that additional roadblocks had been established. A few extra minutes of searching found the location of the owner's residence and his employer. The details were sent to the surveillance teams.

Travel cards were pulled from the airport, border posts, and ferry passenger records, in the hope of tracking down the movements of the owner.

The message came as a shock. The Regional Commander recognized the information—that his roadblock had the right truck in their control a few hours before but had let it go. The militia should have told him earlier. He would have known it immediately, in his position as the Chairman of the Regional Revolutionary Council, a position he intended to keep. When the excitement ended, it would not be long before his superiors in Tripoli realized the mistake his forces had made... *a life-threatening mistake.*

But luck was with him. Tripoli was looking for the truck still, giving him a chance to redeem himself. If it came this way once, perhaps it would return by the same route.

Carver's all-clear signal reached the Highgate mansion command post first, followed immediately by the Libyan alert intercept.

Garnett was impressed by the stamina of the older man. Not once had he displayed fatigue of any kind—he had not disappeared to any of the numerous bedrooms to rest or taken any sort of substantive nourishment. What seemed to sustain him was a steady flow of excellent French red wines; Bordeaux seemed to be the favorite. Garnett

was tried, sore, and had partaken of the bountiful food tray at will—
at the very least to dampen the boredom created by endless silence
between messages. The Chairman of the LFF was nowhere to be seen,
returning only when alerted a message had arrived.

"So what do *you* think?" Henslow asked, passing the cable to each
of them.

The Chairman studied each word carefully, as if it held some coded
secret.

"Abdallah is safely onboard, and our LFF assets have completed
their mission. I believe that is all good news. Promises kept."

"What do you think?" Garnett's turn. Henslow was probing for an
answer, but Garnett could not find a fault in the Chairman's analysis.

"Seems about right. Did we miss something?" A truthful admission
of possible ignorance.

Henslow took a slow, long sip of wine, more to think than to enjoy
the taste.

"No. It sounds right...but something feels wrong." The final sip.
He waved his now empty glass in the air, like a conductor using a
baton in front of an invisible orchestra. "If our man listened to Carver,
he switched vehicles and is bunkered down in Benghazi, safe for the
moment. Something feels wrong."

"The LFF is exposed as well," the Chairman added, a little too
pompously for Henslow.

"The LFF is always exposed. If they do what you told them, they
are fine. Something else is wrong. We are missing it. What is going
through Megrahi's head? He is pissed off and will tear the desert apart
to find heads to cut off to show his asshole leader. He hasn't survived
this long by being stupid."

Henslow stopped with the glass in mid-downbeat and tapped the
radioman on the shoulder.

"Get me the commander of the Sixth Fleet."

CHAPTER SIXTY-FIVE

The phone in the control tower began to ring. He stared at it, trying to decide whether he should pick it up. It was a good day, despite the embargoes, attacks, and orders from Tripoli he was ignoring. The cargo ships churning the waters of Benghazi harbor were loaded and on time. He had to keep his eyes on them in the unlikely event one decided to run aground or collide. On the ninth ring, he grabbed the phone, keeping his other hand tight around the binoculars he held to his eyes.

"Central Control, harbormaster."

"This is Major Megrahi. Do you know who I am?"

He lowered his binoculars at the name. "Yes."

"All ships will remain in port until further notice. None are to leave. The Port of Benghazi is closed. Do you understand?"

"That is a very difficult thing—"

"Closed"

"Yes, closed. I will inform the captains."

"Tell them their ships will be searched. Nothing will go in or out of the area." Out his window, the Harbormaster saw military vehicles pull up outside his building. Dozens of army men jumped out.

"Have you let any ships leave this morning?" the voice demanded.

Pause.

"Only one," the Harbormaster answered, raising his binoculars. In the distance he could still read the white-on-black lettering spelling out *Mediterranean Gold Napoli* on the stern of the ship.

The receiver crackled in the radio room located just behind the bridge of the *Mediterranean Gold*. The radioman adjusted the headphones closer to his ears and copied down the orders.

He found his captain outside, watching the small dot behind him get closer. It had appeared after they had cleared the harbor, less than two kilometers off the coast.

"Message, *Captaino*," the radioman said, handing the captain the note. "Turn the ship around and return to port immediately." The radioman stood waiting for a response.

"Ask for them to retransmit. Tell them we have been having radio problems."

"But the radio is working fine. I am certain."

"Ask anyway." The Captain gave the young seaman a stern look.

"Yes, sir."

The Captain checked the diminishing coastline and then the position of the oncoming boat. He recognized a Combattante attack boat heading at full speed in his direction. Judging by how fast the boat was closing, it would overtake his slow-moving tanker in five minutes. The captain entered the bridge.

"*Completa velocità*," the Captain said calmly as the ship accelerated to full speed.

"*Sì, Capitano*," the Executive Officer responded. *It is too soon to go to full speed, but the captain is experienced and knows best.*

"Distance from port?"

"Approximately one and a half kilometers." Not quite far enough. *Five minutes is not enough.* He was promised help if something ever went wrong. For years, he had helped shuttle men and materials in the belly of his ship, back and forth across the sea. For his loyalty, the check would arrive in his mother's account, just enough to help her since his father had died. Never had there been a moment of trouble, until now.

"Are we at full speed?"

"Yes, sir."

"Sir, the message has been confirmed." It was the young radioman.

"*Grazie.*"

The Captain leaned his head out the bridge window. The attack boat was only a hundred meters behind now. He could plainly see the gunners ready at their positions, their weapons aiming at his ship.

"No reply...sir?" the radioman asked nervously.

"Attention aboard the ship. Stop immediately and prepare to be boarded," an amplified voice cried out from the smaller ship. They bounced up and down in the seas. He could see his crew lining the rails of the deck, gesturing over the port side.

"What do they want? Should we stop, Captain?" the Executive Officer asked next.

He could stop, but he had few choices. "What is our posit—"

The roar of jet engines drowned out his last syllables. In an instant, the officers and crew of the tanker watched the deck of the small boat splinter as machine gun fire rained out of the sky. The attack boat started to smoke and veer away as a small explosion sent debris skyward from the aft portion of the boat. It was dead in the water. As cheers rose from the crew, the Captain looked up to see the two small dots disappear into the sky.

"Continue on course, full speed," he commanded.

"*America*, this is Whiskey-1. Sunset Wonder, over."

"Roger, Whiskey-1. Charlie Mike, over."

Whiskey-1 and Whiskey-2 continued their recon mission, having radioed the coded message that a mission that "officially" had never occurred had been successfully completed.

"Now...he is safe," Henslow declared when the code from the aircraft reached him. Henslow, realizing how exhausted he was, dropped into one of the large, well-cushioned room chairs, sitting for the first time in hours. The fatigue, lack of food, and flowing wine were catching up to him. He felt tired, old, and exhilarated.

"Well done," the Chairman said to the room, walking in circles enthusiastically.

Settling farther into the chair, Henslow allowed a few moments of celebration among them, which also called for another bottle of fine French wine.

"We will have our work cut out for us when he gets here. That's you," he said to Garnett, his glass a baton again.

"Whatever I can do to help." Garnett was enjoying the festival atmosphere over days of pressure, trauma, and tension. "Mrs. Mukhtar will be very happy, for sure."

"Yes, she will—we need to move on to the next phase."

CHAPTER SIXTY-SIX

The Oilman drove his newly acquired van past the safe house, a rundown two-story building in the middle of dozens of look-alike rundown two-story buildings. A few blocks down, he pulled over and sat. It was time to rest, focus, and just let his mind wander.

If he wanted to hide, that would be the place. The problem was he did not want to hide. He had been thinking about the warehouse conversation. All the arguments made perfect sense, except that this was Libya. He also didn't like the van. He felt disloyal to the Toyota that had served him faithfully for years, the kind of guilt you get when you go to another barbershop to try them out. The seats were not broken in, the handling was too tight, and worst of all, there wasn't a cassette player for Frank. He hated it.

As he recalculated his assignment, the math didn't add up.

His first survival instinct told him to leave the country as soon as he could. He really wanted them to change their minds and come and get him. If not, sitting in Benghazi was the next-best option. If they were looking for him, he would be safe. If it was too dangerous after a few weeks, he could still leave. But if he did still have a role to play, then leaving could do more harm.

He relived every moment since he had started the operation, trying to recall anything that would jeopardize him. If there were an informant within the opposition ranks, it would have been over at the roadblock on the main highway. Since they made it past it, the next equation was the chance that the patrol had made a report. The variables were that it was dark, everyone was tired, and it had been quick.

His decided to go back to Tripoli. If he left immediately he could make it by midnight. But, as stupid as it was, and worse, dangerous, he wanted his Toyota back. The thought of not being accompanied by the "companion" he had logged thousands of miles with, shared the viewing of ancient ruins with, and crossed deserts and frontiers in, made his anxiety worse than the thought of what might happen if he was captured. Sometimes, he conceded, emotions get the best of logic.

He only hoped it was still there. Retracing his route back to the warehouse, he pulled up—the area was quiet. If the doors were locked, he was prepared to break in. As luck would have it, the doors were open, and his prize was sitting just where he had left it. In a few minutes, he was on the road, as happy as he had been in days.

The early afternoon traffic was heavy and slow in both directions, and the truck crawled west just as the sun started taking its toll on every living thing behind him. Waves of heat rolled off the asphalt, turning the road into a long, black oven.

The first military patrol passed him an hour west of Benghazi, moving in the opposite direction. His heart started to pound when it slowed after it passed him. Soon, he saw flashing lights on the horizon and several more jeeps parked along both sides of the road. He could feel the eyes of the young men dressed in green fatigues staring directly at him. When the jeeps pulled into the traffic behind him, the confidence in his anonymity cracked. As the lights neared, he made a quick left turn across the highway, forcing an oncoming truck to hit his brakes. He stomped on the accelerator and sped the truck down the hard strip of sand off the main road, figuring he would rejoin the main highway in a few kilometers, near Ajdabiya. *The roads will be clear by then.*

When he reentered the main highway, it was obvious he had made the wrong choice. In front of him, a dozen trucks blocked the road a hundred meters away, surrounded by what looked like the entire Libyan military. For a moment, he considered his options logically, but logic lost its relevance and was relegated to a supporting role. The combination of fear and fatigue got the better of his thinking. Throwing the truck into reverse, he floored the accelerator, spinning his tires and throwing up clouds of blue-black smoke. In his mirrors, he saw the army closing in behind him.

"Stop! Stop!" The uniformed sentries ran toward him, waving their weapons at his truck.

Ignoring the shouts that rang clear in his ears even through the roar of his overheating engine, he turned toward the open desert just as he heard the first bullets strike the rear of the Toyota.

The Regional Commander watched the act play out in front of him. The driver was behaving as he had predicted, ever since he had made the mistake of turning off the main road. The truck took on a life and rhythm of its own, high-pitched dings of bullets ricocheting off the metal, the wheels spinning and then braking, digging into the road with an ear-shattering squeal, circling and stopping liked a caged animal. All the while, he watched his men close in. He told them to stop the truck using whatever means necessary, and they were following his orders exactly. *Fool. Nothing is getting by us this time.*

It seemed to him that all the soldiers had decided to empty their weapons into his truck simultaneously. Flames shot out from under the hood, as every inch of the Toyota's body seemed to explode with bullet holes. The burning wreck rolled slowly backward off the side of the road until a eucalyptus bush stopped its momentum. Before the soldiers could get close, death finally consumed the vehicle as it exploded into a fireball, sending debris into the air.

It would take over an hour before the fire was put out. The regional commander nervously radioed Tripoli that the remains of only one body had been found in the wreckage.

BOOK 6

MAY 1986

The truth is the best picture, the best propaganda.

—*Robert Capa*

CHAPTER SIXTY-SEVEN

There is a mumbling sound.

It was the first thing his brain had comprehended in hours, maybe days. *Mumbling, people talking?* He listened for only the seconds his concentration allowed, then commanded his eyes to open. Only one responded, slightly. There was something in his mouth and throat.

"Well—are—feeling? Pret—lousy—bet." His ears tried to recognize the garbled sounds, and then he heard something familiar—laughter. His functioning eye gradually focused on a man standing over him. Another figure, taller than the other became visible.

"Hello, Abdallah."

The chest of the injured man rose and fell. He nodded his bandaged head slightly at the face, tried to speak, but whatever was in his mouth prevented it.

"Can we get that out?" Henslow asked.

"Yes, he should be OK." The white-coated man reached toward Mukhtar's face. "When I count to three, blow hard."

On the count, he blew as instructed. He coughed hard and then felt the rush of cool air fill his lungs.

A nurse already had a glass and straw at his lips. The small sip of water tasted like a banquet, as the cool feeling running over his throat stirred broken senses. He tried to remember anything, but little came. The prison, the chair, the torture he remembered, although even that was like a haze on the desert. There was something else—oil, diesel, and a sound beating his skull, even while he slept. Nothing else.

"What's his condition now, Doctor?" Henslow asked as he stared down at the man.

"Well, in addition to the various infections, dehydration, sprains and muscle pulls, cuts and abrasions, burns, animal bites…" He looked at Henslow in disgust, then continued reading from the patient chart. "He has a detached retina of the left eye, two broken fingers, and a minor dislocation of the left shoulder. These can all be treated with time. He may suffer some vision difficulties from that eye, but we'll have the base ophthalmologist take a closer look." The doctor stood beside his patient, pulling up the sheets to get a look at the leg. He felt along a swollen mass of flesh. "But I am most concerned about this knee."

"My leg…"

"We are giving you something for the pain. Can you feel this?" Henslow watched the doctor touch the black area of the knee with his pen.

"No."

Again. "This?"

The man shook his head negative.

The doctor let out a sigh and replaced the sheet. He looked at the medical chart hanging from the foot of the bed. Then he took an X-ray from a packet and briefly held it to the light.

"Were you taking anything for osteoarthritis?"

"Aspirins. I used to play football. Not anymore."

They all smiled, the first time in a while.

"We can't do much for that; it's a degenerative condition. But you have a massive infection in the bursa. We already inserted a drain tube to remove fluids, so we expect it to clear, with the help of the antibiotics. Add to this massive cartilage damage, tears of the medial collateral and anterior collateral ligaments, and a severed meniscus. These will require more major surgery. The conditions by themselves are each treatable. Taken together, you have a long, painful recovery ahead, I'm afraid. You will need a wheelchair, most likely. Walking will be difficult for some time." He gave a doctor's reassuring smile and a pat on the shoulder.

Mukhtar took the news without a sign of emotion.

"Thank you, Doctor." Henslow stared at him.

"I will be back to check on you." He motioned to the nurse, and they left.

Henslow waited a moment and then locked the door. Positioning a chair closer to the left side of the bed, he eased himself in so they were looking at each other eye to eye. He sat in silence, staring at the man for a minute.

"You are in the medical services area of a US Navy base in Naples, Italy. If they can't treat you properly here, I will have you transferred to a hospital in Germany," he finally said.

Mukhtar nodded as much as he could in appreciation.

Henslow had an incredible capacity to identify, catalogue, and squeeze the slightest weakness in another human to his own advantage. Never one to miss an opportunity to take advantage of a situation, he had to push, so everyone knew who was in charge.

"I must tell you, Abdallah, you have been quite an international celebrity. Everyone wants to know where you are." Henslow sat back in his chair. "Really, all those years, you insisted that quiet, thoughtful diplomacy would effect all the changes you sought. You're alive today because I decided to save you. You will want our protection, perhaps even asylum…"

Nod.

"But there are a few things we need to take care of. Things we don't have a lot of time to deal with."

Advantage Henslow.

"We want to inform the president of the real situation in Libya. None of that oil data you dropped on me. Seeing as you aren't capable of too much moving around, we'd like to get it recorded. Your own words and feelings. Something we can hand to President Reagan. I have heard he is interested in your condition also. Besides, I'd like to hear the story myself." *And see how close we got to whacking the SOB.* "Agreed?"

Another head nod.

But Henslow considered himself a compassionate man too.

"Let's not talk today. Save your strength. We can start tomorrow. First, I have a surprise for you, if you're up to it."

Henslow walked to the door and unlocked it. "Perhaps you can muster the strength," he said as he opened the door.

She was not certain why she had been moved from Rome to Naples. For days she had been kept mostly in her room, like a prison. But when she entered the room, shock covered her face, and tears immediately streamed out of Marwa's eyes. Mukhtar let the stress and emotion out and began to uncontrollably weep. Even Henslow felt something.

The couple didn't notice Garnett and John with their cameras recording their tearful reunion.

After ten minutes of tears and muffled sobs were captured on tape, Henslow placed his hand on Garnett's shoulder and gave the sign to John to stop. John turned the camera off and followed him out of the room.

CHAPTER SIXTY-EIGHT

The mood in the People's Palace always depended on the personality of its single-most important resident.

Staff working within the building, who dealt with the force of that personality, secretly appreciated the rare times when he was in a somber and reflective mood. A real sense of safety would, however briefly, inoculate the workforce, creating an atmosphere of efficiency and teamwork that actually would grow into a sense of urgency for their jobs. Papers would be processed, and the usually boring, stagnant business of the country would creep forward. If someone mentioned it, even the slightest reference, a finger would quickly be raised to the lips—the sign that they would not speak another word. No, they would collectively sense the peace and take advantage of it as much as they possibly could.

As they watched him exit the large office on the top floor, no one looked in his direction.

The recriminations took longer to arrive than Megrahi had expected—over two weeks. If they were sent out on his order, the attack would have started much sooner. But as it was, when they reared their heads, they struck Megrahi with the subtlety of a knife being driven unknowingly between the shoulder blades. The attack was simple and elegant. Megrahi had to wonder who in his own department had organized it.

He knew the propaganda and personal destruction process in fine detail. After all, he had spent most of his life perfecting it. It had guaranteed his rise to power and ensured he remained there. Others around him had fallen to the public torture of humiliation, many the target of the effectively brutal propaganda section of the Megrahi's internal security organization. He had discovered early in his career that men who one day may possess the power to order the deaths of enemies near and far could be reduced to crying, whimpering children with a well-placed news article, followed by seclusion, then Abu Salim. So that bright morning, as Megrahi read the news reports, he realized his turn had come. And even with all his experience, he was unprepared for the alienation that swept over him like the warm Sahara wind.

The process to discredit him was only beginning and those orchestrating it anticipated it would eventually force him into seclusion, the special refuge for those damaged by "scandal" but much too powerful to disappear. Megrahi was expected not to fight for his public image, issue any clarifications, and eventually relinquish his duties.

Megrahi had no intention of giving in to the pathetic attempts to remove him. It was not even going to be a fair fight, in his opinion. He had made the rules and knew how to destroy them, and anyone who believed those rules could be used against him was mistaken. Megrahi still had power across virtually the entire security and intelligence apparatus of the country. Throughout the years, he had placed his tribal friends and allies into strategic positions in those organizations.

When he received a message that he was summoned to see the Brother Leader, right on schedule, the urge to smile was more than he could resist. He couldn't wait.

"Touching, huh?" John said.

"They love each other." Garnett could not tell whether his colleague was serious or sarcastic. They were huddled in an empty office in a room Henslow had arranged as their media operations center.

"I want an operation put together. A big one," Henslow said, his eyes glistening as the images passed by. "We have a high-level official, a defector now as a result of a successful covert-action operation. He knows who, what, and where. This is an intel coup we need to exploit. Reagan will love it. Stick it to Congress by displaying a defector from the Mad Dog's regime working for the United States," Henslow said.

"Reagan? President Reagan? Well, this is nice." John looked at Garnett, his eyes wide.

Henslow started walking quickly down the dim, empty hospital corridor. There were no other patients in this particular wing after Henslow had had them moved days earlier. Only a few of the hospital staff were allowed past the security checkpoint. Garnett and John were trying to keep pace behind him, the sound of pounding feet on the hard floor echoing through the empty space.

"We're careful about any wide operations like that. Blowback policy. We will need oversight approval. Ok?"

Henslow stopped suddenly. His voice was a whisper.

"You've done your job...and it might just save a few American lives. The good guys might stop, and kill, a few terrorists." Garnett saw color rush into the normally chalky face of Henslow, the first time since he had met him. "That man"—his finger pointed back down the corridor in the direction of Mukhtar's room—"is going to make that happen. Follow or ignore any fucking policy you want. Understand?"

Garnett stared at Henslow, watching the face quickly return to its normal gray. "Do you think he knows?"

"Knows what?"

"About the video. Our role?"

"I don't give a rat's ass if he does; it doesn't matter."

"He was pretty much an innocent bystander before all this started, really."

"Innocent? You must be tired. Abdallah Mukhtar is no innocent man. He has been part of a regime that has been repressing and killing people for years. Until now, he has done little to nothing to stop it. If he had worked for us any of the times I asked, none of this would have happened."

Henslow stared intently at Garnett.

"What's the matter, son? Not used to seeing the results of your work up close and personal? It's pretty easy to do what you do from long distances and ship it out. Nice and clean. Well, when you work up close, it gets shitty."

The words hit Garnett in the face like the heat from a blast furnace. It was the first time Garnett had actually seen Mukhtar in person. He had needed to create a fiction in order to make him react the way Henslow wanted. The man had always been nothing more than particles on magnetic tape forming an image on a screen, no more— hours of film and tape to learn, memorize, and manipulate. Now, just a few feet away, the image was a real human being, lying beaten and bandaged right in front of him. Hugging and kissing his wife, a woman Garnett had given even less attention to, until she had taken form in a small room outside of Rome. All because Garnett had been asked to do his job. *Is there a reason to care one way or another what happens to them?*

"How well did you know him—before?" Garnett asked as Henslow continued down the corridor.

"Fuck that. Get it done." Henslow said as he walked away without looking back.

His car was waiting for him, but instead of sitting in back, he walked to the driver's side and motioned the surprised man to get out and his security detail to wait.

Tossing a newspaper onto the passenger seat, Megrahi sat down behind the wheel, leaving the security men standing idle in the sunshine like weeds. As he pulled the sedan into traffic, his head was spinning, and there was a lead weight crushing his chest. He could not remember when he had last felt this way and willed his senses to ignore the emotions, which was successful—a lifetime of control. He glanced at the paper and knew the words were as dangerous as the deadliest snake. The attacks continued, directly from the Leader's organization, which annoyed Megrahi even more.

This from the man who needs me to run his country. Why does he think that the Americans consider him so important?

After the attack, the citizens had seen hours of images of the Leader on television, dressed in the flowing white robes of a Bedouin, smiling, shaking hands with men in uniform, arms raised above his head, hands clenched together in victory. However, no one was allowed to visit him, including Megrahi, which wasn't a surprise. Now he understood why. The Leader needed to hide his troubles, and Megrahi, who had made just enough mistakes, was the perfect scapegoat. He had prepared for this possibility and was ready to defend his position, and more, if needed.

The first public indication of a fracture between the two most powerful men in the country came in the form of a published "speech" by the Leader—a speech that Megrahi knew he had never been given to write or review, which was the custom. It accused Megrahi of not really supporting the September 1969 coup. Only the insistence of the young Leader, who had moved the revolution forward over the strong objections of Megrahi, had made it a success. The speech continued, "Some in the government are no longer capable of continuing along the revolutionary path set forth in 1969." The final barrage attacked "certain military leaders" who were not qualified to run a country and had failed the people.

Megrahi carefully pored over the nuances of each word, admiring the pathetic nature of the attack. The Libyans were accustomed to the public destruction of key officials. The comment on Megrahi's alleged hesitancy to start the coup called into question his judgment. The other references attempted to discredit him as the senior official in the country.

A tap on his window brought Megrahi's focus back to the road. He was startled—only momentarily, as he regained control—to find his car in front of the main gate of Al-Azziziyah. The heavily armed guard was just as shocked to see the face looking back at him through the driver's window. He immediately signaled for the gate to open, and Megrahi pulled the car forward into the compound. Unfilled bomb craters, bullet holes, and scorch marks lay as evidence of the American attack weeks ago. "Reagan Murderer" and other banners and slogans covered what seemed like every available spot on the walls. Schoolchildren were already taking field trips to the barracks as part of their education to see firsthand the evils of the West and the courage of their Leader. Everywhere, he saw the guards and felt their eyes looking at him.

It was becoming something of a tourist attraction, but he was not a tourist.

CHAPTER SIXTY-NINE

Content for this new propaganda operation required one important prop—a functional Mukhtar. Garnett feared that his condition, combined with an overly protective medical staff, would make this a difficult task. After a call directly from Henslow to the Chief of Medical Operations, they were promised an hour in the room. Whatever they could shoot would have to be enough. *The more the better.*

Once inside, they needed to move fast and efficiently. Marwa was still by his side, looking as if she hadn't moved since he left. John held the Sony camera, as Garnett closed the window shades. Then he set up two lights stands, one in front, and the other behind and to the side of the couple. John checked the light level of the camera. When he was satisfied with the settings he took some establishing shots of the room.

"Good to see you again, Mrs. Mukhtar," Garnett said, smiling. On the bed stand he noticed the silver picture frame he had seen her handle while in Rome.

She nodded at him, not looking pleased that the CIA men were bothering her husband, taking away her private time. Mukhtar, looking marginally better than he had the previous day, tried to prop himself up a little in his bed. He couldn't do it with his broken fingers, tubes seemingly coming from every part of his body, and his leg elevated. She put her hand on his shoulder, and he gave up. He didn't even try to apply makeup. The bruises told a story unto themselves.

"We want to capture your story. It is fascinating, and we think it can be useful to help decision makers understand what is happening." *Not a total lie.*

"Story? Shall it be fact or fiction?" he asked.

"Facts are appreciated…we may add a little fiction," Garnett said, trying to add some humor, which they understood with a slight smile.

It seemed a natural question to Garnett, given the circumstances. *Henslow wouldn't have told Mukhtar the truth about any of this?* That would be quite a breach of security, but not beyond the man who had spent his life with terrorists and who had orchestrated the entire operation.

"CIA propaganda," Mukhtar said. It was more a statement than a question. It was obvious that the mind of the man was recovering—sharp and focused.

"I prefer to call it the truth with a dose of deception. A piece of the old cliché 'perception is reality.' The truth, I've found, is never black or white, but a shade of gray. Although, the truth sometimes has an impact greater than anything we can create."

"You are proud."

"Proud? I guess. It's what I do."

"Then you should be proud. Manipulation is a skill. I know. I have been associated with some very talented practitioners during my career…and may have been the target of this type of manipulation myself."

"I am not here to lie in the normal sense. I control the way it looks and feels and who sees it. Today, you have control." That was not really true either. Another deception.

"So you justify your deceptions by saying you are only creating distortions of the truth?"

Garnett never thought of his work in exactly those terms. He had always taken pride in his profession, which had helped him to advance quickly in an organization that was renowned for slow promotions. Now, faced with the physically damaged product of this skill, Garnett momentarily wanted to escape.

"I have a job to do."

"You must be very good, as our Mr. Henslow would not have it any other way."

Time to retake control of this.

"We need to get started. Just talk to the camera. I'll ask a few questions to get us moving. Let's see what happens. OK?"

JOE GOLDBERG

Garnett watched in awe at the transformation in Mukhtar, as he refocused on the camera. His damaged body straightened as much as possible, his head cocked to the side, and his chin lifted slightly. The voice changed from the *victim* to what Garnett sensed was the *diplomat.*

"One must understand that the blame my country currently receives is the by-product of politics, economics, and terrorism intersecting as the world was leading, misleading, calculating, and miscalculating."

"I don't understand. What do you mean?" Garnett asked.

"We overthrew a monarchy. We were a bunch of young men filled with a belief in our destiny. Discipline. Diplomacy for me. Megrahi, control. Qadhafi was a charismatic, arrogant, brash, self-absorbed ideologue. He wanted to establish our new country and allow us to take a place among the community of nations. We had oil. We were not a threat. The West, the CIA, never understood that. We were all doing what we thought was right. Just like you are now."

"Something changed?"

"He took America's lack of interest personally, so he tried to coerce the region to be more confrontational with the United States. Megrahi supported his maneuvers even when terror was brought to our arsenal. It is a very inexpensive, powerful tool. They saw it as a great equalizer against the huge military might of the West, whose patience ran out. It was time to retaliate."

"Why?"

"Because we were a minor player in the world using our wealth to purchase arms—a huge, senseless arsenal, from both the West and East. Economics and politics connected. He did not understand until bombs dropped on him that when a minor player makes moves into the world of international affairs, there are rules of diplomacy, many unarticulated, which must be followed. I tried to warn them the situation was changing, but they ignored me, I grew weary."

"What happened?"

He stopped and took a sip from a glass of water. Stalling.

"The people. When we started, there was prosperity. Free medicine. Free education. Homes. But with prosperity came the repression. The people were suffering. Spending on weapons. Megrahi, his Revolutionary Councils, Internal Security, and fear."

"So you tried to kill him because of that?"

"No. No. No. Many have tried to kill him. Others want to rule for their own selfish reasons. They have little regard for others, friend or stranger." *Megrahi.*

He was silent momentarily. Garnett felt awkward asking the question, trying to pry out the answer he wanted. *Does he suspect?*

"So why then?"

"My son. Tareq. Do you know what happened to him?"

"He was killed, wasn't he?" Not a total deception.

At the mention of her son's name, Marwa walked to look out the window, her back to the men. "He was an officer in the army. He was loyal to his country, wanted to make it better. We were told he died in a helicopter crash…they were lying. I saw him being murdered…on a video. He would have been about your age."

He paused and looked at Garnett.

"That was the incident that started the events that have led me to leave my country and you to be sitting here today."

"I am sorry." Garnett meant it. Garnett had listened so intently that his muscles hurt from lack of movement. Still, he didn't want to move too much, as if he might lose his concentration. He needed to keep his focus.

"Will you miss Libya?"

"Of course. It is my home. I will miss the sounds of the streets, the bouquet of colors in the bazaar, the smell of the desert at night. I miss my son."

"Anything else?" He had to probe. There was more, Garnett could tell.

"I know about the terror. The terrorists. The funding. Berlin. Rome. Vienna. I will tell it all."

They stared at each other for a moment, until a figure over the man's shoulder distracted Garnett. Marwa stood staring at him, her face pale and wet with tears. Mukhtar turned to look at her.

"I am tired now. I would like to stop. We can talk later, perhaps? I apologize."

"Yes, of course. We have enough, for now." Garnett nodded toward John, who kept the camera running. "May I ask what your plans are?"

"Work for those who cannot. Around the world, too many innocent people are being imprisoned, tortured, or are starving. There is much to do. I will speak with you later. I am sure there will be interest."

"Thank you, sir."

"One more thing, son."

"Yes, sir?"

More?

"All of this," he weakly gestured to nothing in particular, "is not your fault. Do not blame yourself."

CHAPTER SEVENTY

"**Y**ou are here. I have been waiting for days, and you are only here now." There would be none of the normal greetings today.

Megrahi said nothing. *Let him play and enjoy himself while he thinks he controls me.*

The thick burning incense covered everything like dust. The green painted walls were cracked and chipped. Under his feet, the floor was angled, like the shore sloping to the sea. The wall behind the man was covered with dozens of crooked photographs, some with the glass cracked inside their frames, documenting the Leader's meetings with world dignitaries—Nasser, Arafat, Idi Amin, al-Assad. Megrahi was in many of them, with a face much younger than the one reflecting in the cracked glass.

"Help my understanding." The Leader sat on the deep cushioned chair next to a small table, which prominently displayed a copy of *JANA*, and he turned to the specific article. His voice was quiet yet firm. "What shall become of this?"

"We must do what we can for the people. If so, then we each have a role to play." Megrahi said. The Leader never once looked him in the eyes, focusing his gaze instead over Megrahi's shoulder, or to the floor. There had once been a sincere friendship, a brotherhood, and if Megrahi searched his soul, he would have to admit that he truly loved the man at whose side he had been standing, and whose life he had been protecting, for years.

"Why the misunderstandings—you and I? It should be us against the Zionists, America—enemies waging war against us. We advanced the road to freedom, the path of unity and social justice. Now I am attacked, from the world and from within," the Leader continued in a monotone.

"I have no misunderstanding. Mukhtar lost his way. I have not... neither should you." It was a half-truth and a truth, falling on deaf ears.

"He was a loyal ally, turned against me. Why?"

"I do not know, and it is not important—" Megrahi started.

"I—I am the Leader of the Revolution." He cut Megrahi off with a voice more calm and rejuvenated. "The people chant for me. *The Green Book* tells them this is the way the People's Government is meant to be."

The heat had become oppressive in the room, and the incense had become so thick his eyes stung. Megrahi had heard enough.

"Do not make a mistake by assuming I am like the others. I am not disappearing and if I did, my many friends would know who to blame. No more accusations. No more attacks. I suggest you focus on the future of the Jamahiriyah...focus on *your* future. Do you understand?" Megrahi asked calmly.

The Leader paused, he could sense the tension, then slowly approached Megrahi, as close as he had stood to him in years. Finally, he raised his head, looking directly at him.

"You have run the country...the committees...for me. I allowed it so that I may dedicate my time to supporting the world's revolutionaries. You have been loyal, but so was Mukhtar. Are you still?"

"Yes, Brother Leader. From the beginning and always." Megrahi looked back at him, directly in his eyes, only the muscles in his lips moving—anger, hate, love, and power flowed from him.

"Then I will allow you to stay." The eyes blinked at Megrahi in return, and the Leader tilted his head back at the ceiling, staring at nothing.

Megrahi walked from the room without a word. Not one to ever second-guess himself, he was furious for having relied on the Mossad, America bombs, or Mukhtar.

Stay. Yes, we will see who will be allowed to stay.

CHAPTER SEVENTY-ONE

G arnett watched John working his magic, his fingers moving like a skilled surgeon across the tools of the small editing board, mumbling to himself the entire time. Garnett relied on John's expertise, which was sometimes frustrating, given the perfection of a creative artist, cutting it too close to the deadlines many times. His dedication was only fully appreciated in the espionage clutch. Garnett also appreciated that John had stowed all the Mukhtar file footage with their equipment before they left. Without it, they were screwed.

For two days, Garnett and John had locked themselves in a converted storage room within the Navy hospital constructing several news stories of various lengths, each showing a damaged Mukhtar and his wife—their pain and hope. Garnett spent his time writing accompanying scripts for the world's reporters to read over the footage. The words and videos were powerful, emotional, and thematically hammered Qadhafi.

John hit the eject button on the editor and handed the tape to Garnett, who stuffed it into a sleek black box with a label that said only "Mukhtar: News Masters. 20 Minutes Total."

"You're beautiful," Garnett told John.

"You're right."

Henslow stayed away the entire two days, but at the exact moment time ran out, the door opened.

"Let's see it."

Nerves were tight as the senior official watched the segments as Garnett played newsman and read the matching scripts. Garnett couldn't help but be impressed by the technical aspects of the tape— good color, nice framing, perfect lighting—another professional composition by John. But this time, the words and the face added authenticity to the story.

Henslow watched intently, as if they weren't there, glancing up only occasionally from the thirteen-inch color television.

"Damn good job. Wait a week, and then I want all this out; fucking bury Qadhafi." He turned and walked away, clutching the propaganda materials as if they were gold—Reagan and Casey would think the same thing. He stopped at the door.

"One more thing."

"Yes." Garnett nodded.

"It stinks in there. Take a bath." He smiled, closing the door behind him.

Garnett's release of the propaganda segments was preceded by a trip to the Select Intelligence Committees on the Hill to brief them on the potentiality that the product of American intelligence covert action might blow back on the United States. It helped that Mukhtar's fate was a popular subject in the diplomatic community and certain international press outlets.

Garnett orchestrated the leak through tried-and-true operating procedures. The "defection" was first made "public" by a CIA-controlled German news reporter who was given a "scoop"—one of the brief segments of the missing former foreign minister now safe in the West. Attributing the report to an unnamed source in the Middle East, the segment was replayed across a global network of news services, solidifying the impact and credibility to the deception and giving the German reporter newly acquired respect among his peers. Within days, the propaganda had appeared on television screens and in headlines around the world.

The leak and follow-on segments continued for weeks as Garnett activated new key covert media assets, each picking up the dramatic story. Mukhtar was an international hero—an ally to freedom.

Libya made no official announcement.

He had parked his car on the far side of the Square. It was a beautiful day, and the sun felt warm on his skin. Since his meeting, the attacks had stopped as quickly as they had started. He had convened meetings of several committees to reassert control and make it known he still held power—anyone who wanted to doubt that could test him. No one did.

He had secretly set in motion actions to rectify his situation, but at this moment, there was only one task.

Megrahi entered Green Square in complete confidence, his still present security personnel giving him space, as commanded. Megrahi let it be known explicitly through channels that he would not tolerate any interference in his actions. Anyone who dared attempt to take advantage of his supposed weakness would be punished.

He had to wait a minute while the man finished his business with another patron. When the transaction was complete, Megrahi stepped up to the counter.

"Do you have any horses today?" Megrahi asked.

"Yes, we had a request for them last week," the Shopkeeper replied nervously.

"I would like one, please."

The messenger delivered the telegram to the small A-frame house on the mountainside north of Leysin Village, Switzerland.

The knock on the door woke him from his afternoon nap, a habit he had developed early in his career. It was not that he was old and required sleep; rather, it helped with the stress of his life. After taking the yellow envelope, Specter handed the messenger a Swiss twenty-franc note and watched from the door to ensure the stranger departed down the narrow paved road toward the village. He kept one hand behind the doorframe to shield the automatic pistol from view.

Hidden in the middle of the Swiss Alps, the small house had become his favorite—a dark-green, cool mountain contrast to the shades of brown and the heat of home. The view of the Alps was peaceful, providing him the rest and solitude he needed. As well, Leysin Village afforded him the protection and security he required.

Small amounts of money removed from the vaults of Geneva banks 120 kilometers to the west guaranteed that the people in the village paid him little attention. *The small Arab man who stays here when there is no good snow for skiing.*

Special attention was given also to train conductors, taxi drivers, and certain police officials farther down the mountain, fifteen kilometers away in the stop-off point of Aigle. A phone call would inform him of anyone inquiring from the village below. Leysin Village was accessible only by a winding twenty-minute drive or by a small railway that ran up the side of the mountain. Either would give him sufficient time to establish a defensive or offensive position, depending on his mood to kill that day.

It was time for his tea and toast, so the correspondence would have to wait. After all, only a few people even knew of his existence, and fewer of the Alps hideaway.

When he was finished, he wiped the butter residue from his knife, slit open the telegram, and took out the message. There were few words. It would be difficult, almost impossible, taking months of planning for sure, making the challenge even more appealing to a master terrorist—one that he would gladly accept.

The notoriety of the target made it worth the effort.

CHAPTER SEVENTY-TWO

"These are all the tapes and scripts? Everything?"

"That's it. Masters of everything." Garnett handed Henslow the tape labeled *Mukhtar Project Master Tapes: Tareq. Safe House Interviews. News segments.*

Garnett was sitting in Henslow's CTC office, talking to a man who looked more relaxed than Garnett could recall. Carver, leaning against the wall, looked equally comfortable. Without a word, Carver opened a drawer in Henslow's desk and pulled out a bottle and three glasses. Chivas Regal. He looked at Garnett, who shook his head in response.

"You know this is against the policy." Henslow smirked.

"Would hate to violate a policy," he said, handing his friend a glass with a generous helping of Chivas.

"Success." He raised his glass in a toast. Carver's glass followed.

"Some would say we failed. Qadhafi is still in power. Megrahi seems to have survived," Garnett countered.

Henslow sipped his drink and smiled at him.

"True enough—but not a failure. Reagan loved it. The press is eating it up. Everyone is happy."

"What is the truth?" No deception this time. Garnett needed to know. *What was the point of any of this?*

Henslow turned to look out the window. "The truth, son?" He looked at Carver, who nodded back.

"Truth. We've always had two missions regarding Libya: One—Protect. Protect America. Our friends. The region. Oil. Two—Stop the fucking communists. That was it. From the start of their little coup, we, Mr. Carver, and I"—they toasted each other and took a drink—"had to understand what the coup and his so-called Free Officers Movement were all about. They went from a country we backed to a declared radical state."

It was Carver's turn.

"They told us they hated the Soviets—too atheist. But we had to pay more attention when Qadhafi starting building links with them, not to mention the Chinese. Fortunately, the moron brother has been a crazy, green-loving, meditating, mumbling incompetent son of a bitch since they day they shoved out King Idris."

Henslow nodded, and took his turn at truth-telling.

"But he did have a vision, a global personality cult, and money. So innocent people started dying, as he funded some of the worst pieces of terror shit in the world. Powerful tools. Nothing to underestimate. The only competent leadership decision he ever made was to not kill his capable friends—Mukhtar, who was a better negotiator, and Megrahi, who was clearly more pragmatic. If it weren't for them, that People's Government would probably have fallen into the toilet years ago. He was lucky."

"Until Mukhtar was alienated and Megrahi got tired of it," Carver added, refilling their glasses. The drinks were taking their effect.

"And we were helping them all along?" Garnett asked, wanting to keep the conversation bouncing between them until he could ask the only question he had left.

"We were...talking. Cooperating. We targeted Mukhtar. Mossad was running Megrahi, and feeding us the intel. We were all doing exactly what was needed, with the hope we could do more." Henslow was enjoying the reminiscing.

"Welcome to espionage. Same story—there were choices. Israel wanted security. Libya needed oil to flow. The United States needed both and more. Terrorism needed to be stopped. They could have been more helpful when we asked; many people who are dead or injured would be alive. The Mossad confirmed Megrahi was running the country better than his boss ever could. Mukhtar was a good guy, a diplomat doing the rest, but he had had enough. They both came to realize—separately, I speculate—that their old friend had to go."

Garnett couldn't wait any longer. It was time.

"So the point of the video, all the theatrics, was about getting Mukhtar to assassinate Qadhafi?"

"Finally. I've been waiting for that. Took your time. I know it has been bothering you." He looked at Garnett. Smiled. "No. Not officially. Ms. Harper had been quite clear on that. It's the law, but really she didn't give a fuck. But if you must know, I thought he would kill Megrahi. Qadhafi would take out Mukhtar and the Brother Idiot would be left all alone to fail. His country would be in the toilet and the people would rise up. That would be all nice and legal, sort of."

Sip. Wink. Smile.

"That changed, unofficially, when Mukhtar reacted in the least anticipated, more violent way. Then, Megrahi figured out what we were up to, and didn't stand in the way. In fact, he seemed to have manipulated Mukhtar. Quite helpful. He always was the smarter, more ruthless one. The only thing that went wrong was bad timing, interrupting Mukhtar at the same time we missed Qadhafi with a shitload of tonnage. But it isn't a total loss. Mukhtar is pressuring from the outside. Megrahi is disenchanted, wants his boss dead and may be more receptive to our help now."

"And the frosting? The opposition is much stronger. Regime change is the next option, and it's only a matter of time," Carved added, raising his glass in another toast. Henslow raised his and smiled in reply.

"You did a hell of a job, son. You might not always like what we have to do here, but it is important. Here, this is for you, for a job well done."

Henslow held up two large white envelopes. Garnett took them, looking quizzically at Henslow.

"What are these?"

"Appreciation for you and your branch from the United States Government. There should also be a few thousand dollars extra in this month's paycheck, before taxes. Like I said, your work is appreciated. Should help with the new baby."

"Thanks. Any recognition is always appreciated."

Garnett hadn't mentioned to Henslow that his wife was expecting their second child. *I wonder how he knew?*

Without a word, Garnett turned toward the door.

"Mike."

It was Carver, standing right behind him, hand extended.

"You are a patriot."

"Thanks."

Garnett shook his hand and left.

Back in his own office, Garnett reached across his desk and picked up the Middle East and Africa television and radio news report from FBIS, the quasi-governmental international news monitoring and English-language translation service. He flipped through the yellow-covered report open until he found the item he had marked.

28 MAY 1986 0927GMT LIBYAN RADIO JANA NEWS SERVICE/ AP. (begins) Deputy Chairman Major Abdul Megrahi was seen in Tripoli today. The Brother Commander denounced the false-hoods toward "his trusted friend" who remains in command of the Revolutionary Councils. 0931GMT (ends)

Garnett tossed the booklet on his desk, next to the certificates…*The United States of America…Performance Award…Michael Garnett. Electronic Media Branch. Meritorious Unit Citation…*

The contradictions made his brain hurt. Other awards hung on his wall, honest recognition for a growing career devoted to deception. He was proud of EMB, as Henslow said he should be. Henslow and Carver were right. There were choices in this job—tough choices. Gray choices.

Choices at what price?

Swiveling his chair around, he moved some books off the second shelf of the surplus OTS bookcase behind him. Reaching his hand under the shelf, he released a hidden latch while simultaneously pushing the left side panel, until it pulled away from the case on hinges. Garnett turned and unlocked the bottom drawer of his desk and pulled out a tape marked *Mukhtar Project Master Tapes: Tareq. Safe House Interviews. News segments.*

Sliding it into the gap, there was just enough space to re-latch the panel of the concealment device back in place.

Hiding it there was a good choice.

EPILOGUE

SEPTEMBER 30, 1986

Nothing is so difficult as not deceiving oneself.

—*Ludwig Wittgenstein*

"**I**ntelligence is a world of data and information gathered and analyzed in response to policy-maker directives. Propaganda is a world of deception, specter, illusion, and sleight of hand. This office has been charged, through covert means, to cause…our…enemies… pain."

Garnett began his usual speech for what felt like, and probably was, the hundredth time. His fist made the familiar thud on the podium as he emphasized the final words, as always. It was earlier than normal for these briefings—scheduling issues—so the noise kept everyone awake.

"Most DI analysts have never…" he continued on autopilot. The faces in front of him, sitting in the dim light of his small auditorium, possessed the same "what the hell does this have to do with intelligence?" look they always had until he hit them with the video clips of the day.

"As you must realize, I can't tell you that much about our covert action capabilities, but I assure you all covert programs are within presidential findings…"

Garnett's mind occasionally wandered to *The Project*, as EMB had code-named the Mukhtar operation. The Meritorious Citation hung outside his office—so all could see the accomplishments of the branch.

"To show that video is a valuable intelligence tool, as valuable as a written report…"

Garnett backed away as the lights dimmed and the curtains pulled apart, knowing the impact the dramatic change in atmosphere would have. The now familiar voice of Rolf Olson filled the room, and the audience watched the images of South Africa and terrified people running by burning tires.

Garnett had seen Henslow only a few nonoperational times since, each a brief encounter. The last was when they passed by each other in the Studies in Intelligence section of the first-floor library. Garnett saw him first and watched the man meticulously search the stacks of books, taking one book off the shelf, opening it—randomly, it appeared— reading for a moment, and then replacing the book. Garnett hid in the stacks for fifteen minutes watching the procedure being repeated, and then, as Henslow got closer, Garnett decided to leave. Henslow saw Garnett and nodded.

"Hello, son."

"Hello," Garnett replied.

And it was over.

Once Rolf ended, the next clip, marked "CNN: Terrorism—France" started. The anchor read the lead-in to the story, and an over-the-shoulder graphic of a big red target proclaimed "Terrorism" with the word *Libya* created to look as if it were written in blood angled across it. Garnett immediately turned and stared at the images coming from the screen. "Our CNN Paris bureau chief reports," the anchor finished his lead-in.

The segment opened with the reporter standing on a street corner; a light rain was falling.

"Officials in Paris are investigating an explosion last night which killed human-rights leader Abdallah Mukhtar. and his wife in their Arrondissement de Passy residence. The prominent former Libyan foreign minister has been in the world spotlight for months, since his escape from Libya and his disclosures of the Libya's ties to terrorism and human rights violations."

Cut to images along a streetlight-illuminated residential street at a crowded corner, debris littering the glistening streets, with a half dozen imposing French gendarmes gathering evidence and questioning witnesses. The camera zoomed in to a close-up of broken glass and pieces of brick and concrete.

"Mukhtar was a close ally of Libyan strongman Muammar Qadhafi, who led the coup that overthrew the monarchy in 1969."

The images cut to reveal black-and-white stock footage of a smiling, younger Qadhafi in his military uniform fighting through a cheering mob, shaking his fist high in the air. This was followed by a series of current shots of an older Qadhafi, dressed in long white robes, shouting into a microphone.

"Mukhtar, who escaped from Libya earlier this year, had just spoken at the inaugural meeting of the Mukhtar Middle East and Human

Rights Institute, an organization he formed with his wife, Marwa. Sources have told CNN that several witnesses saw Mukhtar and his wife arriving at their Paris home around ten in the evening."

Next, CNN sat on an exterior image of the old but stylish InterContinental Hotel, in the light of early morning—rain was falling. Recent Mukhtar video appeared, with his wife being interviewed in a hospital. Garnett recognized the footage immediately. Cut to various angles of the demolished sitting room—books scattered, lamps shattered, chairs smashed, and mangled round pieces of metal that resembled the lower portion of a wheelchair.

"An apparent act of terrorism, Colonel Qadhafi has targeted many other Libyan opposition leaders for assassination."

When the camera moved into the bedroom and panned across the room, Garnett saw it in the background—on the floor. None of the police officers were paying attention to the small bent silver frame that surrounded a slightly burnt picture of a family enjoying themselves on a boat.

The lights came up in the theater, but Garnett didn't notice, as his gaze was fixed on the screen and what he had just seen. He didn't recall walking back to his desk or sitting and replaying the CNN story several more times, as if one of the rewinds would change the outcome.

Finally, he dialed his secure line.

"Yes."

"Did you see it?" Garnett asked, assuming he knew what he was referencing.

"Yes. I have cables from Paris. What have you got?" Henslow asked.

"CNN report. Video of the damage…hang on." Garnett took the receiver and placed it by the TV monitor and turned up the volume. He hit play again, and the CNN segment Garnett had watched many times began. When it was done, he hit pause.

"Got that?"

"Yes." There was a noticeable hesitation. "Send me that…and any others." Pause. "You OK?" Henslow asked, with the sound of genuine concern.

Garnett waited before answering, looking at the image of a demolished apartment frozen on his screen.

"Yes," Garnett said.

"Good." The line went dead.

One more deception.

ABOUT THE AUTHOR

Joe Goldberg spent eight years working for the Central Intelligence Agency where he engaged in covert action as well as information collection and analysis. During his tenure he earned a Meritorious Unit Citation and three Performance Awards.

A recipient of numerous prestigious awards over his thirty years of working in intelligence, Goldberg is a published author and frequent speaker on intelligence subjects.

A graduate of the University of Iowa, Goldberg currently resides in Wheaton, Illinois, with his wife, Lynda, who is an elementary school teacher. Together they have three grown children, and a dog named Ollie.

Made in the USA
Lexington, KY
05 January 2015